THE HARLEQUIN CREW SERIES

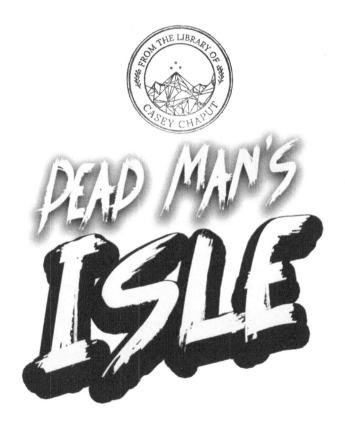

DEAD MAN'S ISLE

THE HARLEQUIN CREW SERIES

CAROLINE PECKHAM
&
SUSANNE VALENTI

This book is dedicated to the starfishes who are forced to work for JJ and swallow down body parts they have no appetite for.
Sorry lil Starfish Pete and Starfish Jeff.
You didn't wanna eat that man's finger or that other guy's toe.
But you did.
And now you're back in the ocean with the horrors of gang life to scar you and your starfish family will never understand your dark past.
God speed, lil starfishes. You're the true heroes of this story and we salute you.

CHAPTER ONE

Maverick was silent as the small boat we were on bounced across the choppy waves and thunder rumbled in the distance. It was pitch black out here, the stars and moon covered in a blanket of storm clouds so thick that it was a struggle to see anything beyond the deck of this little vessel. A freezing wind whipped my rainbow coloured hair around my face and sent a chill racing down to my bones. I was still wearing the fancy French designer outfit Chase had gotten me for our newlywed cover story for the job, but the harem pants and crop top were now marked with engine oil from Maverick's bike and general grime from the holding cell I'd spent the day rotting in.

Maverick was silent, a heavy, furious energy about him that warned me away even though I was stuck here in his company. He stood at the helm, powering across black waves beneath an ominous sky that promised the oncoming storm.

Lightning forked through the clouds overhead and I flinched as it lit up the tips of the dark waves which surrounded us a few seconds before thunder crashed. It was insanity to be out here when the weather was on the turn like this. No doubt my bad luck was only about to get worse and I'd end this shit fest of a day face down in the water while a shark took great pleasure in eating my dead ass. But this ass was too nice to end up as shark chow. I'd been doing my squats again…that one time…a few weeks ago. But still, the payoff was clear to see and required the slap of a rough palm or the grip of brutal fingers, not the sharp slice of shark teeth into my perfectly round flesh.

"How much further is it?" I demanded, wrapping my arms around myself and trying to rub my skin to banish the gooseflesh that was covering my body.

"You scared, beautiful?" Maverick asked, his low voice almost lost to the roar of the engine as he failed to so much as glance around at me where I sat in the back of the small vessel, my knees knocking against his motorbike which took up almost the entire deck. He'd been in that exact same position since he dumped me onboard and we'd sped out onto the water. I'd considered jumping and swimming for shore, but I got the feeling I couldn't out-swim a boat, so it had seemed like a dumb idea.

"Dead girls don't fear death," I replied bitterly, looking away from him towards the ocean even though it was impossible to see anything out there besides the inky darkness. Maverick had a spotlight aimed at the waves ahead of us, but even that hardly showed a thing in the gloom beyond a reflection on the water.

"I know the feeling," Maverick replied, glancing over his shoulder and narrowing his dark eyes on me.

I held his gaze, chin high and defiant, begging him to do his worst because at this point, I couldn't get any lower anyway. Hell, maybe he hadn't brought me out here to return me to his hideaway on Dead Man's Isle. Maybe he'd just brought me out here to drown me and end this eternal loop of suffering I was caught in. Wouldn't that be fitting? For this whole thing to end in the water I'd once loved so much. The same water where we'd all come to try and dump a body all those years ago. I'd stood on a boat not much bigger than this one that night, surrounded by my boys as they rallied around me and helped me to try and cover up what I'd done. I'd been attacked, almost raped, had killed a man then had to dispose of his body. And yet when I'd been standing between the four of them, I hadn't even felt fear over any of it. I'd foolishly stood there with them, looking around at the four pieces of my heart and had believed it would all be okay because I had them and nothing could ever take that away

8

from me. I'd believed that with all I had and all I was – little did I know they were less than a day away from ripping that reality away from me and proving how wrong I was.

Sometimes I wished I could go back in time and be that naive girl standing amongst her boys again, feel the love I'd believed they held for me and the solid thump of my own heart which had beat just for them. But then I remembered it had all been a pretty lie I'd clearly been tricked into believing. When it came down to it, I wasn't the choice they'd made. I was disposable just like that dead body we'd dumped. And today they'd only proven that fact more thoroughly by throwing me away all over again.

The boat hit a wave hard, the nose lurching up into the air and my heart leapt as I was forced to release my grip on myself and grab the metal bar which ringed the line of seats I was perched on.

Maverick returned his attention to steering us through the storm as thunder boomed across the sky once again, splitting the clouds apart so that rain crashed down over us.

I cursed as my fingers curled tighter around the slick metal bar and the boat continued to bounce more and more violently over the caps of the waves. I only hoped that meant we were closing in on the shore, because this storm would chew us up and spit us out if we didn't escape it soon.

I closed my eyes against the pounding rain and the view of nothing as my stomach swooped over and over and my memories cast me back to a time I worked so hard not to remember.

"Run, beautiful! I'll lead them away!" Rick cried, jerking to a halt and tossing me the paper bag we'd just stolen so that the heat of the contents smacked against my chest and I caught it automatically.

"No," I growled, reaching out and grabbing the back of his shirt in my fist to stop him from turning back the way we'd come. "We're in it together. All of us."

His dark eyes raked over me as a thousand arguments moved to his lips, but he clearly read my refusal in my eyes and his grin widened as he gave in.

"Come on then. We'll head for the boardwalk." He grabbed the bag back out of my arms, and snatched my hand before taking off again, the sounds of the mall security assholes yelling for us seeming way too close for comfort.

The others hadn't noticed us hesitating at first, but as we made it to the end of the alley, the three of them appeared, running back our way.

"Shit," JJ breathed. "I thought you guys had been caught for a second then."

"We were gonna beat the fuck outa those security assholes to set you free," Chase agreed, sweeping his curly hair out of his eyes before jerking his chin to get us all moving and racing away again.

"Stop!" a man yelled behind us and I half squealed, half laughed, but mostly just pushed my legs as fast as they could go.

Fox caught my free hand and tugged on it like he thought we could move even faster if he just yanked on me, despite the fact I was the fastest of us all and he damn well knew it.

We spilled out of the alley into the sunshine, our feet hitting the wooden boardwalk which ran along The Mile and the sight of the cerulean sea brought a smile to my face. They held a little market down here a couple of times a month and as today was market day, the place was heaving.

There were people everywhere and more than a few of them tossed glances our way as we took off, racing between the crowd at full speed. I tugged my hands free of the boys' and ran flat out, racing to overtake JJ who was in the lead.

My long, brunette hair billowed out behind me and a laugh fell from my lips.

A woman stepped out of a store right ahead of me and I slammed into her before I could stop myself, the two of us hitting the wooden boards in a heap.

"Get off of me, you little gutter rat!" she squawked as I shoved myself upright.

"Shut your mouth you dried out old tampon," Fox spat at her as he grabbed my arm to heave me up and Maverick caught my other arm to help him.

"You speak about our girl like that again and I'll turn up at your house while you're sleeping and set your fake ass hair on fire," Rick agreed as the woman gasped in outrage.

I grinned big at her, shrugging the boys off and snatching her purse from the ground as we took off running again. Her howls of outrage merged with the yells from the mall assholes as we sprinted away between the crowd and the boys threw grins my way as they stayed either side of me.

We passed a dude who was selling all kinds of fruit and I caught sight of Chase and JJ half a second before they upended a box of oranges and it spilled everywhere behind us. People yelled and scrambled aside or tried to help and best of all, the assholes chasing us were most definitely going to have a hard time getting past that quickly.

The five of us whooped and cheered and I looked up, spotting the Ferris wheel at the end of the pier ahead of us as Sinners' Playground beckoned us home and the sun shone down so brightly it lit me up from the inside out.

As we reached the end of The Mile, we dove off of the boardwalk and onto the golden sand below. The five of us ran into the shadows beneath the pier, scrambling into the tightest, darkest space at the very end of it and cramming ourselves in together.

Rick was butted up against me on my left and Chase on my right and the five of us stifled our laughter as the sounds of the men who had been chasing us drew closer, their curses at having lost us making me crack up.

Maverick placed a hand over my mouth, grinning widely. "Stay quiet, beautiful," he whispered and my heart thrashed for a whole new reason as I looked into his dark eyes.

The men finally moved away and Rick pulled back, opening up the paper bag as the five of us spread out a little, taking seats on the cool sand.

"I'm so freaking hungry," I sighed, eyeing the bag of doughnuts and groaning at the scent wafting from them.

Rick and Fox easily could have afforded to buy their own with the money Daddy Harlequin gave them, but they knew the rest of us didn't like accepting their charity, so they preferred to join us in thieving. It was more fun anyway.

Maverick opened the bag and held it out between all of us and we dove forward to claim the spoils of war.

We pushed and shoved and I growled while JJ gnashed his teeth at me playfully and we finally emerged with a sugary donut each, still warm from the fryer and making my stomach rumble.

"I bet this beats the shit you got for breakfast in the group home this

11

morning, huh?" Maverick teased me as I took a huge bite and I closed my eyes to savour the taste.

"I wasn't allowed any breakfast today," I said around a mouthful of deep-fried goodness. "I went over my time slot in the shower last night because I needed to wash my hair and you know what an asshole Mary Beth is about that kind of thing."

The boys all frowned at me as I admitted that and I suddenly found myself the subject of their stares, eyes flashing with outrage on my behalf and making my heart swell with love for them.

"It's okay." I shrugged. "The breakfast is the same shitty old oatmeal every day and it's not exactly filling anyway. There's never enough to go around. Besides, all the other girls in our class keep telling me they wish they had my figure - so I guess the half-starved thing is working for me."

My joke fell flat and the four of them exchanged looks. It wasn't like this was really news to them and Chase arguably had it worse than me, his parents letting him go without food way too often thanks to his deadbeat dad having no job. JJ's mom was a bit of a shit show too, but at least she always made sure he was fed.

I finished the last bite of my food and my stomach growled loud enough for everyone to hear. Four half-eaten donuts were suddenly placed in my lap. My lips popped open on a protest, but they all spoke over me, demanding I eat and not argue. Chase even assured me that he'd already stolen himself some breakfast today as my gaze met his and I knew he wasn't bullshitting me.

I should have said no. But instead I just smiled, letting them do this for me and bathing in the feeling of their love for me as I demolished their leftovers and they all beamed like feeding me was one of their favourite pastimes.

"We've got you, beautiful," Maverick promised. "Always."

I opened my eyes again, taking in a deep breath as I looked at the stranger that boy had become while he battled the storm and drove us towards the shore. The rain continued to lash down on us and the coldness that had been clinging to my flesh had long since sunk into my bones to take root in my soul.

The ring of a bell drew my attention over the crash of the waves, and I looked beyond the strange new silhouette of the boy I'd once loved and noticed light piercing the pounding rain somewhere ahead of us. That had to be the island. We'd made it. Thank fuck for that.

Maverick guided the boat up to the dock and I gripped the slick bar I'd been clinging onto tighter just as the hull smacked against the jetty.

Men were shouting and Rick barked orders at them to secure the boat and get his bike unloaded and the next thing I knew, he was standing over me, holding a tattooed hand out and watching me with that penetrating gaze of his.

"Are you going to make this difficult?" he asked, seeming not to mind one way or another.

"You know me, Rick," I replied, ignoring his hand which almost looked like it was dripping ink as the rain ran over the black tattoos lining his flesh and pushing to my feet. "Difficult is my middle name."

His gaze slid over me as I shivered before him, unable to move away while he boxed me in with his bulk and the rain washed down over his dark hair and across his leather jacket.

I tried not to shiver but failed and before I knew what was happening, he'd stripped the jacket off and had thrown it around my shoulders. I was too cold to protest against it and as his fingers linked with mine, I let him take my hand and pull me towards the jetty.

I slipped as I tried to climb out of the boat but he yanked me close, keeping me on my feet and practically lifting me up beside him. Then we were walking. Marching really. And his grip on my hand was an iron hold, a means to ensure I couldn't run, a fucking shackle.

Men and women shot curious looks my way as they hurried past us to secure the boat as he'd instructed, but Maverick ignored them completely, striding on with purposeful steps as the rain quickly drenched his black shirt and plastered it to his huge frame.

The moment we stepped through the enormous entrance to the hotel he'd claimed for his own personal palace, I sighed in relief, the warmth and light enveloping us as we left the raging storm outside.

Maverick didn't release my hand and I didn't try to pull away. It wasn't like I could run in that storm, and though there was no tenderness to the way he held me, there was something familiar to it all the same. And while my battered, broken heart was hurting so deeply over what Fox and the others had done to me today, I was all in favour of taking some small comfort from their enemy. Even though I knew he was no more of a friend to me than they were.

Maverick didn't slow until he pushed through the doors into the spa on the bottom level of the hotel where he led me up to a bubbling hot tub before stopping abruptly and releasing his grip on me. The room was lavish, decked out with grey and white tiles and housing a sauna and steam room too, but there were no windows. No way out at all aside from the door we'd just entered through.

"Warm up in the water, or don't," Maverick said flatly, not looking at me or anything else here really. "I need to arrange your accommodation."

Maverick turned and strode away from me again and I frowned at the dismissal, chasing after him and catching his arm.

"That's it?" I asked in surprise as he turned to look down at me.

Maverick ran his gaze over me slowly, drinking in the sight of me like he was trying to align this new version of me with the girl he remembered from our past. "Oh no, beautiful, this isn't it. This doesn't even come close. You may have been kept as a pampered pet by those Harlequin assholes, but believe me when I say I'm a whole other breed of captor. You and me have a lot of unfinished business and I'm going to be making good on every promise I've made over the last ten years. So enjoy your spa time, sweetheart, because it's about to get a whole lot less pleasant from here on out."

He pulled his arm out of my grip and strode through the exit before I could say a word in reply to that. And as the sound of the lock turning in the door followed him, my heart sank like a stone in my chest.

"Here stands the corpse of Rogue Easton," I muttered to myself, looking around at the bubbling water as steam rose from it in a cloud. My fancy French outfit was now dripping wet as well as stained and I would have wanted it off of me even if it hadn't been. It was a reminder of what I'd done today. A reminder of where I'd been and who I'd so foolishly trusted. Again. I mean, what the fuck was wrong with me?

It hurt too bad to even think about the three boys who had once been mine though so I closed my eyes, stripped off every scrap of clothing I wore and moved to climb into the hot tub with a determination in my soul which swore to keep me moving until I could break in peace. Because that was where this night ended. I was going to break all over again unless I could lock it down and I sure as fuck needed something dark to cling onto to make sure I didn't. Something like revenge. "I guess I should make the most of limbo before I'm dragged back into hell."

CHAPTER TWO

S moke coated my tongue as I heaved down lungful after lungful of cancer and pictured my insides turning black and hollow. My fingers were locked around the spare phone I'd taken from home, my gaze set on the windscreen of the black Ford I'd boosted as rain beat heavily down on the glass. I remembered sitting here in my mom's car in the rain after I'd stolen the keys in the middle of the night all those years ago. Rogue had been texting me, saying she wasn't tired enough to sleep and Rosie's snores were sending earthquakes through her pillow, so I'd told her I'd come pick her up. I'd thought I was real fucking cool driving that car and heading off to save my girl.

"Come on," I called out the window, smirking my ass off as Rogue ran towards me across the grass in front of her group home. She had a denim jacket held over her head as the rain beat down on her and I swung the passenger door wide. The second she was in, I hit the gas and tore down the road like I was some badass getaway driver.

"Holy shit," Rogue laughed, scrambling to get her door closed and tossing her wet denim jacket into the backseat. "Your dad's gonna kill you."

"He'll never know," I said dismissively, but the tug in my chest said he

would. But I didn't care, I just wanted to live in the moment and face his fists tomorrow.

I drove us up to Carnival Hill and blasted the heating to dry Rogue off. The wind made the car sway a little and I grinned at the chaos of the night.

My stomach growled almost as loud as the thunder that crashed through the sky a second later, speaking of a missed dinner. And alright, lunch too. Momma had said Dad was coming home with some fish, but by the time he did, it was almost ten and he was blind drunk, no fish in sight. I hated the relief I'd felt when he'd stumbled in the door, grabbed Momma by the hand and dragged her upstairs, not paying me any notice at all. Momma said she was happy, but I knew happy. Happy was surfing with my friends and feeling like there was nothing you could say or do that would make them hurt me. Not being afraid of your own words or even the looks you gave someone in case they lost their shit over them.

"Here." Rogue produced some gummy bears from her pocket, holding them out to me in an offering.

"They're yours," I said dismissively, pushing them back at her. I was well aware she didn't get three square meals a day herself.

"Share them with me," she demanded, tearing into them and placing the bag between us in the cupholder. I couldn't argue with the insistence in her eyes and gave in, taking a couple of them and savouring their sweetness on my tongue. We'd soon devoured every last one of them and the packet lay abandoned between us as we chatted about nothing and everything.

As Rogue started bitching about how Mary-Beth had found a pack of cigarettes in her jeans and taken them away, I gasped in realisation of something. I climbed through into the back seats of the car, opening the middle seat and reaching through into the trunk.

"What are you doing?" Rogue climbed after me and a second later, I had a pack of cigarettes and a lighter in my hand, waving them at her.

"One of dad's stashes," I announced with a mischievous grin.

"You're so dead, Chase Cohen," she warned and I shrugged, opening the pack and pushing one between my lips.

"You can't stop living life just because you know a storm's coming," I said and lightning flashed through the sky as if to agree with me, lighting up *our little haven in the back of my mom's car for a split second.*

Rogue took a cigarette as I offered her one, grinning to herself. "I guess you're right. So does this make you brave or stupid?"

"Neither, little one," I said. "It makes me all powerful." I put on a ridiculous voice like a super villain and she laughed. I drank in every drop of this moment, not letting thoughts of tomorrow ruin a single second of it. There was just here and now and us.

I fell prey to that memory and ached with the desire to go back. Fuck, I'd do so many things differently. I'd have driven that car to my friends' houses, picked them all up and headed on a road trip across the country to somewhere we'd never return from.

I looked down at the phone in my hand in frustration.

Call me, motherfucker.

Every muscle in my body was coiled and knotted, the only part of me moving the frantic, furious animal in my chest which was my heart. It wanted to escape me, fight free of this treacherous body and return to the girl it belonged to. But my heart didn't get a say anymore. I'd locked it up in my chest along with everything it desired a long time ago. And it could thrash and hurt me all it liked now, but it was too fucking late.

What have I done?

What have I fucking done?

My phone buzzed violently in my hand and I answered it instantly, taking the cigarette from my lips in the same moment.

"Tell me good news, Quaid," I snarled down the line at my shady ass lawyer.

"The deal is done," he confirmed in his nasally voice and the breath went out of me, my lungs practically collapsing.

"She's gone?" I demanded, needing to know, desperate to be sure she was finally out of our lives while equally panicking over the thought of never seeing her again.

"Yes, sir, she took the money and the car and I followed her to the edge of the town to make sure she left. She seemed quite confident she would never come back, Mr Cohen. In fact, as soon as I bailed her out, she seemed keen to take anything I had on offer to get her away from Sunset Cove."

Fuck. It's done. She's gone.

That had been easier than I'd expected but I guessed she just wanted this over now that she'd seen how bad this life could get.

My heart rioted and I promised it oblivion in the form of alcohol soon enough. It was pretty much all I could do for it now.

"Good," I said heavily. "Night, Quaid." I hung up, tossing my phone onto the passenger seat before grabbing the brown paper bag in the footwell with the rum in it.

I took the bottle out, shoved the door open and stepped into the hammering rain as I twisted the cap off and started guzzling as much as I could get into my system. I swallowed mouthfuls down until half the rum was gone and the alcohol burned in my stomach.

The rain poured over me in a sheet and I gasped down the wet air as I took the bottle from my lips and stared out over the edge of the cliff I was standing on. One, two, three, steps was all it would take to dive off of it. The wind was at my back, urging me to do it. And maybe I should have. Mother nature clearly wanted me to. She could see exactly what I was; a tarnished soul escaped from hell to reside here and suffer over *her*.

I spun one of my leather bracelets around my wrist. This was my prison, my home, the only place in the world where someone wanted me. Without Fox and JJ, I was nothing. A desolate island where nothing could grow.

I just had to keep assuring myself that I'd done the right thing. It had only been a matter of time before Rogue ripped us apart again. If Fox had found out about her and JJ, it would've been game over for them. And then what? Would I have been forced to choose between them? Lose another of my brothers? Another member of my family? They were all I had in the world and they'd suffered over Rogue as much as I had. She would ruin us if she stayed here. So this was the right thing to do. But then why did it feel like carving my heart from my chest with a blunt knife?

"Take it!" I roared at the sky, the alcohol flooding my body but doing nothing to dull my pain. The only way out now was sleep, but I'd have to drink and drink until that was possible. "Have my fucking heart if you want it, but don't take my brothers!" I roared at no one. Because no god in this world listened to the people of Sunset Cove. This was a lawless land where gods were made. And so long as I had Fox and JJ, I was one of them. I could make a mark right here. I could be…something. The only thing worth being in my pointless existence. A Harlequin. One of them. My boys. And I'd vowed a long time ago when Luther had dragged us out to the woods and made us become a part of his gang, that I would protect my brothers at any cost. But the price that was being paid now was the worst yet. Because losing her again, hurting her, betraying her, was unbearable. So I welcomed the pain that cursed my heart, and let the icy rain chill me through until I was shivering. Then I drank until my mind was just a blur of rainbow hair and hateful eyes. She despised me before and I just gave her a dozen more reasons to despise me deeper. So what did it even matter?

And with that thought spinning in my mind, I stumbled back to the car, fell inside and passed the fuck out.

An incessant buzzing sounded in my aching brain and rattled around my entire skull. I grunted, disorientated as I came to and lifted my head, finding my phone beneath it with ten missed calls from Fox and several text messages from JJ.

Fox was calling again and I blinked groggily against the morning sunlight as it poured through the car, pushing myself upright and glancing back at my soaked feet which were sticking out of the open door. A seagull swooped over and shat on my leg and I mentally saluted it, unsurprised by the local wildlife offering me a casual fuck you. Animals could always sense shitty people. It was why the stray cats near where I grew up never came sniffing at my father's door for scraps. That and the fact that he threw a shoe at them once.

Rogue and I had made a shelter for them out of old driftwood and blankets we stole from her group home. A cat had had kittens in there one summer and we'd taken them to the animal shelter in a cardboard box, riding the bus all the way up there with bare, sandy feet and stupid smiles on our faces while we named all of them. We'd half wanted to keep them, but we knew they'd be better off out of the Cove. I squeezed my eyes shut and held onto that memory as tight as possible, feeling it slipping away already as I wished I could go back to that moment and keep riding that bus into eternity.

I shoved myself upright, tugging the door closed and flexing my neck which was stiff as hell. The pain didn't have anything on what I felt in my heart though, but at least the alcohol was working overtime to keep it distracted.

I grabbed my cigarettes from the dash, tucking one into the corner of my mouth and lighting it up before answering my phone.

"Hey," I said, my voice sounding like a fucking eighty-year-old man's with throat cancer.

"Where are you?" Fox demanded, a note of concern in his voice. *Good ol' Foxy.*

"The Ventosa Cliffs. I passed out. You okay, bro?" I asked, pain flashing through me at knowing how hard this was gonna hit him. But it had to be better than if she'd stuck around and fucked us over later.

"Come home," he ordered, not answering, but the sharpness to his voice said it all.

He was in meltdown mode. And I had no doubt he'd been out searching for her long into the night, trying to figure out which precinct she'd ended up in. But I'd gotten her out of dodge long before he would have found that answer.

Lying to my brothers was up there with betraying Rogue when it came to my shittiest actions. I officially despised myself. The checklist of my redeeming qualities was set at an unsurprising zero.

Bile rose up in my throat as my own body rejected itself and before I could answer Fox, I lunged out the door, vomiting on the dirt.

"Ace?" Fox called, the phone still loosely held between my fingers.

I wiped my mouth with the back of my hand, slumping into my seat as Fox called out to me and I managed to lift the phone to my ear again.

"I'm alright," I slurred. Another lie. *How'd that one taste, motherfucker?*

"Just get home," he growled. "We're gonna regroup. Someone's gotten her out of the precinct."

"What?" I rasped, feigning surprise. But that someone had been me and I'd sent her on her merry way with a pocket full of cash and every reason to keep running and never look back just like I'd planned. She had to believe we'd all decided to betray her, and no matter how fucked up that might have been, at least this way I knew she'd never return to Sunset Cove. Fox would hunt for her of course. But Rogue Easton had made a life out of being a ghost and I was certain she'd be able to evade his best efforts.

"Just get home," he barked and hung up.

I grabbed the rum, taking a swig, swilling it around my mouth and spitting it onto the ground to take the taste of vomit away. My life was real pretty.

The seagull who'd shat on me came down to land and made a feast out of my puke, so I guessed at least someone was benefiting from my existence this morning.

I coughed heavily, my lungs feeling like they were gonna pop as I started up the car and turned it around, my gaze hooking on the seagull in my wing mirror as it rejected the free meal. *Yeah, I don't blame you, bud. Nothing in there but regret and alcohol.*

I drove back to town, bleary eyed and hanging outa my asshole as I finally made it to Harlequin House and headed through the gates. I parked up in the garage, stumbled towards the stairs and paused as my phone buzzed in my pocket.

I hooked it out and read the message waiting for me.

Quaid:
Slight issue.
It turns out the girl I bribed the cops to release got arrested again last night over in Hawksville for drunk driving.

My heart froze. My brain took several seconds to comprehend those words and in that time, Quaid sent over a mugshot of the girl and my lips parted in confusion.

Hang the fuck on…

Chase:

That's not her. Is that the girl you bailed out??????

Quaid:

Yes. She was the only girl at the north precinct, sir.

Chase:

YOU FUCKING MORON. WHAT PART OF RAINBOW HAIR DID YOU NOT UNDERSTAND!????

Quaid:

She had some pink in it…

Chase:

FUCK YOU QUAID!

I fought the urge to throw my phone at the wall and took a breath as my alcohol-infused brain tried to figure out what had happened. Fox said Rogue was free. So if my lawyer didn't get her out, who the fuck did? And how the fuck did they get there before me?

"Jesus fucking Christ," I hissed, carving my fingers through my dark curls as my heart beat out a panicked tune. *Where is she? Who is she with?*

Maybe she called someone. Maybe one of her trailer park friends got there first, somehow put the cash together to bribe the cops…

Not good. Not good. Not good.

My heart beat out a hopeful little tune at the idea of her still being in town, of seeing her again, even with utter rage in her eyes. But I smothered that hope like it was my blood-bound enemy and let my brain think on that further. If she was still in town, she could tell Fox and JJ we got split up, that I didn't go back for her. That I fucking left her there.

No, no, no.

"Ace?" The door wrenched open at the top of the stairs and JJ appeared there with Mutt in his arms.

The dog started yapping at me and I couldn't blame the beast for hating me, the look in its shiny little eyes telling me it knew the kind of monster I was. He knew what I'd done without having to hear the words or see the truth.

I jogged up the stairs, my shoulder bashing against the wall as I made it to the top.

"Are you drunk?" he growled, yanking me out into the hall close enough for Mutt to sink his teeth into my arm. I let the little dog go to town until it drew blood and JJ yanked him out of reach.

JJ slapped me hard across the face and I focused my gaze on him, wincing against the sunlight streaming through the hallway.

"Get it together," he demanded. "Fox is losing his mind. And I'm not far off it either. We've searched everywhere we can think of, I've called every one of her friends, but no one's giving her up. Did you find anything?"

"No," I grunted, dropping my gaze.

In the wake of the guilt, the panic, the fear, came the worst thing of all. Shame. I'd lied to my brothers. And now I was so deeply wrapped up in this lie that I could never let it out, because it held the weight of my entire family with it. If it got out, I'd lose them. No doubt about it. They'd never forgive me for this. And I wouldn't fucking blame them.

"We'll get her back, brother," JJ swore to me, clapping his hand down on my shoulder and my features pinched as I said nothing. "I know you two have issues, but you care about her just as much as me and Fox. You don't have to admit it, you can even tell me to get fucked, but I know you. And I know *us*. We all loved her once, that doesn't just go away. We're just all dealing with it…differently."

I tried to swallow the hard and unyielding lump in my throat as I gazed at my brother and felt so unworthy of his understanding, his love, that I just wanted the floor to open up and drag me down to hell already.

I managed a nod and he broke a sad smile before turning and leading the way down the hall.

Fox was in the kitchen with a map of Sunset Cove spread over the counter. He was striking out sections of it with a pen, marking each and every place they'd already searched from Rejects Park to Afterlife, Sinners' Playground,

Carnival Hill, all our old haunts. Fox looked as worn out as JJ, both of their eyes ringed with dark circles speaking of a night without sleep.

"Chase," Fox snapped, beckoning me over. "Look at the town, where would she go?" he demanded, jabbing his finger down on the map.

I frowned, taking a breath as I tried to align my thoughts and I looked down at the town we called home and wondered where she'd be. Maybe she didn't want to be found. She'd hate us for leaving her. She'd blame us all. So maybe she'd jacked a car and left us all behind, but as my gaze moved to the dog in JJ's arms, I knew she wouldn't have abandoned him like I had her.

"She'll be laying low somewhere," I said darkly as JJ placed Mutt down and started brewing some coffee for us all.

"Why?" Fox snapped.

"Isn't it obvious?" I snarled. "She'll blame us for her getting caught."

JJ groaned, sounding in agony then his fist snapped out and cracked against one of the cupboards. "She'll think we fucking abandoned her. Again."

Fox looked like his head was about to explode, his knuckles turning white as he gripped the counter. "So we need to find her and fucking explain. Where the hell would she go? And what's she thinking now? What's her goddamn plan?" He glared down at the map in fury like it was keeping the information from him.

I stepped closer with a sigh. "My guess? She'll go to ground for a few days then try to come back for the dog and skip town once she has him."

Fox processed that for a long moment before nodding. He scrubbed at the stubble on his jaw, not looking directly at me. He was pissed at me. I'd fucked up royally in his eyes. And I'd pay for it soon enough in more than just the bruises lining my flesh from his rage last night. But his focus was on the hunt now, and he wasn't going to let anything cloud his vision on that.

Fox's jaw worked as his eyes moved from one road to the next on the map, calculating the odds of her being at each location. I reached out and pressed my hand to his shoulder and he shrugged it off, his eyes snapping up to meet mine.

"If we lose her again, I'll never forgive you," he bit out and my heart hammered frantically as those words settled over me. "Either we find her or you're out of the Harlequins," he said icily and dread washed down my spine like ice.

"Fox-" I rasped, but he just slammed his finger down on the map again, pointing to New Palm Lane. "Start there. Knock on doors. Ask anyone you see. I don't care what it takes, you don't have a bed in this house until I get some news on where she is from your tongue."

He pointed me in the direction of the garage, his eyes dark and full of a murderous fury that I'd only ever seen aimed at our enemies.

I met JJ's gaze for a moment then he hung his head, his brow creased. My chest compressed and I backed up, my fate closing in on me and my truest fears being realised right before my eyes.

Losing Rogue had broken me, but losing them too would be the end of me. And now finding her was the only way I could keep my home, my brothers.

Fate had twisted up everything I'd done and thrown it back in my face. I'd fucked up so badly that all I could do was keep digging myself into this hole and pray the bottom of it held an answer. But I had the feeling that I was going to keep digging my way into the endless, lonely dark and never find a way back to the light. And that might just be the punishment I deserved.

Rejects Park

ROGUE

CHAPTER THREE

Maverick's angry shouts were more than enough to draw me out of my hiding place within the sauna where I'd chosen to heat myself up for most of the night. I'd just turned the temperature down after initially banishing the cold from the storm and had made myself a bed out of towels on one of the benches when it had become clear he wasn't planning on coming back for me any time soon. I probably should have thought to hang my wet clothes up in here to dry last night too, but I'd been more interested in warming myself up, so they still sat in a heap out by the hot tub and I was butt naked inside my nest.

I snatched a fluffy white towel from the pile I'd slept in to wind around my warm body and stepped out of the sauna to stand beside the hot tub half a second before Maverick burst through the door.

He'd gotten changed into a pair of black sweats and a khaki t-shirt, though his midnight hair still shone with moisture from a shower and the penetrating hunger in his gaze made me fight a squirm.

I hadn't caught the words that went with his tirade as I'd been hurrying to tie my towel in place, but as a woman's yells followed him through the door, my jaw tightened with irritation.

"I don't see why I have to stay away," Mia snarled, the door flying open at his back as she stalked in, wearing a set of black underwear with a transparent dressing gown hanging open over it. Her short, dark hair made her modelesque features seem sharp like a bird of prey and she narrowed heavily shadowed eyes on me the moment she spotted me. "We can just play with her together," she pouted.

Maverick didn't reply, his gaze fixed on me though I could have sworn annoyance was tightening his jaw as Mia moved to run a hand down his arm.

"Wouldn't you like that, baby? I could help you get whatever information out of her you need. Or if you want to have some more exciting fun, maybe we could take her upstairs to our room?"

"It's not your room," Maverick grunted, folding his arms impatiently like he was just waiting for her to be done here. But I couldn't figure out why he was indulging her at all. Wasn't he the big bad boss man? Shouldn't she have been backing the fuck off instead of stepping over the line he'd clearly drawn here?

"Your room then," Mia conceded. "I'm sure we could persuade her to join in with us. Girls like her always have a price. Wouldn't you like to watch her eat me out? Maybe you could fuck her while she's doing it?"

"Girls like me?" I asked dryly. "Believe me, sweetheart, there isn't enough money in the world to make me want to lick your crusty cunt. And don't go thinking that's because I have anything against pussy – I just have standards which you fall far beneath. Unlike Maverick here who will apparently stick his cock in anything on offer."

Mia laughed like I was joking, but my gaze wasn't on her. I was watching the man in the room, waiting for him to make his move and put his bitch in line. He didn't have long though, because if he didn't do it himself soon, I'd be taking on the job for him.

Maverick's gaze never shifted from me and I arched an eyebrow at him, daring him to do his worst.

Mia took the stand-off between us as some kind of invitation and she prowled towards me, drawing my attention from the main man as she cocked her head and considered me.

"She looks like such an innocent little thing," she commented like I was a show pony and she was considering purchasing me. "All of that cotton candy hair and those big blue eyes begging the world to go easy on her even though it won't. I think she might just be a little too broken, even for you, baby."

Mia reached out to grip the top of my towel and tried to tug it free, but I batted her hand away from me and gave her my best resting bitch face. It wasn't a glare or a snarl or anything like that, just a look of utter disdain which promised her skanky ass that I could beat her dumb face in if she kept pushing me.

"See?" Mia purred. "I bet she wouldn't even-"

"I want clothes," I interrupted, ignoring the twat in favour of pinning Maverick in my gaze. "You wanted me here, so here I am. But I don't need to be naked for whatever the hell you have planned next, because believe me when I tell you I have no interest in catching genital warts from your skanky girlfriend."

Mia lunged at me with a snarl and a flash of psycho in her eyes but I'd been expecting it and I ducked aside, making her stumble as she failed to grab me.

My fist cracked her in the mouth as she tried to recover and busted her lip open as she whirled on me again. Her body collided with mine a second later as she threw me back against the wall and I cursed as I fought to keep her fucking fingernails away from my face.

Mia went the girl fight bullshit route and grabbed a fistful of my hair, yanking hard and making me snarl at her as I kneed her in the vag then threw my forehead into her face.

She fell back with a scream, grabbing my towel and ripping it off of me as she went flying down onto her ass on the tiles with blood streaming down her face.

I lurched forward with the full intention of giving her a good kicking, but suddenly Maverick was right in my space, a hand locking around my throat and my back colliding with the wall once more.

The cold tiles bit against my bare flesh as my spine was pressed to them and Maverick leaned right in so that our breath was mixing and I couldn't even keep my focus on the ink that decorated his neck because I was caught in the intensity of his deep, dark eyes.

"That's enough. You and I are overdue a conversation, beautiful," he growled, his deep voice all I could hear despite Mia's continued agonised wails. I didn't know why she was bitching so freaking much though - I was almost certain I hadn't actually broken her nose, so it was just a little blood.

"I vowed to kill the last man who laid his hands on me like this, Rick," I hissed as his fingers flexed around my throat and something dark and twisted writhed within the confines of his eyes. "So unlike that fucker, if you plan on killing me, you'd better do a better job of it. Because if I come back to haunt your ass, I'll make you regret it more fiercely than anything you've ever known."

"Well you don't need to worry about that," Maverick replied, squeezing hard enough to cut off my oxygen and reminding me forcibly of the fear I'd felt when fucking Shawn had done that very thing to me. When I'd seen my death reflected back to me in those cold, brutal eyes of his and had realised I couldn't fight him off. "If I decide to kill someone, there's no chance of them recovering from it."

My heart was racing as Maverick leaned in impossibly closer and the desire to lock my hands around his wrist and start clawing and fighting to try and get him off of me rose like bile in my throat.

My ears were ringing with the sounds of my screams and the way I'd begged Shawn not to hurt me before his hand had latched so tight around my throat that I couldn't breathe. My pulse was thundering like mad and I was back there, back in that moment when I'd looked my death in the eye and had to face the reality of just how fucking empty my life had been. I was a lost and broken girl, wandering from one place to the next and never really belonging. Because the only place I'd ever belonged was right here in Sunset Cove where the sea was as blue as the sky and the sun shone down on my skin, warming me all the way to my soul. Where my boys had surrounded me and protected me from the countless bad things my life had wanted to offer me, and I could just be me and that was enough. Or at least it had been. Once. The only time I'd ever really felt alive. Perhaps I'd been a dead girl long before Shawn had ever tried to kill me.

Tears burned the backs of my eyes at how fucking pointless my existence had been and as I tried to force the memories aside and focus on the dark eyes of the man who now held me at his mercy, I found myself calming. I still couldn't breathe, my heart still raced and my death may very well have still been looking back at me. But I found that I preferred it to be wearing this face. At least if it was him then it meant something. To me. To him. To all of us and to this place we'd once ruled with nothing at all but the freedom of youth and the impossible belief that everything would always be okay just so long as we had each other.

Maverick's free hand curled around my hip and my skin seemed to burn at his touch, goosebumps tearing across my flesh and making my back arch. I wasn't supposed to like this, but for some reason, some deep, dark part of me did. Some fucked up, broken piece of me was relishing this moment where he held my death in his grasp and I clenched my thighs together as I was overwhelmed by the insanity of that.

He relaxed his grip on my throat and I sucked in a breath, my chest rising heavily between us and drawing his gaze down to my naked body. He'd looked at me like this once before. And yet not like this at all. Back then his eyes had raked over my body with the excited desire of youth, but now I felt his gaze like a dark promise of my own destruction. And instead of wanting to fight him off and run as far and fast as I could, I found myself wanting to invite that destruction upon my flesh. To let him ruin me as best he could and see what was left of the broken pieces which I taped together so frequently when he was done.

"It seems like you think you enjoy playing with the devil in me, beautiful," Maverick growled so low that I was sure Mia couldn't hear him over her continued sobs. "Let's see how long that lasts."

If I'd had anything to say in response to that, he didn't give me a moment to voice it because before I knew what was happening, he'd hoisted me off of my feet and thrown my naked ass over his shoulder.

"Put me down," I snarled, thumping his back. But the dude was like a slab of solid muscle, and I wasn't even convinced he felt my attacks as I thrashed and kicked. He just held me in place with an arm banded around the backs of my thighs and strode right on out into the corridor where plenty of his men were ready for the primetime show of my motherfucking ass being pointed up in the air at them.

"I told you. We have things to discuss. And I'm getting the impression you aren't taking your situation seriously enough." Maverick kept walking, leaving the sobbing Mia exactly where I'd put her bitch ass - bleeding and crying on the floor - as he continued to stride through the enormous hotel he'd claimed for his stronghold.

Blood rushed to my head and I gave up on trying to fight as I looked down at the inked backs of his legs while he walked, my rainbow hair trailing towards the ground as we passed countless people and they all got a good look at my naked butt. I tried to figure out what the Green Power Ranger would do in my position, but I was coming up blank as I tried to remember an episode where he'd been stripped naked and hauled about by a hulking Rita Repulsa as she kept him captive in her lair. *Dammit.*

We took a set of stairs down into the basement of the building and I craned my neck to see as we passed through a commercial kitchen and finally arrived in a dark space where the temperature dropped noticeably around us.

I was flipped right way up again and my ass hit a cold wooden chair a second before a handcuff snapped shut around my wrist, locking it in place on the armrest to my right.

"Rick," I gasped, trying to yank my arm free and making the metal bite into my skin as he caught my other wrist and promptly snapped a handcuff around that one too, locking it to the other arm of the chair and immobilising me.

He didn't even look at me as he reached for my ankle and my fight or flight instincts finally caught up to what was going on. I'd learned that running tended to be my forte over the last ten years, but I was more than capable of fighting if that wasn't an option and I screamed at him as I wrenched my ankle out of his grip and kicked with both legs in a desperate bid for freedom.

Maverick cursed as my bare foot caught him in the jaw, but the impact threw me back in my chair and suddenly the whole thing fell backwards.

I hit the ground hard, pain ricocheting through the back of my skull and making my ears ring for a moment as I blinked spots of darkness from my vision.

Maverick moved fast, taking advantage of my moment of pained hesitation and by the time I started fighting again, he'd already tied my left ankle to the leg of the chair using rough rope.

He grunted in irritation as I managed to kick him with my free leg a few more times before he finally caught it and tied it to the other leg of the chair, forcing my thighs apart and making my heart race with fear.

Maverick stood back as soon as I was restrained, and my chest heaved with panicked breaths as I stared up at the lone strobe light overhead and took in my surroundings properly for the first time. I was inside what looked like a commercial sized freezer, my breaths rising in puffs of vapour before me as the cold pricked at my skin and made me shiver. Empty stainless-steel racks lined the wall to my right, but on my left were meat hooks and specks of red which I got the impression hadn't been left there by traditional meat.

Maverick walked around me until he could grasp the back of my chair and lifted me upright again, setting it down on its feet with a bang that echoed in the confined space.

When he circled around to face me again, I swallowed down the lump of fear in my throat and forced myself to meet his gaze. He licked his bottom lip slowly, tasting the blood that was coating it from the kick I'd managed to land to his face and fear trickled through me at the murderous look in his eyes.

"Get on with it then, Rick. I have an appointment at the beauty salon to get my roots touched up and I promised a seagull I'd meet him for a chat down on the beach at noon. I'm a busy woman these days," I spat, falling back on my standard big mouth and letting it run away with me.

Maverick remained silent for several achingly long seconds, his gaze roaming over my exposed body like a wolf starving for a meal, his eyes fixing on my tattoos just as much as my rock-hard nipples and the space between my parted thighs. I clenched my fists, forcing myself to take a deep breath and just let him look. What did I care anyway? It was just flesh, just the shell I'd been born in and made use of for the last twenty-six years. And I got the feeling I had a lot more to fear from the man my boy had become than the feeling of his gaze roaming over my body.

"If anyone else had betrayed me the way you did with that bullshit over the cocaine destroyed in my warehouse, I'd spend a week cutting pieces off of their body and making them watch as I fed them to the sharks," Maverick said in a tone which promised me he'd done that before and made it hard to hold his gaze. But I did. I kept my eyes steady on his and held my tongue, knowing he would keep talking if I let him and wanting to hear him say his piece. "You came to my house. Made a fool of my men. Stole my key and then set me up to lose thousands of dollars worth of merchandise, and for what? Fox Harlequin and his loyal guard dogs?" Maverick spat that name like it burned his tongue and I wet my dry lips as I tried not to shiver before him from the cold.

"It sounds bad when you put it that way," I replied evenly.

Maverick narrowed his eyes and took a knife from his pocket before stepping towards me. The light caught on the blade and I couldn't help the way my heart raced at the sight of it. As much as I wanted to believe I knew the man standing before me, the last ten years had clearly done a number on the two of us and I knew I couldn't trust anything based off of the things I used to know about him.

"I will admit I wanted your key," I said quickly, sensing his patience was wearing thin and wondering if there was enough of the boy I'd once loved left in him to hear me out. "And to be honest, the making a fool of your men thing was actually pretty hilarious - that asshole seriously thought I was going to suck his cock just because he helped me out with a bit of engine trouble and I-"

"In four days' time, the cartel are expecting me to deliver the cocaine I'd been storing for them to their people. If I don't show up with their merchandise, they'll come here and find me. They'll find my men. And I'm sure they'll find whatever is left of you too. And then they'll skin each and every one of us alive - and that's assuming we get off lightly." Maverick moved to place a hand on the back of my chair and leaned down to look right at me, the tip of his blade pressing to my left thigh above my knee and making a shiver run through me which had nothing to do with the cold.

"I don't want that," I breathed, looking into his eyes and wondering what was going on within them. Was he looking at the girl he'd once sworn to love and protect forever? Or was I just a stranger with the face of a memory to him now?

"So tell me," Maverick asked slowly, dragging the knife up my thigh so that the kiss of the blade awoke every nerve ending in my body as he danced a thin line with the pressure he was exerting so that it didn't quite pierce my skin. "When Foxy boy was slamming his cock into that wet pussy of yours, did he

36

whisper my name in your ear? Did he convince you to come to my home and fuck me even harder than you were fucking him? Did he put you up to your little charade in the hopes of making the cartel do his dirty work for him?"

Maverick skimmed the knife down the inside of my thigh and I gasped as the blade touched to my core, the bite of the cold metal making my heart thrash as he pressed it to me a little harder, warning me not to lie to him.

"It was my idea, not Fox's," I whispered, my muscles coiling with tension as I fought against the urge to panic. I was utterly at his mercy here and there was nothing I could do about it aside from offering him the truth. "And I...didn't really think much beyond them burning a bit of your stock. I just thought you'd replace it or whatever. That drawing your men away from the warehouse would mean less death..."

"So you chose *them*?" he growled. "You chose the three of them when they were the ones who threw you away in the first place? You show up back here after all that time and part your thighs like the good little whore Fox always wanted you to be for him and-"

"I'm not fucking Fox," I snapped. "But maybe you need to ask yourself why you're so caught up on the idea of that, Rick."

"So why is he still telling everyone in the entire town that you belong to him then?" Maverick asked cruelly, giving me a look which said he didn't believe me, but fuck him. I had no shame over sex or who I chose to share my body with, but I sure as fuck wasn't going to sit here like some beat down little bitch and let him throw anger in my face over lies and bullshit.

"Fox has been telling the whole world I'm his girl since I first got back here," I replied scathingly. "He likes to talk a big game and play the boss man with everyone, but he isn't the boss of me. I made it more than clear to him that I wasn't his at every given opportunity and I don't need to sit here and listen to even more bullshit from you. I already gave you this answer the last time I was here and you clearly decided my word means shit. You're asking me for the truth and I'm giving it to you. If you won't listen, then I won't waste my breath."

Maverick regarded me for several long seconds before moving the blade which was still pressed against my pussy and slowly dragging it up the centre of my body. I gasped as he slid it over my clit, the sharp tip almost cutting that sensitive flesh and making my pulse thunder as I tried to clamp my thighs closed but couldn't thanks to the restraints.

"So you were only fucking JJ then?" Maverick asked, arching a brow like he was waiting for me to lie to him but I'd promised him the truth so he could have it. He moved the knife up my body again, curving it around my tits.

"Yeah. Johnny James grew up into a talented man," I replied. "He fucked me until I saw stars and even then, he wasn't done with me. It's just a pity he's a treacherous motherfucker like the rest of them or maybe I could have made more use of him."

Maverick's upper lip peeled back and the knife slipped, making me hiss as he spilled a small line of blood across the curve of my right breast. It wasn't deep, but it stung. Though that small pain had nothing to the hurt in my heart over the Harlequin boys and what they'd done to me again.

"Don't tell me your heart is breaking for that asshole," Maverick snarled, his eyes flashing with malice as he moved the bloodied blade and pressed it to my throat.

I tipped my chin higher, meeting his gaze and letting him see that I didn't fear death at his hands. It would probably be a mercy after all this time. To just let go of the ache in my unwanted heart and fall away into darkness.

"My heart broke for all four of you once upon a time. What they did yesterday only ripped the shattered pieces back apart again."

"What did they do?" he asked, something in the set of his features making me feel like he really did want to know.

"Surely your pet cop told you all about it?"

"I just got a call to say the girl I'd been keeping tabs on was locked up in a cell. All I know is that you were found with stolen goods and it cost me ten grand to make them forget they'd ever arrested you and hand you over to me. I'm still trying to figure out if I got a bargain or if I was ripped off."

"Well let me know when you figure it out," I replied bitterly.

"Spit it out then. What did the three assholes do to put that hurt in your big blues, beautiful?"

My tongue sat thick and heavy in my mouth as I stared up at him, his entire body caging me in and that knife against my throat like the sweetest promise I'd ever been given. He owned me in that moment. My life was his to

38

take or give. And I found the burden of no longer being responsible for it was a relief.

"They made me their fall guy," I said, my eyes burning at the pain of that betrayal.

There was a time when I never could have imagined any one of us leaving another behind and yet it was clear they'd planned it that way. The boats had been gone. They'd saved their own asses and abandoned mine like I was nothing at all to them. And the worst thing was that I had actually been gutted by that. Shocked. Like some naive fucking fool, I'd actually begun to believe in the bullshit they'd been spewing since I'd returned here. Despite my best intentions, a part of me had clearly thought they would have my back like old times. It was so fucking pathetic that I couldn't even argue with fate for landing me where I was now. This was the least I deserved for letting myself fall for their shit and be sucked in by their lies.

"I was the one who got thrown to the wolves all over again. Though fuck knows why that surprised me. You all showed me what you thought of me when it came down to it ten years ago. Fool me once, shame on you. Fool me twice, shame on me," I muttered, dropping my gaze for the first time and studying the ink on Maverick's arm instead of his face.

He had a shrunken head with its hair clasped in the fist of a skeletal hand dominating his forearm and I looked into its dead eyes, wondering if I might find anything hiding in there which mirrored my own soul.

"*They* were the ones who let you down," Maverick said, leaning close and speaking into my ear so that the scent of wood, leather and pure fucking danger coiled all around me. His stubble grazed against my neck and the shiver that raced through my body had nothing to do with the cold. "But I never let you go, beautiful. I came for you. And yeah, I might have fucked it up, but don't go lumping me in with the rest of them. They threw me away just like they did you. They left us both to rot. But we didn't, did we?" He moved the knife away from my throat and used the knuckles of the fist holding it to tip my chin up and make me look at him again. "We grew tougher skin and learned the truth of what we were made of. We came back stronger than before and ready to prove to them that they made a mistake when they chose to cross us."

I met his dark eyes as clouds of our breath mingled between us and suddenly I could see him there, that boy I'd loved with all of my heart. The one who had taken a kicking for me when the asshole from the hardware store caught me stealing from him. The one who had always gone well out of his way so that he could give me a ride on the back of his motorcycle instead of letting me ride my skateboard to meet them. The one who had held my hair back when we'd gotten wasted on a bottle of stolen vodka and I'd spent hours puking it all back up again. The one who had come looking for me when the rest of them had left me all alone in this world.

"I'm sorry, Rick," I whispered. "I'm sorry for not knowing what happened to you back then. I'm sorry you took the fall for something I'd done. And I'm sorry for the warehouse too...I just thought that if I kept you occupied then none of you would get hurt. I knew I couldn't stop them from striking at you and the thought of the four of you taking shots at each other terrifies me. I might hate all of you, but I don't want you to die."

Maverick's brow pinched at the honesty in my words and for a moment I thought he was going to say something that might change everything. Like the world was balancing on the edge of a dime and at any moment he'd make a choice which could send my entire existence tumbling down one path or another.

But before he could do that, he jerked back suddenly, backing up so that the chill of the freezer enveloped me again and I was left shivering before him as he pointed the blade still wet with my blood at me.

"Prove it then," he growled. "If you're so sorry then you can help me fix it."

"Fix what?" I asked.

"My little issue with the cartel. Like I said, if they find out I let their supply burn then I'm going to be held accountable for it. And as much as I hate this fucking miserable life I'm living, I don't think I'm done with it yet."

"How the hell are you going to make them forget that you had all of that cocaine?" I asked him, shaking my head. "I doubt you have the cash to cover it, so unless you happen to have a backup hoard of the white stuff-"

"I don't," he interrupted me. "But I happen to know someone who does."

"Who?" I asked, my fists tightening as I fought a chatter in my teeth. It was fucking freezing in here and I was already missing any sense of feeling in my toes. Perhaps I could ask Maverick to start cutting my extremities off first if he really did follow through on that threat to chop me up - at least that way I wouldn't be able to feel too much of it.

"Shawn Mackenzie," he said, a smirk lifting his lips that was full of danger and made my heart race. "He's the leader of The-"

"Dead Dogs," I interrupted him, because I knew that. Of course I fucking knew that. I might not have had much to do with Shawn's work, but I had been warming his bed for two years. Though I hadn't realised his gang would mean a whole lot to the gangs out here in Sunset Cove. His turf was miles away, inland and based in the town of Sterling. But the question was, did I want to help Maverick break into his drug supplies and steal a fuck ton of cocaine from him to cover up what Rick had lost from the cartel?

Why yes. Yes I did.

"I'm in."

Maverick arched a brow at me and lowered the knife. "Just like that?"

"Let's just say, I have no love for that particular motherfucker and if we can fuck with his business then I'm all for it. Better yet, if we can take a moment to gut him while we're there, I'm up for that t-too." My teeth gave me away by chattering a little as I finished, so I gave up on trying to fight the urge to shiver as the cold in this fucking place bit deeper into my skin.

"You expect me to just believe you?" he asked, his breath rising before him. "To accept your word after you stole my key and ran off on me the last time I turned my back on you?"

"Believe what you like, Rick. But if you leave me butt naked and tied up in this f-fucking freezer m-much longer then I won't be h-helping you to d-do shit."

Maverick moved towards me slowly, his gaze crawling over my exposed body as he slid the knife back into his pocket and placed his hands around the arms of my chair before my frozen fingers.

"Alright then, beautiful. Here's the deal. I'll let you out of here and lock you up somewhere warmer while I prepare everything we need for this little robbery I have planned to replace my cocaine. But while you're waiting for me to come back to you, you'll bear this in mind." He leaned forward and dropped his mouth over my chest, his hot tongue licking across the line of blood he'd left painted over the curve of my breast and making me gasp as my back arched against the wooden chair automatically. "I've had a taste of your blood now," he purred, looking up at me again and capturing me in his dark gaze. "So I suggest you don't cross me for a second time. Or you're going to find out just how bloodthirsty I can get."

Dead Man's Isle

MAVERICK

CHAPTER FOUR

I lay on the velvet couch in the huge old hotel bar as I waited for night to fall, light streaming in from the arching bay windows all along the south wall, though none of it touched me where I was in the shadows. I had a plan in place to steal Shawn's shipment of cocaine and it was going to be a dirty job that I needed a certain kind of cold, detached mindset for. Luckily for me, that was my permanent frame of mind.

I thought of Rogue in the sauna where I'd put her again, sure I could still taste her blood on my tongue. I replayed the moment in my mind and the way she'd shivered for me which had clearly had nothing to do with the cold.

I considered going to her, then wondered why I'd do something like that. And as time ticked by, my thoughts inevitably drifted to the past so I slipped into the cage of my memories, falling into an inescapable nightmare that followed me everywhere I went in life.

Officer White guided me along, my stomach hurting from where his steel-capped boots had slammed into it just minutes ago. It was late at night, the prison quiet and all cells we passed locked up tight.

My gaze hooked on my cell at the end of the walkway as our footsteps rang out across the metal. It was the one place I could get any relief in this hell, a small, six by eight haven of peace where I could rest. My cellmate was a runt of a guy who barely spoke and most of the time I could just ignore he was there, shut my eyes and think of Rogue. Sometimes I wrote letters to her, filled with all the words I should have said when I got the chance, but I always ended up ripping them to pieces and flushing them away. They were just ammo for Officer White and his friends to use against me if they found them, and though I never named her on paper, I still feared someone seeing my weakness laid out like that. She was my secret, my home. One I'd return to just as soon as I got out of here. I only hoped she knew I was coming for her, no matter how long it took. One day, I'd walk free of this hell, seek her out and pray she hadn't forgotten me.

White dragged me past my cell and I gazed back at it in confusion.

"That was my cell," I told him, though he definitely knew that. He'd dragged me out of it just hours ago.

"Not anymore it isn't," he said darkly, a smile twisting his thin lips.

My heart thumped out a violent tune as he led me past a few more cells and finally radioed his buddy up in the control room to open a door ahead of us. I schooled my features, not letting him see me rattled, but inside I was starting to panic. Everything had been the same for so long. I'd keep my head down in the day, get taken to the trench by Officer White and the others at midnight, but by three I was always back in my cell and I knew they wouldn't come for me again until the following night. I could handle that. I'd adjusted to it. But this change screamed wrong to me.

White pulled the door open and shoved me into the cell. "You're bunking with Krasinski now," he purred in my ear and that name sent dread bleeding into every bone in my body.

I twisted around in desperation, planning to fight my way out, even if I ended up in isolation for it. But anything was better than being in here. White slammed the door in my face before I got close and the lock clunked loudly in the dark.

My breaths came hollowly from my chest, matched by the heavy breathing of the man in the room with me. He was the biggest guy in this prison. Two hundred and fifty pounds of muscle, a bald head and an array of silver capped teeth.

46

"Hello, pretty boy." I felt him draw closer and twisted around, his hulking form approaching in the gloom. I was tall, but during the few months I'd been here I'd lost some weight and now White had ensured I was injured all the fucking time too.

His hand snaked around my wrist and I threw a punch with a cry of fury. He spat a curse as it cracked against his jaw. His grip tightened and his answering punch knocked me flat on my back, my head spinning like it used to on the Waltzers at Sinners' Playground. One of us would sit in the car while the other four would work to spin it as fast as possible until we almost threw up. I felt like that now, the world moving around me at an incredible speed, but only shadows drew closer for a moment before I forced myself to picture the smiling faces of my friends. Then I focused on the one that always called to me, her laughter lighting up the air and making all the darkness recede.

"Maverick?" Mia called, snapping me out of the past and I found her dropping down beside me on the couch with a pout. Her nose was still red from the punch she'd gotten from Rogue and she rubbed it indignantly as I pushed myself up, a dark cloud clinging to me. I couldn't face her now, I needed to be alone. When the dark got in, it wouldn't leave until I looked death in the eye and found purpose again.

"She's a feisty little fucker, huh?" Mia said.

"Mm," I grunted as she moved to straddle me and I gazed past her head as my heart drummed out a furious tune against my ribcage.

Mia captured my cheek, turning my head to make me look at her and my breaths came faster at being touched right now. I pushed her off of my lap and got up, scrubbing my hands over my eyes as my skin crawled and bile rose up in the back of my throat.

"Are you okay, baby?" she asked, coming up behind me and stroking her fingers down my back.

"Don't touch me," I snarled, jerking away and striding to the closest window where the daylight was streaming in. I wasn't sure what I was expecting the sun to do, but maybe I was hoping it would chase away some of the shadows lurking in my soul.

"Oh no, are you…having an episode?" she whispered like those words were dirty and I gritted my jaw, tired of having to indulge her all the time. But

I did. Biting at her now would only mean an apology later. And I really didn't have the patience for those.

"Yes," I forced out. "I need some space. Maybe you should visit your stepfather tonight. I'll be on a job anyway."

"Are you sure you don't want me to stay? I could run us a bath?" she offered. "I've got some new bath salts, there's a Himalayan one which is meant to draw out bad energy. I think it could really do you some good."

Lord give me the fucking patience of a saint. This girl and her herbal, salty, voodoo, crystal bullshit will be the end of me.

"No, Mia. I have work to do," I said sharply. Too sharply. I twisted around, finding her with a pissed off expression and I dug deep for the words I needed to smooth this over before she went off badmouthing me to her step daddy Kaiser Rosewood. "It's just for a night. I'll see you tomorrow. We could have dinner?"

Her features softened at that and she broke a smile, hurrying toward me and tiptoeing up to kiss me. I let her, pecking her lips as I fought off the shudder creeping along my skin.

"I'll see you tomorrow then," she said. "And I'll leave a moonstone crystal under your pillow to help you sleep better."

"Thanks," I forced out through a false smile and she jogged out of the room with her pert ass bouncing in her dress.

The smile instantly fell from my face and I took a knife from my hip, striding up to the nearest chair and stabbing straight into the centre of the seat. I stabbed and fucking stabbed as I pictured Krasinksi and bled my rage into every blow I struck until I was panting and there was stuffing everywhere.

Then I straightened, put my knife away and walked out of the room, heading towards the only distraction I could think of right now. We needed to go soon anyway, so why shouldn't I head there?

I made it to the spa and walked inside, looking around and realising she must be in the sauna so I moved to stand outside the door, listening for any movement within it. Rogue's singing carried to me, her stupid, out of tune voice amusing me as I leaned my shoulder against the wall and listened as she made up the words she didn't know to Plastic Hearts by Miley Cyrus. Having my little lost girl locked up in my compound was a satisfying feeling, like chaining the best piece of my past to my new life and not letting it go.

I gripped the door handle and pushed inside, shutting it behind me as heat washed over me and the darkness seemed to lift a little. Usually only spilling blood would soothe me after a so-called 'episode' but my body was beginning to calm already and maybe it was because I knew how much bloodshed was coming tonight.

Rogue had some serious making up to do before she'd be anywhere near getting into my good graces, but I doubted I was in hers either considering I'd kidnapped her. Amount of fucks I gave on the matter: zero.

I pushed a hand into my hair as I closed in on her, but then I forcibly dropped my hand wondering what the fuck I was doing.

"Hello, songbird," I said, making her jump and turn around.

She was standing up on one of the benches in a black shirt which belonged to me and hung to her mid-thigh and I couldn't say I hated the way it looked on her.

Her eyes dropped to me and her song fell dead on her lips as she gazed coolly at me. "That colour doesn't suit you, Rick. With your skin tone you should go for a dusky pink."

"Say what?" I frowned.

"Your lipstick," she said lightly, but there was a sharp undertone to her voice which I couldn't miss. I knew her too damn well, even now.

I rubbed my thumb over my lower lip and when I took it away it was as ruby red as Mia's lips. I smirked. "Jealous, beautiful?"

"Of that colour? Nah, I'm more of a candyfloss pink girl. You look like a cheap hooker. I wouldn't pay a buck for a night with someone wearing that." She smirked right back and a laugh escaped me.

"Well there go my dreams of being a high end whore," I said, moving further into the room and leaning back against the wall.

"What *are* your dreams, Rick?" She asked, arching an eyebrow at me as she lay down on the bench and my gaze dragged along the length of her body, her bronzed legs stretching out and her toes flexing.

"Right now? Fucking you senseless and sending a video to your boyfriend to make him cry," I replied easily.

"I don't have a boyfriend. Unless you count the Green Power Ranger, but it's really more of a one-way relationship at the moment on account of him not knowing I exist. I'm not sure he'd appreciate the video either way."

"I'm not sure you would either once I was finished with you and wrote my name on your back in my cum," I said thoughtfully.

"Is that your party trick?" she asked. "Not really family friendly."

"Depends whose family you ask. The Addams Family might enjoy it," I shot back and a smile played around the corners of her mouth.

"The Brady Bunch, not so much," she said.

"I dunno, the Amish are probably so horny they're desperate to see a cock that doesn't crow at dawn."

"The Brady Bunch aren't Amish," she snort laughed and it was so fucking adorable it made me miss her. And not just her, us.

It was fucking stupid considering she was right there in front of me, but I missed our old life, I missed her easy smiles and her eyes when they weren't weighed down by shadows. I missed who I was before…everything. But that was way back before I realised that life is nothing but wading through shit. Sunset Cove had been the best brand of shit to wade through once though. Especially while she waded through it with me.

I snubbed the intrusive thoughts as I reminded myself she'd come back to town and chosen Fox and his band of merry assfucks over me. They'd predictably let her down though and I guessed if I was really honest with myself, it just made me want to rip out all of their insides a little more than usual. Fact was, she didn't want to be here, and she didn't want to be there anymore either. Looked like lost girl was lost again.

"You ready to make up for what you cost me, beautiful?" I asked darkly and the light fell from her eyes as she nodded. "Good. You have thirty seconds to get dressed." I kicked the bag of clothes I'd had one of my men pick up for her across the room. "Chop, chop."

She took to the challenge, grabbing a pair of ripped black denim shorts and pulling them on along with a black cami before putting on some socks and sneakers. She tugged her colourful hair out from under the cami, thrusting her tits out as she did so and I cocked my head as I watched her. Her body was almost as inviting as it had been down in the freezer, spread out and bared for me. That was an image I was never going to forget and so long as I remained in

50

this world it was going to be imprinted on the inside of my skull for whenever I got bored.

"Didn't they have anything other than black in the store?" Rogue asked, looking down at her outfit with a frown.

"I guess it was picked to match my soul. Now get over here, we're leaving." I patted my thigh, commanding her like a dog and her eyebrows shot up, her face saying fuck no to that order. Which was just what I'd hoped she'd do. I strode toward her, whipping her up into the air and throwing her over my shoulder. She started swearing at me as I locked my arm over her thighs and carried her out of the sauna.

I walked downstairs and passed a bunch of my men as I exited the foyer, striding towards the black van which was waiting for me. One of my boys slid the side door open for me and I spun her around in my arms, dropping her onto her back inside the van. She gasped as I grabbed her wrists, locking them together with handcuffs which were waiting for me inside the vehicle before she could even try and fight me off. Not that she'd have been able to. I smirked mockingly at her and she bared her teeth at me like a savage.

"Get your hands off of me, you cock-sucking terrapin," she snarled and I roared a laugh.

I flipped her over onto her front and she screamed as I locked her ankles together with another set of cuffs and she rocked wildly from side to side like a beached dolphin as she tried to escape.

I slapped her ass and my men chuckled as she yelped, spitting furious curses at me. I rolled her over again and she bent her knees, kicking me in the chest, but I pressed hard back against her feet until her knees bent all the way back to her stomach again and I was the only thing she could see.

"Get fucked, Rick," she hissed.

"Oh I plan to, beautiful," I said, brushing a couple of pastel pink strands away from her face and narrowly avoiding a bite from her.

I hooked my fingers under her cami, scoring my thumb up her side until her breath snagged in her throat. I grinned at that reaction and her face turned thunderous at being caught out.

"If you put your cock anywhere near me, I'll cut it off," she threatened and I could see she was entirely capable of something like that. My dick throbbed at having her beneath me and even with the threat hanging over it, it seemed more than happy to take the risk of a beheading just to get closer to her.

"Didn't realise you were into knife play, beautiful," I taunted. "At least cut if off after you've come on it a few times. You might as well fulfil the dreams you've had about it."

"You fucking-" I didn't hear the end of that sentence as I picked up the rag lying beside her and forced it into her mouth, lifting her head so I could tie the gag tight in place. She continued to scream against it, but the sound was muffled and as I stepped out of the van and shut the door, I could hardly hear a peep from her.

I climbed into the cab and started the engine, driving down to the dock and boarding the boat waiting for me there. It was a long drive to Sterling, but I had all the time in the world to fuck over my enemies. And tonight, I'd be taking down two birds with one stone.

Rogue had started kicking the walls of the van about an hour back, but I ignored the repetitive thumping as I drove north, turning up my music to drown her out. I played songs I knew she'd hate just to get under her skin and even listened to the entire Les Misérables soundtrack because Rosie Morgan used to watch it on repeat in their group home and drive her crazy. We'd even stolen the DVD from her once and we'd all taken turns hitting it with an old hammer we'd found on the Rosewood Manor grounds. Rosie had somehow gotten her hands on a new one though, playing it in their rec room at all opportunities and declaring how incredible the music was. I remembered Rogue shouting at Rosie, *'I'm Les Miserable enough just by looking at your face, I don't need that shit to make me feel worse!'* before punching her in the nose.

A smile quirked up my lips for a moment and I turned off the track, the warbling tune grating on me. Silence fell and I was sure Rogue was listening as I banged my fist on the back wall of the cab.

"I hope you're enjoying the road trip, beautiful," I called as I accelerated onto the interstate.

A muffled sob sounded in reply and a frown lowered my brow.

I focused on the road as quiet fell once more but then a sob came again, a heartbroken little noise that found the last shard of my heart and attempted to tug on it.

Fuck no. I don't give a shit that she's crying.

The sound came again and I gritted my teeth, focusing on the road ahead, but my eyes flicked to a rest stop up ahead. I drummed my fingers on the wheel as another soft sob reached my ears and I ground my teeth harder before aggressively signalling off the highway and taking the exit.

What the fuck am I doing?

Why am I indulging this?

I drove through the huge parking lot and rounded the back of a burger place, parking there in the shadows. The sun was setting, painting the sky in deepest magenta.

There were no other vehicles here and I did a sweep for cameras before killing the engine, grabbing a gun from the black bag in the passenger footwell and stepping out of the cab. I hesitated outside the side door, wondering why I was even bothering with this. Who gave a shit if she was crying?

I hesitated another few seconds before unlocking the door and yanking it open. She didn't move from where she was facing the back wall, her body curled into a ball. Another sob wracked through her and I climbed into the van, awkward as a duck in a bra as I moved behind her and wondered what the fuck I was even planning to do.

"Rogue?" I muttered gruffly and she released another small sob. "Are you hurt?" She didn't answer and I knelt down, pressing the gun to her back. "Don't scream," I warned before untying her gag and pulling it free.

I rolled her over and she stared up at me in the dark, her eyes glinting. "Go away, Rick," she said in a choked voice.

"Can't do that, beautiful," I said in a low tone. "What's wrong?"

"Like you care," she scoffed. "You're pointing a fucking gun at me. Just go back to driving. I wanna be done with this night." She turned her head away and I stared at her, unsure what to do. But my hands moved of their own accord and I tucked the gun into the back of my jeans then cleared my throat.

I was reminded of the time she'd been stung by a jellyfish when she was ten. I'd carried her out of the water and she'd sobbed in my arms while she worried she'd killed the damn jellyfish because she'd punched it. That was the way of my lost girl, she'd always cared more about other's pain over her own. And for a second, we were just those two kids on the beach again, holding onto each other and discussing whether a jellyfish could survive a fist to the face. Or if they even had faces.

"I don't want you to cry," I said roughly and her lips pursed.

"Well I'm in the back of your psycho van, tied up, my ankles fucking hurt because the cuffs are too tight and I'm stuck with another one of the boys who's determined to make me suffer as much as possible."

I couldn't do much about a lot of that, but I could make one thing better. I grabbed her ankles, taking the key from my pocket and unlocking the cuffs. "There, is that-?"

Her bound fists crashed into my face and as I was forced back a few inches, she leapt out the door, running for her fucking life with a wild laugh.

"Bitch!" I bellowed in fury at her fucking tricking me, chasing after her as she started screaming for help.

My heart beat out a furious, panicked tune, and I went to that cold, dark place inside me where nothing but rage lived. I collided with her, taking her down onto a grassy verge and slamming my palm over her mouth. She bit me like an animal, but I didn't give a shit, dragging her back to the van and throwing her inside.

"Wait!" She yelled before I shut the door in her face.

I hesitated, my lip peeled back in a snarl as I took the gun from the back of my jeans in a warning.

"Let me ride in the cab," she demanded. "This is fucking bullshit. You told me you want me to help you rectify this shit and I agreed. So why am I being carted out on this job like fucking cattle?!"

"Because you could be seen by a Harlequin," I barked. "And I'm too busy for a goddamn ambush."

"We're miles out of town, who the fuck is going to see me now?" she demanded and I had to admit she had a point. "You can tie me to the fucking seat in there if it makes you happy, but if you make me ride back here all the way, I won't help you do shit tonight. In fact, I'll scream the second I see one of Shawn's men and make sure they know who's coming for them."

I growled through my teeth. I didn't even need her on this job, I could just leave her in the van. But fuck it, if letting her ride up front would quit her whining then fine.

I grabbed her leg, yanking her toward me and she punched me in the arm. "I can walk, donkey dick," she snapped and I grunted irritably, moving aside and gesturing for her to get out with a dramatic bow.

"This way, your fucking highness," I growled.

"Thank you, peasant," she said lightly, jumping out of the van and I closed the door before following her around to the passenger's side of the cab, pointing the way with my gun. She climbed inside and I slammed the door behind her, walking around and hopping back into the driver's seat before hitting the door lock button.

"So your crying was an act," I sniped as I grabbed a length of rope from the glove compartment and tied her wrist cuffs to the door beside her. It was long enough that she could still move about a fair bit, but not so long that she could reach me.

"Duh, do you think I'd actually cry over you? Been there, done that, won the *I got dumped by my friends* t-shirt."

"I tried to go after you," I growled.

"I know," she said, her tone softening a fraction. She kicked her feet up on the dashboard and leaned over to swipe my phone from the cup holder.

"Hey," I snarled, reaching for it, but she held it away.

"Oh who do you think I'm gonna call, Rick? Ghostbusters?" She rolled her eyes then picked out Savage by Bahari on my phone, the song filling the car.

"You could call the cops," I pointed out.

"Contrary to what you think, I actually want to go on this trip to fuck over Shawn and get your drugs back. So get driving, and can we pick up some burgers? I'm starved. What kind of road trip is this if we don't have snacks? Have you been in here this whole time just…breathing? Ergh." She looked around hopefully for any sign of snacks, but there was nothing here. I opened the bag in the footwell, pulling out my leather jacket and tossing it over her

55

arms to cover the cuffs and rope.

"Fine, we'll get burgers," I agreed, figuring I was kinda hungry anyway.

"I want chips and dip too. And a cherry soda. And a blueberry muffin."

"A muffin?" I snapped. "Where am I gonna get a fucking muffin?"

"Don't know, don't care. But I want one, and you owe me for being an asshole."

I blew out a derisive breath then started up the engine and drove around to the drive-thru for the burger place. I ordered Rogue a veggie burger with extra fries and mayonnaise then got myself a burger before driving the van over to the convenience store.

"You'll have to untie me," Rogue announced. "I can't eat with my hands all tied up."

I gave her a blank look. "You'll manage."

"Okay then." She opened the box of fries and instantly sent a bunch falling to the floor. "Woopsie." She dropped a few more.

"Oh for fuck's sake." I leaned over, untying the rope. "There, better?"

"The cuffs are the main issue." She batted her lashes.

I made sure the van was locked up tight then took off the cuffs and watched her closely.

Rogue tucked into her burger while I devoured mine in three bites, then I locked her back up in the cuffs and headed into the store to get her fucking snacks. Why was I even agreeing to this? She didn't need snacks. She had a burger. But I needed a piss anyway, so whatever.

When I returned to the van, I found her blasting Blood // Water by Grandson, her eyes closed and her head bobbing to the furious beat. A couple of manbun dickwads in their convertible douche-mobile beside the van were watching her, and as one of them started making a blowjob gesture, sticking his tongue in his cheek and the other laughed loudly, I dropped the bag of snacks onto the hood of the van and casually strode over to them.

"Wait, man-" the first cried as I slammed my fist into his face and broke his nose. The second tried to scramble out over the backseats and I caught him by his belt as he made it to the ground, kicking his legs out from under him and slamming his face into the side of his car and denting the metal. He wailed and I strode away, grabbing the snacks and climbing back into the van.

Rogue's eyes popped open as the song came to an end and I dumped the bag in her lap.

"Can I have my cuffs off again for eating?" she asked sweetly. "I'm hardly gonna dive out of a moving vehicle even if I could get the door open."

I grunted, unlocking them once more before I took off down the road, casually wiping the flecks of blood off of my knuckles onto my jeans. Rogue didn't notice as she tucked into her chips and dips. I'd even gotten her the damn muffin from the bakery.

"You want one?" she asked, offering a chip under my nose piled high with sour cream. I devoured it in one bite and licked her fingers clean of dip, making a sexy little gasp escape her.

"Careful where you put that dip. Wherever it goes, my tongue will follow," I warned.

"I'll be sure to put it on a hobo's asshole at the next rest stop then," she said smoothly and a laugh tumbled from my chest. *Fucking beautiful bitch.*

I drove us north for miles while Rogue made a playlist and acted like we were kids out on an adventure again. She even had a wistful look in her eyes when we started driving through a forest on the outskirts of Sterling, the moonlight bleeding through the trees and painting it all silver. While she watched the world, I stole glances at her, wondering what those ocean blue eyes had seen in all the years we'd been apart. Heat Waves by Glass Animals started up through the speakers and the lyrics were all too close to the truth right then.

"Would you rather be reincarnated as an owl or a goose?" Rogue rounded on me suddenly, catching me staring and my head snapped around to look at the road.

"An owl," I answered easily.

"Because of your owl ears?" She flicked my ear and I batted her hand away.

"I do not have owl ears," I growled. "Owls don't even have ears."

"They have huuuuge ears," she countered. "They're just under a load of feathers."

"Are you saying I have big ears?" I shot at her.

"Not as big as an owl's, I suppose," she mused.

"So I guess you'd be a goose on account of your goose feet," I said, fighting a grin.

"I do not have goose feet!" she laughed.

"You do, and you honk," I said.

"I don't *honk*," she belly laughed and accidentally knocked her muffin flying toward the footwell. My hand shot out on instinct and I caught it in my fist.

"Woah, you saved my muffin," she cooed.

"I guess it's mine now then." I brought it to my lips and took a vicious bite out of it and Rogue gasped, diving at me in fury as she tried to wrestle it out of my grip while I fought to get the rest of it in my mouth.

"You muffin stealing bastard," she hissed, biting my hand as she tried to make me let go of it. Her palm landed right on my cock and I cursed, the muffin falling from my fingers into the footwell between my legs and she dropped down to grab it, her hand still firmly crushing my junk.

"*Rogue*," I grunted, grabbing a fistful of her hair. She was still a nutcase over food apparently. "Either put that hand to good use on my cock or remove it," I snapped, trying to grab her wrist as I watched the road.

"Got it," she said excitedly as her hand slipped off of my dick. Her head snapped up and smacked into the steering wheel, sending her face-planting into my crotch and I laughed, shoving her head down in revenge.

"You're so hungry for my cock, it's embarrassing," I said, rubbing her face against my jeans and my dick got overexcited as I started getting hard.

"You thucking prick, let me up", she said, her voice muffled against my zipper.

"What was that, beautiful?" I taunted, my fingers tightening in her hair. "Are you whispering sweet nothings to my cock?"

She managed to get her hand between my legs and somehow pinched my fucking balls.

The van swerved as I let go of her with a curse and she flew back into her seat, tucking into her muffin as I got the vehicle under control.

"Why does everyone talk about confident people having big balls?" Rogue mused. "Balls are the most vulnerable thing on a man's body. You know what's really powerful? A vag. They push freaking babies out of them. And sure, you can kick a girl in the vag, but it won't cripple her. One kick to a ball though and bam, you're out of the game, dude. It just doesn't make sense."

"True," I agreed.

"Do you think we'll be friends when you come back as an owl and I'm a goose?" she asked, changing the conversation as swiftly as a turning wind. "Do you think we'll get a do-over?"

I clucked my tongue, my mood darkening. "I'm not coming back, beautiful. If I do, I'll keep telling the world to get fucked until it offers me oblivion."

She fell quiet for a long moment and I felt her eyes on me, peeling back the layers of my flesh as she hunted for the reason why I'd said that. Rogue was a pretty little indulgence for now, a flash of colour in my endlessly grey world. But her being here didn't change things. My life was set on one course. Once the Harlequins were dead, I'd fill my revolver with rounds and rig my usual game of roulette in favour of death. There was no other purpose for me anymore. I didn't want this life as much as it didn't want me. And when I examined it close enough, even the rays of sunlight in my youth had always been on a time limit.

I just wished I'd been able to see the timer running down back then so I could have made more out of each moment, tasted the sea salt on my lips a little longer, laughed fuller and harder, taken more photos, captured more of the sweetness to help counter the bitterness that had been coming. I knew regrets were pointless, but I had them all the same. *I guess you never realise how bright the day is until the rain comes.*

"What happened to you in prison, Maverick?" Rogue asked just as I parked up at the edge of a track in the woods and pulled the parking brake.

"We're here," I announced, ignoring her question and stepping straight out of the van so I didn't have to meet her probing gaze.

I walked around to her side, opening the door, grabbing the handcuffs from the footwell and tucking them into my pocket. I took her hand as I drew her out of the van onto the dark road, glancing about for any sign of movement around us.

I shut the door and pushed her up against it, crowding her in close as I stared down at my little unicorn and drove my hips against hers. "If you're going to run, do it now. I need this job to go smoothly and I can't babysit you through it. That means you're free, no chains. But you do as I say, when I say it. If you can't do that then go." I stepped back, gesturing for her to take off into the trees and disappear forever. But she stayed right where she was and I wasn't sure either of us really knew why she did it. It definitely wasn't to make things up to me. Maybe it was to do with the connection we'd always had and the time when we'd been each other's ride or die.

"If the sun rises tomorrow, we'll watch it together," I spoke the words we'd always said to each other whenever we were out causing mischief into the night. I had them inked along my collarbone now, but you'd only find them if you looked hard enough.

Her lips parted at those words and heat began to rise in my body, my heart started to pound and all I could do for two seconds was stare at her mouth and imagine what she tasted like. Our breaths washed together and the silence of the night pressed in. It was just us here, alone, miles and miles away from Sunset Cove, where we'd wished we could be when we were sixteen years old. If I'd just taken her and run, would we be together now, living the life we'd always dreamed of?

I forced myself to pull away, striding to the van door and tugging it open, grabbing out a bag and slinging it over my shoulder. Then I took the gun from the back of my waistband, clicked the safety off and handed it to Rogue. I had too many regrets, and I'd spent endless hours in prison thinking over how things could have been different. But the past was like sand turned to glass; there was no undoing it.

"Shoot me now or forever hold your peace." I stood before her in the dark and she pointed the gun right at my heart. "You'll wanna aim a little higher, beautiful. There's nothing there to pull the trigger on."

She rolled her eyes and lowered the gun, gesturing for me to lead the way ahead. I turned and marched up the dirt track into the woods while Rogue stayed hot on my heels. It was half a mile's walk to my planned location and I checked the GPS on my phone a couple of times when we had to head off the track and carve a path through the trees.

I tapped out a message to the leader of the men I'd hired for this job. They were already here, in position and waiting on my signal, ready to unleash a blaze of fire and blood on The Dead Dogs.

We reached a tall wire fence and I dropped the pack from my shoulder, taking out some bolt cutters and making a way through. I picked up my bag and ducked through first, checking the area before beckoning Rogue after me. All was quiet, but the sound of a river came from up ahead as we kept walking. I crouched down as we reached the top of a hill and gazed into the valley below.

Huge red shipping containers were lined up on a concrete compound surrounded by armed guards. A large boat was bobbing on the river beyond them and floodlights lit up the area.

I pulled Rogue down to the ground with me and opened up my bag, setting up the sniper rifle and placing it in its stand on the ground.

"Stay low," I growled at Rogue as I lay down and moved into position, the gun resting against my shoulder as I gazed down the scope.

"What are you, a fucking mercenary?" she hissed at me.

"Nope, I'm just an asshole with big balls – sorry, a big vag."

She snorted, lying down close beside me, her arm brushing mine and making my skin prickle with rising hairs.

"What's the plan?" she whispered.

"My men are waiting on the river," I murmured, setting my gaze on the boat. "How good's your aim?" I asked.

"Perfect," she said and I leaned back from the scope, taking a flare gun from my bag and sending a message to my men with my phone.

"When I tell you to, shoot a flare at the boat," I said.

"What if I miss?" she hissed.

"Then we're dead," I said with a shrug.

"No pressure then," she muttered and I chuckled a little manically, looking back down the scope, my gaze fixed on the boat as my men climbed onto it in the dark, just shadows moving across the deck and dousing the whole thing in gasoline.

"Ready, beautiful?" I murmured as my men got off the boat and dropped back into the water.

"Ready," she whispered, a note of excitement in her voice.

I lined up my scope on my first victim who was closest to the boat, my pulse thumping harder at the coming chaos.

"Light her up," I commanded and Rogue fired the flare.

It shot out over the compound and a shout of alarm went up as it cascaded through the sky in a stream of red sparks. And while it fell towards its fiery death, I pulled the trigger. The bullet cut through the air and the first man's skull shattered the same moment the flare hit the boat, lighting it up in a burning blaze of hellfire.

A grin pulled at my mouth as my men poured out of the water, shooting at The Dead Dogs while I picked them off like sitting ducks. They dropped like flies as they scrambled to try and make sense of what was happening, but it was far too late already. Between my sniper rifle and the men on the ground, they didn't stand a chance and blood coloured the concrete red as bullets cut through the air and men's screams reached up to the sky.

My heart thundered in my chest and my breaths came heavier as I got off on the absolute bloody mayhem unfolding before me.

As the fight spread across the compound, I swung my rifle around, hunting down one of the men among my own, my gaze sharpening on him as he stabbed and stabbed a man on the ground beneath him. My finger kissed the trigger and my upper lip peeled back as I pulled it. He was thrown backwards to the ground dead, no one around to see him fall. Rogue gasped as she realised what I'd done and I moved to kneel, packing up my rifle and stuffing it into the bag before putting it on my back.

"Come on," I growled, shoving to my feet.

"Why'd you do that?" she demanded, grabbing my arm as I started down the hill towards the complex, taking a knife from my hip. "Rick?" she snapped, but I ignored her, upping my pace as I fixed my gaze on the final Dead Dogs still standing.

Before I made it to the compound, I shoved Rogue up against a tree, grabbing her wrist and locking it in a cuff.

"Hey!" she barked just before I locked the other end to a branch above her head. "Wait!"

I dumped my bag at her feet, grabbing her throat and slamming my mouth to hers, figuring if I was about to die, I'd at least have gotten the taste of her I'd been craving my whole life. She tasted like sunshine and the thousands of days lost between us. It was only a few seconds and our mouths were only crushed together like kids who didn't know how to do it right, but it was the most delicious kiss I'd ever had, and probably ever would have again.

I pulled away as she spit curses at me and I ran out into the light, racing across the concrete and slamming my knife into a Dead Dog's back, bringing him to his knees. I swiped my blade across his throat to finish him and relished the bloodlust coursing through my veins, Rogue Easton's unicorn taste on my lips and an urgent fire in my belly which matched the rising flames on the boat.

I hurried around the closest shipping container, finding myself eye to eye with the barrel of a gun. I knocked it aside just as it went off, the bang echoing through my head before I stabbed my knife into my enemy's chest. He died with a wail and I yanked my blade free, leaping over him as the heat of the fire washed across my skin, warming me right down to my frozen heart.

I rounded another corner and grabbed a guy by the back of the head, slamming his face into a container before driving my knife into the back of his neck. He died at my feet and a few of my hired men nodded to me as they finished off a couple more guys.

Silence fell, the screams lost to the wind and the fight officially won. I wiped blood from my cheek and sought out the leader of this little unit I'd hand-picked to help me tonight.

Colten was a cruel bastard with a constantly sneering face. Ex-army, six-foot-fuck-knew and eyes as dark as sin.

"Bring the boats up the river," I commanded. "I want these containers emptied out in less than thirty minutes."

"Yes, sir," Colten said, saluting me with a smirk. Blood stained his trousers and he drove his knife into a guy twitching on the floor, doing it slow and making the pain last as long as he could.

When he'd had his men bring the boats up the river and the containers were cracked open, I helped load the kilos and kilos of cocaine onto them. It was heavy work, but I relished the strain on my muscles and the heat coursing under my flesh. I soon shed my shirt and tucked it into the back of my pants as I worked, my eyes occasionally flicking to the trees where I'd left Rogue. She didn't call out again, but I kept thinking about the fact that I should have gagged her. I may have been the boss here, but these men weren't part of my gang. And I didn't know how far my authority would extend with someone like Colten.

I did a quick headcount of the men as I helped carry another crate of cocaine onto one of the boats, my heart jack-hammering when I didn't spot the ex-army asshole anywhere.

I whistled at a guy near me, making him take over from me and jogging away through the compound. I just needed to check, just make sure…

My heart thrashed and panic clawed its way up the inside of my skin as I ran into the woods, a dark, male laugh reaching me from within the trees.

No, fuck, no.

I readied my blade, my heart beating frantically. I'd brought her here. I'd put her at risk. It was my responsibility if something happened to her.

"Who left this pretty thing all tied up and ready for me? Guess it's my lucky day," Colten purred and venom poured into my blood.

I made it around the tree, finding Colten there with one hand over Rogue's mouth and the other unbuckling his pants. The world slowed and I saw nothing but rage, a liquid black death seeping through my veins and turning me into the darkest of monsters I could be.

I locked my arm around his throat, cutting off his air supply and driving my blade into his kidney. His scream was kept quiet by the pressure I was applying on his throat, but his elbow came back, using some bullshit army move to get himself free.

He dove on me and we hit the ground, blood spilling from his wound as he took his own blade from his hip and tried to stab it into my throat. I jerked aside and the knife slammed into the ground instead, sinking in deep.

Adrenaline pulsed through my veins as my fist crashed into his ribs and a loud crack made him cry out. My hand slammed over his lips at the same time to muffle the noise and I locked my legs around his waist, rolling us over and shoving his head down in the dirt, his knife lost and my advantage regained.

I brought my own blade up to finish the job but his fingers locked around my wrist, pressing some pressure point that made me release it.

I punched the asshole in the face as he tried to roll us over then my hands latched onto his throat and I knew I'd never let go. He clawed at my arms, fighting and kicking as I clenched my teeth and held on, squeezing and squeezing as my muscles locked in place and every part of me detached from anything human or moral in my brain. He fought until the very last second, but his gaze flashed with fear as he finally realised I wasn't going to release him. And I watched, unblinking as the life was snuffed out like a flame in his eyes and my fingers finally unlocked from his throat.

I stood up, panting as I flexed my hands and gazed down at the scum at my feet, spitting on him for good measure. No one touched Rogue Easton. That was a law I'd lived by for as long as I could remember. That hadn't changed now. And so long as I was still drawing breath on this earth, I'd abide by it.

"Rick," Rogue breathed and I turned, finding her staring at me with wide eyes. She saw me now, unveiled and unchained. The dark creature I was. The beast who would bleed the world dry for her. Even to this day.

I didn't acknowledge her, turning and walking straight past her to check on my shipment. I pulled my shirt back on and hoped no one would notice the new scratches on my forearms as I walked back to the men loading the cocaine. They were just finishing up and filing onto the boats, so I didn't need to linger here any longer.

I clasped my hands behind my back to hide the marks and barked out orders to them. "Colten's driving back with me. Take the shipment to my new warehouse. I want it unloaded before dawn and you will all report to me at Bellow Hill when you're done for your payment," I called.

I chorus of yes sirs carried back to me and I nodded, walking away and weaving through the containers, passing by the guy I'd shot who belonged to their crew. He was an ex-Harlequin, his gang tattoo still in place on his arm. A little birdie had told me he'd run from the wrath of Fox after raping a girl and killing her boyfriend, but The Dead Dogs didn't know that. He was a false message to Shawn, telling him exactly who'd stolen all of these drugs from him. And that certainly wasn't me.

Have fun figuring that shit out, Foxy Boy.

By dawn, every one of the men who'd worked this job for me would be feeding the sharks far off the coast of Sunset Cove. Colten's gang of thugs lived down in Mexico when they weren't being bought off as guns for hire by the shadiest motherfuckers in the US. I'd done my homework and knew what they got up to when they were out of the country. They were a bunch of animals, butchering women, children, raping, stealing, murdering innocents.

So I'd bought their time with a bunch of cash I planned on taking right back out of their pockets the moment they lay bloody at my feet. I didn't need loose ends with flapping tongues that could speak my truth to Shawn Mackenzie. And these assholes were overdue their deaths.

I strode back to Rogue, unlocking her cuffs, picking up my bag and keeping her hand in mine as I towed her up the hill. I felt her eyes on me, but she said nothing as we walked into the dark side by side. And for the first time in a long time, I was certain the sun would return tomorrow and my lost girl would once again be there with me to watch it rise.

Rejects Park

ROGUE

CHAPTER FIVE

Rick hauled me down the path and back to his van with bloody fingers curled tight around my hand and I gritted my teeth as I just let him. It wasn't like I had any choice in it now anyway. We needed to get the fuck out of here and I could wait until we were on the road again for my answers.

He stayed silent as he opened the driver's door and shoved me inside, forcing me to crawl across the seats to my own seat and no doubt giving him a nice look at my ass in the freaking shorts he'd bought me.

I folded my legs beneath me as I took my seat and Rick started up the van, wheeling it around and driving us back out of this little slice of shitsville.

His jaw was locked tight, some demons circling his mind which he clearly didn't want to give voice to, and I looked out into the dark rather than watching him as he drove.

Minutes ticked by one by one until I finally gave in, blowing out a frustrated breath as the silence just stretched on endlessly and I realised he was perfectly willing to leave it that way.

"Why make a deal for me to come with you if you had no intention of using me?" I asked, watching him in the blurry reflection cast against my window instead of turning to look at his stupid face.

"You shot the flare," he pointed out.

"Fuck you. The only thing I did was follow you into danger so that you could string me up to a motherfucking tree where anything could have happened to me."

"I wanted to keep you away from those men. Colten in particular. It was fucking stupid of me to bring you at all. I thought you'd be safe where I left you...I guess I fucked up on that account." Maverick's bloody knuckles flexed against the steering wheel and I huffed out another breath as I turned to look at him.

"Well I guess I should be thanking you for killing that motherfucker," I muttered. I didn't want to think about how terrified I'd been when that asshole had found me, of the vile things he'd promised to do to me or the look in his eyes which said he'd done it a hundred times before. I didn't even want to think about how relieved I'd been to see Maverick or how I'd felt while watching him kill that man for me; the way he'd looked dressed in violence and death, the way his muscles had flexed and his eyes had flared with a passion that burned right the way down into my soul. Nope, wasn't gonna think about it. "Even though I could have easily managed it myself if you hadn't tied me up like that..."

Maverick shot me a dark look and I rolled my eyes.

"What? Are you expecting me to thank you more profusely than that? You want me to suck your dick for you while I'm at it, oh great and wonderful saviour?" I mocked.

"I wouldn't be opposed to it," he replied, gripping his cock through his jeans provocatively. He tossed me a filthy look and I licked my lips slowly, leaning towards him and moving to lean my hands on the seat between us. Maverick watched me with interest, his eyes not staying on the road nearly enough as I leaned in to speak in his ear.

"Pity I'd rather suck on a dead man's dentures then, isn't it?" I flicked him in the ear and jerked back to make sure he couldn't retaliate.

Maverick snorted and cursed me then shot me another look which almost made me feel like he wanted to say something else, but then his gaze fell on the road once more and it was gone.

"If you and your band of merry assholes had died back there, you do realise I would have been left for Shawn to find, right?" I added. "Or did my fate following your death not occur to you when you ran into a gun fight with a knife?"

"Don't be dramatic, beautiful. I was never going to die."

"And I guess that guy you hired never would have raped me either, right?" I clucked my tongue and looked out into the darkness again as I dropped back into my seat.

"Colten and his men are a means to an end. They're a bunch of villainous scum who make me look like a fucking saint. Not one of them will survive tonight, I can assure you of that, baby girl. And if you want me to promise never to handcuff you to a fucking tree again, then fine - I promise. That good enough for you?"

"Depends on what snacks are left," I muttered, leaning down to rummage through the bag of snacks he'd picked up earlier and grinning to myself triumphantly as I found the can of cherry soda. "Okay. I forgive you," I announced. "So what's next?"

"We drive home. Those men will get the shipment of cocaine tucked up safe in my new, better guarded warehouse ready for the cartel to come collect as planned. The motherfuckers in question will never know the drugs I had been holding for them got burned, meaning none of us get skinned alive. I'll kill the assholes I hired for the job to make sure there's no one left who can talk about it. And tomorrow the sun rises over Sunset Cove once more and it's just another day in paradise," Maverick deadpanned.

"You forgot about me," I pointed out. "There's no one left to talk about it, besides *me*."

"You think I should kill you too?" he questioned, his dark gaze moving over me and making me wonder if he might.

"I think there are worse ways I could die," I replied honestly, cracking open my soda and taking a long swig.

Rick side eyed me like I was fucking insane but also like he liked that, so I guessed we were good.

"I'm not gonna kill you tonight, beautiful," he said eventually.

"Good. Then I want out of the sauna. I could have run tonight and I didn't. I could have shot you and I didn't. But you chained me to a tree like a fucking animal and left me for the rapists to find. I deserve a break."

"Christ," he muttered. "How can you just joke about shit like that?"

"Come on, Rick. I think you know as well as I do that life for people like us is full of a lot of dark fucking shit. So I made my mind up a long time ago to sniff that shit real good, take a big old shitty lungful right down into my gut and tell myself it smelled like roses over and over again until I almost believed it. Life might wanna fuck me over, but that doesn't mean it can't get me off while railing me like I'm a good little whore."

Maverick turned to stare at me and I grinned at him over my can of soda. He stared so long that the van veered off the edge of the road and he cursed as he yanked the wheel around to right it again.

I swore as cherry soda sloshed over my fingers and he reached out to catch my wrist, making me transfer the can to my other hand before he sucked my wet fingers into his mouth to clean them off for me. My body heated and a zip of energy raced right through my core until I was clamping my thighs together and snatching my hand back.

"I wake at the slightest thing anyway, so you can sleep in my bed with me," he said. "No chance of you sneaking off on me or pulling any shit in the night."

"You live in a hotel. Surely there's another room that I could-"

"Take it or leave it, beautiful. I'm either locking you up where I know you can't escape from me, or you're bunking in with me so I can keep you under my watch at all times."

I pursed my lips while my traitorous vagina got all caught up in the idea of that. Maverick was the kind of mistake I definitely shouldn't make. Which meant that a girl with my kind of bad shot calling skills could be in real trouble in that scenario. That said, I was pretty sure I could keep Lady V in check for the sake of sleeping in an actual bed.

"I'll take it," I agreed. "But you can keep your monster cock to yourself. The Ride-a-Rogue attraction is closed for business."

"Whatever you say."

We sped off into the night and I settled myself in for the long drive back to the Cove. I didn't really know what way this whole thing was going to play out for me. I still wasn't any closer to achieving what I'd come back here for and I had more than a few vendettas to strike off of my list. But for now, I was comfortable enough right here, as a captive of the boy I'd once known, taking a road trip in the middle of the night and singing I'm Not Mad by Halsey at the top of my freaking lungs. Life might like giving me lemons, but I was a fucking pro at squirting the juice in someone else's eyes and I wasn't gonna stop squeezing now.

I must have fallen asleep at some point on the journey back because when I woke, we were driving the van off of a boat back on Dead Man's Isle and Maverick was utterly covered in blood.

He glanced my way as I pushed myself upright and I arched a brow at his appearance.

"You dealt with the rest of those men then?" I asked in a low voice, unsure how to feel about that.

"I can give you a list of the crimes they've been responsible for if you want it?" he offered. "The six of them were mercenaries for hire, pulling jobs all over the world and taking bonuses in the lives of innocents. One of them was particularly fond of young boys and-"

"I believe you," I said, seeing the truth in his eyes and not wanting to hear the list of atrocities those monsters had been responsible for. The world was clearly better off without them.

"You're just a regular Robin Hood, aren't you, Rick? Stealing from the bad guys and killing sick fuckers for the poor."

"That seems highly inaccurate," he replied, opening the door and jumping out.

I yawned widely but didn't follow him, not wanting to deal with the cold air out there and wondering if I could just doze off in here again instead.

Of course, that wasn't allowed and I cursed as Maverick opened my damn door, tugging me out into his arms and holding me against his chest instead of tossing me over his shoulder like a sack of potatoes for once.

"You still sleep like the fucking dead," he commented as he started walking towards the hotel, his men moving forward to deal with the van which I was guessing needed a clean down thanks to all that blood. "I shot six men and loaded their bodies into the back of that van without you even stirring."

I shrugged. "Rosie used to snore like a fucking pig with a blocked nose back in the group home. If I learned how to sleep through that then I can sleep through anything."

"Apparently so." We made it into an elevator and Rick hit the button for the penthouse suite, barking some orders at his men which I didn't pay attention to as my eyes fell shut once more.

When we made it into his rooms, he walked me straight to the shower and set me on my feet.

"Make it fast, beautiful. Or I'll follow you in there and let you get better acquainted with my cock."

I flipped him off over my shoulder and quickly stripped off, figuring he'd strapped me naked to that fucking chair in the freezer anyway, so it wasn't like I had any modesty left to protect.

"So are you gonna keep on pretending you didn't kiss me out there or are you going to explain why you mouth humped me out of the blue?" I called over the sound of the running water.

"Call it curiosity," Maverick replied. "I wanted to know if you tasted like a candy cane or only looked like one."

"And?"

"You taste like sin, beautiful, which just so happens to be my favourite flavour."

My skin prickled at his words and I decided it was best if I focused on washing the muck and blood off of my body instead of giving them too much of my attention. But as I ran my tongue over my lips, I couldn't help but remember the way his had crushed to mine and the way it had made my stomach flip over like it was on a trampoline.

Bad Rogue. Psychos aren't hot. They're terrible people. Terrible, terrible, really fucking hot people.

Fuck.

I made my shower as quick as possible, washing off the blood that he'd transferred to my skin without thinking about it too much and keeping my hair dry before towelling off.

Maverick reappeared as I finished drying myself. "Sleep naked or help yourself to my clothes. And stay where I can see you - don't wander out of the bedroom."

"Aye aye, Captain Dick Bucket," I said, saluting him with as much sass as I could manage and heading out to steal his shit.

I found a white tank in the top drawer of his dresser and grabbed it, tugging it on before slipping into his bed. Luckily the sheets smelled as fresh as a daisy, so I didn't have to worry about there being any gross Mia contamination on them.

I glanced back through the open door to the bathroom where Maverick stood butt naked in the shower, scrubbing the blood from his flesh and I let myself look for a few minutes to give my dreams some nice ammo. He was smirking like he enjoyed the attention and I sleepily flipped him off while studying his mega cock and sexy as fuck tattoos. Those tribal dick tattoos really must have hurt but I was going to vote for that pain being worth it because I was having trouble looking away from them.

No way I was going to fuck the big, bad, psycho in real life. But dream Rogue could whore out all she liked, so I was dedicating that shit to memory for her.

"Night, asshole," I muttered as my eyes fell closed and his reply followed me into sleep as I drifted away.

"Good night, lost girl."

A shiver danced across my skin and I rolled over, cursing beneath my breath as I reached for the sheets to pull them up around me and found them missing. As my hand swept back and forth across the spot where I expected Maverick to be, I found him missing too and I frowned, cracking my eyes open and looking around at the dark space.

Had he even come to bed? One glance at the clock told me it was almost four in the morning and that shit wasn't cool. I hated early mornings. But the fact that he might not have come to join me at all was weird enough that I made my eyes stay open so I could look for him.

The cool air which had woken me up was coming from the balcony door which was cracked open and as I squinted out at the moonlit balcony beyond, I spotted Maverick standing there in his boxers.

He had something in his hand and as I pushed myself upright, my breath caught as I spotted a revolver in his grasp. I watched him load a single bullet into the chamber and he looked out towards the horizon with tension filling his posture.

Maverick set the chamber spinning as I pushed to my feet and the whirring sound of the metal canister twisting filled the air before he flicked his wrist to lock the bullet inside the gun.

I'd grabbed one of Maverick's tank tops to sleep in without paying it much attention but as I glanced down at it I almost smiled, reminded of a shirt he used to wear when we were kids. It was white with a silhouette of waves scrawled across it and long arm holes which let the cold slip inside all too easily, making my nipples pebble as a shiver teased across my skin.

I made it to the open door, my bare feet silent on the tiles as I tilted my head to the side to see what Maverick was doing. He stood there in his black boxers, the moonlight highlighting the black whorls of countless tattoos which lined his flesh and gleaming off of his muscular body, making my mouth dry out at the sight of him.

He released a long breath, his gaze fixed on the lights of Sunset Cove across the dark water and raised the revolver before pressing it to his temple.

My heart leapt in panic as I took in what I was seeing and I lurched forward, throwing the door wide and jumping at him. My hand smacked against his just as he pulled the trigger, knocking the gun aside. The echoing boom of the gunshot rang out across the sea, making my ears ring as Maverick's free hand locked around my wrist and his eyes widened in shock.

The two of us just stared at each other in stunned silence for a moment before I reached out and snatched the still smoking revolver from his grip.

"What the fuck were you thinking?!" I screamed at him, wrenching my arm back and hurling the gun that had almost ended his fucking life out over the balcony towards the sea with all my strength.

Maverick snarled furiously at me, whirling me around and lifting me off of my feet as he slammed me back against the glass wall which separated the suite from the balcony.

My legs locked around his waist automatically and he pinned my wrist to the glass above my head as he glared down at me.

My lips parted to demand more answers, but before I could even attempt it, his mouth found mine and I moaned into his kiss.

My entire body came alive at the brutality of that kiss and I swear every moment of hurt and heartache and longing for the boy he'd been was drawn to the surface of my skin as I fell into it. I could taste his pain too. Could feel his loneliness and his want and need and all the unsaid things that had hung in the space between us for ten long years. This was my Rick, the soul that belonged with mine and ached for mine and fucking hurt because we'd been apart for too damn long. That kiss said everything that words couldn't. It spoke of how much we'd hurt for each other and hungered for each other and of all the kisses we should have shared in the time we'd been parted.

He released his grip on my wrist and I groaned as his mouth moved from my lips to my neck, sucking and biting and marking my flesh as the thick swell of his cock drove against me between my thighs.

"Rick," I begged, needing him to take all of this pain in my heart and soul and turn it into something else. Something so much fucking better, while I did the same for him.

He gripped my ass and turned us, half heading towards the door but slamming me back against another section of the glass wall instead as his mouth found my nipple through the thin material of my shirt and he bit down hard.

My toes brushed against the back of a rattan couch and I shifted my legs so that instead of being coiled around him, my feet were planted on the back of it and I could help him hold my weight up.

I gripped the waistband of his boxers and shoved them down, my pussy clenching at the thought of claiming this beast of a man, this piece of my heart and cause of my pain. But I didn't care about any of that right now, I just needed him to take me in whatever way he wanted me and to let the ruined parts of me feel whole for at least a little while.

Maverick caught the hem of my shirt and ripped it over my head, making my hair tumble down around me in a fan of pastel colours as he gazed at my naked body with a hungry groan.

"Every day that I was in that place I dreamed of you," he said in a rough voice as he kicked his boxers aside and the solid length of his cock moved between my thighs, rubbing against my wet core and making me moan with need. "Every night I closed my eyes and thought about how it would feel to claim your sweet pussy like this."

I looked up at him as his words set my pulse racing and he fisted his cock as he lined it up with my entrance, the head pushing in the smallest amount and making me gasp at the thickness of him.

"No other pussy could have come close for me. Not after fucking my hand to the thought of yours, night after night," he went on, grasping my ass with bruising fingers as I tried to rock my hips and take him deeper. "Do you understand what I'm saying to you, beautiful?"

"No," I moaned, my head rolling back as I dug my fingernails into his shoulders and tried to drag him closer, force him to sink in deeper.

"I was in prison for six years surrounded by nothing but cocks while thinking about your wet cunt every fucking night. I went in there a virgin, beautiful."

"You're not a virgin now, Rick," I protested, because I'd seen him with Mia and I wasn't a fucking idiot.

"I'm not saying I am," he growled. "I'm saying I've waited a long time to take ownership of a pussy because there's only one I'm interested in owning. So tell me you want me to own it, or I'll fuck you in the ass like all the rest."

My lips popped open as I stared at him, blinking several times as I realised what he was saying. And though it was insane, and I knew a hole was a hole and realistically this shouldn't have meant anything different, I knew it did. He hadn't wanted anyone like this aside from me. He hadn't abandoned me when I'd thought he had. He had been alone and aching for me just the way I had been for him and even when he'd given up hope of ever finding me again, he'd never crossed this line with another.

"Own me, Rick," I said firmly. "Fuck me like you mean it and make me forget the last ten years that separated us."

Maverick groaned hungrily at my words, his hold on my ass so fucking hard that I knew he must have been leaving bruises where he gripped me, but I wanted him to. I wanted him to brand my body in every way he could and to take just as much from me as he gave.

With a jerk of his hips he did exactly that, his thick, solid cock driving so deep inside me that the feel of it ripped my breath away and a cry of pleasure tore from my lips to be stolen by the sky. Maverick groaned deeply as my pussy clenched around him and I hoped that it felt as good as he'd imagined it would to finally claim what he'd been aching for.

His mouth found mine as he drew back and as I cried out again with his next brutal thrust, he swallowed the sounds.

I rocked my hips forward to meet him, using the placement of my feet on the back of the couch to make sure that every clash of our hips had his cock slamming in hard and deep and he kissed me in this brutal, savage way that had me destroyed for him.

His cock was so fucking big that it was making my head spin with every thrust and my fingernails bit into his shoulders as I scratched and marked him at least as much as he was me.

The glass at my back shook and rattled every time he drove into me and a sudden cracking sound made us both freeze as the pane at my back erupted with a spiderweb of cracks that spread out all over it.

I swore, breaking our kiss and looking over my shoulder at the damage to the glass, but Rick barely spared it a glance, dropping his mouth to suck on my nipple hard enough to make me groan before pulling out of me suddenly.

Maverick lifted me away from the damaged window and dropped me to my feet beside the balcony railings. He leaned down to kiss me again, his lips bruising as he pushed his hands into my hair and slowly coiled the length of it around his fist. As soon as he had control of my head, he shoved me to my knees beneath him and tugged on my hair to make me look up at him.

"I'm going to own every piece of your body tonight, beautiful," he growled. "I'm going to own it in all the ways I dreamed of owning it while

I was locked up and aching for you. And you're going to love every fucking second of it, aren't you?"

The defiant little asshole in me wanted to tell him to fuck off and show him just how much I could own him instead, but there was something about him tonight, something in the way I'd caught him with that gun pressed to his temple and the darkness in his eyes that seemed to stretch on forever. He needed this. He needed to claim something from his former life and fulfil this desire in him if there was ever going to be any hope of him reclaiming the life he could have lived.

"Make me love it, baby," I mocked him, licking my swollen lips and eyeing the solid length of his inked cock while he fisted it in his big, tattooed hand. "Do your worst. I'm yours to ruin tonight. Let's see if you can make me feel alive again."

Maverick gave me a look that made my insides clench in the most delicious way as I missed the feeling of his dick inside me. He pressed forward and I opened my mouth like a good girl, licking the head of his cock as he fed it to me, his grip in my hair holding me completely immobile.

But he wasn't fucking around with any kind of build up and with a lust-filled growl, he jerked his hips forward and thrust his cock right in to the back of my throat.

I moaned around his shaft, tasting him and me and sucking on every glorious inch of it as my jaw was forced wide and he began to fuck my mouth with a reckless abandon which had me panting for more.

I gripped his ass to encourage him, my fingernails biting into the toned muscles and as I raised my gaze to meet his where he was watching me, he groaned loudly and came hard.

Hot cum shot to the back of my throat and he held me in place with his dick firmly inside my mouth as he waited for me to swallow it down before unravelling his fist from my hair and pulling back out of me.

His cock was barely even losing any of its hardness and Maverick licked his lips as he tugged me to my feet and led me over to the sun lounger.

"That was the easy one, beautiful," he said in a rough voice that made my nipples tighten and ache. "Now come sit on my face while I get ready for round two."

Ho-ly shit, this man was going to be the death of me and I would lay there in my casket with a big as fuck smile on my dead face and the words 'she was dicked to death and died happy as sin' scrawled across my headstone.

Maverick sat back on the sun lounger, giving me a moment to stare at all of his delicious ink as it shone in the moonlight. Hell, even his cock was a work of art, the leviathan resting between his thighs at half-mast already and making moisture pool between my thighs. This man was a sight to behold. A demon given the skin of a saint, left to corrupt it in all the most delicious ways.

I climbed into his lap and kissed him hard, loving the way he gripped my ass and dug his fingers in hard. Everything about this man was solid and certain and unforgiving. He was rough and brutal and oh so fucking delicious.

Maverick's teeth suddenly sank into my bottom lip and I gasped at the bite of pain, jerking back and tasting blood. I slapped him without even thinking about it and that darkness in his eyes swirled with filthy promises as my palm stung from the blow.

"I told you to sit on my face, not my lap," he warned me, laying back on the sun lounger and lifting me by ass so that he could place my knees down either side of his head. "Defy me again and I'll punish you for it."

"Yes, master," I taunted but the heated look he gave me from beneath my thighs said he didn't mind that one bit. "Or would you rather 'owner'?" I teased and Maverick's grip on my ass tightened as he forced me down so that my wet pussy was positioned exactly where he wanted it and as his mouth closed over my clit, I couldn't help but suck in a sharp breath. He started licking and sucking and oh my fucking life, it felt so good that I couldn't help but moan for him as I began to grind down and ride his face. I pawed at my aching nipples, tugging on them and giving some relief to the needy flesh as I tried to remember what I'd been saying.

"Sir?" I suggested breathily, trying to keep up the game even as his tongue swirled around inside me and I found myself grinding down harder, fucking his face as I chased a release which I knew would destroy me. Maverick took a hand from my ass and slapped it down hard, making me yelp and buck against his mouth. I knew that was my warning, but shit, my pussy had liked that a whole hell of a lot and if spanking was the punishment I could expect for riling him up then I was definitely game.

"My king?" I moaned as he sucked my clit into his mouth and this time he spanked me so hard that my pussy clenched and I almost came instantly, but the fucker released my clit and started lapping at my opening instead, denying me the release.

"Do that again," I begged, rocking my hips and fucking his face and not even giving a shit that anyone could see us up here. I was too far gone for that. Dick blinded, pussy poisoned, who could fucking say? All I knew was that Maverick was licking me out like he was going for gold in the Olympics and I was more than ready to let him claim that fucking prize.

He didn't comply with my request though and his fingers merely bit into my ass as he rocked my hips and refused to spank me again. So I clearly needed to bring out the big guns.

"Spank me, Daddy," I moaned. "Show me you own me like I'm a naughty little-" a cry of surprise escaped me as Maverick thrust two thick fingers straight into my ass and sucked my clit between his teeth in the same move. He pumped his fingers in harder and his tongue lapped over that perfect fucking spot, making me explode for him.

The cry of pleasure that escaped me must have been loud enough for the sharks to hear and I tugged on my nipples as I ground down on Maverick's face to prolong the ecstasy. He yanked his fingers back out of me and spanked me sharply, making my pussy clench and my orgasm intensify as my body fell apart at his command.

Before I even knew what way was up again, Maverick gripped my waist and tossed me face first onto the sun lounger. My ass was in the air and his cock plunging into my pussy a moment later and I gasped as I was forced to grip the edge of the lounger and hold on for dear life.

Maverick gripped my hips and fucked me so hard that I couldn't catch my breath, his huge cock slamming in so deep and brutally that it was all I could do to keep my ass in the air and take every fucking inch of him just the way he wanted me.

He was pinching and squeezing my ass, his hand cracking down against it firmly more than once and his fingers pushing into my tight hole too, making me feel so full that I could barely take it.

I was making so much fucking noise that my throat was already feeling raw and as my pussy began to clench and tighten around him again, I knew I was begging but I just couldn't help it. This felt too fucking good. Too fucking right.

But just as I was certain that we were both about to finish for the final time, Maverick yanked his cock out of me again and pulled me to my feet.

He whipped me around to face him, kissing me deeply, his tongue dominating my mouth as he walked me backwards into his suite and shoved me down onto the bed beneath him.

My legs spread wide as he followed me and he kissed and bit his way back up my body, marking my flesh and branding me with his touch. He sucked and squeezed my tits while his hand found my clit and as he sank his cock into me again, his other hand closed around my throat.

I stilled beneath him, looking up into his dark eyes as he gave me the briefest moment to say no. And I should have been saying no because this was fucked up. Shawn had almost killed me by putting his hand around my neck like that and there was no way it should have been turning me on.

But shit, my pussy was so wet right now, my muscles clenching and heart pounding and for some fucked up reason, I wanted this.

"Show me you own me, Rick," I breathed and that darkness in his gaze flared with triumph as I wound my legs around his waist and he tightened his grip on my throat.

Maverick began to thrust in harder, deeper, his mouth moving to claim a savage kiss from my lips one last time before he drew back, rearing over me and squeezing tight enough to cut off my breath.

My hands locked around his wrist as my pussy tightened around his cock and he drove himself into me harder and harder until my lungs were burning and my head was spinning and I was coming so fucking hard that black spots danced across my eyes.

Maverick loosened his hold on my throat as an animal growl escaped him and my pulsing pussy gripped his cock tight in a demand for every drop of cum he had.

I gasped, sucking in a heady breath as my entire body buzzed with pleasure and his weight drove me down into the sheets.

He fell over me, his dick still buried deep as he kissed me again, his fingers trailing down my side and making my tingling body hum with more pleasure.

This kiss wasn't like the others, it was slower, deeper, full of pain and heartache and all the time we'd been without each other. It said I owned him as much as he'd just owned me.

Maverick drew back slowly, his eyes closing and forehead pressing to mine as we simply stole that moment from the universe. The two of us had suffered at the hands of time over the last ten years and in the darkest depths of the nights when I'd woken up alone or in the bed of a stranger, I'd dreamed of him. Of all my boys holding me close like that and never letting go.

His hand found mine in the tangle of sheets and he threaded his fingers through mine, slowly lifting it above our heads and pressing it to the mattress.

"I always knew I'd find you again one day," he said, breathing in deeply like he was trying to inhale my soul. "We were written in blood and bone. The sum of all we ever were and will be."

"I missed you," I admitted, a tear slipping from the corner of my eye as I tried to steal that feeling of his body pressed to mine and keep it for myself so that I'd never have to feel alone again. "I missed you so bad it broke me, Rick."

He sighed and I swear in that sound alone I could feel the ache in him too, the regret and the knowledge that we could never really reclaim what we'd once had. The future we should have owned together had been stolen from us a long time ago and the people we were now had nothing on the kids we'd once been.

Maverick released me, pushing himself upright and separating our bodies so that cold air washed over my bare flesh once more.

I caught his forearm suddenly, my fingers biting into his skin as I frowned up at him. "Stay," I demanded. "Steal a little more of this lie with me, Rick. I just want to pretend for a bit longer."

A frown pulled at his brow and he looked at the point where I held his arm, causing me to tug on him as I let the wall around my heart crumble just a little for him. Enough to show him how much I wanted this.

Without a word, he caught the sheet beside us and hooked it over our naked bodies as he moved to lay beside me. I let him roll me onto my side and he tugged my ass back against his crotch as he wrapped an inked arm around me and held me tight to his broad chest while letting me use his other bicep as a pillow.

I breathed in deeply as I closed my eyes and Maverick's hand slowly trailed down my side until he was sliding his fingers between my thighs where the sticky mess of his cum was coating my skin.

Shit. I hadn't even fucking thought about contraception and that seriously wasn't good.

"See, beautiful?" Maverick growled in my ear and my skin prickled at the scratch of his stubble against my neck. "This is all mine."

Christ, that really shouldn't have sounded so good, and I definitely should have been freaking out about STIs or tiny people coming out of my vagina or just the fact that I'd allowed myself to get so dick blinded that I'd let him fuck me skin on skin without so much as a thought about it.

But in that moment, his words and the possessive growl to them, the way he was holding me so freaking close and acting like he might just want to keep me there forever made my inner animal purr with satisfaction. So I was going to let her purr because she had spent too fucking long pining. And in the morning I'd deal with the reality of what we'd done. Because right now, I wasn't going to be moving from that spot for all the money in the world.

CHAPTER SIX

I had every one of my men searching the town from the darkest corners of the lower quarter to the shiniest streets of the upper quarter. And I still had nothing. Not one clue to go on. Not a single sighting. Not a fucking hair. But I did have a final lead I was waiting on and today I was hoping to get some answers.

I had connections with a guy who lived out in one of the rich asshole mansions along the beach outside of Sunset Cove who could get hold of the security footage from the precinct for me. He'd moved here with his family last year and approached me first hand to ensure my gang weren't going to be an issue for him. I'd promised that his home and his people were safe so long as he greased my palm well enough and I'd been surprised at the balls on the guy when he'd offered me a monthly payment plan and had made it crystal clear that he not only had extensive connections in the black market, but if I needed any kind of intelligence he was the man to go to - so long as I would be equally willing to help him out if he needed my kind of expertise. So far, neither of us had called in those favours, but it was time to change that.

I wasn't sure how a dude a couple of years younger than me had ended up out here living in a house that looked like a fucking church which he'd named 'The Temple', and frankly I didn't give a fuck to ask. I hadn't planned on mixing it with him at all beyond taking his money, but then I'd gotten desperate when none of my people had the connections needed to provide me with the south precinct's CCTV footage. So here I was, waiting on a call from a guy a million times richer than I'd ever be and praying that whatever he found would return my girl to me.

I sat at the breakfast bar while my food went cold and I twisted my phone around on the surface before me. *Call me, asshole.*

Mutt sat obediently at my feet, his eyes trained on me like he was as anxious for this news as I was. I'd been out half the night again hunting the streets before stumbling into bed at four am for a couple of hours sleep. The clock was just ticking towards seven now and though I knew it was early, the guy I was waiting on had promised me it would be this morning. And that could be any time from now.

JJ appeared in his boxers, rubbing his eyes and moving to join me at the kitchen island, giving me a hopeful look. I shook my head and pushed a bowl of fruit and muesli towards him. He diligently started eating, knowing I'd be pissed if he didn't keep his energy up, but I wasn't exactly setting a good example right now.

"Did you see Chase last night?" I asked in a gruff tone.

JJ nodded as he yawned. "We searched a couple of streets together. He's…not good."

I ground my teeth for a moment. "He deserves to be not fucking good right now."

"True," he said, eating another mouthful of his breakfast.

"Where's he sleeping?" I asked.

I might have been angry at Chase for losing Rogue on that boat and for bringing her on the goddamn job at all, but he was still my brother. I wasn't about to get soft on him and let him come home though.

"At Sinners' Playground," JJ said, releasing a sigh and my chest tightened. "I think he's drunk ninety percent of the time and the other ten he's just…a mess."

"Why's he sleeping down there?" I growled. "He could stay with any of the Harlequins, or even Rosie if he wanted."

JJ shook his head and I frowned at my brother who looked more tired than I'd ever seen him. "I think he's punishing himself."

I released a frustrated breath then my heart jerked as the front door opened down the hall. I rose from my seat, my mind hooking on Rogue, praying she'd come back, or that Chase was walking in here right now to tell me he'd found her. But it wasn't either of those people who appeared.

The air was sucked out of my lungs as my father stepped into the kitchen and immediately dominated the whole room. Luther Harlequin's shadow always seemed twice the size of anyone else I knew and his aura was laced with pure power. He wore a black shirt with his sleeves rolled back to reveal the ink on his forearms, his hair was unkempt and dark blonde like mine, and his dark green eyes were sharp and focused on me. "Morning, son."

"I didn't know you were coming," I said instantly, rising from my seat to put us on more even ground. I was the same height and breadth as my father these days, but something as simple as sitting down always reminded me of feeling small in front of him when I was a kid. My mind wheeled onto Kenny who'd been working with him up in Sterling who always shot me a message in advance to let me know if my father was coming home. Always. *What the fuck Kenny?*

"Hey, boss," JJ said, slapping on one of his easy-going expressions but Luther was dragging his gaze over him in an assessing way, taking everything in.

"You're up early," he said. "Why do you both look like shit?"

I glanced at JJ as my heart warred in my chest and I didn't immediately answer, unsure what my father knew. He never showed all of his cards, I'd learned that the hard way. So I was going to let him reveal a few more before I attempted a lie and got caught out.

"And why've you got a load of my men searching high and low across Sunset Cove for some girl?" He arched a brow curiously at me and I could tell he really didn't understand what was going on. My heart thrashed harder and I fought the urge to look at JJ again, feeling like a couple of teenagers who'd just been caught out. But the consequences of this truth were too high. My dad had sworn to kill Rogue if she ever returned to town, and in all the years I'd known him, I'd never seen him back down on his word.

"She took something from me," I said, raising my chin as I decided how best to play this.

My poker face was far better these days than it used to be, but I swear my dad had the uncanny ability to see right under my skin. For Rogue's sake, I had to make sure he couldn't this time. Technically, I wasn't lying anyway. She had taken something from me. My fucking heart. And I planned on getting both her and it back as soon as possible.

"I see," Luther said, resting his hands on the breakfast bar and I eyed his scarred, tattooed knuckles which had seen a thousand fights. "Well this hunt better not affect our takings for the week, kid. What did she steal that was so important? And how did a girl get close enough to my son to take it?" His expression was stern. Luther Harlequin's number one rule; never let a woman into your house or in your heart. He was too fucked up over Mom leaving him to trust the opposite gender, though I hadn't wanted to hear exactly what had gone down with her. All I needed to know was that she hadn't wanted us anymore. So now I didn't want her either.

Mutt padded over to my dad, sniffing his sneakers suspiciously and Luther frowned down at the little animal. "When did you get a dog?"

"I found him outside the club," JJ said smoothly, which again, technically wasn't a lie. He *had* picked up Rogue and Mutt outside Afterlife.

Luther dropped down, picking Mutt up and stroking his head affectionately while the dog stared at him. I swear its little eyes were narrowed as he tried to work out whether to trust my father or not. I doubted he knew he was in the hands of the most powerful man in the state or that those hands had put countless men in the ground.

Mutt distracted Dad for all of five seconds before he put him down and pressed on with his questioning. "So? What did the bitch steal?"

I bristled at that word but didn't react outwardly. "Money." Truth again. Rogue had been stealing cash off of me for months. Or at least she had been until she'd realised I was leaving it out for her to take and she'd thrown it back in my fucking face, refusing to take any help from me. Honestly, that girl's moral compass was so twisted – of course she'd happily steal from the guy trying to give her a home to live in, but no way would she accept the money if it was offered because that made it charity. Her decisions on that shit left me all kinds of irritated, but I kinda loved how much she wanted to hate me too.

"Hmm." Luther's eyes darkened. "You never listen to me about women, boy. They'll fuck you then they'll fuck you over. JJ's got the right idea." He looked to him with a smirk, clapping a hand down on his shoulder. "Make them pay for your time and don't get attached."

"Yes, sir," JJ said brightly, but the emotion in his eyes told me exactly how attached he was to a certain rainbow haired girl who'd come back into our lives like a sea storm. My gaze lingered on him a moment and I hoped that attachment didn't go deeper than friendship. We'd all adored Rogue when we were younger, but I'd laid my claim on her clearly since she'd returned. I was sure I didn't have to worry anyway; JJ didn't do relationships. Sex was a transaction for him, one he enjoyed and made a living out of. That was unlikely to change after ten years.

"So where's Chase? Still in bed?" Luther asked, before moving to the fridge and helping himself to some orange juice.

"I kicked him out until he finds the girl," I said honestly. "It's his fault we lost her, so he can come home when he finds her."

Luther chuckled. "Good lad." He drained the glass of orange juice, his muscular bicep flexing against the inside of his shirt.

"So why are you back in town?" I asked casually and he placed the glass down on the side, gesturing for me to sit.

I did so a little reluctantly and he slid into the seat next to mine, resting his forearms on the counter.

"I'm here on business," he said. "But maybe I missed my son too, huh?" He elbowed me and I withdrew a little, earning me a frown from him. He cleared his throat and went on, "Shawn Mackenzie has gone underground. He's pissed off the cartel to high hell and they're hunting his ass like a prime buck."

"Well that's good," JJ said excitedly. "Maybe they'll deal with him for us."

Luther pushed a hand through his hair, his brows pulling together. "See, that's what I thought at first. But then some of my men tracked him south leaving his territory. I figured he'd go east and keep running until he went off the grid. But he didn't. The last sighting we had, he was on the border of town."

"This town?" JJ gasped as my gut clenched.

"Yeah," Luther said, his eyes shadowed. "So why would the leader of The Dead Dogs come all the way out of his homeland and into the heart of enemy territory?"

"He's planning something," I growled, my hands curling into fists.

"Exactly," Dad agreed. "So I'm moving some of my men down here."

"You're staying?" I balked, unable to hide my horror at that and Dad's eyes flickered with hurt for a second.

"Yeah, and don't worry, I'm not gonna cramp your style, kid. This is still your empire. I gave it to you fair and square. But The Dead Dogs are my domain and I want Shawn Mackenzie's bloody head in my hands. I've been hungering for his death for a long time."

Shawn was in his late thirties, only ten years or so younger than Dad and he'd been on the scene since back when I was a teenager, causing havoc for my father. He hadn't been the leader of his gang then, but he'd been a ruthless asshole who'd killed a couple of Dad's friends and I knew this was about vengeance as much as anything else. Dad had brokered peace with their gang for several years, but as soon as that motherfucker had risen to power it had all gone to shit.

My phone started ringing and my heart nearly burst right out of my chest as I grabbed it. "I've gotta take this," I said, pushing out of my seat.

"Sure thing, I'll let myself out. And if you're around for lunch later just let me know…" Luther tried to catch my eye, but I just strode out of the room and kept walking until I was on the back porch, answering the call from Saint Memphis.

"Hey, tell me you've got something," I said in place of a greeting.

"I have something," he said in that posh north-western accent of his, his tone measured and deep. "But I'm going to need you to do something for me before I give it to you."

A growl built in my throat. "I don't take orders from anyone. We had a deal, now give me the footage."

"The deal was that I would procure the footage for the right price."

"So name a figure and I'll forward it to your account," I said in frustration.

He laughed coolly. "I don't want your money, Fox." He said my name like it displeased him and I had to assume that it wasn't fancy enough for his tastes.

"So what do you want?" I pressed.

"The neighbour across the street from me has painted a hideous mural on his wall which faces my front gate. It is offensive to my eyes and the eyes of all who see it. Deal with it and ensure he doesn't repeat the monstrosity, then come to my house and I will show you the footage."

"That's it?" I gritted out.

"Yes. See you soon. I'll have tea prepared." He hung up and I rolled my eyes, stepping back into the house and tucking the phone into my jeans' pocket. I returned to the kitchen, finding Luther gone and JJ looking at me with big eyes.

"Anything?" he asked.

"Yeah, get dressed, we're leaving in two minutes," I ordered and he jumped up like his ass was on fire, jogging away toward the laundry room.

Mutt barked excitedly and I grabbed a bag of chicken treats from the cupboard, tossing him one before pushing the bag into my pocket and picking him up. I wasn't going anywhere without this dog since Rogue had vanished. If Chase was right and she was going to try and come back for him then she was going to find him constantly glued to my side when she came looking.

Mutt licked my fingers, his affection for me officially bought by chicken and I headed to the garage just as JJ reappeared in jeans and a bright blue tank top. We hurried downstairs to my truck and I placed Mutt in JJ's lap as I started it up and we headed off of the property onto the road. Luther's car was gone so I guessed he'd headed back to The Oasis – the official Harlequin clubhouse where he always stayed during his visits.

I hightailed it towards the hardware store a few streets away then sent JJ inside with instructions to buy two gallons of white paint. When he returned, I drove us out of town, passing the first of the huge properties which lined the seafront out this way, my heart pounding wildly as I told JJ what Saint had said.

I didn't like being anyone's fucking lackie, but I'd do anything to get my hands on that footage today. It was a fucking rarity to have the king of the Harlequins himself running errands for anyone, but Saint Memphis seemed like the kind of guy who got exactly what he wanted from people. He just needed to realise I was not someone to be messed with.

This footage he had better be the key to finding my girl, or he was going to regret having me run around for him like a trained dog.

We drove along quiet streets where the road ran back down over the cliffs to a stretch of clean white sand. Massive houses were interspersed along the beautiful area, getting bigger the further we went and I soon pulled up between two huge, gated properties, one on the beach front and the other opposite it with a hideous mural on the wall of two giant beachballs.

JJ released a low whistle. "That's one ugly asshole of a painting," he said, shoving the door open and grabbing one of the paint buckets. I picked up the other one and Mutt dove out after me as I exited my truck and stared at the enormous white walled house that could have fit three Harlequin Houses inside. We strode toward it as the sun beat down on us and I casually pressed the buzzer at the gate as JJ opened up his paint can.

"Hello?" a man answered sharply. "Is that you, Raul? You were supposed to be here fifteen minutes ago. I will have to find a new gardener if this behaviour continues."

"It's not Raul," I said dryly, cracking open my own paint can. "It's Fox Harlequin."

Silence. The beautiful, terrified kind.

"E-excuse me? What kind of joke is that?" he stammered.

"The kind that isn't funny," I said simply, standing back so he could see me on the camera properly.

"W-what do you want?" he demanded. "I'll call the police."

"Go ahead," I said with a smirk. "But most of them are in my pocket, and do you really want to risk pissing me off? If I have to come back a second time, I won't be in such a friendly mood."

"Are you here to rob me?" he asked nervously. "I don't keep cash in the house. And there's no way you'll get inside anyway, there's-"

"If you shut your mouth I'll get to the point," I snarled and he fell deathly quiet. I pointed to the mural on his wall. "That painting is as ugly as sin. It offends my eyes. And when my eyes get offended, I get stabby." I stepped closer to the intercom, talking directly into it. "You don't want me to

94

get stabby now, do you buddy?"

"N-no," he rasped. "But I-I assure you the painting is quite unique. I am a prestigious artist, I have credentials!"

"Looks like you're gonna want a refund on those credentials, dude," JJ called as he stood in front of the mural and threw white paint all over it.

"My balls!" the man gasped. "Stop splashing that all over my beautiful balls!"

I took a knife from my belt and let the sun catch on the blade as I used it to pick at my nail beds.

"A-alright, maybe it was a little bright for the area," the man backtracked.

"I thought so too," I agreed, tucking my knife back away and walking over to join JJ. Mutt yipped as I opened my can of paint and threw it all over the ugly balls, covering the vivid stripes on them. When we couldn't see a speck of colour left on the wall, I nodded to JJ and he smirked at me as he wiped his paint flecked hands down his jeans.

"Come on then, let's get our girl back," I said in a low growl and we headed across the street towards the even bigger property which was built to resemble a massive church.

The gates started opening as we approached and I led the way inside, spotting a tall figure standing in a huge window that overlooked the landscaped front garden. His face was shrouded in shadow, and I guessed from that height he might have been able to watch us destroy his neighbour's painting. He moved away into the dark room he was in, disappearing like a wraith and a moment later, the arching front door opened and he stepped out onto the porch.

Saint Memphis was strikingly handsome, his skin dark, his features intensely sharp and his cheeks hollow. He wore a white shirt which was immaculately pressed and light grey chinos and his expression gave nothing away. "Good morning, Fox, Johnny James." He nodded to us, then looked to the dog. "And this is?"

"Mutt," JJ supplied.

"How simple," Saint commented as a black cat stepped out of the house and curled its way around his legs before sitting like a statue and gazing coolly at Mutt. "This is Debussy."

"How pretentious," I remarked and Saint's lips quirked up at the corner.

Mutt growled and JJ picked him up before he lunged, but the cat didn't even blink at his display of aggression.

This guy exuded wealth unlike anyone I'd ever met. He was so refined, I had to think he'd been born in the wrong century. Of course, one internet search had shown up everything I needed to know about his heritage. He was the son of a state governor, owner of several billion-dollar companies, including Rivers Corp. which was the most famous pharmaceutical company in the world after they'd created the vaccine for the Hades Virus which had swept its way across the planet several years ago and seriously fucked with everything and everyone.

"I did as you asked," I said, cutting to the chase as excitement and anxiety blended together inside me. "Show me the footage."

Saint nodded, turning and beckoning us after him into his massive temple. It had to take one really pretentious asshole to live in a church built wholly for him and his family.

We headed inside, following him through to a lounge with gleaming wooden floors and beautiful white furniture. A balcony swung around the top of it, giving a glimpse onto the second level and a chandelier made of twisting iron hung above us. I may have been a king in my world, but I wasn't this kind of king. I was the one who fought alongside his men in the dirt on the front lines, Saint was the kind who never even muddied the finger he used to direct his soldiers.

My gaze hooked on a charcoal sketch on the wall of Sinners' Playground, the light captured beautifully and all of the edges none too perfect, just like the real place was. There were silhouettes of children playing on the beach between the shadows of the pier struts and my heart yanked as blissful memories stole me away. Whoever had drawn this had seen the secrets it hid and the life it held, and somehow they'd bled it all out right onto that canvas.

"You like it," Saint commented, following my gaze and I tugged my eyes away with a shrug.

"I'm not really an art guy," I said.

"There is a type of art for everyone's tastes," Saint countered. "Art doesn't have to be hanging in a gallery for it to be worthy of attention."

"Your neighbour has shitty taste," JJ commented.

"Quite," Saint agreed, his upper lip curling for a moment. "Tea?"

"No," I said, stepping closer to him. "I held up my end of the bargain, now hold up yours."

Saint nodded and picked up an iPad from the mahogany coffee table where a tray of tea was waiting for us. He held it out to me and my heart drummed almost painfully as I took it from him. A video was ready to play on the screen and JJ's shoulder jammed up against mine so that he could watch as I pressed the button.

The footage was dark, but I could make out my girl exiting the precinct into a parking lot. There was no sound on the video, but I didn't need it to understand what happened next. My world twisted upside down as Maverick appeared in the shot. They spoke for a moment before Rogue tried to run and he raced after her. The video switched onto another camera and panic burned every nerve in my body as he got hold of her and forced her onto his bike.

"No," JJ breathed in my ear, my throat tightening as the reality of where she was curled over me like a cresting wave. And then I was drowning, dragged into the depths of the darkest sea where all my fears came to life.

The video ended and I mutely passed the iPad back to Saint.

"His name is Maverick Stone," Saint supplied and my face twisted into a grimace as I looked up. "But you already knew that, didn't you?" his expression was mildly curious, but I said nothing, turning sharply and marching for the door with death on my mind. I'd take a boat to that island and plant every bullet in my possession into Maverick's skull. But what if she was already dead?

I made it to the door, storming outside as JJ called my name and ran after me. I couldn't hear what he was saying, it was all a blur as my mind descended into a bloodthirsty pit where nothing but death lived. I had a thousand reasons to kill him, but this was the one I'd put him in the ground for. My adopted brother had taken the one thing from me that I valued above all else. If he had hurt her, tarnished her, or heaven fucking forbid, killed her, I would make him bleed and bleed until there was nothing left of him but bones.

I made it to my truck, ripping the door open just as JJ caught up to me, gripping my arm and pulling me around to face him.

"Fox," he snapped and I managed to focus as he placed a piece of paper in my hand. "Saint got hold of Maverick's phone number."

I stared down at the digits on the square slip of paper, my mind racing.

"Call him," JJ urged.

"Call him?! I don't want to call him, I want to kill him," I spat. "We need to get home, take the boat-"

"No." JJ gripped my arm tighter. "We have to make sure she's okay."

"I'll find out when I get there," I barked, but JJ didn't let me go, his fingers digging into my arm and Mutt started yapping angrily at the confrontation.

"That could be exactly what he wants!" JJ snapped. "What do you think will happen if we sail over there? We'll be gunned down on sight. And if Rogue's alive, then she'll be left alone with him."

"She has to be alive," I rasped, destroyed by even the thought that she might not be. That my brother could be so vengeful as to kill her because I loved her. But she'd been to that island and survived once. He'd had a chance to take her life before and he hadn't, so maybe there was hope.

"She is," JJ backtracked. "Rick hasn't killed her. Because if he had, he'd have made sure we already knew."

I released a heavy breath, nodding in agreement of that. "You're right."

"So call him," JJ urged and I gritted my jaw, my fingers tightening around the piece of paper that was a link to my lost brother.

"Fine," I bit out, dropping into the car and JJ jogged around to get in the other side.

I took out my phone, aggressively dialling the number and pressing speakerphone as I hit call.

It rang three times before a gravelly voice answered, sending a chill of recognition sweeping through me.

"Who is this?" he demanded.

"Your death if you don't give me back my girl," I warned and he fell quiet for a moment before releasing a booming laugh.

"Hello, brother," Maverick said tauntingly. "I wondered when you'd figure it out. Which rat in my gang did you have to kill for this number?"

"Killing isn't the solution to everything, Maverick," I said tightly. "Although when it comes to dealing with you, it's the only one on the table."

"How terrifying," he said blandly. "So I suppose you want to know what condition your pretty unicorn is in?"

"If you've touched her-" I started, but he cut over me.

"Oh I've touched her alright, brother. I've touched her *everywhere*."

Ice trickled down my spine and anger spiralled through me so fiercely, I couldn't see anything but a cloud of red.

"You fucking monster," I snarled as JJ clawed a hand through his hair, his eyes wide with fear. "I'll slice you apart, I'll fucking gut you for this."

Maverick laughed obnoxiously once more. "It's cute that you think I raped her. The girl was practically drooling over my cock the second I brought her home. I made great use of that wet mouth of hers too."

"Fuck you!" I roared, my fingers squeezing the phone almost hard enough to break it. "You're dead, you're fucking dead!"

JJ snatched the phone from my hand, taking a breath as he worked to keep calmer than I was managing. "Put her on the phone. Prove she's alive."

"Nah," he said lightly. "I don't think I will. She's busy fingering herself to get ready for another round with my cock."

"Shut your filthy mouth," I snarled, grabbing the phone back from JJ as Maverick laughed loudly once more.

"Calm down, Foxy boy," he said mockingly. "Maybe you shouldn't have abandoned your girl if she meant so much to you."

"I didn't fucking abandon her," I snarled and he scoffed.

"That's not what she told me. And she's been telling me a lot of things, brother. Have you been keeping secrets from Daddy dearest? Tut, tut. What ever would he do if he found out Rogue was back in town?"

"You know exactly what he'd do," I spat.

"Yeah, well I guess that's the only two things Luther Harlequin and I have in common. We hold grudges and we keep our promises. I'm gonna ruin your girl then dump her at your door when I'm finished having my fun, then I'm gonna cut through the army of men you hide behind, drag you to Gallows Bridge and hang you there like the traitor you are."

"The only traitor in our family was you," I hissed. "And listen to me very fucking carefully. I'm coming for Rogue Easton, and I will leave your island with her in my arms and your head swinging from my fist."

"Good luck with that," he said lightly. "But I thought you wanted the cartel to kill me off for you like a coward?"

A dark smirk pulled at my lips. "Rumour has it they like to slice people up like salami when they owe them money."

"Ain't that the truth. Oh, but haven't you heard?"

"What?" I gritted out.

"Every kilo of cocaine I lost in that fire miraculously turned back up again in my new warehouse. I guess the drug fairies must have brought it in the night. Aren't I lucky?"

"What are you talking about?" I demanded.

"It's strange that Shawn Mackenzie lost the exact same amount from his storage units though. I guess the cartel will be out for his blood now instead," Maverick mused, clearly enjoying this as a curse left my lips.

The asshole had replaced the drugs, he'd fucking pinned his losses on Shawn. It was infuriatingly genius, and I guessed that explained why the leader of The Dead Dogs had gone underground.

"I made sure there was enough clues there as to who took it too," Maverick said with a smirk in his voice. "Shawn will be so very angry with you, Foxy."

"Shit," JJ muttered as my gut lurched.

Shawn was out for us as it was, now he thought we'd robbed him of all that cocaine and turned the cartel on him. He was on the fucking run, and no doubt on a warpath too. He was gonna be hunting us with the fury of a wild man.

"Anyway, I'd better go," Maverick said. "Rogue's probably as wet as a waterfall right now and I don't wanna keep her waiting."

"You fucking-" I started but he hung up and I threw the phone onto the dashboard with a shout of fury before throwing my fist into the steering wheel. I punched it over and over so the horn went off repeatedly, blinded by utter hate and horror at what he'd said. Was she really fucking him? Did she want him? Was she glad to be away from me?

Mutt barked furiously and JJ dove on me, locking my arms to my sides as I panted furiously, strands of blonde hair falling into my eyes.

"Breathe," he commanded and I did, meeting his gaze and finding my strength there. "He's trying to get in your head."

Slowly, the manic rage in my mind lifted enough to give me some clarity on that. Maverick was surely just fucking with me. She was his prisoner, she had to be. She wouldn't give herself to him. He was just taunting me.

JJ gripped my face hard to keep my eyes locked with his as Mutt got squashed between us. "We will get her back," he swore and I held the back of his neck in return, pressing my forehead to his as that vow flared between us. "But we can't go off half cocked."

I nodded as we released each other and I sat back in my seat and stroked Mutt's head, a little whine leaving him like he knew what we were talking about. "We'll head home, regroup and come up with a strategy to get onto his island."

"Fox...we won't survive it," JJ said seriously. "His compound is locked up tighter than a duck's asshole, he has watch towers, we'll be gunned down in the water before we even get close."

I clenched my jaw, knowing he was right, but I couldn't face the possibility that I had to just wait this out. What if he was torturing her? Raping her? I couldn't just leave her there to that fate. I had to rescue her.

"There has to be a way," I rasped and Mutt gazed up at me like he was desperate for me to come up with an answer too. "Maybe he'll take a trade. We can offer him territory, anything to get her back."

"Yeah," JJ said, though he didn't sound certain. "Let's just go home and talk it out."

I nodded, twisting the key in the ignition and driving down the road. When we eventually approached Harlequin House, I didn't slow, accelerating past it and taking the next left turn towards the beach.

"Where are you going?" JJ asked in surprise.

"To bring our brother home," I said quietly, driving along the seafront in the direction of Sinners' Playground, the old rides on the pier gleaming in the morning sunlight.

I parked up and we headed out across the sandy beach, walking down into the shadow of the amusement park towards the wooden strut where we'd carved a ladder all those years ago.

But before I made it there, Mutt ran off with a bark under the pier and I squinted into the darkest recess at the end of it, spotting someone lying there.

My heart squeezed with worry and JJ cursed as we started running up the sand to where Chase was laying shirtless in the dark with an empty bottle of rum in his hand and a cigarette butt between his lips, ash coating his chest.

I kicked him in the side and he groaned, the butt falling from his lips onto his collar bone. Mutt barked right in his ear and Chase waved a hand vaguely to try and bat him away.

"Dude, get up," JJ said, jabbing him with the toe of his boot.

"Can't," Chase croaked. "There's a volcano erupting in my head."

Mutt barked at him again and Chase groaned in agony.

I folded my arms, taking in my brother with concern rippling through me. Had he been sleeping here every night like a fucking hobo? From the looks of the empty rum bottles littering the place, I was guessing he had.

Mutt pranced around him then cocked his leg and started pissing on his jeans.

"Whassappening?" Chase slurred.

"Mutt's pissing on you," JJ supplied with a snort.

"Argh, nooo." Chase managed to sit up and Mutt bounded away with a yip as Chase stared at the wet patch on his jeans with a look of defeat.

His pants were undone and his curly dark hair was sticking up in every direction. He squinted up at me and he looked so fucking pitiful that I offered him a hand to help him up. He took it and I pulled him to his feet, brushing the sand off of his back for him as he stumbled forward a step.

"I looked everywhere, man," he promised. "I only came here at dawn, I swear."

"I know," I muttered, seeing the truth in his tired eyes. "Come on, you can come home now."

"I can?" he asked hopefully.

"Yeah," I said heavily.

"Does that mean-" he started, but JJ cut in.

"We found her," he said, his gaze intense.

"Where is she?" he demanded in alarm.

"She's with Maverick. He's the one who got her out of jail," I said and he gaped at me.

"What?" he breathed in fear. "Is she alright?" He gripped my arm, his features twisting in terror and I shook my head.

"I don't know, brother," I said darkly. "But if she's not, there's no force in this world that will save Maverick from our wrath."

CHAPTER SEVEN

I watched the view out over the water as I sat on the balcony in Maverick's suite, looking into the distance where I could just make out Sinners' Playground with the sun glinting off of the metal framework of the huge Ferris wheel. I was grinding my teeth. Rage and heartache biting into my soul as I glared towards the town which held the Harlequin Crew at the heart of it.

There was a time when all I'd wanted to do was run from those boys and their betrayal, but that time was gone. Now I wanted vengeance. That was the cold, hard truth of it. I'd been a poor girl with no one to give much of a shit about me when I'd been growing up, but those boys had made that simple, empty life feel so fucking full. And thanks to that I now knew what I was lacking. What I'd always be lacking for the rest of my days. And I intended to take that from them too.

I needed to get back there. I needed to find the rest of their keys and unlock that crypt. Hell hath no fury like a dead girl scorned. And they were going to find that out first hand.

The door opened behind me and I looked around as Maverick stepped out to join me. He'd been gone most of the day and I'd been stuck in here while he left men to guard the doors and man the courtyard beneath me and basically make certain I couldn't leave. At least the day of solitude had given me time to sunbathe naked at long last and bring some of the golden glow back to my skin.

Maverick dropped down on to the cream rattan couch which sat on the other side of the balcony before a glass dining table and placed two bowls of food down. He didn't say a word as he began eating and I grabbed the grey tank top I'd stolen from him and pulled it on to cover myself up. There hadn't been any talk of me getting my own clothes while I was here aside from the outfit I'd worn on that job and I didn't really give a shit about borrowing from him - but I drew the line at the idea of wearing anything of Mia's.

"You didn't want to eat with your girlfriend then?" I asked as I dropped into the seat to his right and tugged my bowl closer. I might have been a captive in this place, but that didn't mean I was going to turn into some meek mouse. Besides, if he wanted me dead, he'd had his chance.

"Believe me, she's not my girlfriend," Maverick grunted, his lip curling in distaste as I took a bite of my pasta.

"So what is she then?" I asked suspiciously because I'd been thinking about that on and off since we'd hooked up and I didn't like the idea of me being the other woman even if Mia was a bitch. "Because I saw her with her hands on your body, Rick. Don't try and pretend you haven't fucked her."

"I never said I haven't. She's a lot easier to tolerate when I have her face rammed into the cushions so that I can fuck her ass in peace."

I narrowed my eyes on him, wondering what I even wanted to gain from this conversation and he sighed, tossing his fork down into his empty bowl and levelling me with a flat look.

"Don't get yourself all worked up about it, beautiful. Mia is a means to an end. That's all."

"So what am I?" I asked, arching a brow at him as he ran his gaze over me.

"*The* end," he said slowly.

I took another bite of my food and mulled that over, trying to figure out exactly what that was supposed to mean.

"I got my period," I said suddenly. "Had to ask one of your men to go find me some tampons - which freaked him the fuck out might I add. He got way too confused about which ones to get and I think he had to go find a woman to help him in the end."

"Is that so?"

"Yeah. I assumed you'd wanna know. Because you fucked me without a condom and all. And I'm guessing you're not ready to play daddy to a little bundle of joy any time soon."

Silence fell between us and I stared at him, wondering what the hell he was even thinking. I knew what I thought of it, that was for sure. I'd been borderline freaking the fuck out over the fact that we'd forgotten about contraception and the idea that I might have landed myself in that kind of situation. So when I'd gone to the bathroom and found the Red Ranger had paid me a visit I'd whooped for freaking joy. I seriously didn't even have my own shit half together, so I knew I had fuck all chance of being a badass bitch of a mom.

"Well, I guess we don't have to worry about that now. Do we?"

"Were you worrying about it at all?" I challenged.

"If I'm honest, I've been more caught up thinking about how slick and hot your pussy felt wrapped tight around my cock and how fucking good it felt filling you up with my cum while you begged me for every drop of it. So no, I hadn't been worrying about the consequences, but I'm sure we would have figured it out if there had been any."

"Figured it out?" I asked, folding my arms and wondering what he meant by that.

"Isn't being a daddy all about fighting to the death to protect your own? Pretty sure I've got that handled, beautiful. I could figure out the diapers and that shit on the job."

I burst out laughing before I could stop myself and Rick hooked a smile at me too. The shithead almost had me going then. And hell, maybe he really did mean it. Dude was fucking insane, but whatever. Shark week had started and I didn't need to worry about babies popping out of me, so I was all good so far as those concerns went.

"Am I going to need to go get myself checked out?" I asked him, spearing some more pasta and almost groaning at how good it tasted.

"I got tested when I left prison," Maverick said, his gaze darkening with some truth he clearly didn't want to go into in any more detail. "Since then,

I can't say I've ever forgone a condom aside from with you so I think you're good."

I nodded and he leaned towards me, dropping his voice. "But maybe *I* need to get tested? You admitted to fucking Johnny James after all and the entire Cove knows he's a whore for sale. I'm guessing he's got a few nasties lurking about him."

"He gets himself tested weekly actually," I replied, narrowing my eyes. "And unlike you, he never forgets a condom. So I'm good."

"You wanna tell me some more about that?" Rick asked, his gaze running down my body with interest.

"About me fucking JJ?"

"Why not? I might hate the little prick, but I hear he's a good lay. I'd be interested to hear how loud he made you scream and how hard he made you come. Hell, it might even turn me on to hear the filthy details. Or maybe he's overpriced and it's all hype?"

My skin prickled as I thought about JJ's body claiming mine but that was quickly followed by the rush of hurt, betrayal and hatred I felt toward him and the rest of the fucking Harlequins for what they'd done to me on that fucking ferry and I just shook my head.

"I don't want to talk about him. Or any of them."

"That's a shame, because I had an interesting phone call today," Maverick said, leaning back in his chair, his dark eyes glimmering with amusement.

"From who?" I demanded.

"Foxy Boy. He's finally figured out where you are, beautiful, and it sounds like he's not at all happy about it. He threatened to do a lot of bad, bad things to me - especially after I informed him about how much you'd enjoyed taking my cock."

My lips popped open in outrage and Rick just smirked at me like a prime asshole.

"Why the fuck would you tell him that?"

"Because he's been telling the whole world you're his and I promised to break you and lay you back at his door beyond repair. Now here you are, your body sore from my time spent owning it and covered in marks I branded onto it, your heart black with hatred for him and his little friends and the fissures

108

that night ten years ago carved into all of our souls officially bleeding once more. I'd say I've more than achieved what I was hoping to with you, baby girl."

"So that's all I am to you? A playing piece for you to set against your enemy?" I asked angrily, tossing my fork down and glaring at him.

"No. But that doesn't mean you can't be that too. Am I lying about any of it? Do you hate him with all your heart?"

"Yes," I hissed, ignoring the little voice in the back of my skull which was weeping for the rest of my boys because that bitch was weak. They'd fucked me over, left me there to take the fall, abandoned me *again*. They'd had their chance to prove their pretty words weren't just bullshit and they'd fucked me over for the final time.

"And do you want to stand at my side and strike back at them?"

"Yes," I said firmly because fuck it - I did want that. I wanted someone in my fucking corner for once and out of all of my boys, Rick was the only one who hadn't actually abandoned me all those years ago. He'd probably suffered worse than I had because of the damn Harlequins and why the fuck shouldn't we band together against them?

"And does that sweet cunt of yours still ache from the feeling of me owning it? Does it throb with the desire for me to do it all over again? Did I lie to him when I said you were begging for it, demanding it, spreading your legs wide and panting for me to give it to you?"

"Fuck you," I said but my voice was kind of breathy and I was clenching my thighs together to try and stamp down my own arousal.

"You already did. But I'm keen for another round, baby girl. Just say the word."

I rolled my eyes at him and he smirked, pushing his chair back and beckoning me over to him with a single finger.

I folded my arms and leaned back in my chair in a clear refusal. I might have liked him manhandling me all over the bedroom, but that did not make me his meek little submissive waiting for him to click his fingers and command me to service his cock.

"Come here, beautiful, I just wanna talk. And I like to look a person in the eyes when I talk to them so that I can see their truth." He patted his thigh and

I pursed my lips.

No fucking way was this that simple, but I had to admit that I was tempted by his offer. He owned that fucking chair the way he'd owned me the other night. His shorts and backwards baseball cap combo made me lick my lips and I let myself appreciate his muscular torso and the countless tattoos which covered his bare chest as I looked him over.

"You want to talk to me, Rick?" I asked him. "Then that truth is gonna go both ways. We can trade truths until one of us doesn't want to give one up and then the loser will have to do a forfeit."

"Fine. When you refuse to tell me something, you can get down on your knees and swallow my cock like a good girl," he replied instantly, never one to back down from anything.

"So predictable. And what will your forfeit be when you refuse to answer one of my questions?"

"Easy. I'll have to fuck you until you remember your manners again."

"How is that a punishment for you?" I asked.

"Well, if you really want it to be a punishment then you don't have to let me come. But I'll work my hardest to convince you not to go with that plan."

I got up slowly and walked towards him, letting him reach for me and clasp my ass in his huge hands as I stood between his thighs and looked down at him.

"Yeah, but you can't exactly fuck me while I'm bleeding, so how long am I going to have to wait for this prize?"

Rick snorted derisively. "You think I won't fuck you bloody?" He pushed my stolen shirt up to reveal my bare ass and moved his fingers between my thighs, making me gasp as he found the tampon string and curled it around his finger, tugging the tiniest amount. "Believe me, beautiful, there is nothing about that that turns me off. So unless it's a problem for you..."

I bit my lip, wondering if it was. Shawn had never wanted anything to do with me when I had my period and I'd never fucked any of my other boyfriends while on it either. But the way Maverick was looking at me while I thought it over made my blood heat and a motherfucking blush rose in my cheeks as I shrugged one shoulder.

"I guess I'm not totally against it," I said slowly, making him growl low in the back of his throat before yanking me down to straddle his lap.

"Come on then, ask me whatever it is that's burning you up inside, because if you don't distract me, I'm going to bend you over that balcony railing and give all of my men a real show."

I laughed and slapped his chest, and he looked at me like he didn't even know what to make of that sound. My laughter fell away and I cupped his cheek, searching for the boy I used to know beneath the layers of pain and anger he'd built up around himself.

"Do you even mean it when you laugh anymore, Rick?" I asked him softly, my fingertips moving across his stubbled jaw.

"No," he replied simply. "My turn. Tell me why you're holding a grudge against Shawn Mackenzie."

I jerked back on instinct, pressing my palm against Maverick's chest as I made a move to stand up, but his grip on my ass tightened and he tutted at me. "Backing down so soon? The Rogue I remember was never afraid to voice her truth for the whole world to hear. Why so shy, baby girl?"

I fell still, frowning at him and wondering if there was some truth to his words. I had changed in the last ten years. I ran from my problems and lied more easily than I spoke the truth. Maybe that was because I used to have my boys at my back, so it had been easier to stand my ground and speak my truth back then. Or maybe I'd just let my pain over losing them turn me into a fucking coward. And I didn't like the idea of that one bit.

"If I tell you, I want you to promise me you won't kill him for me."

"Why would I make a silly promise like that?"

"Because his death is mine. I'm fucking owed it and I'm not looking for a knight in shining armour to do my dirty work for me," I snarled.

Maverick raised a brow at the intensity of my tone then nodded his chin at me, agreeing to my terms and waiting for me to go on.

I searched his eyes for some deception, but I found myself just wanting to trust him. To finally fucking trust someone other than myself. I gave in to that urge because I wanted him to know and I guessed I wanted to test him to. To make sure he would honour my wishes and stick to this agreement between us.

"Shawn and me were...together," I admitted slowly. "I was his girl for about two years."

Maverick fell still. The kind of still a cobra took on right before it struck at its prey. "You let that piece of shit touch you?" he growled dangerously.

"I would have thought that you of all people might have understood that life has fucked me in every imaginable way up until this point. And yeah, that includes me spreading my legs for some questionable characters on more than one occasion. What do you want me to say? He set his eyes on me and he was rich, powerful. He offered me protection and it's not like he's bad to look at. Hell, I can't even say he has a small cock - though he is a selfish fucker when it comes to the way he uses it."

Maverick's gaze stayed fixed with mine and it was clear that he wasn't enamoured with this story, but he was listening at least.

"Anyway. That's where I was before I came back here, kept in one of his apartments and comfortable enough that I wasn't looking too hard for a way out though I wouldn't exactly say I was happy."

"Did you know he was an enemy to the Harlequins?" Maverick asked. "Was it about revenge, or-"

"No. I didn't...what do you mean, enemy? His turf is nowhere near here. Why would he have anything to do with-"

Maverick barked a laugh suddenly and I just stared at him as I tried to process that little nugget of shit he'd just dropped into my lap.

"You should have done your homework better, beautiful. The Dead Dogs have been at war with The Harlequin Crew for a while now. Luther moved upstream, trying to play the big shark and monopolise the movement of half the drugs on the lower side of the west coast. He put his fingers in so many pies and spread his territory so wide that he's been racking up enemies left, right and centre. And Shawn Mackenzie is about the worst of the lot. Didn't he ever tell you about that shit while you were shacked up in his bed?"

"It wasn't like that with me and Shawn. I might have been his girl, but it certainly wasn't love. We went to parties and we fucked. I met his mom a bunch of times because he liked to pretend he was a nice guy for her benefit, but I can't say she bought it. Mostly we just enjoyed each other because I knew no one could touch me while I belonged to him and he knew I was a good lay and I wouldn't start trying to make him wife me. It wasn't particularly romantic, but it worked. Or at least it did until I guess I saw something he didn't want me to and the motherfucker tried to kill me."

"Kill you how?" Rick demanded.

His grip on me tightened and I wondered if I'd made a mistake in admitting this to him. But I was tired. So fucking tired of the lies and the games and the bullshit and I just wanted to tell one fucking person the truth about this.

"He wrapped his hands around my throat and squeezed until I blacked out," I admitted in a low voice and Maverick's gaze trailed from my face to my neck as he took that in. "I guess he thought he'd finished the job so he wrapped me in a potato sack and drove me out here. Buried me in a shallow grave somewhere up the coast from Sinners' Playground. I came to the next morning and dug my ass up out of the dirt like some freaking zombie, realised where he'd dumped me and decided I may as well try and deal with some unfinished business while I was here."

I expected yelling, snarling, some big show of macho posturing with a bunch of death threats thrown in, but Maverick wasn't that kind of creature. I could see the rage there burning in his eyes like a demon, but he was detaching from it, moving it through his brain in a cold and calculating way and filing it away for later. No doubt when he released it again, he would explode into the vengeful monster I'd seen when he'd killed Colten for me, but right here and now he was solid. Silent. A predator biding his time and waiting for the opportune moment to pounce.

"What did you see to make him do that to you?" he asked slowly, his hand trailing up my side and making my skin tingle.

"I don't even know," I admitted irritably. "I'd been out, and I was horny. Like I said, he has a big dick and the feel of it slamming into me always helped build me up even if I inevitably had to finish myself off after he was done. He liked watching me do that - used to say I was so addicted to his cock that I had to finger myself over him even after we were finished. Which was total bullshit, I just needed to come and he never made the effort to get me there, but whatever."

"You put up with shit sex for two years?" Maverick asked and I narrowed my gaze on him.

"Most sex is pretty shit, Rick. Just because you managed to make me come doesn't mean all men can. Anyway, I went over there thinking along those lines and his guys let me in. But when I made it to the door, I heard him talking to someone. Well, it was two people actually. A man and a woman. They said something about things coming together nicely and change being exactly what was needed around here, but that's it. I guess I must have made a noise or something though because suddenly Shawn ripped the door open and he was fucking furious. The woman started shouting something about him promising there would be no witnesses and the guy said the deal would be off if there were and the next thing I knew, Shawn was sighing like, I dunno… kinda like what he had to do was a real pain in the ass. And the next thing I knew he'd lunged at me…" My voice trailed off as the fear I'd felt that night consumed me and Maverick growled angrily, lifting my chin and making me look at him.

"Spit it out, beautiful. Bile only burns worse on the way back down. You gotta get it out or it'll fester in your gut." His fingers moved to wind around my throat and I moaned softly.

The look in his eyes said he knew as well as I did how fucked up it was for me to like him doing that so much, but it was weirdly cathartic. Like allowing him to re-enact my darkest memory in that small way gave me power over it. Trusting him to put his hands on me like that and to reap rewards from it instead of terror and pain helped me process it or some shit. Or maybe I was just broken beyond repair. Either way, I was pretty sure I needed his brutality to help me find my own.

"I ran, grabbed a lamp and hurled it at him then made a run for his bedroom. He had a balcony there and I was pretty sure I could shimmy down the drain and jump from it to the wall which ringed his apartment block then all I'd have to do was run and run until I was lost all over again and he'd never be able to find me. But when I threw his door open, I found the bed he'd fucked me in so many times wasn't empty. There was a girl there, naked and clearly off her fucking face on something as she stared up at the ceiling with full blown pupils and drool running down her cheek. And dumb bitch that I am, that fucking hurt. He'd made it clear to all of his men that I belonged to him, that I was his and no other man could lay a finger on me and the fucking hypocrisy of seeing that freshly fucked bitch in my place hurt just enough to make me pause. The next thing I knew, Shawn was throwing me against the wall. I tried to fight back, but he's a lot bigger than me and when he punched me, I swear I saw stars. Then his hands were around my throat and he was squeezing and squeezing and I could see my death looking right back at me in his icy blue eyes. And all I could think about was this place and the four of you and the life I wished I'd lived. Because the one I'd had instead was so fucking empty and it was ending way too soon."

Maverick was still beneath me, his fingers tightening around my throat, though not in a way to cut off my breath, more like he wanted to hold on tight and never let me go.

"I'm gonna need you to kiss me, beautiful. Otherwise I'm not sure how much longer I'll be able to remain where I am and keep my promise to let you end that piece of shit." He shifted his grip to the back of my neck and I leaned forward, my hands sliding over the hard press of his tense muscles before my mouth found his and I fell into a kiss that swallowed me whole.

Maverick kept his grip tight on the back of my neck, caging me against him as his tongue moved against mine and his heart thumped wildly beneath my palm. When he kissed me like that, the ache in my heart seemed to fall away, like I was pushing it behind a curtain out of sight and almost forgetting it was even there at all. It was me and him surfing with the sun on our backs, scrawling graffiti on freshly painted walls, stealing from assholes who didn't know how fucking good they had it and laughing until our sides hurt because just being together made all the bad stuff fade away.

When I finally pulled back, I found him looking at me like I was the answer to some question he'd been asking for the longest time. But as a frown furrowed his brow, I knew exactly what he was thinking - it didn't change the past.

"Tell me, Rick," I whispered. "I told you, so it's your turn. What happened to you when you were sent down?"

His hands fell to my thighs and he blew out a breath, seeming as though he was going to refuse as his thumb tracked over the skull inked onto my thigh and his gaze fixed on it too.

"Juvie sucked," he said. "But not that much. Mostly I was bored there. It wasn't hard for me to take control of the place, to prove to the other kids that I was the one to fear, the one to keep away from. Hell, I thought I was the big fucking man in there, miserable about being incarcerated but still the ruler of that shitty little empire. When I turned eighteen, they packed me up and shipped me out. Prison was...hell. Not like the bullshit version of it you see on TV where you think about how fucking shitty it might be to be locked up all day and the occasional asshole gets shanked in the corridors. No, for me, walking through those doors and hearing them lock behind me was akin to being tied to a stake and being burned alive from the inside out."

"What happened?" I breathed, my fingers trailing over the ink on his chest, tracing the tally marks he had there and feeling the ridges of scarred flesh that went with them. It was like we couldn't stop touching each other, this gentle movement of our fingers across each other's skin was somehow soothing the hurts inside us and all the time we kept it up, the darkness might just stay away.

"In all the time I'd been in Juvie, I'd denied every request for visits from Luther and from the boys too. The four of them had put me in there, turned their backs on me and left me there to rot, all because I loved you enough to chase you when you needed me. It haunted me knowing you were lost out there somewhere, all alone and fuck knew where. JJ kept writing to me long after the others stopped. Updating me on pointless shit in their lives and in the gang, telling me what he knew about you - which was fuck all. I only read them at all because I was desperate to hear about you, for them to find you and keep you safe. But of course, that information never came and my fury at them only grew. I was locked up, unable to come and find you no matter how much I ached for you, but their chains were made of nothing but fear and cowardice. They could have gone after you. They should have." Maverick's fist clenched against my thigh and I took his hand in mine, lifting it to my lips and pressing a kiss against his inked skin. He watched me for several long seconds before continuing. "Anyway, I guess by the time I was transferred to prison, Luther was losing his patience with me and thought he'd try his hand at forcing the apology he was so desperate for from my lips. He had guards in his pockets. Four of them. And every night from the very first I spent in that place, they came for me, took me from my cell and spent hours beating and torturing me."

Anger burned through me hot and fast as I took that in and my heart

116

began to race at the thought of him suffering like that. Night after night, locked up in that place and enduring all of it - because of me.

"I'm sorry, Rick," I whispered, tears brimming in my eyes as I realised this was all my fault. Everything he'd endured had been down to me because the man he'd been sent down for killing had died by my hands, not his. "I didn't know. But you shouldn't have taken the fall for me. Axel was a rapist piece of shit and I was the one who killed him. I replayed that night so many times in my head and sometimes I think that I should never have called the four of you for help. The asshole had attacked me. It was self-defence. I should have called the cops and told them everything and if Luther had wanted to come after me anyway then at least it wouldn't have been the four of you and-"

"Stop that," Maverick growled. "You know full well that the cops around here are all bought and paid for. You killed a Harlequin, and it doesn't matter if he was a filthy fucking animal who deserved worse than what he got because Luther would have made you pay the price for his life in blood. That's how the Harlequins work. Besides, I didn't go to prison over Axel. I went to prison because Luther likes to play god with the people he thinks he owns. He thought he could force me to beg for my way out. He thought that one day it would get so fucking bad in there that I'd call him up and promise to be a good boy and do whatever the fuck he wanted for the rest of my life just so long as he rescued me from that hell. But I can promise you, that no matter how bad it got, no matter how many beatings I took or how many times I wished I was dead instead of locked up in there enduring all the worst things a man can endure, I never once considered making that call to him."

"Tell me about the men who hurt you, Rick," I demanded, ignoring the tears which had slipped down my cheeks and pressing his palm to my face as I gave him a serious look. "Tell me about them and I'll help you hunt them down and we can make them pay for-"

"Oh don't worry about that, beautiful," he said, a dark look entering his eyes which reminded me all too clearly that this man had made good friends with death in the time he'd spent away from me. "The four guards who enjoyed torturing me oh so much had a few little routines which they shared with me. Once a year - always on the same weekend, the second one in August, I got four days of freedom from their torture because they took an annual fishing trip together. They made sure that the moment they were back I paid for the time off and more, but they were also fucking sloppy when it came to telling me the details of their little trips. So as soon as I got out of that fucking place, I made sure to head on out into the woods they'd told me all about the moment that weekend rolled around again."

I bit my bottom lip as he told this story, the pain and horror of the memories he'd been reliving from his time in prison peeling back as this dark demon rose in him and I could practically taste the bloodlust on my own tongue as he told me about his revenge.

"Did you make it hurt?" I asked breathily, placing my hand over his heart so that I could feel it pounding beneath my palm.

"I made them scream for days," he growled, bringing a dark smile to my lips. "I cut them apart piece by fucking piece and bathed myself in their blood while they begged me for mercy. There was nothing left of them by the time I was done and the official line is that they must have gotten lost out in the wilderness or fallen prey to some kind of animal attack. And I guess that was pretty accurate in the end, because I really was an animal out there."

"Good," I hissed and he gave me a smile that made my toes curl as he ran his thumb across my bottom lip and I dragged it between my teeth before biting down and making him tug it free again. "Is that why you're the way you are now?" I asked slowly, wondering if he'd admit to the coldness that had claimed his heart. "Was the revenge not enough to banish your demons?"

"Are you worrying about that, beautiful?" he deflected, pushing his thumb into my mouth again so that I sucked on it and he watched me with a heated look in his eyes. "Do you think revenge might not be enough to fix your damage?"

I released his thumb from my mouth so that I could reply. "I don't think anything will be enough to fix my damage," I admitted. "But it seems like there's something else causing yours. Something more..."

Maverick looked away from me, out over the rolling waves towards Sunset Cove and I frowned, wondering what could be so bad that he didn't want to voice it after all we'd just shared.

"There is more. But I can't talk about it," he said eventually, his voice rough and shadows dancing across his expression.

"You can tell me anything," I promised him, catching his rough jaw and making him look at me again. There was a war taking place in his dark eyes and it hurt me even though I didn't understand why.

"I don't want you to look at me differently," he said firmly. "Besides, I'm not that person anymore so I think some of the past should stay buried. All I care about now is killing the fucking Harlequins and finishing what I started. Maybe if I really do get revenge on everyone who fucked me over I'll feel some of that relief I'm hunting for so desperately. Or maybe I won't and all of it will have been for nothing."

"All of it?" I asked, my heart tugging painfully at the thought of that and he frowned.

"Maybe not all," he admitted, looking into my eyes. "But seeing as I just lost our little truth game, I think I have to fuck you now, right?"

A laugh escaped me despite the heaviness in my heart and I shook my head. "Maybe later, stud. How about right now we just sit here? We can watch the waves and cuddle like a couple of old people without a care in the fucking world."

"You wanna cuddle with me?" he asked with a snort of amusement.

"Yes, big boy. Even psychos need a cuddle from time to time."

I shifted in his lap so that I was sitting across him instead of straddling him, laying my head against his broad chest and listening to the solid thump of his heartbeat against my ear and he sighed as his arms folded around me.

The two of us really were a pair of damaged creatures. But somehow, when we were together, that fact didn't seem to hurt so much.

Dead Man's Isle

MAVERICK

CHAPTER EIGHT

*A*n unstoppable, unbreakable chain of days and nights slipped by. A month, two, three. Every day was the same hell and the only gleam of light keeping me from ripping my blanket to pieces and forging a rope out of it for my neck was her. I'd made a promise to come for her. And I would. I just wasn't sure how much longer I could survive like this.

I stood in my cell, my face squashed to the wall, Krasinski's hand pressed to my back and keeping me there while I chewed the inside of my cheek until it bled. He was touching himself, and soon he'd touch me and the only place I could escape to was the corners of my mind where distant memories still clung to me. But they were like moths fluttering around the flame of a candle and whenever I tried to see them clearer, they burned up and vanished before my eyes. Each one was precious and harder to hold onto than the last. It wasn't that I was forgetting Rogue, it was that with each time I tried to cling onto those pieces of my past, they seemed more fragmented than before. I couldn't picture myself in them anymore because I was no longer the boy she'd depended on. I'd failed her. And now I was just some convict's bitch with no future and no way to reach her.

So after a while, I sought out a different kind of strength to keep me going. Vengeance. When Krasinski held me down and breathed heavily in my ear, I thought of violence. I imagined firing a bullet into Luther's head, the man who'd abandoned me to this fate, who let Officer White and his Harlequin lackies punish me day after day. And through the storm of hate washing through my mind, I finally found an answer to my problem. It wasn't immediate. But it gave me hope where there had been none before.

The reason Luther controlled me was because he was bigger and badder than me. It was the very same reason that Krasinski controlled me too. So there really was only one way I could destroy both of them. I had to become the biggest, baddest motherfucker in the room. And not just this room, every fucking room.

So I'd train my body daily, work tirelessly, make this my one and only cause in life. Then, when I was strong enough to fight back, I'd let every demon in my head run riot on my enemies. And after I'd cast them from this world, I'd hunt down the only girl who'd stood by me and pray I wasn't too broken to love her.

The morning light spilled through the room, waking me, bringing relief with it. I despised the night. The dark reminded me of them. Officer White, Hughes, Reed and Boyd. But worse than them. Far worse. Krasinski. Once I'd started sharing a cell with him, I prayed for White and the others to come. At midnight they'd steal me from my bed and I relished every punch and kick and jeer. I welcomed the pain because when it stopped, it meant I'd have to return to *him*. And there was no greater nightmare to me than that.

The memories receded faster than usual as the scent of coconut ran under my nose and I found the beautiful creature in my arms who I'd wanted to capture my entire life. Finally, somehow, I had her. And now I was afraid of life stealing her from me just as fast, and this moment becoming another memory I could barely hold onto, taunting me with its brevity.

I drew Rogue tighter against me, the night gone, the daylight burning brighter than it had since I was a child. She'd fallen asleep in my lap last night and I'd carried her inside, stripping down to my boxers and just laying with her in my bed until sleep had finally claimed me too.

When I thought back on that broken boy I'd been in prison, it made me shudder with shame. I may have found my way back to her eventually, but I definitely wasn't the man I'd hoped I'd be when I got here. Now, we were a temporary fire burning in an icy wasteland, the snow already beginning to fall.

I still hadn't fulfilled my wishes of giving death to all those who deserved it. While Luther and his son drew breath, I was cursed to walk this earth, tormented by the pain of my past and the knowledge that I hadn't survived prison with anything left of the boy Rogue had once cared for. I was a cruel stranger inhabiting this body, consuming it, absorbing the desires of that boy and fulfilling them as best I could now, knowing that the clock was already running down on our time together. I wanted to be him more than anything in that moment. But I wasn't and I couldn't ever be again.

There were only a few things certain in life and the hardest one I'd had to swallow was that there was no going back. There was only now. No future, no past, just this moment. And this, and this. So I'd drown myself in each of them and try to stretch each second into two, each minute into five. I'd have bartered with the Devil himself, offered him my blackened soul on a silver platter tomorrow, if only he'd give me more time right here with her.

I dragged my mouth along her neck, raking my teeth over her flesh and fighting the urge to take a deep and bloody bite out of her. How could she sleep so soundly wrapped in the arms of a monster? I doubted she really had any idea of who I was these days. My face was a familiar lie to her. But it was just a mask, beneath it was nothing but sin and wicked deeds, wrapped around the heart of a boy which ached for her as it always had. She'd see soon enough that there was nothing of him left but memories. And she was the owner of the ones which counted.

"I'm going to keep you," I murmured in her ear. "I'm going to lock you up and destroy the key. You're mine, lost girl. I found you. And I'm going to possess you until my final breath, so pray it comes before I break you." My promises were false and petty. I couldn't keep her any more than I could keep the wind contained in a jar. But speaking them aloud felt defiant, like telling the universe it was so.

She released a sleepy moan, her hand moving to cup the back of my neck and pull me closer.

"Do you have any idea who's in this bed with you?" I growled in her ear.

"Hmmm," she sighed, her eyes remaining closed. She patted my head and brushed her fingers over my face like she was trying to work it out. "It's got big ears, it must be an owl."

I released a low laugh, sliding my hand down the length of her body and drawing her back against me by the hip. I examined the array of sea creature tattoos on her arm then rolled her onto her front, pushing up her shirt to trace my fingers over the angel wings on her back.

"Where would you fly to if you had wings?" I asked, scoring my thumb down her spine and making her shiver. *Mine*.

"I'd keep flying into the sky, up and up and up until the world was just a tiny pea. Then I'd crush the pea between my finger and thumb and all my problems would be gone. Poof." She spoke into the pillow and I regarded her, brushing the rainbow hair away from the back of her slender neck.

"You'd solve every problem in the world," I said with a smirk.

"I'm generous like that," she said, goosebumps rising across her body as I pulled the sheet down over her ass, grazing my fingers across every bruise and mark I'd left on her when I'd claimed her and savouring each one.

"You'd kill all the tiny kittens and puppies, you monster," I taunted and she laughed into her pillow.

"They can come into space with me," she said. "I'll make them tiny space suits before I go."

"That so, beautiful?" I smirked and she flopped over onto her back again, curling up against me. She fit so perfectly there, like she was a piece carved off of me at birth, destined to be returned to this very place at my side.

She sighed long and softly. "I guess not. I hate the world and it hates me back, but I wouldn't destroy it."

"Why's that?" I bit her shoulder until she gasped and swatted at me, but I moved over her so she was beneath me, bearing down on her like a cloud shadowing the sun.

Her fingers moved to run over the new tally mark cuts on my chest, inked in to mark my recent kills. "Because the world is bad and dark, but it's good and light too. Maybe the good redeems it just enough, even if that good isn't meant for me." Her eyes flicked up to catch on mine and I wasn't sure we were talking about the world anymore.

"There's no good in me, beautiful," I said, pressing my weight down to

124

pin her in place. My cock swelled against her thigh and she wet her lips in the most seductive way I'd ever seen. "Not anymore."

Her fingers tiptoed up to my cheek, grazing through my stubble then pulling up the corner of my mouth into a crooked smile. "I don't believe you, Rick," she whispered.

"You would shudder at the things I've done," I said, my voice lowering an octave.

"There's only one thing you did that I care about," she said, a crease forming between her eyes. "Though I don't *really* care, but I guess I'm curious. I just can't understand it and I...think I need to understand."

"What?" I pressed.

"You attacked Fox, JJ and Chase the night you got out of prison. They showed me the scars and I saw the truth in their eyes. So why did you do it? What made you hate them like that? I get that you were mad, but enough to kill them?" She shook her head, the sum not adding up in her mind. And she was right. There was more to it than them not fighting harder to keep me out of prison. It wouldn't have mattered either way; Luther would have had me locked up regardless of what they'd done. Mostly, I was just angry that they hadn't gone after Rogue when I couldn't, locked behind bars while they were out in the world free to plan something. I would have found a way, but they didn't. They fucking let her down even worse than I had.

I sighed, rolling off of her onto my back and she pulled the sheet up around us, propping herself up on my chest and gazing down at me.

"When I got out of prison, Fox, JJ and Chase showed up to meet me, but after years of resentment, all I gave a shit about was getting a car and driving straight out of town to find you."

"Chase said you ignored their attempts to contact you," she said with a frown and I clucked my tongue.

"So what?" I scoffed. "They all lost that right the moment they threw me to the cops and used me as their fall guy."

Rogue's eyes sparkled with pain on my behalf. "So what did you do when you saw them outside the prison?"

"I spat at their feet in a simple fuck you and left them there. Then I hitchhiked my way as close to Fairfax as possible then walked seven miles into town to Fox's aunt's house where they'd sent you."

"How'd you know where it was?" she asked.

"Luther took me out there once. He was training me up to be Fox's fucking muscle, his aunt was getting some trouble from a couple of dealers moving in on her turf. So we dragged them into a van, took them to the middle of nowhere and I watched as he scared them shitless with a chainsaw so they'd back off. We had dinner at Fox's aunt's after, casual as anything."

"Why'd you never tell me Luther did shit like that?" she demanded and my gaze slid away from her.

"It was Luther's business, I couldn't talk about it. And you knowing anything would only have put you at risk. Not even Fox knew half of it."

She squeezed my arm and I looked back at her. "When I showed up at his aunt's place looking for you, the old bitch was out in the yard scolding some kid and hitting him with a cane. I snatched it off of her, snapped it in two and threatened her with the sharpened ends to tell me where you were. And you know what she said?"

"What?" Rogue breathed.

"That you were dead, caught in the crossfire of some gang shoot-up a few years back," I spat, the terror I'd felt at that moment driving a shard of ice into my heart once again.

"Why would she say that?" Rogue gasped.

"Luther," I snarled and her brow creased in confusion. I thought back on the crushing moment when I'd believed those words were true, the way the air had been sucked from my body, the way the ground had seemed to spin a hundred miles an hour beneath my feet. "I was so angry, Rogue, blinded by this gnawing rage and grief that was gonna split apart my chest. I told that bitch to give me a gun and she did because I was pretty sure she knew I'd kill her right then if she didn't. It was this old timer revolver that was in a box with a stash of bullets inside, but I wasn't gonna complain. A weapon was a weapon. I left Fairfax, stole a car and drove all the way to Harlequin House with only vengeance in mind. If you were dead, it was on them. If you were dead, we should all be fucking dead. But most of all, Luther needed to be dead." My breaths came unevenly and Rogue watched me intently, hanging on my words. "I pulled up at the gates, got out and walked straight up to the assholes manning them and told them to let me in. They knew who I was, they remembered me and just like that they allowed Luther's death into his palace. I broke through a side window and heard them all fucking laughing out on the patio like they had no cares in the world. And I thought that if they could laugh in a world where you didn't exist, then they didn't deserve to keep breathing. Maybe they didn't know about you, but either way they hadn't saved you. So their fates were sealed."

"Oh my god," Rogue whispered. "What happened?"

"I crept out to the patio and let them see me. I wanted them to know who was here to end them, but all that did was give them a heads up and I wasn't even fucking trained with a gun, but they were. I fired at Fox first, but he lunged aside and my bullet grazed his fucking neck. My hand was shaking and I had this feeling in my chest like…" I shook my head, not wanting to say this because it went against everything I felt about them now.

"What?" Rogue pushed.

"Like I may as well have been firing the gun on myself for how good it felt." I didn't look at her. "Not that that means fucking anything now. Anyway, my next bullets went wide and they got hold of their own guns, shooting back, one of them carved a chunk outa my leg and JJ tried to take me down by swinging a fucking deckchair at my head. I had to run or be killed, and I decided that I'd come back when I was trained and end them for good, but if I stayed any longer I'd waste my blood and be put in the ground before I could avenge you. So, I ran like a fucking coward in the hopes that I could return."

"And that started the war between you all?" she guessed.

"Sort of. Unfortunately that night didn't end there. I managed to get off the property while the guards from the gate were running into the house. I took the stolen car and drove away, realising I had nowhere to go. So I went to the only place I could think of and ended up on the beach near Sinners' Playground. But when I stepped out of the vehicle, I was grabbed, two fucking meatheads waiting for me right there like they'd known I was coming. I was disarmed and shoved in the trunk of a car and I thought that was it, I was gonna be driven somewhere and put to death by the Harlequins, and the only thing comforting about that was that I'd be with you soon enough."

"Rick…" Rogue said sadly and I brushed my knuckles along her cheekbone.

"When the car stopped, the trunk opened and I found myself gazing up at Luther, my adopted fucking father come to put me to death himself. He pulled me out of the car and yelled at me for a long fucking time about me trying to kill the others and I just glared at the asshole with hatred thrumming through my veins. When he was done, I spat at the motherfucker and cursed him for causing your death. And then he laughed. Laughed like a fucking psycho who'd had the longest night of his life, grabbed hold of me by the shoulders, looked me dead in the eyes and said you were very much alive and that he'd told his sister to tell that story if anyone came looking for you in case any of us showed up there."

"Fucking Luther," Rogue growled.

"Yeah," I said coldly. "Asshole almost got all of them killed for that lie. He spent the next hour trying to convince me to come home while I ran my mouth at him for being the most worthless father I ever could have asked for. It was all too fucking late for playing happy families, those boys had abandoned you regardless and Luther was the root cause for everything I'd faced in prison. So I declared war on him there and then, told him I was a damned man and I'd be making damned men of him and his boys soon enough too. Luther said I was crazy, drove me to an apartment he had on the east side of town and left me there under the supervision of three of his men. I was a prisoner once again, locked in some random goddamn place I had no intention of staying in. So I needed a plan to get out, and when those assholes brought home a bunch of hookers the following night and started beating the shit out of them like they were nothing, touching them when they told them to stop, begging for someone to save them, I stole a gun off of one of their drunk asses and I didn't miss when I fired a bullet into each of their skulls at close range."

"Jesus," Rogue breathed.

"Mhm," I said, a smile curling my lips at their deaths. "I took their wallets, guns, phones and any other shit they had which could help me survive long enough to kill those motherfucker Harlequins. One of them was carrying the revolver I'd used to shoot at Fox and the others and I felt a sort of attachment to it that made me sure it was going to be the one I ended their lives with."

"Is that the same gun you…"

"Yeah," I growled, moving swiftly on from my little Russian roulette hobby. "Anyway, I dragged the three of them out to Gallows Bridge and strung them up there just to drive my message home then got out of there. I knew I needed to find some place away from the Harlequins where I'd have time to prepare to win a fight against them. I spent a few weeks living on the edge of town, sleeping in a shitty hotel. There was this old guy in the room next door to me who always wanted to talk, he went on and on about all the gossip in Sunset Cove and I lapped up every scrap of it, hoping it would give me some edge on Luther or Fox, anything that could give me a glimpse into their routines. He didn't do that, but he did tell me about Dead Man's Isle, he knew all about the big old hotel which was abandoned out here, said the guy who'd owned it and planned a refurbishment had up and died and the place had been left to rot. It sounded like fate to me. So I took a chance one night, stole a boat and found my way to the isle, broke into this hotel and called myself king of this land just like that."

"How did you form your gang?"

"News of my attack on the Harlequins slipped through town and eventually I had people seeking me out. I used to head back to the mainland for food and I'd go to The Dungeon for a drink sometimes. I had men coming up to me, guys who'd been rejected from the Harlequins or had been pissed off by them in some way. Once I had a few guys around me, it didn't take long for them to start recruiting for me and soon I had my own little crew. I started carving out territory, taking pieces of Sunset Cove from Luther and laughing at every mile I claimed from him. He continued to ignore my efforts for a long time, trying to summon me home, telling his men to keep out of my way and just let me fucking be. More fool him because eventually they had to take notice of the threat I posed and when I headed to town to kill Luther for good one day, a lot of blood was shed between our people. And that was it. The Harlequins were officially against me and I had the war I'd wanted all along. I was a lonely king with one purpose and it didn't matter what it took to get it done."

Rogue cupped my cheek, giving me a woeful look and I growled, despising that. I shoved her off of me, forcing her to roll over and smacking her ass so hard she yelped. "Don't you go pitying me, woman."

I moved onto my knees and squeezed her ass, parting her legs as I moved between them. I freed my cock and squeezed the base of it as it hardened in my grip.

"Wait," she said breathily, propping herself up on her arms and turning her head to look back at me. "We should use protection."

"Hm," I grunted. Call me an asshole, but using a condom with her was about as appealing as wrapping my dick in three inches of cotton wool before ploughing it into her. I'd waited for her pussy for ten years and it had not disappointed. The feel of her hot, wet flesh wrapped around me was better than any ass I'd ever fucked by a mile. I didn't know if that was just because it was a pussy or if it was because it was *her* pussy. But I had the feeling it was the latter.

I couldn't exactly fuck her unprotected forever though.

"Alright, I'll just get you off before I go down to the supply room for some condoms."

"Don't you keep some in here for Mia?" Rogue asked icily and I growled at the mention of her name right now, squeezing a fistful of her ass in anger.

"She deals with that. Now just shut up and come for me like a good girl." I propped her up onto her knees, spreading her cheeks and running my hand between her thighs, feeling the string of her tampon there.

"Hang on, why do I need a condom anyway? You're on the rag."

"Ergh, don't call it that." She twisted around to swat at me, trying to scramble away.

"And are you sure you aren't grossed out by the blood and stuff?"

"I waited forever for your body to be mine, beautiful. A little blood isn't going to keep you away from me. I came home dripping in the blood of six men the other night, I'd pay good money to be covered in yours."

"Rick!" she gasped, trying to smack my hands off of her hips, but I held on tight, leaning down and running my fingers up the centre of her. She shuddered, moaning and pressing her ass back instantly, her protests dying just like that.

"I'm going to lose myself in you all day," I growled into her neck as I teased her clit and she sighed my name. "Again and again until you can't stand. Neither of us are leaving this room until I've had you every way known to man."

"Jesus," she moaned and I dragged out her tampon, tossing it who knew where before I slid my fingers into her tight pussy. I drove them in and out before adding a third and driving them in deep, proving how much I wanted this. She gasped, her hips rocking in time with my hand as I worked her body, giving her my hand in just the way she wanted until she was clamping down tight and coming on my fingers, collapsing down onto the bed.

I flipped her over, squeezing her perfect tits as her thighs fell open either side of me.

"Shouldn't we get a towel or something?" she panted and my eyebrows arched.

"No," I growled impatiently.

"Most guys would probably want a towel down," she pointed out.

"I'm not most guys, beautiful." I hooked her legs over my shoulders as I lined my solid cock up with her throbbing pussy. "And I won't be happy 'til my white sheets are bright red."

"Animal," she gasped as I thrust inside her, tossing the pillows out from beneath her so she was flat on her back.

I pressed my weight down as I gripped the headboard and fucked the life out of her. Her screams filled every corner of my room and I hoped everyone in this hotel could hear exactly how much she enjoyed my company as I claimed her body. She wrapped her thighs around me and I showed her no mercy as I pounded into her perfect pussy, making my head spark with pleasure as her nails sliced into my arms and drew blood.

I shifted us onto the edge of the bed, flipping her up to sit on my lap and gripping her ass as she straddled me. She held onto my shoulders as she rocked her pussy up and down my cock, tipping her head back and moaning loudly as I thrust my hips up to hit some sweet spot inside her that made her cry out even louder.

I worked harder to keep fucking her right in that place, watching as her tits bounced and I leaned down to suck and bite her nipple as she clawed at my back. She started trembling and pressed her forehead to mine, her pussy clamping down on my cock and making me curse as pleasure ricocheted through my shaft. My balls tightened and I shoved her hips down, filling her completely as I came, thrusting in one more forceful time as she took all of my cum and sighed my name in my ear.

I caught her chin, bringing her mouth to mine as her eyes become hooded with sleepiness again and I smirked against her full lips, taking a hungry kiss from them. Her tongue tangled with mine and I held her hard against my chest, her heart pounding furiously in time with my own.

My mind was struggling to catch up to the fact that I really had Rogue Easton right here in my arms. She was everything I'd ever wanted. The *only* thing I'd ever wanted. And nothing and no one was going to ruin this moment.

"What. The. Fuck?!" Mia shrieked and Rogue's head snapped around, breaking our kiss.

"Shit," I growled as I looked over Rogue's shoulder, finding Mia standing there in a tight blue dress with her hands on her hips and her face pinched in absolute rage.

Rogue climbed off of my lap and I threw the sheet over her as I searched for my boxers, but I couldn't spot them anywhere. Mia's eyes fell to my thoroughly spent dick and the period blood coating it which told her exactly where it had just been.

"You fucked her? Like, in the vag fucked her?" she screamed. "You won't fuck me anywhere but my ass, but you'll fuck this ho on her freaking period?!"

"Don't call her that," I snapped.

Where are my fucking boxers?

"Oh my god is that a tampon on my salt rock crystal!?" Mia screamed, pointing to the stupid rock beside the bed and solving the mystery of the missing tampon. It was like starring in an Agatha Christie novel.

I looked around in frustration as Rogue got out of bed, snagging my shirt from the floor and pulling it on with a tight look on her face.

"I'll give you guys some space." She headed to the door, but I caught her arm as panic flared inside me at the thought of her leaving. But then my gaze flicked to Mia and I hated my fucking life, but I had to calm her down. If I sent her away now, she was never going to come back.

"Stay," I commanded Rogue, trying to meet her eye but she wouldn't look at me.

No. Why now? Why couldn't I just get one single day with her without it being ruined?

I released a noise of fury then let her go and took hold of Mia's arm instead, dragging her out of the room, shutting the door behind me and snarling my frustration. Rogue was a flight risk at the best of times but right now she was a Boeing 747 ready for take-off to fucking anywhere. And I couldn't let her get away. *Not again.*

"Put some fucking clothes on!" Mia shrieked at me, yanking her arm out of my grip as we made it out of my suite and I locked the door, turning her back on me.

I stalked down the hall, shoving through the door into a storage closet and grabbing some sweatpants from a pile. I tugged them on, carving my fingers through my hair. I had to keep it together, act like I gave shit about Mia's feelings and somehow smooth this over. She liked bringing other women to bed sometimes, she'd even suggested it with Rogue, so maybe I could swing this some kind of way to make her think this was for her benefit. Fuck if I knew how though.

"She's Fox Harlequin's girl, baby," I said, landing on the first thing I could come up with and she frowned at me.

"And what?" she snapped. "Now you're sharing a pussy with your enemy?"

"No." I stepped toward her as she folded her arms and glared at me. "I made a vow to ruin her for Fox. The girl's obsessed with me. I told Fox I'd fuck her in every way I wanted and destroy her for him, that's all."

"That's it?" She pursed her lips. "Then how come you don't fuck *my* pussy?"

"Because your ass is so fucking perfect and pussy does nothing for me." I moved into her personal space, reaching around to squeeze it and I could see my plan was working as a small smile tried to pull at her lips.

"Better than the rainbow chick's vag?"

"So much better," I lied. Rogue's pussy was the best thing I'd ever felt. End of discussion. But that was not knowledge for Mia's ears. "I'm just breaking Fox's girl's heart, Mia. She's already half way in love with me, a couple more nights in my bed and she'll be so far gone I'll be able to hear her heart crack in two when I dump her cheap ass back outside Fox's door." Those words tasted vile on my tongue, but I needed to keep Mia on side, so I spat them out anyway.

She bit her lip then a giggle escaped her as she pressed a hand to her arm. "You're a bad man."

"The baddest," I agreed with a smirk and she leaned up to rake her tongue up my neck. "Can I help break her?" she whispered excitedly.

"She's not into chicks," I said as her hand slid down my chest towards my cock and I caught it in my grip, bringing it to my mouth and kissing her knuckles to cover for stopping her.

"Boo." She pushed her lips out.

"I'm gonna need a little more time with her, but when I'm done I'll come right back to my favourite girl." I twisted my fingers in her hair and pulled tight enough to make her gasp. "And you're gonna remind me what I've been missing, aren't you?"

"Yes," she said breathily. "I'll suck your cock so good, Rick."

"I'll think about that next time I'm inside the little unicorn," I said darkly, though I absolutely wouldn't do any such fucking thing.

She chuckled wickedly. "Do you have to go back to her just yet?"

I considered palming her off, but I couldn't risk her getting pissy at me again. "No, let the unicorn wait. I wanna eat breakfast with my girl." I slid my arm around her, drawing her down the hall and fighting the urge to look back as my heart yanked me in the opposite direction to the way I was going. But I needed to do some damage control, so I sent one of my men down the hall to guard the room before leading Mia into the stairwell.

I couldn't help but smirk quietly to myself as I walked. Mia had swallowed my lie way too easily and now I even had her cheering me on to fuck Rogue senseless. I was one serious asshole of a guy, and I didn't give a single flying fuck about that.

Rejects Park

ROGUE

CHAPTER NINE

I had the world's angriest fucking shower as I scrubbed the blood and Maverick's fucking cum and every filthy deed we'd gotten up to off of my flesh. But of course when I stepped out of the shower and caught a glimpse of myself in the floor length mirror I found bruises, hickies, teeth marks and plenty of other evidence of what he'd been doing to me still staining my skin.

I huffed irritably, found a tampon and inserted it so angrily that a squeak of pain escaped me. Fucking vagina javelin. Who the fuck invented that shit? Might as well stick a cactus up my cooch and be done with it.

I dried off quickly, dumping the towel on the wet floor like a brat and stomped out into Maverick's bedroom where I stole a pair of bright blue basketball shorts and a red tank top to wear from his drawer. Then I tossed the rest of his shit out on the floor and stuck the empty tampon canister into the box of revolver bullets which he kept in his nightstand.

The gun hadn't reappeared since I'd caught him playing Russian roulette and I was hopeful that meant I'd succeeded in delivering it to the sea. Not that he'd confirm anything about that fun hobby with me when I'd tried to force him to tell me about it. I just had to chalk it up to his damage and wait for him to be ready to share, but even the idea of him risking his life like that left a foul taste in my mouth.

I spied an elastic band and tied my rainbow hair in a knot on the top of my head. When I turned to look at myself in the mirror I was pleased to see I looked like utter shit which was a nice reflection of how I felt.

I was hungry. And mad. And like a tiny bit hormonal thanks to Aunt Flow visiting and me being ditched like a used condom before I'd even managed to come down from my orgasm high.

I started rummaging through drawers and cupboards, but it quickly became painfully clear that there was no food in this place so I strode over to the door and banged my fist against it instead.

"What?" a gruff voice came from whatever watchdog Maverick had chosen to leave guarding me.

"I'm hungry. I want to go look for some food. Let me out," I called back.

"No can do. Boss said you gotta stay in there."

"Oh, so he can fuck me on my period, but he can't provide me with chocolate when his monster cock makes my cramps worse?" I yelled back. I mean, they weren't really any worse but that didn't make me want chocolate any less, so I didn't give a shit.

The watchdog spluttered something unintelligible but didn't open the door. Fine. Fuck him.

I looked around with narrowed eyes, my gaze falling on the balcony door which was cracked open. *Guess I'm taking the back door then.*

I stripped Maverick's somewhat ruined – alright, violently bloodstained - sheets from his bed, accidentally knocking a potted plant flying with my ass as I worked so that the vase smashed and spilled soil all over the floor. *Woops.*

I hip-bumped the balcony door open and looked down at the five floor drop to the pool, spotting a drain pipe off to the right of the balcony below this one.

I quickly tied the sheet to the railing then hopped up and over it, ignoring the swoop in my gut as I began shimmying down to the lower level. Maverick needed a reminder that I wasn't some toy to be kept in a cupboard and played with when he got bored. I was a creature of the sea and I wouldn't be kept locked up in a goldfish tank. Let alone put up with him going for a dip with a dogfish while my back was turned. Or maybe she was more of a shark with a clam for a vagina. Yeah, that sounded about right. Stupid, clammy vag bitch. If he was still with her, he shouldn't have been with me. He could keep his wandering sea cucumber to himself from now on. Gah.

My feet met with the tiles which lined the balcony beneath Maverick's, and I grinned to myself as I spotted a bottle of ketchup which had been left on the little table there. I quickly wrote a message with it across the tiles for the douche of the hour to find when he followed me.

Go back to your clam vag.

Nice. Although as I looked at it, I realised the ketchup was running in the heat of the sun and it was pretty illegible already. *Dammit.* I quickly drew a huge cock with an arrow pointing to it and the word 'you' which was easier to interpret then moved to tackle the drainpipe.

Breaking and entering wasn't my usual bag, but I had mastered the art of escaping a long damn time ago and the drainpipe was a lifelong friend of mine by now. The trick was checking that it was secured to the wall nice and tight - I learned that one the hard way when one I'd been scaling gave way and I fell six foot into a rose bush. I swear I'd still been pulling thorns out of my ass a week later and I wasn't going to make that mistake twice.

So after giving the drain pipe a good shake to check it was bolted down well, I hopped over the railing and quickly shimmied down.

A few of Maverick's little gangbanger boys looked my way as I strode out to the poolside bar and moved around behind it, but I ignored their grumpy asses and just went about my business, letting them decide for themselves whether or not they should be interrupting me.

I ducked behind the sadly unmanned bar - *I guess bartenders don't get many shifts in gang compounds* - then began to rummage. *Jackpot!* There was a fridge behind the bar and I found a box inside with some cheese salad sandwiches in it and the name 'Dave' written in sharpie on the top of it. Who knew gangsters brought packed lunches? But even better than that was the jumbo bar of chocolate sitting in the clear box alongside his sandwiches. *Mine.*

Sorry not sorry, Dave.

I tucked the bar of chocolate into my pocket and my sandwiches into the other one which made Maverick's shorts slide halfway down my ass with the weight of it, then turned to look at my choices of beverage. A bottle of Malibu whispered my name on the breeze and I snatched it, striding back out into the sun again as more gang members looked my way.

"What are you doing out here?" one of them called and I levelled him with a dark look before striding over to stand before him. He was kinda huge, built like a fucking bull and covered in even more tattoos than Maverick. I probably should have been terrified of him and all that, but honestly, I'd been running with dudes like this for so long that I knew the drill. They were just sheep in the flock and the only one I really had to watch out for was the wolf who controlled them. And seeing as Maverick had made the mistake of making it clear he had no plans to kill me, I found myself utterly at ease amongst his band of scary cronies.

"Rick told me to come relax in the pool. He also told me that none of you assholes would bother me and that I should tell him if you did. So, are you bothering me, Rupert?"

"That's not my-"

"I need some sunglasses." I reached up and took his from his face before placing them on mine and flashing him a smile. "Be a lamb and hold that rubber ring in place for me, yeah?" I pointed at the black ring which was floating in the pool beside us and he frowned. "Chop, chop, Rupert, if I have to tell Rick you fucked up my morning he will have your balls for it and we both know that's true."

"My name is Dave," he ground out, dropping to one knee to hold the ring for me while a few of the other gangsters exchanged glances. Ooooh, this dude was gonna hate me so hard when he realised I was not only bullshitting him but that I had stolen his fancy lunchbox. *Sorry Rupert.*

I dropped my ass into the hole in the rubber ring, sucking in a breath at the feeling of the cool water soaking into the ass of my stolen shorts before relaxing back into it and kicking off the edge of the pool.

"Crank up the music, Rupert. I don't wanna be able to hear myself think while I'm relaxing. And make sure you choose some decent songs or I'll be pissed."

Dave scowled at me but moved away to set some songs playing over the speaker system that surrounded the pool. I grinned as Sweet Melody by Little Mix came on and I kicked my feet in the water in some vague semblance of dancing. *Nice choice, Rupert.*

I drifted away from the edge and pulled the sandwiches from my pocket, eating them quickly before the water sogged them up. Then I hooked out my jumbo bar of chocolate and started in on the real feast, alternating between devouring squares of it and sinking mouthfuls of Malibu until I had a nice buzz going and my cramps were easing off. That just left me with the delicious tenderness my body experienced post fucking Maverick which I was equally pleased with and pissed about.

I wondered if he was off fucking *her* now. Was he trying out another pussy now he'd gotten what he wanted by claiming mine? Did I even have any right to be pissed over the idea of that? He wasn't mine. Not anymore. Probably never had been. And he hadn't made me any promises of monogamy. Hell, I didn't even want him to. Did I?

I ignored the sharp tug of jealousy in my gut and the urge to cut a bitch, trying not to picture them together. Okay, so maybe I was full of shit but I was gonna have to own that because my pissed off vibe wasn't dulling.

I used my hand to set the rubber ring spinning in a lazy circle and watched the sky as it turned above me, giving me a view of the hotel half the time then nothing but blue sky and fluffy white clouds the other half. Around and around until the chocolate was all gone and the wrapper was floating away from me, the rum was half gone too and I was somewhat drunkenly singing along to Daisy by Ashnikko which was seriously in line with my current mood. I was in some form of blotting-out-my-problems heaven. Or at least I was until my view suddenly included one seriously pissed off looking gang leader as he glared at me from his position standing at the edge of the pool.

"Get out, Rogue," Maverick growled as I met his gaze through my stolen sunglasses.

"Why don't you get *in*, Rick?" I suggested, kicking some water at him and making his scowl deepen.

"We need to talk."

"Fuck your words. I just wanna lay here in the sun and drink until I drown. Is that so much to ask?" I raised the bottle of Malibu to my lips and smirked at him over it as I took a nice big gulp.

"All of you, fuck off. Now," Maverick barked and I leaned up to get a look as his men all scampered. Rupert tossed me a glare as he hurried away with his empty lunchbox in hand and I snorted a laugh as I kicked some more water at Rick.

"Are you coming in then?" I called provocatively.

"If I have to, you'll regret it."

"Add it to the fucking list," I muttered. "I regret damn near every decision I've ever made, so what's one more?"

The look Maverick gave me promised me death by his hand. Or at least a severe spanking and my heart leapt as my pussy clenched and my brain shouted *abort mission* but was drowned out by the booze induced giggles of my libido. Well damn. I was done for.

I watched as he yanked his shirt off and tossed it aside before diving into the water and disappearing beneath the surface.

Several seconds passed and I couldn't help but hum the Jaws theme tune as I pushed myself up a little to try and spot where he was going to surface. I was shark chow for sure, but the way my heart was racing said I wasn't entirely opposed to being eaten by him.

I screamed as he appeared beneath me, throwing my rubber ring into the air and dunking me in the water. I sank to the bottom like a stone, losing my bottle of Malibu and my new sunglasses with a pang of regret.

I used my arms to keep myself down there, looking around through the cloud of rainbow hair which surrounded me for any sign of his next attack.

A hand suddenly locked around my wrist and I was yanked towards the surface, my head breaching it as I was dragged to the edge of the pool where it was just deep enough for me to touch my toes to the bottom.

Rick shoved me against the tiled wall of the pool and I pushed my hair back out of my face as he caged me in there with water running over his inked up arms and bulging chest muscles. I was going to lick him. Not yet though. But soon.

"Spit it out, Rogue. You never could hold your tongue anyway so just give it to me," he demanded and I raised my chin as I glared at him.

"Why is she still here? I thought you sent her away."

"She came back," he replied unhelpfully.

"So what does that make me? Your bit on the side? The other woman? Something to pass the time while she was gone?"

"If you wanted to be my girlfriend maybe you should have asked," he replied darkly.

"I don't. And you don't want me to be either, do you?" I replied instantly. "It's like you told me and Fox - you just want to fuck me and use me and break me and dump me back at his door. Well, you found me broken to begin with and you did a good job of fucking me, so I guess it's time you dump me back there."

"Fuck, I forgot how infuriating you can be when you lose your shit," Maverick growled. "Do you seriously believe any of the crap pouring out of your mouth or are you just spitting venom at me because of the Mia thing?"

"I don't know what to think. You wouldn't be the first guy to lie their way into my panties."

Maverick surged forward, his chest pressing to mine, his lips against my lips and pure rage resounding off of his body. "Tell me what you feel when I'm here with you like this," he growled. "Tell me how I could lie about that."

My body was trembling, my heart racing and my soul aching and no more words would fall from my mouth. I closed my eyes and breathed him in, licking my lips and accidentally licking his too because of how close he stood.

"It's no lie, beautiful. You run through my blood. There ain't no way to lie about that. I told you to let me own you, to give yourself to me, but that was bullshit. Because I owned you before you said the words, just like you own me. Like you always have. Like you do for the rest of those assholes over in Sunset Cove too. Every fucking one of us knows it."

"They abandoned me," I growled, the pain of that cutting me deep every time I let myself think of it. "They left me on that fucking boat."

"Yeah. They abandoned me too," he agreed. "So let's not stand here and argue about shit that doesn't even fucking matter."

"It matters to me," I protested firmly, finding some ounce of strength as I placed my hands against his chest and pushed him back. He gave me a few inches, but his hands stayed locked against the edge of the pool either side of me. "Tell me why that clam vag was back here."

Maverick pushed his tongue into his cheek, clearly not liking me making demands of him but then he shrugged like he'd decided he didn't even give a shit and gave in. "She's a job. Not that she knows that. But she's Kaiser Rosewood's stepdaughter and my way in to his fucking estate if I play it right. I can't just stroll on over there what with it being on fucking Harlequin turf, but I want what's locked up in his crypt. *Our* crypt. I want to crack it open and take out those secrets and use them to destroy Foxy boy and his little minions as well. And I think you might just want the same thing."

My lips parted at that admission and I wasn't sure if it was the booze or the sun or the look in his gorgeously dark eyes, but I found myself nodding, admitting it, agreeing to something without even saying a word.

"How many of their keys have you got?" he asked, his gaze heating excitedly as he realised I was trying to play this game the exact same way that he had been. That maybe, just maybe, the two of us were up to the very same thing.

"Only yours and mine," I replied. "Hidden in my trailer. Though it might not be mine anymore because my rent is overdue and I can't exactly pay it from here."

"But you've been trying to find theirs too?" he pressed and I nodded again.

"I want revenge, Rick," I breathed. "I know you said it didn't fix everything for you and maybe it won't for me either. But if that secret gets out, they'll have no choice but to run from this town which they valued so much more than me. Than *us*. I can take something from them which will come as close to equalling what they took from me then maybe I'll be able to find some fucking peace afterwards."

"You really think you can get their keys?" he asked curiously and I chewed on my bottom lip as I considered it.

"Maybe. It was clear enough that Fox wanted me back even if it was only to fuck me. And JJ..." I trailed off because it just hurt so fucking much. I still couldn't really understand it. I'd felt like I was making real progress with them, all of them. Sure, we hadn't been anywhere close to returning to the way we'd once been, but I still couldn't believe they'd cut me loose so easily. What the fuck was that about? The things JJ had said to me before it all happened just didn't tally up to his actions, but I'd lived through their betrayal so maybe I was just a fool to think I was missing something.

"Of course Fox wants to fuck you, beautiful. They all do. You were the ultimate fantasy for all four of us for a long fucking time and that shit doesn't just disappear."

"What am I supposed to do with that? Even if it was true-"

"Don't bullshit yourself, baby girl, you know it's true. And I'm willing to bet you thought about fucking all of them more times than you can count too. It was there for all of us. We were just too young and fucking dumb to figure out what to do about it without destroying ourselves. The question is, do you still fantasise about that, or can you keep a clear head and go get those keys for us?"

"You want me to go back to them?" I asked in surprise.

"Want isn't the word I'd use," he replied. "But it seems to me that if the two of us work at this problem we have to come out on top in the end."

"Meaning you'll keep playing the Mia angle while I go and try to get their keys?" I asked, scowling at the idea of him still stringing her along, playing her, kissing her, fucking her.

"Well I'm hardly going to let all of my hard work with her go to waste on the off chance that you can pull this off," he replied scathingly. "But if you can pull your end off quickly then I won't have to keep her dangling for long. So what do you say? Do you wanna team up with me against the Harlequins, beautiful? Do you wanna help me make them pay?"

There was a little voice in the back of my head which was shouting out for my attention, trying to make me think of the reasons why I should have been saying no. Begging me to think this through. To see this deal with the Devil for what it was and turn it down. But another, hurting, more vengeful part of me was shouting even louder for me to bite his fucking arm off.

The Harlequin boys didn't deserve any better than this from me. They didn't deserve any loyalty or pity or anything from me at all aside from this. If we cracked open that crypt I would have more than enough money to set myself up somewhere far away from here with a new name and a new life. And they would be forced to face the same reality that they'd presented me with ten years ago when I'd been cast adrift and forced to run from every single thing I'd ever known and loved.

"I'm in," I growled, the Malibu helping deaden the sounds of the sad little girl crying for the boys she'd once loved with all of her heart. "But that means you'll have to let me go, Rick."

Maverick regarded me with an intent look and moved his hands from the edge of the pool to hold my face between them. "I'll never let you go again, beautiful," he growled. "But that doesn't mean I have to keep you in a cage."

I swallowed thickly, liking the sound of that a little too much and when he leaned in to kiss me, I was helpless to resist him. He guided my mouth up to meet his and I fell into that kiss, drowning against him and swallowing him whole.

I wasn't sure if I was doing the right thing or if it would just turn into another regret for me to ache over, but I did know that being here in his arms felt right. And as our kiss deepened, I let myself forget about everything that existed outside of it, because while I was locked in it, nothing else mattered anyway.

CHAPTER TEN

I was in trouble in all senses of the word. My heart was in danger of combusting over losing Rogue and my head was a helicopter in a tailspin, tumbling towards sharp rocks. Not only did I have to work to keep Fox from taking a boat in the night and sailing over to Dead Man's Isle on a suicide mission, I now had Luther on my ass looking for the cash I owed him for this month's work. And as I hadn't been taking any escort jobs since I'd fucked Rogue, my pockets were terrifyingly dry and I was down to my final twenty four hours to come up with the extra few grand I needed to make up my cut. I knew Fox would have leant me the cash, but that would lead to questions. And if he started digging too deep into my current predicament, I was gonna have to start lying to him and I couldn't bear to do that to my brother. I knew it was stupid. I'd already fucked the girl he'd claimed as his own. But it was Rogue. She wasn't just any girl. How was I supposed to keep my hands off of her after I found out that she wanted me? My dick may have had superpowers, but it wasn't capable of being *that* much of a hero.

The thing about me was, I'd always been a sap for Rogue. And I guess that was why a chunk of the money I could have given to Luther was currently tucked in my pocket about to pay her rent on the little trailer she had down at

Rejects Park. Di and Lyla had mentioned it was due and I couldn't make ends meet either way, so why not spend a little of my weekly earnings on keeping the place she'd wanted for herself?

Oh man, I'm fucked, I'm so fucked.

The worst thing about Rogue being out on that island stuck with that asshole, was not knowing what was happening to her. And the fact that she probably despised me again which was a hard, jagged pill to swallow. Like one of those round, uncoated pain killer tablets that always got stuck in your throat – who made that shit anyway? Satan?

I pulled up in the parking lot outside the trailer park and walked in, heading along the winding track to her little blue trailer and opening it with the spare key Fox had acquired. I stepped inside and was immediately hit by her coconut scent and the absolute sweetness of her.

I pulled the door shut behind me, moving through the small space she called home and stepping into her bedroom. The bed was unmade and there was a little yellow dream catcher hanging above the bed. I wondered if I'd ever featured in her dreams over the years, or if she'd worked to forget me as quickly as possible the moment she thought I wasn't coming for her. How was she sleeping now? Alone? In some cold, dark place?

My hands balled and violence rippled under my skin. I held onto one small comfort, that I truly didn't believe Maverick would hurt her. As much as Fox and Chase feared it, I was quietly assured that he wouldn't. She'd already been to his island and returned unscathed. And if that wasn't proof enough then all I had to do was remember the way he'd looked at her as a kid and the answer was there. But she *had* fucked him over, and surely he wasn't going to let that lie?

Maybe I was just a fool who saw the good in people too easily, especially after all Maverick had done. But some part of me felt sure he still had a heart, and maybe a few pieces of it still resembled the one that had belonged to the brother of my past.

I didn't wanna go all Fox on this place and rifle through her drawers, but I felt like I wanted to do something for when she came home. So I moved forward and made the bed, running my hands over the sheets to smooth them out. It was stupid and small, but it felt like getting it ready for her return.

Because she would return. She had to.

I sighed, heading into the bathroom and taking a piss while I mulled over how I was going to come up with the money for Luther and when exactly life was ever going to stop being so complicated. The room was so small that I practically filled every inch of it and as I washed my hands and swung around, my hip hit the door and sent it flying into the wall beside the shower. A vent above it popped open and something bronze caught my eye.

"What the..."

I frowned, reaching up into it and taking out two familiar keys. My eyebrows arched as I twisted them between my fingers. These were Rogue and Maverick's keys to the Rosewood crypt. They matched the other three in every way, but each of them had a tiny animal engraved at the base of the stem which differentiated them. Maverick's had a shark and Rogue's had a turtle.

I examined them for a moment then put them in my pocket, my heart pounding a little faster. Was Rogue really planning to get into the crypt? The thought unsettled me. It wasn't like she'd ever manage to get hold of the rest of our keys anyway, but still... did she hate us that much that she wanted to unleash the secrets waiting in there? Surely not. There were valuables in there too, some jewellery, anything we'd robbed over the years which had been too hot to sell on at the time. Maybe she was after that. I hoped so, because I didn't like the idea that she hated us so much that she'd be willing to set us all aflame and burn right along with us for the sake of her revenge.

I headed out of the trailer, locking up and walking back to my orange Mustang GT. Then I drove to Afterlife and pulled up in the parking lot ready for rehearsals. But time was ticking on my deadline for Luther and I really wasn't sure how the fuck I was going to come up with the money by tomorrow. I could pull a job, steal a car and try to sell it quick, but Chase was the best at boosting vehicles and I didn't wanna get him involved. Especially as he was often so drunk lately that I didn't trust him to keep a secret when he could barely even walk in a straight line half the time. He spent most of his days down at Raiders Gym, then stumbled home at random hours of the night. I barely saw him, and I was seriously worried about him. I just had my own problems to deal with right now.

I headed into the club and found my dancers waiting on stage. Texas was shirtless, trying to teach Adam how to pop his pecs, Olly was in a raging argument with Bella at the side of the stage and Jessie was twirling a strawberry condom around her finger as she batted her lashes at Ruben while Estelle plaited Jessie's long dark hair.

I clapped my hands. "Alright, boys only. Estelle, can you put Old Town Road by Lil Nas X and Billy Ray Cyrus on?" I called and Estelle nodded, hurrying off stage to start up the music.

Di and Lyla appeared from the direction she went in, wearing crop tops and low riding sweatpants, smiling at me tightly before moving into one of the booths beside the stage. They texted me every day asking for information on Rogue, but I never had any to give them. I could only tell them we didn't have her back yet, which was true, but I wasn't going to be telling anyone about her being on Dead Man's Isle. That was a problem for me, Fox and Chase alone. There were already too many questions about the girl we were hunting for flying around and we couldn't risk Luther taking more of an interest in the situation and figuring out that Rogue had returned to the Cove.

"Olly," I barked as he continued to lay into Bella about some shit. "If you don't shut your mouth and get in position, you can skip the next show."

Olly sighed, clawing a hand through his long black hair then walking over to join Ruben and Texas on stage.

"Nice to see you here for rehearsals for once, Bella," I said and she smiled, looking a little red-eyed but definitely sober for once. She moved to join Di and Lyla with Jessie bounding after her, looking disappointedly at the condom in her hand. I wasn't sure why she had to unwrap the things before she'd secured herself a cock to suck, but I guessed she was just that self-assured she'd find one if she put her mind to it. To be fair to her, I'd never seen her fail to find a cock yet.

Old Town Road started up and the boys fell into the new routine I'd taught them last week as I watched and barked out corrections.

"Roll your hips, Adam," I ordered and he tried the move again but failed.

I sighed, jumping up on stage and moving behind him, dragging his ass against my crotch and forcing his hips to roll in time with mine. "Like that, you got it?"

"Yes, boss," he said, trying it again and his abs flexed perfectly too as he tried it.

"Better." I clapped him on the shoulder. "Okay, from the top." I moved to the front of the troupe as Estelle started up the song again.

I fell into the rhythm of the music, glancing at the others as they hit every beat and satisfaction ran through me. We'd pair this number with cowboy outfits and finish it with pulling girls from the audience and making sure they fulfilled their dreams of riding a cowboy.

When the song came to an end, I beckoned Lyla onto the stage. "Adam, show me what you've got."

He nodded, his cheeks touching with a little colour as he grabbed Lyla's hips and threw her onto the floor, dropping down to grind over her and she arched her back into the movement with a laugh. He rolled her over once more so she was on top of him and he rode her over his cock, bouncing his hips as she swung an imaginary lasso.

Di and the other girls started cheering and laughing and a smirk pulled at my lips. Kid was getting good. And he was a decent listener too. He absorbed every tip I gave him without question.

We finished up rehearsals and I headed backstage for a shower, feeling better for the workout even though my head was still fucked and the knot of anxiety in my chest was still firmly intact.

"Hey boss, can I have a word?" Ruben poked his head in the bathroom as I wrapped a towel around my waist. His hair was coppery brown and his eyes were golden, his money maker face deeply bronzed and coated in a neat beard.

"What's up, man?" I asked and he slipped into the room, pushing the door shut behind him. He'd changed into a black tank top and white sweatpants, his skin gleaming from his favourite moisturiser which he'd applied all over.

"I got a job offer I wanna discuss with you. I don't wanna take it if it's gonna be a conflict of interest, but it won't affect my hours here, I swear," he said.

"Oh yeah? Why would it be a conflict of interest?" I frowned.

"It's at the Dollhouse," he said a little guiltily. "I'm not dancing," he said quickly. "You know I wouldn't do that, but they've got this new…fetish room."

"Keep talking," I urged.

"The clients want all kind of weird shit, feet tickling, being whipped with sticks, there's even a guy who wants to be treated like a baby, diaper changes and all."

I wrinkled my nose. I wasn't a prude, but that baby shit was messed up.

"Thing is, it's a strictly no sexual contact job and you know I don't like the escorting…but my mom's sick and I need the extra cash to pay her hospital bills. The clients offer up to three hundred a job, but apparently they tip like crazy too." His brows pulled together. "So, would it be okay if I took it? They said I can start tonight."

"Three hundred?" I breathed. "How many jobs can you do in a night?" I demanded, my heart beating harder with hope.

"As many as you want, I guess," he said with a shrug.

"Holy shit." I strode forward, grabbing his face between my hands. "Are they still hiring, Ruben?" I asked in desperation.

"Er, I think so?" he said, his lips squished together by my grip on his cheeks.

"Then you can have the job, dude, but only if you get me one too and keep it a damn secret," I whispered, my eyes whipping to the door and back.

"You wanna…work there, boss?" He frowned, his lips still puckered out like a fish.

"Yeah, but no one can know. Like you said, conflict of interest. Not for you 'cause I don't give a shit, but it would look bad on my business if I was seen working for the competition. I could wear a mask or something, right? I'll be like Zorro, only instead of a sword, I'll have a branch to whip people's asses with. You won't sell me out, will you Ruben?"

He shook his head. "No, boss. I'd be living on the streets if it wasn't for you."

I released his face, but clapped his cheek a few times. "Good boy. What time are you going up there?"

"Eight," he said.

"Pick me up from the parking lot on the way."

"Don't you need to like…have an interview?" he asked.

"No, the Granvilles have been dying to get a piece of me for years. They'll love having this over me." I grimaced, but it was what it was. I needed the cash and I needed it without selling my cock. Johnny D was suspiciously quiet on the matter, in a fucking mood. He'd had to form a reluctant relationship with my right hand since Rogue, and he wasn't best pleased with that considering he'd now had a taste of the Holy Grail of pussies. He only agreed to it at all so long as I was thinking about her - which I was constantly so at least that worked out.

But despite the shit storm that was my life right now and my dick being pissed off with me, things were looking up. Because I'd just secured myself a job tickling feet and fulfilling all kinds of creepy fantasies. *Hashtag winning.*

"You want a job?" Jolene asked with a smug smile on her full red lips as she sat across her desk from me in her powder pink office. Her long blonde hair had been straightened ruthlessly and her dress was a shocking neon yellow colour that offended my eyes.

"Yeah," I said, folding my arms. "But I'm not taking a contract. I'll give you your cut, show up under a fake name and wear a mask. It'll be part of my act here."

Jolene chuckled, inspecting her long, tiger print nails. "What kind of mask?"

"I dunno, what mask do you want me to wear?" I demanded, but immediately regretted it as her smile widened.

"Hmm, I'm sure I can find something suitable."

"I need to start tonight though," I said, shifting in my seat.

"Are you in some kind of financial trouble, Johnny James?" she asked in a mocking purr. She was loving this. Me coming to her for charity.

"That's none of your business," I said simply, my jaw tightening.

"Surely my nephew can help you out if you're in trouble?" She pushed, arching a perfectly manicured brow.

"He can't know about this," I said seriously. "None of the Harlequins can. It's between you and me, alright? Or there's no deal."

155

She considered that for a moment then nodded. "Alright, you can start now. I'll need your shift schedule from Afterlife so I can work in hours for you later. How many do you want?"

"As many as you have going spare," I said, raising my chin.

"Okay, sugar." She smiled brightly. "Come with me." She got to her feet, moving to the back wall behind her desk and pressing her hand to it.

A secret door swung inward and I followed her through it in surprise, heading along a dark corridor. She pushed through another door where a stone stairway led us down under the massive house and we soon stepped out into a large storage room full of costumes, makeup and decorations for various themed parties.

Jolene took a black crow mask from a box and held it out to me. "Is this to your tastes, Johnny James?" she asked and I shrugged, putting it on and eyeing myself in a broken mirror on the wall. It had a large shiny black beak and feathers that tickled my neck. It covered my whole face, so it was good enough. "We'll call you Crow while you're here then," she decided then her gaze slid down my body. "We have a client coming in in twenty minutes who has a fondness for alien tentacles."

Oh goody.

She moved to a rack of costumes and plucked out a gimp suit with bright green tentacles stitched onto it and I sighed internally. *Fuck my life.*

"Nothing sexual," I reiterated and she laughed.

"This is sexual to them, but you won't have to touch them with anything other than the tentacles, okay?"

"Okay," I gritted out.

"You'd better get changed then." She tossed the gimp suit at me, chuckling to herself as she walked to the door. "Oh and you can use the back entrance when you arrive for your shifts if you like? The fire exit lets you in here and I'll leave out the costumes you'll need for each client." She paused, waiting for something and I stared blankly back at her.

"What?" I grunted.

"A thank you would be nice."

I sighed. I guessed she was doing me a solid. "Thank you, Jolene."

"You're welcome." She smirked and slipped out the door as I gazed at the black gimp suit in my hand, thinking of Rogue. If this was what it took to make money and keep my dick clean, then so be it.

I stripped out of my clothes and pulled on the tight leather suit which clung to every inch of my skin. The tentacles dangled around me and the addition of the crow mask made me look fucking psychotic. I went to that detached place inside me, checking out mentally so I could pull this off without a hitch. Then I headed out the door and found Jolene waiting for me, biting her lip on a grin as she took in the outfit.

"Perfect," she announced with a light laugh. "Come on then, he's arrived early."

"Lucky me," I muttered as I followed her along a stone corridor and through a door into a glitzy stairway lit with pink lighting. We headed into a corridor full of doors and she guided me along it, my gazing hooking on Ruben at the far end of it waiting outside a room. He wore a furry wolf suit with a transparent window over his crotch that revealed his bare cock. *Nice.*

He gave me a smile and a nod that was more fitting for soldiers going into war and I might have found it kinda funny if this wasn't my actual life.

Jolene rapped her knuckles on a door to my right and a male voice answered. "Come in, my alien pudding."

"Showtime." Jolene winked at me. "You keep thirty percent of the client's pay and all of your tips, Crow. I hope you find what you want in there." She wiggled her eyebrows teasingly then I pressed my shoulders back and entered the room.

A shirtless man with a large gut and hairy chest waited inside, laid out on a white table under the deep pink lights.

"Oh my, what a mask," he gasped. "And what big tentacles you have." He grinned widely. "What's your name?"

"Crow," I answered in a low voice.

"Well don't just stand there, Crow, tickle me silly," he urged, wetting his lips.

I thought of Rogue, filled my head to the brim with her and moved forward to do as the guy asked, using little rods on the tentacles to control them. The man started giggling like a child as I tickled him and I made sure to do a damn good job too. I needed those damn tips.

"What shall I call you, sir?" I asked.

"Just talk in your alien language to me," he panted as he got hard and started touching himself.

"Gleeb glop ga-loopa," I said in what was a perfect freaking alien voice thank you very much.

"Oh my! Tickle my nipples, Crow," he demanded and I did, tickling those jiggly teets good as his hand worked inside his boxers and he had the time of his life.

I whipped my tentacle across his crotch and he extracted his hand with a gasp and a shiver. I wasn't going to let him come too quickly. If there was one thing I knew about earning good tips with clients like this, it was all about prolonging their release.

"Glabba jabba do-wol," I snapped sternly and his throat bobbed excitedly.

"I've been a bad, bad space cadet," he said breathily. "Imprison me on your ship and teach me the manners of your species."

I whipped him across his thighs and he cried out in pleasure.

Well, it looks like I'm officially going to alien spaceman hell. But I'm still as loyal as a dog to Rogue. So it's totally worth it.

CHAPTER ELEVEN

The roar of the speedboat's engine had electricity thrumming through my veins as I stood beside Maverick while we cut across the waves and tore towards Sunset Cove.

"You sure you wanna do it this way, beautiful?" he called to me over the noise while I held my arm out to feel the spray of the water against my skin.

"It's gonna be pretty obvious that you and I aren't enemies if you drop me off safe and sound at their front door, Rick," I replied and he nodded, turning the boat south so that I had to look back over my shoulder to keep my gaze locked on Sinners' Playground.

It was a beautiful day, the sun baking down on me and my skin tingling from the kiss of its rays. I was wearing one of Rick's tanks again and I had to admit that I'd been getting used to the free and breezy fit of his clothes, but my tits could definitely do with a bra day or two before they decided to start making friends with my knees.

We sped down the coast until we weren't too far out from an empty patch of shore a few miles outside of the town and Maverick cut the engine.

He turned to face me, looking down at me from behind his mirrored aviator sunglasses and my heart began to pound as I looked back up at him.

"You got my number memorised, baby girl?" he asked me, his hands finding my hips as he drew me to him and I was filled with this intense sense of foreboding.

I didn't know when I'd see him again after this. I couldn't exactly go for a visit and if he set foot in Harlequin territory then he was as good as dead. But we'd agreed to try and figure out a way once I was able to slip away. Who knew how long that might take though, especially with how possessive Fox could be.

I repeated his number back to him and he nodded, yanking me closer so that he could claim a kiss from my needy lips. It was closing in on sunset already and the plan had been for me to head over here mid morning, but then we'd realised that not seeing each other meant not fucking each other and one thing had led to another...and another, and, well, here we were five hours later.

I drew him close and he groaned as he tugged the hem of my shirt up, pushing his fingers inside the boxers I'd borrowed from him in place of my own underwear. But trailing through Sunset Cove with my cooch uncovered probably wasn't the best idea, so this shirt and boxers combo which could almost pass for a dress was what I'd landed on.

"Rick," I protested as his fingers worked their way between my thighs and he moved his mouth down my jaw.

"Are you going to let them touch you like this too?" he asked me in a rough voice just as he sank two fingers into me and I gasped, gripping his arms in an attempt to push him back, but he gripped my ass in his free hand and held me in place. My period was over so I was tampon free - not that that would have stopped him but it made this easier logistically. And I was all about the logistics. "Are you going to fuck them before you fuck them over?"

"Why are you asking me that?" I demanded as he pumped his fingers again, his thumb finding my clit and pressing down hard.

"Why are you getting even wetter at the thought of it?" he asked right back, his teeth nipping my earlobe and making me hiss.

"I'm not," I protested, trying to push him back again but as his fingers sank in deeper and as his thumb circled my clit like a fucking pro, a moan escaped me too.

"Don't lie to me, beautiful. I've had years to think about this. To wonder what the answer was to the question we all asked ourselves a thousand times - which one of us would you pick?"

"I never wanted to pick," I growled but my pussy clamped his fingers tightly and I was pulling him closer instead of pushing him back now. Damn him.

"I know. That's what I realised. The innocent girl we used to know might never have picked because you loved us all so sweetly. But this version of you, this jaded, damaged, fucking beautiful version knows how to claim all the best things in life. And that got me thinking about you coming all over JJ's cock-"

I tried to say something to that, but he drove his fingers in harder and all that escaped me was a wanton moan as my fingernails bit into his arm and my wet pussy begged for more.

"-and it made me think about you not picking in a whole different way. Because now I'm thinking you might just be a greedy girl. And no, you won't pick one of us. You'll just pick us all."

"Maverick," I panted as his thumb circled harder, his fingers plunged deeper and his teeth sank into my neck hard enough for me to know he'd marked me with them.

"So when you give in to that desire, baby girl, and you let one of them sink their filthy, Harlequin cock into this greedy, greedy cunt of yours. I want you to remember who owns it. I want you to remember that it's mine and when you're coming for them, you're still coming for me. And I'll be back to claim what I own in blood one day very soon."

Maverick turned his head and kissed me hard, his hand moving faster as he drove his fingers inside me and punished my clit for this imagined betrayal and the moment I was coming and moaning for him, he bit down on my lip hard enough to draw blood.

I jerked my head back, cursing at him as my pussy squeezed hard around his fingers and trapped them deep inside me while it took and fucking took from him. He moved his free hand from my ass and snatched a fistful of my hair, yanking it back so that I was looking up at my own reflection in his mirrored glasses. My lips were parted and bloody, my pupils wide and my chest heaving. I was destroyed for him, ruined, owned and he fucking knew it.

"Say it, beautiful," he growled, anger lacing his tone like he had already decided the truth of what would happen next.

"You own it," I panted, knowing that was what he wanted to hear and feeling the truth of it while his fingers remained so deep inside me.

He smirked at me, clearly satisfied by that as he let me go and drew his fingers back out of me, sucking my taste from them and watching me from behind those fucking glasses.

"If you're so sure I'll be fucking the rest of the boys, does that mean you'll be fucking Mia again the moment I'm gone?" I demanded, straightening out my borrowed clothes and trying to regain some control of this goddamn situation.

"No," he replied simply and I was surprised by how relieved I felt at that. "I have to get back to Dead Man's Isle first, don't I, baby girl?"

I took a swing at him and he barked a humourless laugh as he dodged it before grabbing me and whirling me around to look at the sandy beach which I was going to have to swim to. It wasn't that far and the tide was low which meant I would probably be able to wade back for more than half of it.

"None of that shit matters, beautiful," Maverick said in rough voice as he held me against his chest and lowered his mouth to my ear. His stubble grazed my skin as he spoke and my heart raced for him even though I still wanted to dick kick him. "Eyes on the prize. This right here is no man's land we're entering. Both of us will do whatever we have to to come out the other side of it victorious. You do what you have to do to tear them apart from the inside out and find those fucking keys. And if for any reason you can't manage that then I'll do whatever I have to to get into that crypt using Mia. That's the focus here, right?"

I looked at the Ferris wheel in the distance and my heart twisted with pain as I thought about them abandoning me on that fucking ferry. A part of me felt all kinds of shitty about what I was planning, but all I had to do was focus on what they'd done to me and I was certain I could follow through with it. So that meant Rick was right, didn't it? Getting into the crypt was all that mattered. And I had to concentrate on that.

"We could just run away," I breathed, wondering why I was even saying it out loud because I already knew his answer.

"It's too late for that, beautiful," Rick growled but there was a strange amount of sadness to his tone which told me he almost wished he could say yes to me instead. "Don't you feel it? The pull of this place calling to you? We were born and bred for Sunset Cove. We'll live and die here one way or another. There is no turning back from this, our paths are all set. So we just have to look this fate in the eye and deal with it. There's no changing our minds now."

I nodded sadly, knowing he was right. I'd been running for ten long years and no matter how much I'd always denied it, a part of me had always known I'd end up back here. This really was our unfinished business and one way or another me and my boys were going to have to deal with it.

I turned and looked up at him, a bitter, angry creature rising between us which neither of us could vanquish. But this was it, I was leaving and with the life he led, I wasn't going to just turn my back and refuse to offer him a goodbye.

I reached out to grip the back of his neck then tiptoed up, taking those fucking sunglasses from his face and tossing them aside so that he was forced to look me in the eye.

"You'd better believe I own your dick if you own my pussy, Maverick Stone," I growled. "And if I have to cut a bitch for getting close to it before I come back to claim it, then I am more than willing to do that. And I might take a fucking ball from you too."

A dark smile tugged at his mouth which didn't offer me any promises and I shoved his chest angrily before pressing a rough and brutal kiss to his lips.

"Take this," he said, reaching into his pocket and pulling out the pink phone Fox had gotten me which I hadn't seen since the night Maverick stole me from the cops. "It's dead but you can charge it once you get back. It's no use to me anyway." I nodded, tucking it into the side of the boxers I was wearing and feeling glad once again that the badger had forked out for the waterproof model.

Before he got the chance to get me any more riled up, I turned my back on him and dove off of the boat.

Salt water enveloped me and I focused on kicking to the surface and starting to swim without letting myself think about the fact that I was heading back into the heart of my enemies and leaving my only ally behind.

I swam and swam and it didn't take long before my toes were brushing the sand and I was wading towards the shore instead of swimming.

When I stepped onto dry sand, I turned to look back, watching as Maverick started the speedboat up, our gazes locking one final time before he whirled it around and sped away across the waves.

My heart pattered to an uncomfortable beat as I watched him go and I licked my salty lips before wringing the worst of the water from my hair and clothes and starting off up the beach.

It was going to be a long walk back to the Cove, but I was willing to bet I could boost a car or hitch a ride along the way at some point.

For now I just started walking down the golden beach with my toes in the water and the sun beating down on me to dry me through.

While I walked I tried to think through my plan. It was all well and good for me to say I was going to return to the Harlequins, but the reality of that meant allowing the men who had betrayed me all over again to take possession of me. And as much as I had faith in my amazing acting skills and outstanding poker face, there was no way I was going to be able to just play nice with them after that shit. Although, as I considered it, I guessed that wouldn't really be a problem. It wasn't like I'd been playing all that nice before they'd dumped me on that ferry so I could probably just present them with my real emotions on what they'd done to me then let the wind blow me where it would from there.

Fox had made it clear he wanted to keep me around so no doubt he would do that regardless of how I felt about it anyway even if it was only in aid of getting his dick into me. Of course, I had the small and no doubt thrilling obstacle of him knowing that I'd fucked Maverick to contend with now too. That was going to be one hell of a reunion. Though as I thought on it, I could admit that I wasn't exactly dreading going to bat with the badger. A small, clearly insane part of me actually kinda loved our back and forth arguing bullshit.

"Can I help you?" a girl's voice drew my attention and I looked up from my feet where I'd been watching the waves rush over them while I walked and spotted her laying on a sun lounger further up the beach. She was wearing a white bikini and had long, blonde, perfectly perfect hair that hung around a stupidly pretty face.

"Help me what?" I asked in confusion, glancing around to see if there was someone else here who she might have been talking to. But no, it was just little old me out here alone with her, but as my gaze moved beyond her to take in the mega mansion behind her I realised what the issue was. I'd just wandered into this Barbie Doll's Dream House and my poor ass feet shouldn't be walking on her private beach.

The girl pushed herself to sit upright, taking off a pair of big, black sunglasses and glancing back over her shoulder towards the megalodon of a house which actually had a spire like a church sitting on top of it. Wow, rich people were insane - had these people seriously designed their home to look like a place of worship like they were gods forced to live down here on earth amongst the masses?

"Come have a margarita with me," she called, surprising me. "If my boyfriend sees you wandering across our beach, he'll lose his shit. But if you're day drinking with me then it's just a friend of mine who's come over for a visit."

I probably should have been telling the posh bitch to keep her fancy drinks for her fancy friends, but this was free booze she was offering, and I was not the kind of girl dumb enough to say no to that.

I started walking up the beach to join her and she grinned at me, flashing a set of perfect teeth as she grabbed the margarita mixer from an ice bucket which was sat beneath her parasol in the shade and quickly poured me a glass to match her own.

I dropped down onto the sun lounger beside hers as I reached her and took in her perfectly put together appearance. Shit, this girl could have been a damn model. She was all long legs and big blue eyes and had something about her that would have been enough to make me go a round for the other team if I didn't love the D so fucking much.

"I'm Tatum," she said, passing me the drink.

"Rogue," I replied, adjusting my borrowed boxer briefs and wincing at the wetness of them.

"Wanna tell me why you're wandering along the beach looking like you're lost?" Tatum asked as she leaned back on her sun lounger and took a sip of her drink.

"I was kidnapped by a guy I used to know and spent the last ten days on his island fortress," I said, pointing out over the water towards Dead Man's Isle across the waves. "But I have some unfinished business back here in town and a nice big dose of revenge to dish out, so I came back."

Tatum laughed, but not like she didn't believe me, more like she could see how much I meant that and was cheering me on.

"I'm guessing the kidnapper thought lending you his clothes was cute instead of just giving you your own then?"

"Mostly I think he liked me being naked, so I guess buying me stuff that actually fit me didn't occur to him," I replied with a shrug and she smirked at me.

"So are you planning on walking all the way back to town? Because that's a long ass walk in this heat."

I shrugged. "I figured I'd swim occasionally to cool down, maybe boost a car from some rich asshole who doesn't need it as much as I do."

Tatum laughed again and I found myself liking her as I sank my margarita in one long hit.

"Go long, Tate!" a dude's voice drew my attention half a beat before a frisbee smacked into the sand between our sun loungers. A tall guy with dark hair swept back in that perfect preppy rich boy way jogged down the beach after it, pausing as he spotted me.

He was stupidly attractive, like the kind of guy you saw on swimwear commercials with a surfer in the background but who never actually got wet himself. Hot, but not rough enough around the edges for me.

"I can't play with you right now, golden boy, I'm having drinks with a friend," Tatum explained as he jogged up to us and the dude turned his bright green eyes on me.

"Oh, hey. Sorry, I didn't know there was someone here...how did you sneak through the house without me noticing?"

"I didn't," I replied. "But if I had I would have robbed you blind while I was in there, so it's probably a good thing that I arrived via the beach."

The guy grinned and Tatum laughed loudly.

"Well, I'm gonna go and see if I can convince one of the guys to come play with me then. Unless you girls want in?" He grabbed the frisbee and waggled it temptingly but Tatum shook her head.

"I hardly ever get to hang out with girlfriends. You go play over there so we can talk about boys without you eavesdropping."

The guy grinned and leaned down to press a heated kiss to her lips before jogging away from us and yelling back towards the house in the hopes of tempting someone else out to play with him instead.

"Your boyfriend doesn't seem so scary," I pointed out, wondering why she'd thought he'd flip out if he saw me wandering along his private beach.

"Oh no, that one isn't," she agreed. "I was talking about Saint." She turned to look back towards the house and pointed, making me look around too. There was a guy standing up on the long balcony which ringed the second floor now, a phone pressed to his ear while he looked out over the sea and gave off a seriously pissed off vibe. He was wearing a pair of chinos and a linen shirt which looked freaking tailored, and I swear he was actually oozing money and privilege. He wasn't looking our way but even from looking at his profile, I could tell he was just as attractive as the first dude. His dark skin and chiselled features made him hard to look away from, but there was a coldness to him that made me think he'd kill your grandma with a letter opener if she pissed him off. "But don't mind him. I've been training him up and he can almost hold a full conversation with non-billionaires without his upper lip peeling back these days."

I snorted and took another healthy swig of my drink as I lay back in my lounger. "So how does that multiple boyfriends thing work for you then?" I asked, processing what she'd said. "Do they have a bunch of other girlfriends too, or-"

"No," she replied firmly and I couldn't help but smirk at that possessive bite to her tone.

"Hey, there's no need to get defensive," I said, raising a hand in surrender. "I have way too much dick drama of my own. I'm not scoping out any of your men. On that note though, how many men are we talking here?"

Tatum shrugged, pretending to go all coy on me but then she leaned closer and lowered her voice. "I'm at my limit with them, but any time I get caught up in the idea that it might be insane for me to have so many hot men all to myself, the group sex helps me remember that it's the kind of insane I can handle being. Just about."

"Hmm." I drained the last of my drink as I let that tempting little sausage float about in my brain and I tried to figure out how many cocks would be too many cocks. I started off by counting holes, but then I had to account for hands. And of course, if it came down to turn taking then realistically the sky was the limit. But then when would my poor lady V get a break if she was taking part in a ten cock rotation?

A girl could dream though. And I had to say that the idea of choking on a cock while getting railed by another guy did seem pretty fucking hot to me. Then again, recently it felt like my damn libido was working on overdrive, so maybe my pussy had just gotten sun stroke and was having an episode. Surely it wouldn't remain this fucking thirsty for long. I guessed it was my own fucked up way of self-medicating. I certainly couldn't afford counselling to help get me through the turbulent waters of Sunset Cove, but a prescription of regular dick did help me to forget my problems pretty well.

Tatum's phone pinged beside her and she picked it up, sighing as she read the message. "Saint has some business thing to go deal with," she explained as she quickly tapped out a reply. I caught sight of the squid emoji she sent him before she locked the screen and dropped the phone down beside her again. Girl after my own heart. Everyone loved the squid emoji. I was pretty certain it was the best emoji there was.

"How about I make you a deal?" Tatum offered. "You hang out here and get day drunk with me this afternoon and I'll get one of the guys to give you a ride into town in a couple hours to wherever you need to go. We've only been living here for around six months and I haven't made many girlfriends out here yet, so you'd be doing me a favour. I can even lend you a bikini if you wanna get out of those boxers?"

"Well, I was enjoying the way the wet, sandy material was chafing my ass crack, but now that you mention it, a bikini does sound good."

"Perfect." Tatum reached out to refill my drink before clinking her glass against mine and I couldn't help but grin at her.

I might have had a bunch of gangster assholes to get back to, but a few drinks on a private beach with a new friend couldn't hurt. Besides, I deserved some down time. Because once I was back in the hands of the Harlequins, I knew the shit was really going to hit the fan.

Four margaritas later, a lot of laughter, a brand spanking new designer bikini which apparently I was welcome to keep because Tatum claimed it suited me better than her anyway, and way more detailed discussions than I'd ever thought I'd have about the joys of double penetration and I found myself sat in the back of a fancy ass Audi something while yet another one of this girl's boyfriends gave me a ride back to Sunset Cove.

I relaxed back into the new leather smell of the seats and watched the town I knew so well pass me by from the comfort of the A/C while we listened to Joke's On You by Charlotte Lawrence on the radio and Tatum and her man practically bounced in their seats over their destination tonight. The two of them were heading into the lower quarter, much to my surprise but it hadn't taken me long to figure out that this girl wasn't your regular boring rich bitch anyway. They were going to an underground cage fight and though I had been sorely tempted to join them, I had revenge to get on with.

I had to direct them down the graffiti covered streets towards Rejects Park and when we finally pulled up outside it, I could tell they were more than a little out of their usual comfort zones, but neither of them commented on the state of the place. And to be fair to them, there were already working girls cat calling the car as well as a dude in a hoody who had perked up way too much at the sight of them and I would bet my left butt cheek he was selling some less than legal substances tonight. But it was still home to me, so I grinned as I made a move to jump out of the car, thanking them for the ride.

"Give me your hand," Tatum demanded as she held a pen ready and leaned back through the seats. I obliged her and she quickly scrawled her phone number onto my flesh. "Call me and we can set up that night out."

"Okay. But you're going to have to party like a sinner if you wanna come out dancing around here, rich girl, or everyone will see what you are from a mile off," I teased.

"I think I can handle that," she promised with a grin and I flashed her a smile before hopping out into the balmy air.

It was dusk already, the sun slowly stripping from the sky and leaving trails of dusky pink across the horizon.

I glanced about, making sure I couldn't spot any lurking Harlequins before I headed into the trailer park and set a beeline for my little blue trailer. I just hoped that Joe McCreepy hadn't turfed me out the second my rent went a day overdue. On that note, I needed to sort out paying for the weeks I'd missed and maybe one or two in advance before I headed back to Harlequin House, because knowing Badger the way I did, he was bound to lock me up in his stupid house again the moment I arrived.

There were a few people out smoking on the little decks which fronted their trailers, but the park was pretty quiet for the most part and I smiled to myself at the sense of homecoming I got as I closed in on my place.

I broke into a jog as I got close, rounding the side of my trailer and dropping down to retrieve my key from where I'd stashed it beneath a rock there.

I hurried back around to let myself in and sighed as I closed the door behind me. The place was quiet, empty and a pang in my chest made me miss my little dog. I'd asked Lyla to keep an eye on him for me if I didn't come back from my job with Chase the day the Harlequin boys had fucked me over on that ferry so I'd known he would be okay, but I still wanted him here.

I flicked the lights on, a prickle running down my spine as I looked around at the familiar space. I couldn't place my finger on it, but something made me feel like the trailer wasn't exactly the way I'd left it. Like someone had been here while I was gone. But as I looked around at the space, I couldn't figure out what that might be.

I moved through the small kitchen area and into my bedroom, stopping abruptly and gasping at the sight of the perfectly made-up bed I found there. Bed making was for heathens with nothing better to do with their lives than straighten out blankets! Someone had been in my fucking home.

My heart began to pound as the reality of who that must have been settled over me. There were only a few douchebags who kept forcing their goddamn noses into my business after all, so it wasn't hard to figure out that it must have been one of them.

My mind shot to the keys I'd left hidden inside the vent in my little bathroom and I broke into a run, throwing the door open to the shower room and letting it bang against the wall as I flicked the light on.

My heart plummeted right down into my ass and beyond as I stared up at the vent above the shower. It had been left open, the grate pushed aside and even before I shoved my hand in there and felt all around inside, I knew what I was going to find. Nothing. Not a fucking thing. My key and Maverick's were gone. And one of the assholes I needed to use them against had taken them.

My mind whirled with that and I chewed on my bottom lip, trying to figure out what the fuck I was going to do now. This changed everything. They might have guessed I was after their keys before, but finding Maverick's alongside mine would have banished any doubts they may have had about how serious I was about claiming them. They knew I was after the contents of that crypt. Which meant they knew I was out to get them. Could I really risk heading back into the lion's den with them knowing that?

I needed to think. And I probably needed to talk to Maverick, though using my cell phone to call him was beyond risky. I already knew that Fox had put a tracker on the damn thing and for all I could tell he would be able to trace my calls and shit too. Was that likely? Who fucking knew. But I was starting to think I might have to risk it.

I took the sparkly, pink mermaid phone out of the side of my bikini strap where I'd wedged it and headed back into the living area of my trailer before plugging it in to charge.

I didn't know what the hell to do now. Was it too much of a risk heading back to the Harlequins now? But what was I really risking anyway? I was pretty certain by this point that they had no intention of killing me which meant I was only really risking them being mad. And did I give a shit about that? Not one. Because I was pretty fucking mad at them myself.

A loud knock came at the door and I froze. *Shit*. I wasn't ready to face them yet. How the hell had they figured out I was back so quickly?

"Rogue?" Di yelled. "I know it's you. No one else has crazy hair like you do, bitch!"

A breath of laughter escaped me and I moved to open the door for my friend, my smile widening as I found Lyla and Bella right behind her.

"You're lucky," Di announced, shouldering her way in before I even got the chance to shift my ass aside for her. "We were just arriving back with our pizza when we spotted your unicorn hair heading this way. I figured if we feed you, you'd give us all the info on the drama you're in with the Harlequin Crew."

I inhaled deeply as she carried the pizza boxes over my threshold and moved aside for the other girls. "You would be correct in that assumption." I caught Lyla's arm before I closed the door and she turned to look at me, her honey blonde hair falling down her back at the movement. "Can we go grab Mutt quickly before we eat?"

Lyla winced and my heart sank, knowing what she was about to say before it even passed her lips. "I'm so sorry, Rogue. But Fox Harlequin damn near busted my door down and he was yelling threats at me, demanding to know if I'd seen you. I tried telling him that you'd asked me to look after Mutt if you didn't make it back that night but he-"

"It's fine," I cut her off, sighing as I swung the door closed. "He'll be looking after him. He's just using him as bait to make me come back to him."

"Details," Di demanded, moving to take a seat on the little table to the right of my living space. Bella squeezed in beside her and flipped the lid of the pizza box open and I followed Lyla as we took the seats opposite them.

"Well, I don't really know where to start," I admitted. "Why don't you tell me what's been going on here and I'll fill in whatever blanks I can." I grabbed a slice of pizza and sighed contentedly as I took a big bite.

"JJ has every sex worker in the town looking for you. Any whispers of a girl with rainbow hair have to be reported to him immediately," Bella said before dropping her voice conspiratorially. "He said he doesn't care if there is a dick buried in us at the time - we have to pick up the fucking phone and dial."

"Yeah, and Fox has every member of his gang hunting the streets. Honestly dude, I wouldn't be surprised if someone hasn't already ratted you out to them. He's offering ten grand for information that helps him get you back. We've all been freaking out over what the hell must have happened to you," Di added, her eyes filled with concern and my heart swelled a little as I realised that the three of them had chosen to come and talk to me rather than rat me out for that pay day. Loyalty really did matter to these girls and I was damn pleased that they'd decided to count me in on their ride or die mentality.

"I don't get it," I admitted, chewing that information over more thoroughly than I was chewing my food. "They took me out on a job and let me be the fall guy. They knew I was arrested, so why the big freak out over where I was? They clearly didn't give a shit about letting the cops catch me so why make such a big deal over finding me after I got out of the holding cell?"

The girls exchanged a look and Lyla started shaking her head. "That doesn't sound right to me, babe. Fox Harlequin was legit losing his shit over trying to find you. If I didn't know that man has a heart carved from ice, I'd have said he was head over heels in love with you. No fucking way do I believe he sold you down the river. If you ask me, he'd have killed a cop rather than let them take you."

I scrunched my nose up at that assessment, but the others were nodding along.

"JJ too," Bella said. "I've seen him on the war path more than once. He looks after his working girls and if any of us get hurt on the job he goes full fucking psycho. But the way he's been over finding you is next level. I'm telling you, if he could rip the sky apart to find you, he'd have done it. Damn the consequences. As far as I see it, he'd have rather died than let those cops take you. No way did they let you take the fall intentionally."

"But they did," I said firmly. "The four of us were pulling a job on the ferry to Belina Island. We got separated and..." I trailed off as I thought it through. Chase had been with me while we led the guards away from the others. He'd been using his phone to stay in contact with Fox, but I hadn't actually seen what he'd been saying to him.

"What about Chase?" I asked slowly, piecing together a puzzle which was beginning to fit into place all too fucking easily. "What's he been doing?"

"Shit dude, there was such a scandal over him. No one knows for sure what he did, but it seemed like Fox kicked him out of Harlequin House," Di said in a low tone, her eyes darting towards the door like she thought someone might be listening. "And then, he didn't go stay with his girlfriend or with one of the other gang members or anything like that."

"So where did he go?" I asked, sensing how juicy they felt this bit of information was by the way the three of them were all tensing up, looking ready to burst with it.

"He spent three nights sleeping rough under the old pier down on the beach," Lyla said, sounding scandalised.

"He was drunk off his ass the whole time too," Bella added, twirling a lock of red hair around her finger. "I saw him there myself. One of my johns took me down to the beach to fuck me and I looked right at him, laying there beside a bottle of jack and a puddle of vomit."

I pursed my lips as I thought on that. So poor little Chase had been kicked out of the house by the big, bad badger for letting the cops catch little old me. Unless I was being totally conceited about it - but it sure sounded that way. The other two had been hunting for me and he was cast out in the cold. The question was, had he done it on purpose or was it really all just some big fuck up? Had he lost me onboard that boat and not been able to find me before the guards caught up to me? Or had he chosen to leave me there?

"What is it, Rogue?" Di asked, reading the suspicions etched all over my face.

"I'm thinking," I said, devouring another slice of pizza. "And if I'm right then this kind of changes everything."

They all exchanged looks but none of them pushed me to be more specific. They knew I was in deep with the Harlequin Crew and they knew that there was a line drawn in the sand unless they wanted to get in as deep as me too. You didn't ask questions about the Harlequins in Sunset Cove unless you had a death wish. Their business was their own and if I knew something about them, then the chances were that it was best for their sakes if they didn't have any responsibility for that information.

The suspicions building within me kept growing while we ate our pizza and I filled them in on where I'd been. Di whistled long and low when she realised I'd been messing with The Damned Men too and their questions quickly dried up. I didn't blame them. They didn't want to be caught in the crossfire between the two gangs and I was more than happy to protect them from it.

By the time we'd eaten every scrap of food and they'd finished catching me up on the things they'd been up to while I was gone, I had a pretty strong idea about what had really happened on that boat.

The girls called it a night, wishing me luck with the Harlequins tomorrow and just about managing to conceal their concern for me. It was sweet that they were worried about what Fox might do when he found me standing on his doorstep, but I wasn't concerned about that. I was a dead girl walking after all and what didn't kill me again only made me stronger.

When I locked the door behind them, I took my time walking over to the pink cell phone which I'd left charging on the kitchen side before taking it into my grasp and moving into my bedroom.

I changed into a band tee and a pair of shorts to sleep in and slipped beneath the sheets, pulling them up over my head before powering on the phone.

Messages and missed calls started pouring in and my pulse thumped heavily in my chest as I opened up the messages which dated back to the night of the ferry job.

Badger:

Where are you?

Badger:

Are you clear?

JJ:

Where are you, pretty girl?

Badger:

I need to know you're okay, hummingbird.

Badger:

Just let me know you're alright.

JJ:

We're starting to freak out over here...

On and on the messages went, getting more and more irate and my pulse kept pounding a solid tune in my chest as I let my gaze run over them one by one before hitting call on my voicemail next.

"Where the fuck are you?" Fox's freaked out voice came down the speaker. "*Fuck*, I knew this was a bad idea. I need to see you, hummingbird. I need you back here. Call me."

The truth settled over me like the softest caress on my soul and the darkest stab of hurt my heart had ever known. Because message after message poured in from Fox and JJ, most of them from that night, the two of them panicked and fearful, begging me to be okay and to come back to them. But then there were more as the days passed and they failed to find me. JJ's voice cracking as he told me he couldn't survive losing me again.

But the final nail fell in the coffin of my suspicions as I listened to a voicemail from an unknown number and Chase's rough and clearly drunk tone filled my ear.

"Fuck you for ever coming back here," he slurred. "From the moment I laid eyes on your face again after all those years I knew you'd be the death of me. I knew you'd carve my beating heart from my chest and spit on it the same way you did back then. I knew you'd always make the other choice. The choice that fucking ruined me..." The line went quiet and a choked noise escaped him that spoke of his pain and anger and made my own heart crack open like an egg and bleed all that I was onto the ground, impossible to put back where it had begun. When he spoke again, his words were like a dagger directed at my soul. "Fuck you for making me do it. Fuck you for being so fucking hard to hate... just...fuck you, Rogue Easton. Loving you was always going to break me. So I guess I broke you first."

The line went dead and I switched the phone off again, plunging myself into darkness beneath the sheets.

There were tears lining my cheeks but there was a dark truth lining my soul now too. The Harlequin boys hadn't betrayed me. Only one of them had. The one of them who I'd once wanted to rescue more than any other had thrown me to the wolves to save his own skin. Worse than that. He'd done this on purpose. I wasn't just the fall guy. He'd wanted me gone for good.

Well tough luck, Chase Cohen, because I wasn't going anywhere. And tomorrow he was going to find out exactly what payback looked like.

CHAPTER TWELVE

I wasn't sure which was worse. The guilt or the anxiety. I was in turmoil. If I'd thought I knew hell after Rogue had been ripped out of our lives all those years ago, now the world was proving that I hadn't even been close. Knowing she'd been stolen away by Maverick all because of my actions was a special kind of agony that left me in a fucking state.

The rum wasn't even much of a help until it knocked me out. Every waking, conscious moment of my mind was now laced with an acute suffering which made me want to tear the broken pieces of my heart out just so that I didn't have to deal with the way they throbbed and burned anymore. I'd cast them into the sea and pray this pain went with them. Unfortunately, the organ had other uses, like keeping blood moving around my body, and though I wasn't afraid of choking on my own vomit in my sleep, or falling off my motorbike and hitting the sidewalk, or a shark dragging me underwater in the sea while I was surfing, I wasn't the type to just up and end my life. I'd dealt with pain my whole existence, and there really wasn't a flavour of it I couldn't bear the brunt of. I would have welcomed a gunshot wound over heartache though.

Mostly, I tried to avoid Fox and JJ, fearing my truth would be written into my face, but if I was being totally honest, it was because I knew I'd let them down. I'd fucked everything up and I'd put Rogue's life in danger in the process. I'd never wanted that. This wasn't how it was supposed to go. But maybe I really was just as useless as my father had always believed.

"You piece of shit," Dad spat at me. Drunk again, the scent of PBR on his breath, his teeth yellow and bared at me while his hand locked around my throat. "What do I go working all those hours out fishing for, huh? For my little rat of a son to rob me blind?"

"It was just a couple of cigarettes," I growled, but I knew that wasn't gonna fly. I could have stolen a piece of lint from him and he'd have been out for my blood for what I owed him.

"You don't take what's mine, boy," he snarled, his fingernails biting into my neck. "I work for every penny I have and I spend 'em on what I want."

"Got it," I forced out as his fingers tightened and started to cut off my air supply.

"I don't think you do," he hissed.

My momma was out of the house for once, fetching groceries from the local store. And my dad was always ten times more dangerous when she wasn't around to take his attention from me. But I didn't want her doing that anyway. I wanted her to divorce his ass and run for the damn hills. She was either too fucking loyal to him, or too afraid he'd find her. I was only fifteen, I wasn't able to get her out of here myself. But a couple more years and maybe I could get a job, rent some place she could escape to.

"I think you've got all kinds of thoughts in your head, boy. You've been hanging around with Fox Harlequin too long and his arrogance is rubbing off on you. But you know the difference between you and him?" He got even closer to my face, nose to nose with me as his too-long fingernails drew blood from my skin. "He's going places. He's got good reason to lord it around this town like he's gonna own it someday. 'Cause the fact is, he is. And you'll be left in the dirt for him to walk all over and use how he likes, 'cause you're worth nothin' to no one."

My jaw gritted as I gazed into his eyes and tried not to believe those words, but they cut too deep, slicing into my insecurities and making them bleed.

"It's why he keeps you around, you know?" Dad continued. "He can use you how he likes, get you runnin' around for him, doin' his dirty work. But his daddy will soon teach him there ain't no point keepin' boys like you around for any other reason than you catchin' a bullet in your skull to protect him."

"Fox is my friend," I snarled, though the doubts were creeping in, crawling under my flesh like ants. "And his dad's a better one than you'll ever be."

My heart beat furiously in my chest as Dad swung me around and slammed me down onto the kitchen table. The back of my head impacted with the wood and my skull rang from the collision.

I pushed his shoulders, terrified of what he might do as his eyes swirled with darkness and rage. But he was too strong and his body was fuelled by the fury of alcohol.

"You worthless piece of shit," he snapped, his fist cracking into my left eye as his other hand released my throat.

He kept beating me until his anger was sated then left me on the table to bleed into the wood.

When I was sure he was gone, I slid off of it, staggering toward the back door and taking in a desperate breath of the morning air as I made it outside. I grabbed my bike, hurried through the side gate and peddled down to Sinners' Playground as fast as I could, gritting my teeth through the pain of my injuries.

I hid my bike under the pier then made my way to the ladder we'd carved into one of the struts which would get me up into the amusement park, clutching my aching side. I tried to climb it three times before I had to give up, the pain in my body too much and not allowing me to make it.

I gazed at the amusement park above with an ache in my soul, wondering if my father had been right and I really was just going to remain down in the dirt my whole life. Fox wouldn't use me though, he was one of my best friends. Nothing was going to change that.

"Ace?" Rogue called to me from behind and I stilled, heat rushing to my cheeks in embarrassment at her finding me here like a tenderised piece of meat. She'd seen my bruises plenty of times before but today was an extra shitty example of my weakness, so I remained facing the pier strut, not wanting to turn and let her see the state of my face. I hadn't even seen it myself yet, but the way my left eye was throbbing, I was sure it was swelling up like a bitch.

Her hand suddenly took mine and all the warmth in the world seemed to flow into me from her. I turned my head away as she tried to get a look at me, my stomach in knots.

"Lemme see," she said gently, already knowing exactly what had happened.

"I don't want you to see," I admitted, but she cupped my cheek gently, turning my head towards her.

Her ocean blue eyes glistened, but she didn't look sad or pitying, she looked furious, a whole sea storm raging within her gaze. "Wait here," she said decisively then let go of my hand and ran away up the beach.

I moved into the shadows beneath the pier, my ribs hurting like hell as I sat down and rested my back against one of the struts. Rogue soon returned with a tub of Phish Food flavoured Ben and Jerry's ice cream.

"Where'd you get that?" I smirked, though that movement just made my face hurt even more.

"Stole it off a vendor while he was looking down some girl's shirt," she said with a grin.

She reached out and gently pressed the tub to my puffy eye and my brows arched at the reason she'd stolen it. She moved up close beside me, just holding it there while I stared at her and my heart rate slowed to this calm, flowing beat that made me forget all the pain in my body. But then I shifted a little and winced, clutching my ribs.

"Shit, let me have a look," Rogue said, biting her lip as she lifted my hand and placed it over the ice cream tub to hold it against my face.

"It's fine," I gritted out.

"It's not if something's broken," she said seriously and I humoured her, letting her pull my shirt up and start tiptoeing her fingers over my ribs, applying a little pressure to each one.

I was so distracted by her hands on my skin that I didn't even give a shit about the pain blossoming over that area.

"I think they're just bruised," I murmured, but she didn't stop her inspection, working back down my ribs again and skating her fingertips along each one. Her dark hair brushed her sun kissed cheek and I had the urge to

184

push it behind her ear and find out how it felt between my fingers.

"Looks like you dodged a bullet." Her eyes suddenly snapped up to meet mine and she dropped my shirt, nestling against me once more. "Fuck your dad."

"Yeah," I muttered, lowering the ice cream from my face and popping the lid off of it. It was starting to melt but it looked like the best food I'd seen in a long time. I dipped my fingers into it, sucking them clean as the sugar burst over my tongue then offered it to Rogue. She did the same and we sat there eating it like that, watching the tide roll out and taking all of my anxiety with it.

I crept downstairs in my gym clothes at quarter to six before the others woke up, my eyes burning from a hangover and lack of sleep. I was living on the odd takeaway meal, but mostly I didn't eat. I just drank until my stomach didn't growl anymore.

I stepped into the kitchen, desperate for a glass of water, but found Fox and JJ there, standing shoulder to shoulder in front of the sink in their boxers, their arms folded and eyes narrowed. My heart jerked uncomfortably and I frowned.

"What's going on?" I asked, my voice gravelly from the countless cigarettes I'd chain-smoked last night.

"At the risk of me sounding like a middle aged woman trying to deal with her kid's weed habit - this is an intervention," Fox said simply, his green eyes sharpening on my gym bag.

I tucked it a little tighter under my arm. "For what?" I scoffed.

"Give me the bag," Fox growled and Rogue's little dog barked like he fucking agreed as he came to stand by Fox's feet.

"No," I said simply. "I'm going to work."

"Come on, Ace," JJ said gently. "Just hand it over. We don't wanna do this the hard way, but we will."

"I dunno what you're talking about." I waved a hand dismissively, turning around and heading for the door, but two sets of strong arms accosted me, dragging me back into the room and wrestling the bag from my grip while the fucking dog bit my ankles.

"For fuck's sake," I growled.

JJ kept a tight hold of my arm, wheeling me back around and I cursed as

Fox dropped the bag onto the kitchen island with a loud donk.

"This is ridiculous," I muttered as he unzipped the bag and produced a bottle of rum from within the folds of my clothes. Then another, and another. And okay, another.

Mutt caught my attention as he sat on his furry ass and cocked his head to one side with the most judgmental fucking look I'd ever seen on a dog.

"You're gonna kill yourself, brother," Fox snarled furiously, but when his eyes flashed onto me, there was only concern there. "This isn't the answer to getting her back."

"You think that's what I want?" I laughed dryly. "Her back in this house, back in the middle of us ready to rip us all apart?"

My gaze flicked to JJ and his eyes implored me not to tell Fox his dirty little secret. The fact that he thought I would showed how little he thought of me right now. But the whole point of this was to try and keep us three together. I'd do anything for my brothers and I wasn't going to tell Fox he'd laid his hands on Rogue. Ever. That would be akin to setting a grenade off right here in this kitchen, and frankly the critical hits would probably be lower by comparison.

"I'm not gonna argue with you about Rogue right now," Fox said evenly, walking to the sink with the rum bottles and placing them down on the side. He twisted off the cap of the first and poured it down the drain, the glug, glug, glug of the rum spilling out of the bottle filling my ears. I could get more, he knew that. But he was making a point, and I got it. I really did. But if I didn't have alcohol to numb my pain, I was going to have to face it. And fuck, I really didn't wanna do that.

While Fox's back was turned, JJ mouthed, "Don't tell him," to me and I pressed my hand to his shoulder, giving him a look that swore I wouldn't. I hated lying to Fox, but I wasn't an idiot. My only goal was keeping us as one unit and that truth would be the end of us. Fox would never forgive JJ for it. It would ruin them. Us. Which was exactly why she'd had to go.

"Gimme your wallet," Fox gritted out when he was done pouring the rum away, facing me and holding out his hand.

"Come on, man," I tried, but he just closed in on me while JJ moved to block the nearest exit.

I blew out a breath of frustration then took my wallet from my pocket and placed it in Fox's hand. "What now? Am I grounded?" I rolled my eyes as Fox placed it on the counter and picked up a box beside it, taking something out of it.

I frowned at the handheld device with a little tube extending from the side of it. I knew what that was. A breathalyser.

"I'm hungover as shit, I'm not gonna pass that test, brother," I laughed dryly but neither of them cracked a smile.

"I know," Fox said. "I just want you to say hello to your new best friend." He gave me a dark smile and my heart sank. "You're gonna keep this breathalyser on you wherever you go. And if I text you asking for a reading, you're gonna send me a video of you taking it. And I want those numbers on dead zeros after the alcohol has left your system today, do you understand me, Chase?" He asked in his most dominating tone.

I ground my teeth, my breaths coming heavier. Alright, so maybe I'd gotten a little too reliant on the booze lately. But I wasn't an alcoholic. I wasn't my fucking dad. This was just a phase, a blip. I didn't *need* rum, it just... helped.

"This is extreme," I said. "I don't have a problem."

"That's what someone with a problem would say," JJ said, moving to my side and giving me a worried look.

"Fuck off." I shoved his arm then looked back at Fox. "This is too much, bro. I'll cut down to a couple of drinks a day, but I'm no T-totaller." I laughed, they didn't, my stomach knotted.

Fox folded his arms. "If you don't give me dead zero readings from tomorrow onwards, you're out of the Harlequins."

My heart thundered in my ears as I glared at him. "You're really pulling that shit with me again?" I growled. "Are you just gonna threaten me with that every time you want me to jump through one of your hoops, asshole? You don't own me."

He strode up to me, chest to chest with me and his eyes endlessly dark. "I don't need a drunk in my crew," he said in a deadly low voice. "You're a liability. You're not just a danger to yourself, you're a danger to anyone you're out on a job with. So until you can prove to me that you can keep your head straight and deal with your own shit, you're not going on jobs and you're not taking part in Crew meetings either. You show me you can stay sober for two weeks and I might let you start climbing the ranks again, but until then, you're a pledge and I expect you to prove your worth to me and my gang." He stepped past me, sweeping out of the room and slamming the door behind him to emphasise his point.

Mutt barked again then hopped up into a potted plant and took a piss and I swear the little fucker held my eye the entire time like that was aimed at me.

Rage coiled through every fibre in my body and I began to shake with it. He couldn't do that. I'd been a part of this crew as long as he had. Luther had initiated me, not him. I wheeled towards JJ, looking for at least some glint of him having my back in this. Fox had gone too far, but JJ just frowned sadly at me and hung his head like an obedient little lapdog and I growled through my teeth.

"You can't seriously think this is okay?" I snarled.

"You need to look after yourself, Ace," he said, reaching out to me, but I jerked away from his touch.

"Fuck you," I snapped, grabbing my gym bag from the island and heading through the door towards the garage. I grabbed my motorcycle key from the box as I jogged downstairs, putting my bag on my back. I jogged over to my Suzuki and swung my leg over it, starting her up.

The electric door opened and I flew out of it at high speed, tearing towards the gate as a couple of Harlequin guards scrambled to open it in time. I sped through it, the engine roaring as I shot down the street with the wind twisting through my hair, weaving through the traffic before loosening the throttle as I hit The Mile.

I went as fast as possible, the world becoming a blur, everything just merging into a sheet of colour either side of me.

I parked up outside Raiders Gym and kicked the stand down on my bike as I dismounted before unlocking the doors and marching inside. I'd work out until my muscles screamed and everything burned. If my heart was going to hurt like this, then the rest of my body might as well follow.

Fox:

Take it.

I ground my teeth, my phone locked in my hand as I guzzled water, sitting on the floor in the boxing ring after a third round with Terry. Sweat dripped down my spine and the pain in my skull from the alcohol last night was finally easing, its place taken by my aching muscles instead.

I considered refusing him, I really fucking did. But that was just the stubborn asshole in me. After a few hours, I'd calmed down enough to know I was going to do exactly as he asked, because I knew he was just psychotic enough to really kick me out of the Harlequins if I didn't obey his every word and the thought of that was terrifying. I'd lose my brothers, my home. And there wasn't anything I wouldn't do to stop that from happening.

I pushed to my feet, heading into the office and asking Brandy to give me some space. She jumped up from behind her desk and tottered out into the gym on her vibrant orange heels, shutting the door behind her. I dropped down into my seat and set up my phone on the desk to record me as I took the breathalyser test, casually flipping Fox off as I did so then stopping blowing into the device when it beeped. I showed him the low reading he was hoping for and switched off the camera before sending the video to him.

Even as I sat there for a couple of minutes, the anxiety kicked back in hard and the guilt over Rogue started gnawing at my gut again. I chewed the inside of my cheek, my instincts telling me that rum was the answer. But it couldn't be now. So I was just going to have to suffer through this and hate myself.

By lunchtime, after I'd worked every muscle in my body, showered and changed into some navy shorts and a white tank top, I knew I had to eat. I was shaking from the lack of food and my head was spinning like a motherfucker. Before I could make up my mind on which takeout I was gonna go eat alone on the beach, Fox messaged me once more.

Come home for lunch. You officially eat all of your meals with me.

I cursed him under my breath, then stormed out of the gym and got on my bike to ride home.

When I walked back into Harlequin House, Cuban music was playing and I headed to the kitchen, finding the sliding doors open and Fox out on the patio, sitting at the table under an umbrella with all kinds of breads, cheeses, fruits and salad laid out in front of him.

He was wearing aviator Ray Bans that reflected my exhausted looking self in them and Mutt was on his lap as he casually stroked his head and I swear the dog scowled at me. Fox's tanned chest looked like it had been gilded by the sun this morning and the artful ink dotted around his body seemed to shine brighter than usual.

"Help yourself," he said, pushing a very green looking smoothie across the table towards me. "And drink up."

"What are you, my momma?" I asked, striding over to sit down opposite him and inspecting the smoothie.

"We both know your momma never made you anything this good, brother," he said, not to mock me, just stating plain old facts.

"Lunch!" JJ bounded out onto the patio and Mutt wagged his tail, though he seemed content to stay on Fox's lap for some reason.

I was pretty sure he'd taken to carrying treats around in his pocket to buy the pup's favour. But I didn't think the dog would like me even if I had a prime rib in my pocket. I didn't know how the little beast knew that I was responsible for getting rid of his owner, but he did. I could tell. And I swear he was out to get me for it too.

JJ sat down beside me, grabbing a plate and starting to pile it high with food.

"You only ever make us food on Sundays." I narrowed my eyes on Fox.

"Well lucky you, now I'm going to make you every meal," Fox said, popping a grape in his mouth and crushing it between his teeth.

"You don't have to babysit me," I bit out, still not touching anything despite the way my stomach growled for food.

"Oh, on the contrary, Ace, I abso-fucking-lutely do," Fox said, eyeing me with a challenge in his gaze and sipping his smoothie. "Drink. Up."

I blew out a breath then picked up the smoothie and downed a mouthful of it. It tasted like a vegan's asshole, but I drained every drop of it then wiped away the green slush from my lips and grabbed a plate, heaping it high with food and acting like a savage as I ate my way through it. If he wanted to be my personal chef, then fine. I wasn't gonna complain about that.

"Did Luther pick up his cut yesterday?" JJ asked Fox.

"Yeah, and he's gonna up it this month by five percent," Fox announced.

"What, why?" JJ gasped.

"Because he thinks Shawn Mackenzie is going to strike at us hard soon and we need to buy more weapons. Plus, we lost out on the extra cash we would have had from the ferry job," he said with a frown. "It'll only be temporary. You can just take on some extra escort jobs to make up the difference, right?"

"Oh er...yeah, of course," JJ said, going quiet as he tucked into some more food.

"I can increase the membership a little at Raiders," I said. "And we could get working on the next job-"

"I told you, you're not running jobs right now," Fox clipped and my jaw worked furiously.

"Oh come on, you need me. Who's gonna get the vehicles? Who's gonna drive the getaway car?"

"Basset," Fox said simply.

"Fucking Basset?" I snapped. "He hasn't even got half the talent I have boosting cars."

"Fair point," JJ agreed.

"He's good enough, and maybe the extra practice will bring him up to par," Fox said with a shrug.

I slammed my hand down on the table, sending a papaya flying off of it onto the ground. Mutt barked at me, baring his teeth as I bared mine at the guy holding him.

"So now you're gonna replace me?" I demanded, my heart warring and panic tearing up the centre of me. This was the only thing I was good at, and Fox was just dismissing it like even fucking Basset could learn to reach my standard. "Is that how disposable I am to this crew?"

My father's words echoed in my head and I tried to force them out, but they were carved into my mind and I couldn't get rid of them. *Worthless. Useless. Nothing.*

"No one said you're disposable," JJ tried, but Fox cut in, pointing at me.

"You wanna be valued here, then prove your worth," he growled. "Basset is a hundred times more reliable than you are lately and I don't give a fuck if it takes him twice as long as you to steal a car and he stops at every red light during a getaway because there's more to a Harlequin than just being good at one thing. You need to show up on time, you need to have a clear head, you need to have your crew members' backs no matter what." His eyes were furious and the accusation cut deep. He thought I'd abandoned Rogue, and that I might do the very same thing to him or JJ. But he didn't understand, it wasn't like that. I would never leave them, and under any normal circumstances I wouldn't have left her either. But I'd thought it was the only answer to getting things back to normal. How wrong I'd fucking been.

I didn't snap back at him, I just gazed down at the half eaten food on my plate as my appetite died and I realised he was right. About all of this. He was trying to give me a chance I didn't deserve. And it was one he wouldn't have offered to anyone else if it hadn't been me. So if I wanted to stay here, I really was going to have to prove my worth. The problem was, I just wasn't sure I had any to offer.

The doorbell rang and I frowned in confusion, the three of us looking between each other as if doing a headcount.

"Who the fuck is that?" JJ muttered.

"Luther wouldn't knock," I said.

"Only a Harlequin would get through the gate," Fox said thoughtfully.

"I'll get it." I pushed out of my seat as Mutt growled at me and Fox stroked his head to shush him.

I headed through the house to the front door, unbolting it and pulling it open.

I froze, turned to a statue of ice as my mind took far too many seconds to catch up with who I found standing there.

Rogue was on our porch wearing ripped denim shorts and a white baggy cropped shirt with a picture of a hand with its middle finger up.

"Hello, asshole," she said brightly then punched me in the dick.

I stumbled back with a wheeze, clutching my bruised junk and cursing under my breath as white spots burst before my eyes. It took several long seconds for me to recover, in which time she stepped into the house, kicked the door shut behind her and fluffed up her rainbow hair while looking in a mirror on the wall.

I finally stood upright and all my instincts went to shit as I still couldn't quite comprehend that she was here, despite the very real pain in my balls which said she was.

I lunged at her, pulling her into my arms and crushing her against my chest in a fierce hug which I wasn't going to overthink as she wriggled violently to try and get free. She smelled like coconut and hope and all the good things I'd been missing ever since I'd lost her as a teenager. All the things that didn't belong to me and never would.

Fury bubbled under my flesh at this whole situation and as she tried to knee me in my tender balls, I pushed her back, keeping a tight hold her shoulders.

"Did he hurt you?" I demanded, searching her eyes for the broken girl I'd thought she'd be after her time on Maverick's island. But she looked fiercer than ever and all I found in her shimmering blue gaze was hatred.

"Only in the good ways," she tossed at me and I released her like she'd burned me.

My heart beat out a panicked tune and all the anger I'd felt at her choosing Maverick over the rest of us when we were sixteen came flaring up and tearing through every inch of my soul.

"You fucked him?" I spat.

"That's really none of your business." Her eyes narrowed and suddenly I was panicking for a thousand more reasons as she lowered her voice to a whisper and moved into my personal space.

"By the way…I know what you did, *Ace*," she hissed. "I know you left me on purpose. I know that you worked alone. That you wanted me gone and thought you'd pack me off to prison to solve your little problem. And I know that Fox and JJ don't know."

A lump of freezing ice lodged in my throat as those words rang in my head and I saw the Devil in her eyes. She was going to ruin us, rip us apart for good. That was her vengeance on us and she was here to deliver it. *No.*

She moved to step past me and I dove into her way, blocking her path. "Please, wait," I begged in a low and desperate tone. She was going to take everything from me, expose me to my brothers and turn them on me like rabid dogs. "Rogue, please don't do this."

She gave me a bitter look, all her disregard for me clear and it hurt more than I could have predicted. I hadn't expected to ever see her again when I'd decided to leave her on that ferry, hadn't thought I'd have to deal with that look from her. But now she was here and I had to face it. The venom she pointed my way seeped deep under my skin and made all my organs rupture.

"Why would I tell them?" she questioned sweetly, taunting me as she curled a lock of lilac hair around her finger. "When I can watch you squirm like this for as long as I like?"

"Rogue," I warned. "You can't do this, or I'll-"

"Are you sure you wanna fuck with me, Chase? Because your first move kinda backfired, and now I'm in the driver's seat and it looks like you're my little bitch. Unless you want me to just get it over with and tell the others what you did right now?"

"Fuck you, ghost," I snarled and she smiled darkly, making my blood rise and fury tangle with the very essence of my soul. This girl was my personal poltergeist, here to haunt and terrorise me. She was a demon with the face of an angel and the body of a goddess. I was both captivated and captured by her.

I pushed her against the wall with a snarl. "You can still walk out that door and take the first bus out of town," I growled. "If you play this game with me, you won't win."

"Well let's find out, shall we?" she whispered, her breath brushing my lips and tasting like a sin I wanted to commit over and over again.

She was going to torture me until the end of time. I was cursed to walk this earth and pine for a girl who despised me to her core, while desperately trying to hate her back. But when she was this close, her curves moulded to my muscles, my fingers on her flesh, I lost sense of all that hate and desire rose like a flame in its place. My cock twitched in hope of something it was never gonna get. I hadn't touched a single girl since I'd left her on that ferry, she consumed my thoughts again as she always had. And I was plagued to want her as keenly as I didn't want her.

"Which one of you took the keys?" she asked sharply.

"What keys?" I frowned.

"The Rosewood crypt keys," she said, her eyes accusing. "Mine and Maverick's went missing from my trailer."

"I don't know anything about that," I said dismissively, still trying to work out how I was going to deal with her now. Could I get her down into the garage, bundle her into the back of Fox's truck, drive her out of here and dump her somewhere out of state? She'd just come back though, the promise of vengeance in her eyes told me that much.

"Well you're gonna find out," she insisted. "And you're gonna help me get my hands on all the other keys too."

"No," I said instantly, my heart jack-hammering.

"Yes," she tossed back. "Because if you don't, I'm going to expose you for the rat you are, Chase. So you can start by giving me yours."

My teeth ground in my mouth as I glared at her, trying to think up a way out of this, but she had me by the balls. I couldn't risk her telling Fox and JJ what I'd done. Fox already had me on probation, if he knew I'd intentionally left Rogue on that boat, he'd kick me out of the Crew for good. Maybe even the whole of Sunset Cove. I'd lose my family, I'd lose *everything*.

"Fine," I forced out.

I heard footsteps pounding this way and withdrew from her just before Fox and JJ rounded into the hall. Rogue was quick to school her features, casually stepping away from the wall as my boys' eyes fell on her.

Mutt yipped desperately, trying to fight his way out of Fox's hands, but he didn't let go, holding the beast like he was the only thing stopping Rogue from evaporating before his eyes.

"You're back," JJ rasped then ran forward, pulling her into his arms and Rogue hugged him tight, her fingers knotting in his shirt.

I could see the genuine relief she felt to be in his arms again and my heart twisted as I took another step back.

Fox was there in a heartbeat, placing Mutt in my hands and giving me a look that said *if you let him go I'll gut you*, then turning and pulling Rogue from JJ's hands, cupping her face and starting to inspect every inch of her.

Mutt bit me everywhere he could and I cursed as his sharp little teeth drew blood.

"Did he hurt you?" Fox asked her, practically begging, fear flaring in his eyes.

"Not in any way I couldn't handle," she said seriously, but his fingers traced over bruises on her neck then paused on a hickie. His muscles bunched and he fell unnaturally still as her gaze flicked up to meet his.

Rogue took hold of his hand, giving him an intent look. "I don't want to talk about that. And if you try to make me, I'm going to leave again."

Fox's jaw worked and his fingers threaded with hers, clearly calling on every ounce of self control he possessed not to lose his shit. But he would. I knew Fox, and he was going to explode the moment he could. But right now, keeping her here was more important.

"Lock the door," Fox threw at me as he led her down the corridor.

"I want my dog," she said, reaching for him and he whimpered in my bleeding arms.

Fox nodded to me and I placed Mutt in her hands. He went crazy licking her and she laughed as she hugged him tight, her hand still firmly gripped by Fox's.

JJ watched her, barely blinking like he thought she might vanish if he looked away for too long.

I locked the door up tight and pocketed the key, staring after them as they flanked her and walked down the corridor. She threw a look back over her shoulder at me, her long rainbow hair brushing her spine and drawing my gaze to the bare, tanned flesh of her lower back and the base of the angel wing tattoos she had inked there. She smirked at me and my heart shredded in my chest. My balls were officially in her hands. And not in the way I'd dreamed about once.

She'd just turned me into a snake in the grass, an enemy against my own brothers. I had to help her try and get their keys. And I would. But when I had them, I'd take hers too, head to the Rosewood crypt and destroy the evidence lying inside it which could end my family.

If she wanted a war, then she could have one. But she'd just taken on a man who knew no limits, and would go to the depths of hell and back for his brothers. *So game on, little one.*

Rejects Park

ROGUE

CHAPTER THIRTEEN

Fox kept a tight hold of my hand while Mutt continued to lick me like crazy and I couldn't help but grin at the dog's antics as he celebrated my return. Maybe I'd been wrong to assume the little fella would be done with me at the first sign of something better after all. He was my ride or die pup and I was pretty confident that we were in this for the long haul now.

"Are you hungry?" JJ asked, moving to my other side, his arm brushing against mine as he crowded in close, and I had to fight the way my heart wanted to swell in response to being back here again amongst them. The scent of almonds reached me from his flesh and fuck, I'd missed that. But I'd never admit it.

There was food laid out on the table by the pool and Fox dragged me into a seat beside him before scooting his own chair so close to me that I was surprised he hadn't just dumped me in his lap in the first place.

He was wearing a pair of aviator sunglasses which I swear were the exact same as the one's Maverick had been wearing when he gave me a ride back on his boat yesterday. But I was willing to bet Fox wouldn't appreciate me pointing out the fact that he had the same taste as his adopted brother, so I kept my lips sealed on that.

JJ dragged his chair around the table so that he was rammed up close on my other side and he shoved a half-eaten plate of food away from me as he called out to Chase to get me my own plate.

"I guess I'll go get myself a new chair then too," Chase muttered irritably, letting me know that I'd just taken his spot and I gave him a cherry pie smile before he stalked back inside.

"How did you escape?" JJ asked.

"What did he do to you?" Fox added.

"Do you swear he didn't hurt you?"

"Is your lip split?"

"Where did you sleep?"

"Did he give you decent food?"

"Did he try and make you tell him anything about this place?"

"Did he punish you for being ours?"

"Jesus, let a girl breathe, why don't you?" I interrupted them, leaning back in my seat and wafting them away so that I could get a breath of fresh air which wasn't laced with testosterone.

I let Mutt hop up onto the table and he quickly made his way over to Chase's half eaten meal and started in on his cheese selection. I fucking loved that dog.

Chase reappeared with my plate while Fox and JJ managed to force themselves to lean back a little and give me some room.

"Thank you, Ace," I said sweetly and Fox cut him a glare as he snatched the plate from him and took on the job of loading it up with food for me.

"Don't think he hasn't been punished for losing you on that ferry," Fox growled, plenty loud enough for Chase to hear as he moved to get himself a chair and pulled it up on the opposite side of the table. With how close the others had moved to me there was a pretty big us and him vibe going on and I could see how much that pissed him off.

"Aww, that's sweet you're putting all the blame on him," I said, picking up a few crisp grapes and popping one into my mouth.

"We're so sorry, pretty girl," JJ rasped, his hand landing on my thigh as he leaned in close to me and I arched a brow.

"It's like déjà vu all over again, isn't it?" I asked, my tone sweet but meaning acidic.

"Take your hand off of her," Fox snarled, his arm closing around the back of my chair and making me feel like a bone being fought over by dogs.

JJ glared right back at him, his fingers biting into my thigh in a way that I didn't entirely hate, but I wasn't in the mood to become the central attraction in a tug of war.

I sighed dramatically and pushed to my feet, knocking the chair back and causing JJ's hand to fall from my leg while Fox's was pushed back with my seat.

"Here's the short version. You three left me on that ferry for the cops." My gaze met Chase's just to drive the point home to him that I knew precisely who was to blame for that particular offence. "I was arrested with thousands of dollars worth of stolen merchandise. Then I was dumped in a holding cell while they processed me. But then my fairy godmother - who apparently rides a motorcycle and has a shit load of ink - showed up to save the day and the charges against me went *poof*." I snapped my fingers while the three of them just stared up at me, drinking in my words. "Must be nice to be a super scary, gangster. Apparently the rules just don't apply to any of you, do they?"

"So Maverick paid them off then took you back to Dead Man's Isle?" JJ asked, concern colouring his features.

"Yep. We had a great time. He tied me to a chair in his murder freezer while I was butt naked, we bonded over the way people who promised to love us enjoy throwing us away all the goddamn time yada, yada, yada. But when it came down to it, I just didn't want to be his toy any more than I wanna be anyone else's. So I ran away and came back here for my dog."

Fox snatched Mutt into his arms so fast that my little buddy yelped in surprise and farted. A piece of Chase's lunch fell from his jaws and my nemesis cursed as he glared between the dog and me.

"You just came back for Mutt?" JJ asked, reaching out for me again and giving me a look that made my heart twist.

I shrugged one shoulder then tugged my shirt over my head to reveal the seriously hot black bikini Tatum had gifted me. "Not sure yet. I guess it depends how enjoyable my stay is here."

"How did you escape from Maverick?" Chase demanded and I sighed.

"I snuck out onto the beach in the dead of night then sang a song for a dolphin who offered me a ride in return for my sweet melodies."

"The real story, pretty girl," JJ said firmly, because I clearly responded so well to a firm hand.

"I jacked a boat of course. And swam some. Then I made a new friend, drank some Margaritas, got a ride back to town and hung out at Rejects Park for the night – thanks for paying for my trailer there by the way."

"No problem," JJ muttered.

"Least you could do after ditching my ass." I shrugged, shooting Chase a death glare that let him know he'd be paying for my rent there from now on. Or if the glare wasn't clear enough, I'd spell it out later to be sure. "Now I'm gonna cool down in the pool while the three of you finish your little freak out and when I come back I wanna eat my lunch without anyone mouth breathing in my damn ear. Kay?"

They all just stared at me like they had no fucking idea what to think of this and I smiled big as I hung my shirt over the back of my chair and unbuttoned my shorts. I dropped them to my feet, kicking my sneakers off before bending down to grab my shorts so I could toss them on the chair too.

As I moved to stand upright, Fox's hand slapped down on the small of my back and I cursed in surprise as I was forced to grab the edge of the table to stop myself from face planting.

His fingers brushed against my right ass cheek, making my skin tingle and I looked over my shoulder at him, finding him inspecting a bruise which had most definitely been left there by a set of teeth.

I slapped his hand off of me and stood upright, turning to look down at him again and arching an eyebrow at him as he glared at me through those sunglasses.

"Problem?" I asked while a vein in his temple began to pulse and I could practically see him choking on all the words he wanted to throw my way.

"Fucking hell, pretty girl," JJ muttered, dropping back in his chair as he carved a hand through his inky hair.

Chase was glaring at me. I didn't need to look his way to know that because I could feel his eyeballs trying to burn their way through my skin.

Fox stood suddenly, sending his chair crashing to the ground before he threw his sunglasses down on the table hard enough to crack them. His forest green gaze met mine for the briefest of pain filled, furious seconds before he turned and strode away into the house.

"She doesn't leave!" he barked loudly in a clear command for JJ and Chase and the next thing I knew the sounds of shit getting destroyed began to tangle with the air.

I released the breath I'd been holding while waiting for him to lose his shit then turned and strutted my designer bikini covered ass over to the pool.

I dove in like a freaking pro thank you very much, and I lost myself beneath the water as I began to swim.

Fuck I loved that feeling. Always had. And I'd missed it when I'd been away from here. I'd missed the sea most of all, but just being able to swim was like a balm to the scars on my tattered heart.

I cut through the water and made it to the far side of the pool before I surfaced again. The sounds of shit getting ruined still rang through the house while Chase and JJ had some hissed conversation which I clearly wasn't invited to join in on.

I turned and pushed off of the wall, swimming beneath the surface again as I headed back over to them and when I grasped the edge of the pool and pulled myself up to lean my forearms on the tiles, I found Chase there waiting for me.

One glance over his shoulder told me JJ had gone to try and calm down the raging badger and Chase's gritted jaw promised he had a whole lot of angry shit to spew my way.

"No thanks," I said quickly, before he could get the chance to start in on me.

"What?" he growled in confusion and I smiled at him. The kind of smile a shark would give a tasty little sealion. Or maybe the kind a siren would offer a pirate right before she drowned him for being a cock sucking motherfucker who had tried to fuck her over for the last damn time.

I hauled myself up out of the water and Chase rose to his full height again, his bronze skin gleaming in the sunshine as his muscular chest tensed and no doubt all of the hateful things he wanted to say to me circled in his head.

"Listen to me, Ace," I said, taunting him with that nickname because we both knew I didn't say it with any fondness. "And I really suggest you don't do anything dumb, like interrupt me or call me names."

He ground his jaw but held his tongue and I smirked at him in triumph. Fuck yes, payback really was a bitch, and I was going to enjoy wearing her face for him.

"You and me just became best friends," I informed him as I took a step closer, moving right into his personal space and reaching out to press two fingers to the bullet scar he had on his lower abs. I pitched my voice low just for him as I spoke again. "I want those keys. And today, you're going to show me just how committed you are to this little deal of ours by giving me yours."

"It's not here, ghost," he ground out as I slid my fingers down to the other bullet scar on his abdomen, the one which sat just above the waistband of his shorts. His skin was so hot to the touch, his muscles hard and inviting beneath my fingertips, but there was no way I was going to be dick blinded by this particular asshole.

"Where is it then?" I asked sweetly.

"Somewhere safe."

I tutted at him like he was some disappointing naughty child and slid my fingers from his skin, down over the front of his shorts. He froze solid, his muscles tensing up as a grunt escaped him and my fingers came damn close to brushing against his cock, but that wasn't my destination even if I did have his metaphorical balls in my fist right now. I slipped my fingers into his pocket instead and tugged out the pack of cigarettes I'd known would be there.

I took a smoke from the pack and held it between my fingers before tossing the box in the vague direction of the table behind him.

"Here's how this will go. Tonight, after the others are all tucked up in bed-"

"JJ's working tonight," he interrupted like JJ not being in his bed made the blindest bit of difference to my plan.

"Maybe just leave the talking to me, yeah?" I suggested. "You can nod to let me know you understand."

"Do you want me to kiss your fucking feet too?" Chase snapped.

"Don't tempt me."

He glared at me like I was the reason for every bad thing in his life and

204

I just kept on smiling because I was pretty sure that if I didn't, I might crack. I might remember the boy he'd been and how much I'd loved him. I might remember how fucking shit he'd had it and how often I wished I could help him find a way out. And I didn't want to remember any of that. I wanted to remember the fact that he'd left me on that fucking ferry and had been willing to let me go to prison for years rather than have me back here when I'd done nothing at all to him.

I placed the cigarette between my lips and arched a brow at him, waiting for him to get the hint.

Chase cursed as he snagged his zippo lighter from his pocket and flicked it open, holding the flame out for me while I inhaled deeply to get it to light. Being my little bitch looked good on him.

I plucked the cigarette from my lips again and breathed my smoke into his face. "Tonight, you and I will go on a little adventure and you're going to take me to get your key," I said firmly. "And if you don't, I'll tell Fox exactly what you did to me on that ferry. Now, I'm guessing you might be wondering whether or not you could just lie and say I'm crazy, but don't you worry your pretty little head about that, Ace. Because I have the voicemail you left me to back me up."

"What voicemail?" he grunted, his brow furrowing.

"I'm not all that surprised you don't remember, because it was pretty obvious that you were shit faced at the time. But never fear because in amongst your ramblings you managed to make it dead clear how much you'd wanted me gone. So there won't be any confusion at all over that if I play it for your fearless leader. So tell me, Ace, do you want to find out what Fox might make of that? Or do you wanna play nice with me and give me that itty, bitty key?"

His jaw was tight and fists balled, but I could see my answer in his sea blue eyes as I took another drag on my stolen cigarette.

"Fine," he gritted out just as the sound of JJ and Fox returning drew our attention.

"Good boy." I flicked the cigarette at his feet and tossed him a wink before sidestepping him and heading back over to get some food.

JJ and Fox reappeared and apparently we were all just going to ignore Fox's bleeding knuckles and what I was willing to bet was a house full of fairly destroyed furniture too.

Chase's gaze burned a hole in the back of my head as I took my seat at the table again but we both knew there wasn't anything he could do now apart from play my game. And though I was certain he was trying to come up with a hundred strategies to beat me at it, I was confident that I would be the one who came out on top in the end.

So I sat down to enjoy my lunch with the feeling of the sun on my skin and smiled to myself because this day was going even better than I could have planned.

I sat in the chair by the window, looking out of my locked balcony door, watching the dark sea rolling up on the shore beneath the darker sky and waiting.

I didn't doubt that he would come. I had him all figured out now and for all of his pretty words about only wanting to rescue his brothers from the heartache of me tearing them apart, I knew what he was. And that was a fucking coward. He'd taken one look at me after all those years and had seen nothing but a threat to the little slice of calm he'd carved out for himself. And I could understand that. He had it good here. He had his boys and he had power, somewhere safe to call home and no one to push him around. He hadn't wanted me causing ripples. But that had never been his choice.

I'd had a place right here for just as long as he had. The only difference was that my spot had been left empty for a long damn time. But I was starting to think he was realising just how easily this perfect little family could turn on each other.

They'd turned on me and then Maverick a long time ago. Their love was a fickle, selfish thing and if it suited them to turn on him next then they would. I saw that now and he did too. Which was why I knew he'd come.

The door pushed open behind me and Mutt growled low from his position in my lap, knowing what Chase was just as well as I did. I smoothed a hand down his back, tickling his little white ears to calm him. I wasn't afraid of the mean old Harlequin. He was my little bitch boy now.

"Are we doing this or what?" Chase hissed as I looked over my shoulder at him and I got to my feet, placing my dog down in the warm spot I'd vacated.

I was dressed already and waiting for him, my white Converse Allstars silent as I crossed the carpet to join him. Although it was late, the day had been hot so I'd chosen a pair of stonewashed denim shorts to go with it and a Nirvana band tee which belonged to JJ. I'd tied a knot in the shirt beside my right hip to make it fit me better, but the way Chase was scowling at it told me he knew who it belonged to and he didn't like me borrowing JJ's clothes.

He jerked his chin at me like I was some dog for him to command at will then turned and strode away down the corridor. I glanced at Fox's door as we passed it, but all was silent inside.

We descended the stairs and I followed Chase through the living space towards the garage door which he unlocked using a key in his pocket.

I stayed silent as he crossed the space to his bike which was parked up near the exit and I watched him as he grabbed a leather jacket from the hook on the wall and shrugged it on so that it hugged his muscular body and stretched over his broad shoulders.

He took a second jacket from the hook and tossed it to me without really looking my way and I caught it automatically.

The tags told me it was new and I arched a brow as I found it in my size, clearly bought specifically for me, the brown leather supple and expensive.

"You worried about me, Ace?" I mocked, snapping the tags out and shrugging it on.

He tossed a glance my way, his gaze appraising as he took in the look of it on me before shaking his head.

"You can thank Fox for your wardrobe. He bought that before you ran off on us in case you ever needed to come out on my bike with me."

"Ran off? That's cute," I mocked, taking the white helmet he offered me next and fighting a smirk at the skull printed on the back of it.

Chase secured his own helmet then climbed on and waited for me. I had no desire to get any closer to him than absolutely necessary, but I wanted this damn key so I wasn't going to let a little asshole aversion put me off.

I climbed on behind him and wound my arms around his waist tightly, feeling him stiffen at the contact like even that was too much of me.

His abs were firm beneath my hold and my thighs hugged the backs of his, making me all too aware of the powerful body I was currently wrapped around, but I chose to ignore that.

Chase started the engine up and a heartbeat later we were tearing up the ramp and out of the underground garage towards the exit. The men posted at the gates pulled them wide for us and Chase let the throttle go as we raced out of them and turned right towards the town.

The wind whipped around us, a taste of coolness to it blowing in off of the sea which made salt coat my lips and fill my lungs with the taste of home. Fuck, I hated that. Why did the one place I felt settled in this miserable world have to be the one inhabited by the men who had destroyed me?

Chase rode fast and angrily, weaving around any cars we happened to meet on the dark roads at high speed and causing adrenaline to crash through my body as I had no choice but to cling on tight and just wait for us to reach our destination.

I wasn't even sure why I was surprised when we finally pulled up at the end of The Mile and Chase cut the engine, parking as close to Sinners' Playground as we could get on the road.

I released him and got off of the bike, unclipping my helmet and tossing it to him as he followed me.

He tugged his own helmet off too and hung both of them on the handlebars, his dark curls falling haphazardly for a few moments and reminding me of the boy he'd once been before he pushed a hand through them to tame them again.

"Why am I not surprised?" I asked, my gaze moving from the face of the man who'd betrayed me to the pier which stretched out into the sea. I shrugged out of my jacket and tossed it on the bike where he'd already left his. It was too hot in the Cove for it tonight.

"Because some things are better left in the past. Like this place and those keys too."

"And me too, right?" I added and the dark look he gave me said he wished that were so.

"Let's just get this over with." He turned his back on me and tried to walk away but I caught his arm just above his elbow, his bicep flexing as he looked down at me in surprise.

"Oh no, Ace, this isn't over after tonight. I told you, I want all of the keys. Which means giving me yours won't even come close to buying my silence. Don't go thinking you can blow me off or waste my time over this. You wanted to know what I've been doing in all the time we spent apart and I can sum that up pretty simply for you. Because what I learned was how to be ruthless. How to set my gaze on what I need and take it. So don't go kidding yourself that I won't follow through on my threat to you. And that means your choice is simple. Your boys or your keys. Because if you don't give me one, I'll take the other."

I released him as suddenly as I'd grabbed him and strode past him, hopping the low wall which separated the beach from the road and landing in the white sand and memories on the other side of it.

I kept going, heading straight for the pillar where we'd carved those handholds so long ago and heaving myself up them all the way to the top until I was climbing through the railings and pulling myself upright on the pier.

Chase wasn't far behind me and when he reached the top, he had to climb right over the railings rather than scramble through them thanks to his bulk. He met my gaze and took a cigarette from his pocket, cupping his hand around it as he lit it up.

I watched him take a drag which lit his face for a moment as the cherry flared and his gaze moved down over my shirt like he was itching to ask me something about it. But if he wanted me to tell him something then those words were very much going to need to escape his lips. I wasn't offering him shit for free.

Whatever it was clearly didn't make it beyond the dark thoughts swirling inside his mind and he turned away from me, leading the way along the old boards and heading into the amusement arcade.

He didn't hold the door for me and the fucking thing nearly hit me in the face, causing me to stumble back and curse him.

A snort of amusement escaped him and I scowled, shoving the door wide and snatching a moth eaten gorilla teddy that sat on a shelf there before throwing it at the back of his head.

A cloud of mildewy smelling dust enveloped his head and he swore as he jerked aside, turning a glare on me while I shrugged innocently.

"Let's hurry this up, ghost," he muttered, clearly wanting to spend as little time in my company as he could.

"Fine by me."

He moved further into the dark, nothing piercing it aside from the faintest sliver of moonlight which made it through the filthy windows and the orange glow from his cigarette.

He led the way to the gap between the old Space Invaders and Pacman machines and I glanced at the heap of blankets there, wondering if they were the same ones I'd slept in the last time I'd felt whole.

I should have fucking known to check here. This place had been special to all of us but to Chase it was a refuge. When his dad lost his shit, he could come here and know that no one would ever find him. He could be safe from that monster even if it was only for a little while and that meant more to him than I knew he'd ever have admitted.

I watched as he dragged the Space Invaders machine away from the wall and dropped down to one knee as he popped the rear panel off of it. He leaned forward, reaching an arm inside and when he finally drew back, a heavy sigh escaped him.

I waited him out. The scent of his cigarette reaching me and the darkness coiling around us like it was trying to conceal us from the world.

Chase got to his feet again and stepped towards me, his gaze hard and locked on mine.

"Promise me you won't use this to hurt them," he growled like my word would mean shit to him. His certainly didn't mean anything to me.

"I got you, Ace," I said, my voice echoing the past as I stepped up to him and cupped his cheek in my hand. He let me, that darkness in him seeming to give way to pain for a moment, so brief I wasn't certain I even saw it. We were just two kids with no one in the fucking world to care about us aside from each other and our crew. I'd found him in this very spot once, his jaw bruised and mouth bloody after his dad had punched him so hard he'd knocked out one of his back teeth. I hadn't said a word about that because he never wanted any of us to. He hated feeling pitied almost as much as he hated the animal who had done that to him. "Just tell me what you need to make it better," I added just like I had that day when the boy I'd loved so fiercely had been hurting so much. It wasn't even the physical pain which had been destroying him, it was that hopeless fear which enveloped him in that fucking house.

I could see the reply he'd given me then sitting on his tongue, wanting to spill free as this brutal man just stared at me and saw the girl I was.

"You," he breathed, his voice barely more than a whisper which cut me deeper than any memories ever could.

"You used to tell me such pretty lies, didn't you?" I asked, my heart pounding like I'd run a marathon. "So I guess you're just going to have to wait and see whether I'm as full of shit as you were."

I plucked the key from his hand but before I could pull away from him, he was on me, the cigarette falling to the floor and his hands snaring my hips. He whirled me around and shoved me face first against the Pacman machine, driving my cheek against the glass as my hips were crushed between the metal games console and his solid body.

His hand fisted in my hair and his mouth moved to my ear as he snarled his words with a hateful anger. "Don't think I won't kill you myself if I have to, little one. I may have to play along with your games for now, but that doesn't mean I'll let this go too far. I'm trying to protect what me and my brothers have left. So for now, I'll go along with your bullshit to keep this secret from them because I don't want it to hurt them. But if it comes down to you or them then I'll happily sell myself down the river. If I have to lose them to protect them then that's the choice I'll make. And you'd do well to realise that I'm not the scared boy you remember. I bought my position with blood and foul deeds and I'm not some little bitch for you to force beneath your heel. I'm a fucking Harlequin, love. And we don't take shit from anyone."

A laugh escaped me as my fist tightened around the key he'd handed over and I pushed my ass back against him, making him grunt as he maintained his hold on me.

"Careful, Ace," I warned. "If you think Fox will be pissed to find out you tried to get rid of me, imagine how angry he would be if he found out you laid your hands on me."

"Are you trying to say you don't like it rough, Rogue? Because we all saw the marks Maverick left on your body while you were over there having a little vacation with him. So I find that a little hard to believe. Tell me, did ten years give him time to practice and make it better for you? Or was it just like old times?"

"Is that what has you so worked up, Ace?" I taunted, pushing my ass back against him again. "Isn't Rosie keeping you satisfied? Or is there some other reason you're so interested in my fucking sex life?"

"Like I give a shit about who you fuck. The point is that Fox does. He says you're his girl and yet you went over there and fucked his enemy and the way that you and J-"

"What?" I demanded when he cut himself off.

"Nothing," he spat. "I just don't want you ruining everything we've got going here with your fucking wandering pussy."

"That might sound a little more convincing if your dick wasn't trying to bury itself in my ass right now, champ," I laughed and he shoved away from me suddenly, releasing his hold on me and stamping out the still smouldering cigarette on the floor.

I pushed a hand through my hair as I turned to look at him, my scalp tingling from his hold and my nipples aching against my shirt.

"I should cut your fucking throat and rid us all of you for good," he hissed, snatching another cigarette from the pack in his pocket and lighting it up.

I strode towards him, swinging my hips like I didn't have a care in the fucking world and stopping right in his personal space. "You should," I agreed. "But you won't. Wanna know why?"

"Go on then, little one, enlighten me."

"Because that really would be the end for you and your boys, and you know it. You kill me and they'll never forgive you. In fact, I'm pretty sure they'd kill you in return. So even if me being gone is what's best for them, you won't do it. Because when it comes down to it, this isn't about them. It's about *you*. And, selfish creature that you are, you don't want to lose them." I tiptoed up, plucking the smoke from his lips and taking a drag as he glowered at me. I didn't know why it was so freaking satisfying to steal his cigarettes but dammit it was. "That's why I'm not afraid of you, Ace. And that's why I'm so sure you'll be a good boy and get me what I want. Because you're not trying to protect them from the truth. You're just trying to save your own ass." I blew my smoke in his face and flicked the cigarette at his chest, sidestepping him and striding away towards the exit.

I didn't look back because I didn't need to. Heavy footsteps told me he was following and I was confident that he'd be helping me track down the rest of those keys too. It was all just a matter of time.

Chase didn't say another word as we rode back to Harlequin House and I was happy to leave the tension hanging between us. I didn't care if he was feeling butt hurt and salty. I was the one who had been left on that fucking ferry. If he'd gotten his way, I could be looking at years in prison. He'd set me up and had been willing to let me drown, so I hoped he gave himself a stomach ulcer worrying about the things I might say or do next.

I hadn't been able to sleep since we'd gotten back though. His key was burning a hole in my pocket and I couldn't help but worry about my key and Maverick's which were yet to make an appearance. I was convinced that Chase didn't have them because his poker face wasn't as strong as he thought it was when he was caught off guard, and I'd been looking him in the eyes when I asked if he'd been the one to take them. So that left me with two suspects.

I heard Fox's door opening down the corridor and finally decided to give up on sleep altogether, pushing out of bed and heading to my own door with Mutt leaping up excitedly too. The little monster always loved it when I got up because he knew that signalled breakfast.

I pulled my door open and shrieked in alarm as I found Fox right on the other side of it like he'd been about to knock or come in or maybe like he'd just been listening at my door like a fucking creeper.

"You nearly gave me a damn heart attack," I scolded, slapping his big, naked chest and making my hand sting from the impact.

"I was just coming to see if you wanted to come for a run with me?" he offered but I smelled bullshit.

"I don't run for pleasure, Badger, only to escape."

His eyes moved over me slowly, taking in JJ's Nirvana band tee which had become my pyjamas after I'd gotten back, matched with a pair of Green Power Ranger panties which I freaking loved.

"Do you need more clothes to sleep in?" he asked me and I frowned.

"Do you object to the Green Power Ranger? Because if you think we had problems before, that won't have anything on the shit storm you're about to bring down on your head if you start trying to tell me Red is better."

Fox snorted in amusement, leaning in close and having to duck to put us on eye level. "Everyone knows the Red Ranger is the best, hummingbird. You're just so defensive about it because you know you're wrong."

I clutched my chest and gasped in horror and he laughed as he turned and strode away from me, leaving me there to reel in the terrifying reality that he'd just spouted those poisonous words right in my face. And I'd thought our relationship was balancing on a knife edge before. What the fuck was the world coming to?

"Hurry up if you want me to make you pancakes," Fox called over his shoulder. "That ass of yours won't stay so round if you start skipping meals."

"Err, I'll have you know that my ass is sustained via a diet of regular junk food and a strict squat routine which I carry out at least once a month. Besides, I've seen you staring at it often enough to know there is zero chance of you starving it out of spite." I chased him down the stairs, but I lost sight of him as he headed away into the kitchen. "And I'm not just going to let you get away with that Red Ranger bullshit either, Badger. Because you know as well as I do that Green is-" A yelp escaped me as I stormed into the kitchen and something whipped against my ass with a sharp snap.

I leapt away from the source of the pain and found Fox grinning at me as he snapped the dishcloth my way again and a snarl escaped my lips.

"You'll pay for that, Fox Harlequin," I warned, snatching a spatula from the drawer and brandishing it at him threateningly.

"So you just got over the fact that she spent the last ten days taking Maverick's cock like a pro then, did you?" Chase interrupted us as he strode into the room in a pair of low hanging gym shorts that showed off the beautiful

V that dipped below his waistband. He did not deserve that V and I cut him a glare for it and his words.

The humour fell from Fox's face and I couldn't miss the hurt that lined his features a second before he turned away from me to start grabbing ingredients from the fridge.

"Don't speak about her like that again or you'll fucking pay for it," he snapped, throwing a box of eggs down on the counter hard enough that one of them cracked and started leaking out of the box.

For some unknown reason the badger's defence of me made my gut twist uncomfortably and I blew out a breath, moving closer to Fox and nudging him.

"No one ever taught me how to make pancakes," I said, looking up at him and making him fall still as he placed a bag of flour down with a little less rage to his movements. "And when I was sitting in that police cell, waiting to get sent to prison after the three of you left me behind on that ferry-" I met Chase's gaze and he gritted his teeth. "I couldn't help but think about all the awful breakfasts I'd have to eat in prison for year after year after-"

Fox caught my chin and turned me to look up at him. "That never would have been your fate, hummingbird," he growled and suddenly I wasn't looking at the man I thought I knew. I was looking into the eyes of one of the leaders of the most notorious gangs in the country and I knew he meant every damn word. When Fox Harlequin made a vow like this, he would move heaven and earth to make it happen. "I would have gotten you out of there long before Maverick showed up if only I'd known where they'd taken you."

I wetted my lips and nodded slowly, knowing that he meant that and trying not to get lost in all the implications which went with that vow.

"So show me how to make pancakes then, Fox," I asked again. "Remind me what the good life tastes like."

Fox gave me a half smile and released me, giving my thrumming heart a moment of respite as he started passing me ingredients while I placed them in the batter bowl. When they needed mixing, he moved to stand at my back, his arms around me and his body pressed flush to mine while his hand covered mine where I gripped the whisk.

It was utterly unnecessary, but some combination of the death glares

Chase was giving me and the rich cedar scent of home which enveloped me while Fox held me like that had me staying right where I was. And the sexy chef fantasies didn't hurt. Maybe he could wear one of those white hats and knead my dough while I battered his...sausage. Damn. Where was my sexy fantasy head at these days? Now I couldn't even make cake sound sexy and everyone knew how fucking sexy cake was.

Soon we were plating up pancakes and I was passing a plate to Chase, giving him a sweet as pie smile while telling him with my eyes that I hoped he choked on them.

The garage door clicked as it was unlocked from the other side and I looked up as JJ stepped into the room. He had dark rings under his eyes and his chest was bare and gleaming with sweat. A black feather clung to his neck and Fox barked a laugh as he looked at him.

"Gave you a rough ride did she, brother?" he teased, pushing another plate of pancakes across the kitchen island for JJ to claim.

"Who?" I asked curiously.

"Our boy's been out working all night, haven't you, you dirty fucker?" Chase joked and JJ snorted a laugh too as he took his seat.

"It's hard work, but someone's gotta do it," he said vaguely, his gaze falling to his pancakes as something cold and squirming started writhing in my gut.

"Come on, how many of them did you have screaming your name last night?" Fox pressed him, chuckling as he started to help me plate up my own food. I was pretty sure the only reason I was moving at all was because Fox's hand was curled tight around my fist to guide the spatula and without him, I would have fallen deathly still.

"Let's see all that green then," Chase added, lunging at JJ who tried to bat him off before yanking a fistful of cash from his pocket and dumping it down on the breakfast bar with a low whistle. "Shit, that's gotta be at least five clients, right? How the hell do you manage to get hard for them all one after another like that? You gotta be using Viagra, right?"

"Nah," Fox answered before JJ could. "He's just a horny motherfucker. Any hole's a goal for you, isn't that right, J? You'll fuck any woman who gets close enough for too long."

"For the right price," Chase added and the two of them laughed loudly while I died a little inside.

It wasn't that I had anything against the sex trade, but since the two of us had been together I guessed I'd been fooling myself into thinking that it might have meant something to him. But maybe I'd just been the closest hole after all. It clearly wasn't like he'd stopped working while I was missing. I mean, I'd been enjoying the warmth of Maverick's bed while I'd been away, but that was different. For one, I'd thought JJ had dumped me on that ferry, and for two, well…it was Rick. He meant as much to me as JJ did and maybe that was messed up, but when it came to the five of us, normal rules just didn't apply.

Fox gave me a shove to make me go and sit down with my food and I found myself right beside JJ as the scent of latex and sex sailed off of his skin.

"Good morning, pretty girl," he said to me in a low voice, trying to catch my eye and I just nodded, unable to look at him and focusing on my food instead. Not that I had any kind of appetite anymore.

"What's the feather about, dude?" Chase asked. "You been doing fetish shit again?"

"Err, yeah," JJ said, his gaze still burning into the side of my head while I just stared at the utterly unappetising looking pancakes.

The sound of the front door unlocking interrupted all of us and suddenly the three of them were on their feet, panic coating the air and making me look up in fright.

"What is-" I began but JJ yanked me out of my chair and slapped a hand over my mouth as the sound of the front door opening reached us.

I was hauled off of my feet and JJ broke into a run, yanking open the door to the basement and shoving me through it with a wild look in his eyes. My lips popped open as I stumbled and almost fell down the freaking stairs but JJ steadied me, his hand still clamped tight over my mouth. Mutt shot in behind me, growling low at JJ for the manhandling while I tried to figure out what the fuck was happening.

"Do I smell pancakes?" Luther Harlequin's voice stole my breath and sent ice flooding through my veins and the terrified look in JJ's eyes suddenly made all kinds of sense.

He released me slowly as the sound of Fox responding to his dad came in reply and Chase greeted the man who had promised me my death if he ever laid eyes on me again too.

JJ pressed a finger to my lips as he released me and I nodded because I wasn't a fucking fool. I didn't have a death wish and I wasn't about to give myself away.

JJ backed up, the warmth of his skin against mine disappearing and leaving me cold, the fear in his honey brown eyes paralysing me as the door swung closed between us.

I stayed frozen there in the dark with my heart thrashing and fear speeding through me like poison. I might have been a dead girl walking, but that wouldn't be the case for a single second longer if Luther Harlequin laid eyes on me. My death sat eating breakfast in the other room and if I wanted to keep lingering on in this miserable life of mine then I needed to pray that he didn't figure out I was here.

CHAPTER FOURTEEN

*H*oly fucking shit.

My heart hammered like crazy as Luther sat down at the breakfast island as JJ walked back into the room and shared a look with us. The others schooled their expressions quickly, falling into polite small talk with my dad as I washed up some of the utensils I'd used.

Heat burned a line up the back of my neck as I tried to focus on what I was doing, but all I could think of was how close Rogue had just come to being caught. This shit was too dangerous. I needed an advance warning on Luther's movements. *Dammit Kenny, what the fuck are you playing at?*

I made a mental note to call Kenny later and make sure he paid for not tipping me off. Again. I wasn't going to go easy on him either. This was the second huge failure on his part and I wasn't bribing his ass for nothing. I needed Luther's location at all fucking times while he was in Sunset Cove, it was life or fucking death. Literally.

While I was distracted, I nearly burned my own pancakes but saved them last minute. Luther pulled the plate which had been Rogue's closer with his tattooed fingers, picking up the syrup and squeezing a healthy dose all over them. He looked tired, his blonde hair was getting too long and it didn't look like he'd shaved in a week. My parents had been young when they'd had me, so he was only twenty two years older than I was and sometimes I wondered how different my life might have been if Rogue hadn't had to run all those years ago. Would I have gotten her knocked up young too? Might there be mini versions of us ready to grow up and wreak havoc across the Cove? I'd never wanted kids because my dad would see them as heirs to the Crew. But the one thing I knew for certain was that I wouldn't chain any child of mine to this life if I ever did have any. And she was the only girl I would ever have even considered having any with. But if that reality came to pass, I'd let them make the choices which were stolen from me and hopefully my relationship with them would be a whole lot better than mine was with this man.

"What's the news?" I asked, trying to focus as I sat down beside him and picked up my fork. But fuck if I was hungry anymore.

Luther took his time eating a large mouthful of pancake, his brows pulling together like something displeased him. Maybe I'd burned them while I was distracted with the feeling of Rogue's ass rubbing against my dick. "You get your cooking talent from your mother."

Silence burned a hole in my ears and I sensed JJ and Chase shifting awkwardly in their seats as I stared at my dad. He never mentioned Mom, it was a cardinal rule in this house. And I didn't much care to think about her either. She'd left us, end of story. I didn't wanna know if I shared this thing in common with her, it wasn't relevant. She'd made it irrelevant when she'd abandoned us.

Luther cleared his throat. "Why'd you make four portions of pancakes when there's only three of you?"

Ever the fucking observant asshole.

"I'm bulking," Chase said, the lie coming out as smoothly as a breath. "Fox has been helping me carb load."

"Pancakes is no way to build muscle," Luther scoffed.

"They're organic and I used a protein powder in the base." I shrugged and JJ nodded along, scooping a large forkful into his mouth so he didn't have to add anything. It wasn't even bullshit. My pancakes were healthy as fuck and just as delicious as regular ones. Better actually.

Luther chuckled. "Well, I guess you kids know more about all the

222

modern fitness mumbo jumbo than I do these days." He ate another mouthful of his pancakes, his eyes suddenly darkening. "Anyway, I'm here on business I'm afraid, boys. Three of my men were killed last night on the edge of town. They were picking up arms from the Garcia brothers. All of them were shot dead, and our guns were fucking stolen." His hand tightened around his fork.

"You think Shawn Mackenzie did it?" I asked venomously.

Luther nodded firmly. "I know so, because he carved The Dead Dogs symbol into all of their fucking faces before he left." His upper lip peeled back and disgust ran through me. "The message is clear enough. He's moving in on our turf down here and he wants a war."

War. The word buzzed in my head as I remembered it written across the Harlequin gates in blood. Maybe Maverick had been telling the truth about that, maybe he really hadn't beheaded Piston and Rodriguez. But had Shawn Mackenzie or his men really gotten that close to our home? The thought was unnerving and I made a mental note to up security on the place, especially with Rogue staying here.

"Finding Shawn seems pretty impossible, but I've got a few photos of his people from when we were back in Sterling. These are some of his top boys. Do you recognise any of them from around town? I have a feeling he's placed eyes close to us and I want to catch me a rat so I can squeeze Shawn's location out of its throat." He took his phone from his pocket, opening the photos and sliding it towards me. I took it as Chase and JJ stood up, moving either side of me so they could see too.

I scrolled through the photographs, studying each face and making sure my boys got a good look as well.

"The last photo's of him and his girl. The one that went missing," Luther said. "But he didn't bring her out to the kinds of places I could get eyes on often and that's the only picture my men ever got of her. I doubt she's much of an issue, but she could easily be planted as a spy and she hasn't been seen for a while, so I'm concerned she's already been moved down here."

I scrolled onto the photo and my heart stopped beating. JJ's hand landed on my back in warning and I took a slow breath to stop myself from reacting. But what. The actual. *Fuck?*

It was taken from behind so you couldn't see her face, her hair long and dark, tumbling down her back and brushing against the angel wing tattoos peeking out from her crop top. I'd know her anywhere, in any photo, taken from a thousand miles away. So what the hell was my girl doing in the arms of Shawn motherfucking Mackenzie?!

"Sorry, boss," Chase said smoothly, plucking the phone from my locked fist and passing it back to Luther. "Haven't seen any of them, but we'll keep an eye out."

"If you forward me the photos I can have my security on alert at Afterlife, so if any of them come in, we'll know," JJ offered while I tried to form a coherent thought. But all that existed in my head right then was a hydrogen bomb going off and a mushroom cloud filling up every space in my brain.

"Thanks, kid," Luther said.

Mutt barked suddenly, jolting me out of my frozen state and I glanced at the others for information on where he was. *Please tell me he's not with Rogue.*

"Aww, where's the little guy?" my dad asked, pushing out of his seat.

"Err..." JJ started as Luther strode out of the room. "Fuck," he cursed under his breath and I jumped up, my heart jolting with panic as his face told me exactly where the dog was.

Jesus Christ, how many fires did we have to put out today?

I practically ran after my dad, following him down the hall toward the basement where Mutt was yapping loudly.

"Why's he down there?" Luther clipped at me like I was abusing the damn animal.

"He keeps getting stuck in there," I said quickly. "Gotta stop leaving the door open. I'll get him." I quickened my pace to try and overtake him, but my dad moved like the fucking wind, making it to the door before me and yanking it wide.

A bark came from downstairs and Luther moved to step inside. I dove into his way like I was taking a bullet, scrambling for a reason as to why I was acting like a lunatic.

"Wait," I gasped. "There's a dodgy step," I blurted, catching JJ and Chase's wide eyes over my dad's shoulder.

Luther's features softened and he pressed a hand to my shoulder then shoved me aside, flicked the light on and strode down the stairs. "It'll take more than a dodgy step to kill old Luther Harlequin, son," he called back over his shoulder with a laugh and I shared a panicked look with my brothers. Chase darted to the cupboard beside the basement door, taking out a handgun stashed there and my heart beat furiously as I turned and raced after Luther.

I'm not gonna let him kill my dad, am I?

But what if he finds Rogue, what if he tries to kill her?

I hated Luther, but I wasn't sure I could watch him die. If it came down to him or Rogue though, I knew who I'd choose. And it wasn't him.

As he made it to the bottom of the stairs, I almost crashed into him as he whistled for Mutt. "Where are you, boy? Did my wretched son lock you down here?"

"I didn't," I gritted out, looking around the place for Rogue. Where the hell was she?

Mutt came bounding over, his little paws tapping across the floorboards as he ran at Luther and dove into his arms.

"Who's a good boy? Yes you are, yes you are," Dad cooed like an idiot and I frowned at the great Luther Harlequin who was apparently a complete sap for that dog. "Is my son not taking care of you? Do you want me to lock him up and beat his head in for you? Yes you do."

Ah, there's the man I know and hate.

Mutt licked his hands and wagged his little tail like crazy as Luther scooped him into his arms and turned to me with a stern look.

"You need to take care of your animals, kid. I raised you better than that," he said sharply and the air got choked out of my lungs as I spotted Rogue's legs dropping down from the ceiling behind a wooden beam. Her body followed and her legs kicked frantically as she tried to get back up to wherever the hell she'd been hiding, but her strength was clearly failing her. Had she gotten up into the damn piping in the ceiling?

"Sure, yeah," I forced out at my dad, my eyes snapping firmly back onto him.

"It's not right, is it Mutt?" he said to the dog then glared at me again. "And give him a proper name."

The rest of Rogue's body came into view and I could see she was about to let go, panic sending my heart into overdrive.

"MUTTLEY!" Chase bellowed just as Rogue lost her grip and dropped to the floor, his voice covering the sound of her feet hitting the floor as she stared at us in horror.

"Why the fuck are you shouting?" Luther demanded.

"I just got…overexcited," Chase said. "We could call him Muttley?"

"That's a shitty name," Luther muttered, frowning at Chase like he was a weirdo.

"I think Mutt might need to go pee," JJ said, jerking his head at the stairs. "He's got that look in his eyes, don't you boy?" He gave the dog a look and Mutt whined as if playing along with the lie.

Luther scratched his ears before heading past us with a tut and carrying him upstairs.

I looked back at Rogue as she bit her lip anxiously, desperate to go to her, but I just pressed my finger to my lips and led my boys back upstairs.

I locked the basement tight and released a breath of relief as I followed Luther back to the kitchen where he was opening the sliding door to let Mutt out.

We finished our breakfast and he soon headed off, leaving us with orders to hunt for Shawn and his men. My head was still reeling from the fact that Rogue had been that twisted motherfucker's girl. It made me sick. Had she really hated us that much that she'd gone to our enemy's bed? And as I thought of that, my mind latched onto Maverick and I picked up one of the island stools and hurled it out the door. It hit the concrete and bounced into the pool as my breaths came in furious pants.

"Let's just hear her out," JJ reasoned.

"Bring her to me," I commanded through my teeth and JJ hurried off to fetch her.

I took out my phone, dialling Kenny's number as my pulse thundered in my ears. It went to voicemail and I practically spat venom. "You listen here, you useless little shit. I'm going to rip out your intestines and strangle you with them if you don't call me back before sundown."

I cut the call and shoved my phone into my pocket as Chase pushed a cigarette into the corner of his mouth. I snatched it from his lips, putting it in my mouth and swiping his lighter from his other hand. I didn't smoke anymore, but I was being pushed to my fucking limits today as I tried to remain 'reasonable', and I just needed to do some damage to myself right now to stop me from doing damage to someone else. Chase gaped at me as I dragged the smoke down into my lungs and I cursed the world for how fucking good that was.

Chase lit up his own cigarette then folded his arms and leaned back against the wall, his aura dark.

"Shawn," I spat his name. "Fucking Shawn?"

"Fucking Shawn," Chase confirmed with a nod, his jaw working.

"How could she?" I snarled.

"How could I fuck a beautiful bastard with a big dick and a nice, comfy bed I got to sleep in every night? Hm, seemed like a viable lifestyle once," Rogue mused as she stepped into the kitchen.

JJ flanked her like a bodyguard and I gave him a dry look. What did he think I was gonna do? Hit her? I'd sooner cut my own hand off.

"Are we all smoking?" Rogue asked lightly, bouncing past me to Chase and stealing the cigarettes from his pocket. He offered her the lighter, his gaze cold and hard as he stared at her lips around the smoke and JJ strode forward to grab one too.

"Well now we're all firmly back to being sixteen years old, let's play the truth game," I said icily, working very fucking hard to keep my anger in check, but it wasn't working.

"What's the forfeit?" Rogue asked, sweet as pie like she gave no shits that we'd exposed the truth about her and Shawn Mackenzie. But she did, I could see it in the depths of her ocean blues. And I was going to get every dirty piece of it.

"Whoever refuses the truth first has to sleep in the basement. Naked," I said.

"And tied up," Chase threw in with a smirk.

"Fine," Rogue said with a shrug, turning her back on us and walking outside. We all followed. "What's on your mind, Badger?"

"How long were you Shawn Mackenzie's girl for?" I demanded.

"Two years," she said then whipped her dress off to reveal a tiny blue bikini and the fading marks all over her body from Maverick's touch. I nearly lost it there and then, blinded by rage, hatred. How could she want him? I knew what she'd thought I'd done when she'd been arrested, but that didn't make it feel any better. She'd cut my heart open the second she'd gotten into bed with him and she knew it. She fucking *knew* it.

"How big's your dick?" she asked me lightly, throwing me for a fucking loop as she dropped down onto one of the sun loungers and picked up a bottle of sun lotion.

JJ laughed and I shot him a glare that shut him right up.

"Nine inches," I answered. "Did you fuck Shawn just to get back at us?"

"Nope, I had no idea he was your enemy," she said easily with no hint of a lie, her eyes falling to my crotch with a raised eyebrow like she was trying to tell if I'd lied.

"They've been an enemy of the Harlequins on and off for years," I snarled.

"I don't keep track of all your gang shit. I swear every gang you hate is called something beginning with D. The Dog Dicks, the Damned Dicks, The Dead Dicks, I don't fucking know," she said earnestly. "So how many girls have you fucked?"

Chase pulled up a seat for the show, seeming angry as hell and I glowered at my girl, knowing she was just trying to screw with me.

"I dunno," I said.

"Take a ballpark guess," she encouraged.

"Thirty," I threw at her. "Is Shawn Mackenzie the one who left those bruises on your throat when you showed up here?"

"Yup," she said and I felt a vein throbbing in my temple that was definitely going to burst.

I went to the most villainous place inside me and made a vow to kill that motherfucker so good that his death would go down in history in this town. JJ and Chase looked ready to pack some weapons and get bloody right there with me too.

"Have you ever had a bi-curious experience?" Rogue asked me, making my head rattle.

"What? No," I balked.

"You let me hold your dick that time you needed to pee when you were too drunk to do it yourself," JJ pointed out unhelpfully and Rogue tipped her head back as she laughed.

"Thanks, J," I deadpanned. "I don't think that's quite the same as a bi-curious experience."

He shrugged, then looked back at Rogue with a frown on his brow. He always used humour to hide his mood, but his eyes said it all. The fact that she'd been with Shawn was gutting him deep. It was a betrayal on a level she clearly couldn't even comprehend. The guy was like fifteen years older than her too. What the fuck had she been thinking?

"Did you love him?" I demanded of Rogue and she tsked.

"No. What is love?" she tossed back with a shrug and I took it as her next question, striding toward her until she was in my shadow.

"Love is obsession. Love's the thing you can't control, that binds you to someone whether they want you or not. It's a gift to those who feel it towards each other, and the most excruciating curse when it's unrequited." I leaned down, gripping her chin and making her look at me. "You made love your enemy, hummingbird. You rejected it with all your soul because you think you're not worthy of it. But I've never seen a girl more worthy in my life."

Her eyes softened for half a second before she jerked her head out of my grip. "Next question," she pushed.

"Did you fuck Maverick?" I asked in a low voice just for her, but I could feel Chase and JJ listening in.

"Yes," she said without hesitation and my world crumbled, the single crumb of doubt I'd had on the matter flying away on the wind.

Mutt jumped up at my legs, sniffing my pockets as he hunted for treats.

"Do you want him? Is that why you came back to town?" I asked, desperate for that answer as much as I feared hearing it.

"It's my turn to ask a question," she said, her voice thick with emotion which she didn't let spill over.

Her eyes moved to meet mine and the breath got trapped in my lungs as I waited for some stupid question and got lost in the depths of those eyes I'd missed so much, for so damn long.

"Did you try your hardest to find me when your dad sent me away? Did you do everything within your power to look for me?" she asked, her throat bobbing and I could tell how much she needed this answer. The pain in her eyes made my anger ebb away just enough for me to reach out and take her hand.

"Yes," I swore. "I searched for you for ten years in every place I could think of, but the only place I ever found you was in my dreams."

Her features pinched and she hooked my sunglasses off the table beside her, putting them on to hide, taking a drag of her cigarette. "Ask me again then."

I swallowed the sharp lump in my throat as I prepared myself for a truth that would ruin me. "Did you come back to Sunset Cove for Maverick?"

"No," she said. "Shawn tried to kill me, left me on the edge of town and I figured coming back here was my only option. I didn't come here for Maverick."

"What did you come here for?" I rasped.

"To rip your heart from your chest," she admitted.

"Well good work, hummingbird." I stood upright, done with this game. "It looks like you got what you wanted then."

I stubbed my cigarette out in an ashtray and strode inside, heading down into the garage and grabbing my truck keys on the way.

I drove into town with one face in my head and a gun loaded on the passenger seat beside me. I was going to find Shawn Mackenzie and skin him alive for laying his hands on Rogue. It was the only thing that would sate this beast in me. *Besides, no one hurts her and gets away with it.*

I set every one of my men out hunting Sunset Cove for signs of Shawn and his thugs, but the day had turned to night and I hadn't yet found one lead to go on.

I returned home just after sunset, weary and with several missed calls on my phone from Chase and JJ wondering if I was alright and I finally shot back a couple of texts to say I was. I stepped into the house and headed to the kitchen, immediately starting to cook dinner for everyone. As I was babysitting

Chase, I might as well cook enough for the household, so I soon had a stir fry ready for all of us.

Chase appeared at the scent of food, wearing low riding black gym shorts and a grey wifebeater, his hair a mess like he'd been taking a nap. He looked better already from a couple of days of good food and no alcohol in his system.

"Show me," I demanded as I dished up a plate for him and he rolled his eyes before taking the breathalyser from his pocket and breathing into it. It beeped a moment later and he showed me the neutral reading which helped ease the knot in my chest a little. "Good. Where's JJ and Rogue?"

"Rogue's in her room and JJ's working," he said as he started eating like the food was about to vanish before his eyes.

He always did that. I guessed it came from having hardly any meals on the table when he was a kid. His parents had failed him on so many levels, it still made me angry to this day. If it was up to me, I would have shot his old man a long time ago for what he'd done to my brother. But Chase wanted him to linger on in loneliness with only the company of his bad leg and dodgy lungs, and I guessed that was a sweeter kind of justice.

"Any sign of Shawn?" he asked hopefully.

I knew he'd been out searching himself this afternoon even though I hadn't given him the order to do it. I'd seen him down at the beach questioning people and I wasn't going to call him out on it because frankly, he'd just deny that he was as desperate to find him as I was. He wanted to make Shawn pay for Rogue's sake, and no doubt JJ did too. I'd made sure J had stayed home to keep an eye on my girl though. Or fuck…was she even my girl anymore? Had she ever been? Me laying a claim on her hadn't made a bit of difference to how much she wanted me in return. I just didn't know what I was doing when it came to her and maybe it was time I tried reading one of JJ's mommy porn books because I really didn't know where else to turn.

After my rage had simmered down this afternoon, I knew I couldn't just give up on her. No, I had to up my game. Make her see why we were meant to be together. I still planned on gutting Maverick for laying his hands on her, but she was in my house now, not his. And I had to find a way to make her see how perfect we were for each other so she could choose me for herself.

"Are you babysitting her tonight?" Chase asked. "I've gotta go to Raiders."

"Yeah, I'll stay home," I said and he nodded, getting to his feet and moving to load his plate in the dishwasher.

"I could um, do a sweep of town before I come home later, check in with some of the Crew and see if they've gotten any leads on Shawn?" he offered, looking hopefully at me to set him a job.

I eyed him for a moment, considering that. "Alright," I agreed. "Be home by midnight though."

"Yes, Dad," he mocked and I rolled my eyes as he headed out of the kitchen towards the garage.

I dished up a plate of food for Rogue, placed it on a tray with a glass of apple juice, some cutlery and a chicken treat for Mutt then headed upstairs and placed it down outside her room. This was probably a douche move, but whatever.

I knocked on her door then walked away and slipped into my bedroom, shutting it tight and listening as she opened her door. There was a pause and Mutt yipped enthusiastically.

"I know you're there, Badger," she sang, but I didn't answer. She didn't know shit.

The sound of her door pulling shut reached me and I cracked my door open, finding she'd taken the food. Maybe all I had to do was cook my way into her heart; she certainly loved food more than she loved me. So I could try and associate the two.

I crept back out of my room, heading into JJ's and walking up to the black bookshelf he had against one wall. My gaze roamed over the book titles and I frowned, having no fucking idea where to start. The only one I'd heard of was Twilight, so I plucked that off the shelf, figuring it was as good a place as any to begin and headed back to my room.

Three hours later, I was confused.

I'd pretty much been doing exactly what Edward had done to win Bella over. Following her everywhere, protecting her at all costs, stopping her from seeing hot werewolves - AKA other men. I supposed the one thing I hadn't done was the gentleman thing. The old fashioned dating stuff which I was a complete amateur at.

Alright then, Edward Cullen, teach me your sparkly vampire ways.

I read on a few more chapters until an idea came to me and I shot a text to Saint Memphis for a little help on something I was pretty sure the posh bastard would know about.

Fox:

Hey dude. Any chance a guy like you knows what kind of classical music is the most romantic?

Saint:

Hello, 'Dude',

I require more information. Do you mean romantic as in the western classical music associated with the period of the nineteenth century – more commonly referred to as the 'Romantic Era'? Or are you referring to the definition of romantic as in expressing affection to one's counterpart?

Hell, was this guy for real?

Fox:

The second one I think.

Saint:

Suite Bergamasque – Claud Debussy
The Carnival of the Animals - Camille Saint-Saëns
Vesper – New Tide Orquesta
Ombra Mai Fu – Malena Ernman
Serenade, Opus 20: II – Edward Elgar

Fox:

That's a lot of weird words, bro, but thanks.

Saint:

Squid emoji

Fox:

??

Saint:

Forgive me, my girl got hold of my phone.
You are quite welcome. Good night.

I blew out a breath of amusement then built a playlist on my phone from what he'd suggested and headed to my closet, rummaging through all the casual shit I owned until I found one smart white shirt and some nice black pants.

I took a shower and changed into them, styling my hair and eyeing myself in the mirror. I looked...fucking stupid, but I guessed I was Edward Cullen worthy minus the fangs and glittery skin. I flattened a crease in my shirt which hadn't seen daylight since my Great Aunt Nelly's funeral two years ago and kicked on the shiny shoes that went with this outfit.

I headed downstairs and opened the sliding door onto the patio, turning the fairy lights on around the decked area, then grabbing a new box of them which JJ had planned to put up. I strung them across the ground, making a sort of fairylight pathway from the door towards the table. It looked...shit. But maybe Rogue would like it.

I fetched a bottle of wine from the fridge that had been left there since the last party we'd had. I inspected the year on it, but I wasn't sure why as I knew nothing about wine. It was white and looked sort of nice, so I hoped it would taste alright.

I grabbed a couple of wine glasses from the cupboard and headed outside, setting them up on the table before starting the classical music up through the Bluetooth speakers.

Okay...now I just need Rogue.

I shot her a text, wondering if she'd even bother to answer or if I was just going to be left hanging here like an asshole.

Fox:

Drink on the patio?

Rogue:

Hell yeah, I'll come drink your booze, Badge.

I put my phone back in my pocket and stood there like an idiot, wondering what to do with my hands. What would Edward Cullen do?

I folded them, then unfolded them. Then held them behind my back, but that made me feel like a complete twat, so I just tucked them in my pockets and hoped for the best.

Rogue appeared in a little pink sundress, her feet bare and her hair wild. She looked perfectly imperfect. My heart raced and I offered her the most awkward smile in the world as she took me in with her brows rising towards her colourful hairline.

"Err, sorry I think I've stumbled onto the wrong patio, does this one belong to the Duke of Hastings?" She bowed to me, backing up into the kitchen where Mutt was staring at me in confusion, his head cocked to one side.

"Rogue," I growled irritably as she burst out laughing. *Dammit.*

"Excuse me for the intrusion, sire," she mocked me some more, twisting her hand through the air in a flourish. "I shall take my leave and return to the peasant's quarters."

I ran a hand down the back of my neck, heat blazing up my spine. "Fuck off," I said through a nervous laugh. God, I didn't get nervous, what the fuck was I even doing right now?

"Oh my, what a brash mouth for such an upstanding lord of the land," she gasped, holding a hand to her forehead.

"You're not funny," I said, but my mouth was betraying me as I cracked a smile at her continuing to bow and curtsy her way through the kitchen.

"I am not worthy of your liege's grand eyes!" she said dramatically, covering her face with her hands. "Do not look upon thine face of your lesser, sire!"

I ran at her while she wasn't looking, whipping her off her feet into my arms and walking her out onto the patio as she gasped. "This duke wasn't taught any manners, baby. And I'm afraid he spanks his house staff when they take the piss out of him."

"*Fox*," she laughed, trying to wriggle free, but she wasn't going anywhere.

I flipped her face down onto the table, clapping my hand against the back of her thigh, her dress riding up almost high enough for me to see her panties. She looked back over her shoulder at me with parted lips and my cock twitched excitedly at her flushed expression. Mutt yapped, but one sharp look from me silenced him.

I took my hand from the base of her spine, pointing her into a seat and she slid off the table, wetting her lips as I moved to sit beside her, her leg brushing mine.

"Are you wearing cologne?" She leaned in and sniffed my neck and I gnashed my teeth at her, making her jerk back with a laugh.

"I thought girls liked this shit," I muttered, opening the bottle of wine and pouring us both a glass right up to the brim. I took a large gulp of mine and sat back in my seat, figuring I just had to balls this out now. *Ergh, what the fuck is that after taste about?*

"What shit? You dressing like a duke while playing old people music and drinking fancy grape juice?" She sipped her wine and wrinkled her nose.

"It tastes like ass, doesn't it?" I confirmed and she nodded, turning around and spitting it into a potted plant. "Right, fuck this." I got out of my seat, grabbing both glasses of wine and walking off into the kitchen. I tipped them down the drain, took two bottles of beer from the fridge and ripped the caps off with my teeth.

I was gonna have some very stern words with JJ about this Edward Cullen bullshit. Read mommy porn to know what women want? He was definitely having me on.

I re-joined Rogue outside who was going through the Spotify app on my phone and building a new playlist. She started up ily (I love you baby) by Surf

Mess and Emilee and I smirked as I passed her a beer.

"Just one more thing…" She reached out, unbuttoning my shirt and my dick hardened at the slightest scrape of her nails against my chest. If I wasn't totally shitting myself, I was sure her eyes lingered on my flesh for a second, then she placed her beer down and worked to unbutton my sleeve cuffs and roll them up to my elbows. Finally, she shoved her fingers into my hair and I got fully fucking hard as she clawed her hands through it to mess it up, her tits pressed together as she worked and making me stare like a hungry wolf.

"There," she announced and leaned back, leaving me feeling like I'd just been fucked even though she hadn't done a single sexual thing to me. If I got her beneath me for real, the fire between us would burn us up and I'd die a happy man.

"Thanks, baby," I said in a growl, drinking a long swig of my beer as her eyes watched my throat work.

"Don't ever try to be fancy again," she commanded and I smirked, placing my hand on her knee and her pupils dilated as she looked up at me. I ran my fingers in soft circles on the inside of her thigh and a breathy noise left her before she schooled her expression and drank more beer. She didn't push me off though.

My gaze dipped to the fading hickie on her neck and a growl built in my throat. I wanted more than anything to lean in and mark her for myself, brand her as mine, and as she saw where my attention was, she cocked her head to give me an even better look.

"I was never yours, Fox," she said softly, reading my mind. "I never agreed to anything."

"I know," I bit out, looking away over the rippling blue swimming pool and taking my hand from her knee, despite wanting to push it higher and show her who could really make her scream. She would have forgotten all about Maverick the second I was inside her and she'd remember why we'd always been destined for each other too.

She took my hand, her fingers sliding smoothly between mine and the feel of her silken palm against my rough one made me turn my head to look back at her.

"I wanna be friends," she said. "I can't say I'm not still angry at you for a lot of things, but I think I'd like to try and move past it."

"Friends," I echoed coolly, my eyes moving from her full lips to her bright blue eyes. "I can't do friends." My hand tightened on hers and she pouted.

"Well you managed it once," she said. "Or am I just a pussy to you these days?"

"Don't say that," I snarled. "You're not just anything to me. You're everything. Don't you get that yet?"

She frowned at me, seeming confused by my devotion to her, but it was perfectly simple to me. She was looking for the lie in it all, the scheme. But I wasn't playing her. I wanted her and that was it. I'd do whatever it took to have that, even if I had to look past the fact that she'd screwed Maverick and fucking Shawn.

My chest squeezed like a fist and I looked away again. God it was gonna take a lot to get over it, but I could. I could do anything for her. I'd waited ten years to get her back in my life and if she needed longer to figure out that I was meant for her, then fine. I just had to be sure the side-fucking was done, because I already had Shawn and Maverick marked for death, I didn't need that list growing or my heart breaking any further.

Rogue sighed and leaned against my shoulder and I released her hand so I could wrap my arm around her and pull her closer. *Just see me, baby. I'm right here waiting for you.*

"I miss life being simple," she murmured and I stroked my fingers through her hair with a sigh.

"Me too, hummingbird."

"Do you remember the time we swam out to that old shipwreck beyond the cove?"

"Yeah." I smirked. "We were so fucking convinced it had treasure hidden on it."

"Maybe it did, we just couldn't hold our breaths long enough to find out," she insisted and I laughed.

"Chase nearly made it into the hull, but he got attacked by that fish," I said and she burst out laughing with me.

"Oh yeah! It went psycho on him," she snorted. "Then we named it after his Dad."

Her hand pressed to my chest and my laughter stuttered out as her fingers brushed casually back and forth over my abs.

"Do you think he still lives there? Angry old Dylan down in his shipwreck?" she murmured absentmindedly, probably having no idea what she was doing to me right now. My cock was hard as iron and one look down would show her just how turned on she had me.

"I don't think fish live that long," I said as I struggled to concentrate.

"I heard goldfish can live up to twenty years," she countered.

"But it wasn't a goldfish."

"Coulda been the cousin of a goldfish," she said with a shrug and I smirked.

"Well we'll have to take a boat out there and find out if Dylan lives on then," I said and she looked up at me with a mischievous smile.

"Really?" she asked and I nodded.

"Whatever you want, hummingbird."

She leaned in closer and my heart rioted as she wet her lips and my gaze dropped to them, an ache of desire racing through me.

"I like this," she breathed huskily.

"Like what?" I murmured, closing the distance between our mouths by another inch.

Her gaze dipped to my lips then back up again, her long lashes framing her beautiful eyes. "When you're this Fox...old Fox...my Fox."

My breaths came unevenly at those final two words and I lifted my hand to carve my fingers along her jaw and tilt her head up to line her mouth up with mine.

"I'm always your Fox, even when you hate me," I told her and sadness filled her eyes, ten years worth of regret stored right there for me to see. "I'm sorry I fucked up, I'm sorry I broke every promise I ever made to you. I don't deserve a clean slate, but if you ever decide to give me one I'll never tarnish it again, baby, I swear it. And I know that's the word of someone who let you down before and that you don't have a single reason to trust me, but I plan on giving you some new reasons, and reminding you of the old ones while I'm at it."

"Your lies are so pretty," she whispered, leaning closer, heat blazing in her eyes and the same desperate need I felt in my heart mirrored right back at me within them.

"That's because they're truths," I swore, tasting her on my lips before her mouth even touched mine.

"I don't know what to believe anymore," she admitted, her fingers sliding up my chest and knotting in my shirt as she drew me even closer, just a single whisper parting us. My cock throbbed and I fought the urge to grab her with everything I had, needing her to come to me, to prove she wanted this as much as I did.

"Holy mother of a fuck!" Chase barked followed by a thwack.

Mutt dove into my lap, barking loudly and forcing his head between ours, licking my goddamn mouth as he crushed my dick.

My phone started ringing loudly in my pocket and the moment dissolved into thin air as I whipped around, finding Chase on the floor of the patio, his feet tangled in the fairylights path and his elbow cut open on the tiles.

Mutt dove off of my lap, running over to him and peeing on his leg while he was down.

"Ah no!" Chase cried as he tried to get his feet unlocked from the wire. Mutt turned his back on him, kicking his feet back as if trying to bury his pee and catching Chase in the eye with his foot.

"Argh, you little bastard." Chase lunged for him and Mutt scampered away with a yip.

Rogue laughed as I got up, moving to help him, dragging him to his feet as I got the fairy lights off of him.

"What the fuck, man? Are you booby trapping the house now? Why's it so dark out here?" He demanded, then looked me up and down. "And why are you dressed like the Duke of Hastings?"

"Ha! That's what I said," Rogue laughed.

I clenched my teeth in annoyance then inspected the cut on his arm. It was fine, nothing that would need stitches. "What are you doing back here?"

"I forgot my phone and figured I should have it when I went out on the hunt later in case I find anything," he said and I nodded. I couldn't exactly be angry at him for that, though why he'd chosen that exact moment to come home, I'd never know. "I guess I'll change my damn pants now too." He glared at Mutt who blinked innocently out at him from the kitchen.

My phone stopped ringing then immediately started again and I took it out with a sigh, finding my aunt Jolene calling. I guessed the moment was thoroughly ruined now anyway and my boner was definitely gone.

Rogue swept past me, picking up Mutt as she headed inside and started rummaging in the fridge. My gaze moved down her tanned legs beneath the fridge door as I answered the call.

"Hello?"

Rogue danced on her tiptoes as she hunted the shelves for who knew what, but it was all very distracting.

"Hi Fox," Jolene said. "I'm waiting for my man to show up. He might have some information on the whereabouts of Shawn Mackenzie. I think you should get down here."

My pulse picked up and my thoughts sharpened in an instant. "You're at the Dollhouse?" I confirmed.

"Yes."

"Be there soon." I hung up, looking to Chase. "We gotta go. Grab the emergency bag." He strode off at my word and Rogue looked to me for an explanation as she shut the fridge door.

"What's up?"

"I need to go see my aunt about something." I didn't mention Shawn's name, I knew she wanted his death but there was no way I was risking getting her mixed up with him. If Jolene really was about to get information on his location, no piece of it was going to reach her ears. I'd deal with this with my boys and hand her his head when I was finished.

"Fox," she growled. "You've gone all murdery in your eyes, what's going on?"

"Crew business," I clipped, moving into the house and grabbing her arm before pulling her along. I wasn't going to let her out of my sight until I was sure of Shawn's location. He could be waiting to sneak in my back door for all I knew, and I wasn't going to risk leaving her until I had him pinpointed on a GPS with an arsenal of weapons at my back.

Chase reappeared in fresh pants with the bag and we headed for the

241

garage as Mutt barked at our heels, sensing the change of energy.

"You don't have to drag me, I'm coming anyway," Rogue said, snatching her arm out of my grip.

"Fine, just stay close," I commanded and she kicked some flip-flops on by the stairs.

I noticed Chase flanking her other side before we descended into the garage, sure he didn't even realise how protective he was of her.

I waited for Rogue to get into the middle seat of my truck with Mutt on her lap before getting in the driver's side and Chase pressed up against her, holding a pistol in his grip. His eyes were shadowed and his jaw set. He was on point tonight, my boy wide awake and without the cloud of alcohol in his head for once. This Chase was lethal, sharp witted and one of the best shots I knew.

I strapped Rogue's seatbelt in place before I hit the gas and took off out of the garage, dropping my hand to graze over the gun in my door pocket to reassure myself of its closeness. I was on high alert as we headed out of the gates and pulled up alongside Basset and Eddie, dropping my window and whistling at them to catch their attention. Basset was tall, lanky and blonde and Eddie was a foot shorter but twice as muscly.

"Get in the back." I jerked my thumb at the bed of my truck and they jumped in obediently.

I took a winding route through the backstreets of Sunset Cove for fear of an ambush. I did that whenever I went anywhere lately, making sure I never took the same route too often. I had to be unpredictable, never set a routine that Shawn's men could be taking note of, working a plan around. Nothing that could get me, my boys, or my girl killed.

I soon headed up to the cliffs where the Dollhouse was nestled, the shining lights of it glinting from miles away before we made it there. Music pounded through the air and bikini-clad girls were scattered everywhere around the huge pool out front and along the first level balcony of the massive white walled building. Party goers filled the place, dancing and drinking as they stumbled around.

I parked up on the grass and we poured out of the vehicle, my hand locking around Rogue's. I wasn't sure if it was because she sensed the danger in the air tonight or if she just knew how much I needed to hold onto her right then, but she didn't pull it free. I tucked my gun into the back of my jeans, while Chase kept his in his grip.

Basset and Eddie jumped out of the back of the truck, moving around me like a shield. I wasn't exactly expecting Shawn to show up in the middle of the Dollhouse, but you never could be too careful when a maniac was hunting your ass.

I led Rogue along through the wild party, and people gasped and dove out of our way as their eyes fell on my face. Mutt growled in Rogue's arms, clearly not liking the place and when one girl tried to stroke him, he nearly took her finger off.

I headed up to Jolene's office and knocked firmly on the door.

"Come in!" she called and I turned to Rogue.

"Stay here," I told her. "Basset and Eddie will watch you."

"Can't I just head off for a drink?" she asked, gazing at the party a little wistfully.

"No," I growled then snapped my fingers at my men, pointing at her. They immediately closed in around her and she huffed, blowing a lock of pastel blue hair out of her eyes.

I headed into the office with Chase and he pushed the door closed behind us.

Chester was sitting behind the desk in a vibrant purple shirt that had several buttons undone, revealing his tanned, muscular chest. His blonde moustache looked freshly groomed and his blue eyes immediately whipped to Jolene in the chair beside him for instruction. Her fair hair was pulled up into a ponytail and she was in all black tonight with dark eyeliner to match.

"Evening boys," she said. "I'm afraid my man's not back yet, but it won't be too long." She drummed her nails on the desk, her gaze flicking to the iPad beside her and her drumming fingers halting. "Who's the girl?"

I guessed she had CCTV on her screen, but I couldn't see it from the angle I was at.

"She's mine," I said fiercely and Jolene glanced quickly at Chester before smiling at me.

"She's pretty," my aunt commented.

"She's a goddess," Chase corrected and I shot him a glare as he cleared his throat. He seemed kind of confused as to why he'd said it himself and he just shrugged at me before I turned away.

Jolene's eyes moved from Chase to me as she thought on something. "Is she informed of what's going on?"

"No," I growled. "She's not part of the Crew."

"Ah yes," Jolene clucked her tongue. "No women allowed." She rolled her eyes. "My brother is such a fool."

"Now, now, darling," Chester said, chortling uncomfortably as he patted her hand. "Let's not bad mouth Luther. He has his reasons, doesn't he Fox?" He turned to me with a simpering smile and I shrugged.

"Yes he does, because the only weakness he's ever had is a woman," Jolene said with a light laugh. "Ironic, isn't it? That the terrifying Luther Harlequin is afraid of the opposite sex. He'd do better to realise our power would only strengthen the Harlequins tenfold."

"True, my dear, but let's not question Luther's ways," Chester implored with an undercurrent of *especially not in front of his son.*

"Well I'll be sure to file your complaint to the boss," I said dryly just to make Chester shit his pants and he released a nervous fart that said I'd gotten close.

"Jesus," Chase muttered, wafting his hand in front of his nose and Jolene sighed disappointedly, getting up to crack a window.

"You're dressed very interestingly tonight, nephew," Jolene commented, looking me up and down. My shirt was still hanging open to reveal the tattoos marking my chest and I shrugged, not really giving a shit. Except I wished I'd changed my shoes because if I headed out into a shoot up tonight, I did not wanna be running around in these.

Note to self: take someone's shoes before I leave here.

The door suddenly flew open and a man with scraggly black hair jogged in, shoving the door shut behind him and throwing me a fearful look. He opened and closed his mouth a few times, apparently starstruck and I had the urge to punch him in the face until he got the words out.

"Speak," I commanded and he threw a look at Jolene who nodded firmly in encouragement.

"Go ahead, Cyril," she urged.

"He's staying out in a trailer in the woods behind Carnival Hill," he blurted. "I seen him with my own two eyes." He took a phone from his pocket, bringing up a photo and offering it to me.

I gazed at the photograph of Shawn Mackenzie with his smug handsome face and his stupid stubbled jaw with his shitty dark hair and his fucking smarmy mouth that had gotten way too close to my girl, chatting with a couple of men around a fire outside a trailer in the woods.

"Have you got a location?" I growled, excitement swirling through my blood.

"Yes, sir," he said, taking the phone back and showing it to me on the map. When I had it locked into my own phone, I turned to Chase.

"We'll head down there, bring an army and give him no chance of escape," I said.

"Go with him, Cyril," Jolene commanded her man. "Make sure he finds it."

"Yes, ma'am," he answered.

"You can ride with us," I told him, walking to the door.

"You can leave the girl here at the club if you like? I'll have someone watch her," Jolene called to me and I glanced back with a shake of my head.

"I'll have my men take her home," I growled. "Thanks for the info, Aunt, I'll make sure you're compensated for it if it pays off."

"Be careful, Fox," she called and I nodded, marching to the door with my heart thumping furiously in anticipation of the coming kill. I was going hunting. And tonight, Shawn Mackenzie was going to find out how high the price was for hurting my girl.

CHAPTER FIFTEEN

The door opened and Fox strode out with a face like thunder and Chase right beside him looking just as murderous.

"Where's the fire?" I asked, hopping up from the floor where I'd been playing with Mutt and striding away from the two goons who had been left to watch me.

"Something's come up," Fox growled, his gaze sliding over me before shifting to my watchdogs who had made their way right back to my sides already.

"Basset, Eddie, take her home to Harlequin House and lock her inside. You don't take your fucking eyes off of her." Fox tossed them the keys to his truck and I snatched them out of the air before Basset could catch them.

"Err, no thanks," I interjected. "I'm coming with you."

"Not a chance in hell," Fox growled. "I need you where you're safe." He caught my wrist and forced me to release the key back into his possession before handing it to Basset. "Rogue, if you give even one shit about my authority, you won't make this difficult," he said firmly, tugging me close so that I was engulfed in his shadow. "Just do as you're told and don't mess me about on this. I need to know you're safe tonight. I'm not letting anything happen to my girl."

I pouted at him and he nodded like that was some kind of agreement before shoving me back into Eddie's sweaty hands.

"Be good, little one." Chase winked at me before slapping a hand to Fox's shoulder and turning away with him.

I scowled at their backs as they headed off through the crowd and Eddie forced me to turn another way as he began to lead me towards Fox's truck. I whistled for Mutt and he bounded over, hopping up into my arms and giving me a relieved look. I was pretty sure clubbing wasn't his scene.

I let him push me along until we were out of sight then turned around abruptly, forcing his hands off of me and looking up at him sweetly.

"I need to pee," I said in my most innocent voice. Honestly I was practically passing for a saint right about now. I probably had a halo glowing around my head and everything.

"Hold it," he grunted.

"Rude," I replied. "And no. I have low bladder control and I can't hold it. Fox won't want me to pee in his truck. And if I do, that'll all be on you, bucko."

Eddie glowered at me then cut Basset a look which was met with a shrug.

"Look, there's a sign for the little girl's room. I'll be in and out in a shake of a lamb's tail," I said, pointing across the dimly lit room beyond the gyrating hips of a man in a pink PVC catsuit. He was really working it too and I was kinda jealous of his moves.

"You have two minutes," Eddie growled, nudging me towards the bathroom and earning himself a snarl from Mutt who was still nestled close in my arms.

I skipped away from him and hurried through the room, pushing my way into the bathroom and sidestepping the line of women waiting to pee as the door swung shut between me and my bodyguards.

"Don't mind me, I'm not cutting," I promised the other girls as I made my way around them, glancing at the toilet stalls which held no doors where substances were being snorted and one girl was getting eaten out by another, and one woman was just shamelessly shitting. When you gotta go, you gotta go I guessed.

I slipped past them all, tossed a smile at the women who were reapplying lipstick in the tarnished mirror above the sinks and grinned as I found what I'd been hoping for - a window.

See ya, suckers.

I hopped up onto the sink beneath it and pushed the dark glass wide, my eyebrows arching in confusion as I found an empty corridor beyond it instead of a way outside. Still, it was in the opposite direction to the two assholes Fox had left babysitting me, so I was gonna take it.

I tucked Mutt close under one arm then swung a leg out the window before managing to squeeze my ass through and drop down on the other side.

Mutt wriggled in my grip, so I set him on his little feet and he yipped excitedly before turning left and scampering away. I'd been going to pick right, but I trusted him, so I followed.

He led me along until we reached a staircase which disappeared down into a dark space where the heavy thump of a deep bass reached me.

The sound of angry shouts came from behind me, so it was a no-brainer as I broke into a run and followed Mutt down into the dungeon - I mean basement, but it totally had a dungeon vibe.

At the foot of the stairs, a set of double doors swung open and I sucked in a sharp breath as a woman in a gimp suit stepped through. She flinched as she spotted me then shook her head like I was irritating her.

"Hurry up, the show is about to start." She pointed behind her and I quickly ran through the door with Mutt close at my heels, finding a corridor beyond it with a line of closed doors either side of it.

"Come on," a dude called, giving me an impatient look as he held a door open for me halfway along the corridor and I jogged up to him as the sound of Basset and Eddie's hunt drew closer to me from outside.

I slipped into the dark room which was only lit by a few dark purple strobe lights and the guy pointed me towards the one empty chair left of the six, all of them circling a small stage where a man stood with his back to me. It was too dark for me to see much of him aside from the fact that he was wearing some kind of huge mask, but I focused on getting my ass in a chair because the men and women spread out in the other seats all seemed to be waiting for me.

Mutt scampered under my seat and the dude who had been holding the door moved towards me, pushing a small cart.

"The show is an even hundred," he said to me in a low voice. "Each splosh you partake in is an extra twenty if you toss it, and fifty if you apply it by hand. Got it?"

I parted my lips to ask what a splosh was, but he was already hurrying away and I was left to inspect the contents of the cart he'd left parked up before me.

Music started and the lights above the dancer waiting on the stage brightened as he began to flex and grind with his ass pointed at me, but my gaze was fixed on the selection of items before me.

There was a tin of red paint and a tin of green. A tube of chocolate sauce and a can of squirty cream as well as a bowl of jelly, some custard and several other wet concoctions which I couldn't easily name.

Before I had to call out to ask what all of that shit was for, something wet splashed against my cheek and I gasped as I looked up, finding the woman on the opposite side of the stage to me had just thrown a tin of blue paint at the dancer's crotch and I'd been caught in the crossfire.

The large man to my right groaned loudly, filling his hand with squirty cream before sliding it inside his pants.

My eyebrows arched all the way up to my rainbow hairline as I quickly looked away from that unsavoury show and looked back at the dancer.

He'd dropped to his hands and knees before me, his ass flexing up and down in a pair of black latex boxer briefs and a giant, black crow's face mask on his head bobbing up and down.

He crawled towards the woman who had thrown the paint and she tipped her bowl of chocolate sauce into her hand before running her palm down from his shoulder to his wrist with a sigh. "You like getting all dirty for us, don't you, big boy?"

The dancer remained silent as he continued to bounce his ass to the music before dropping into a press-up which contained a hip roll against the floor and ended in him hopping back to his feet.

More of the men and women threw the contents of their trays at him and he began to rub it over his bare flash as the dude who had let me in here took note of everything on a clipboard, no doubt to charge these fuckers for every drop spilled before they left.

Good luck to him getting any money out of me though. I was fresh out. But I was fast so I wasn't worried.

The dancer turned to his left, rotating on the stage so that everyone could get a good look at his body from every angle and as he moved to face me, I sucked in a sharp breath which left my jaw hanging open.

"No, fucking, way," I breathed, spotting the swallow tattoos that dove beneath his waistband just as JJ started rubbing the whipped cream down his chest with both hands.

He froze solid, hips thrusted towards me, paint and food dripping down onto the stage and the eyes of the crow mask he wore to conceal his face seeming to bug out of its ghastly head.

Mutt barked excitedly, choosing that moment to leap up onto the stage and lick some cream from the top of JJ's bare foot and the music just so happened to come to an end.

Another track began to play, but the clipboard dude seemed to have noticed JJ's inanimate state, not to mention the dog on stage and he quickly shut it off, clapping loudly just as the cream pants dude came with a loud groan to my left.

The other patrons all clapped a little belatedly, some pouting and others seeming to be pleased that they'd gotten what they came for.

A big, fat, motherfucker of a grin pulled at my lips and I started clapping too, nice big claps, spaced out long enough to break the tension in JJ's pose as he quickly bowed for the others like the act had always meant to end there.

"Gimme a minute with this one," JJ's muffled voice came from within the mask as I just kept grinning and the clipboard dude nodded while ushering the others out.

"Hey, I thought you said he wasn't for sale?" one of the women complained as she was forced to leave too but the door swung shut before I could hear the guy's reply to her.

"Rogue," JJ croaked out, reaching up to grasp the sides of his mask, but I held up a finger.

"One sec," I commanded, snatching my sparkly pink cell phone out of my bra and quickly snapping a shot of him standing there all smothered in food and paint.

"Delete that," JJ growled, yanking the crow mask off and tossing it aside. His raven hair was all tussled within it, a faint line of sweat coating his brow. "What are you doing here?"

"Shit, Johnny James, I knew you were a kinky fucker, but is there even a name for what I just witnessed?" I asked him, snorting a laugh as he tried to swipe the worst of it from his skin.

"Yes," he growled. "It's called sploshing. Now answer my question."

"Fox told a couple of dickheads to take me home like a good girl while him and Chase went off to play gangster. So obviously I faked a need for a bathroom break, ditched them and then ran down a deserted corridor until I was led into a fetish room which is where I discovered this." I gestured a hand at his filthy body, but before he could answer, the sound of Basset and Eddie yelling my name came from the corridor outside.

"Shit, they can't see me here," JJ growled, hopping down off of the stage and grabbing my wrist before hauling me out through a curtain I hadn't even noticed.

I let him drag me along until we made it to a brightly lit dressing room where men and women were changing into all kinds of weird and wonderful costumes, and he didn't let go of me until we were stood outside a shower unit in the far corner.

JJ set the water running and Mutt yelped in frustration as he leapt away from his whipped cream feast on JJ's foot.

"Fox will lose his shit when he realises you're gone again," JJ growled.

"So tell him I'm with you," I suggested.

"He can't know I'm here. I didn't even bring my phone," JJ replied, dropping his latex boxers so that his beautiful manscaped cock was on show for the world to see as he stepped beneath the flow of hot water to rinse the food and paint from his flesh.

I licked my lips as I watched him scrub his skin clean and the water ran over each defined muscle on his body.

"You like what you see?" he taunted and I shrugged one shoulder.

"You make a living out of knowing how hot you are, Johnny James.

I'm not going to blow more smoke up your ass. I'll leave that to your paying clients." My own words were a stinging reminder of the way Fox had accused JJ of claiming any hole that got near enough to him and I turned away, inspecting the dirty tiles on the wall to my right instead of the demigod washing beside me.

"Do you have a problem with that?" JJ challenged.

"I know that people do what they have to to make a living," I replied with a shrug. "It's not my preference, but you do you, JJ. I can't say I'm much of a one for fetishes, but whatever pays your way I guess."

The water shut off and I refused to look as JJ towelled off and quickly got dressed into a pair of sweats and a tank top in my periphery. He moved up close behind me as he finished, murmuring in my ear. "Everyone has the odd fetish or fantasy, pretty girl. Even you."

I shook my head as I turned to look at him but shouts came from the far end of the dressing room and I heard those assholes calling my name again.

"Let's go," JJ hissed, taking my hand and tugging me down so that we were ducking as we scrambled across the room towards a door which was half hidden behind a rack of sparkling costumes.

A woman was standing by the door and as we made it to her she smiled at us, not seeming to notice the fact that we were trying to hide as she passed JJ a fistful of cash and told him she looked forward to seeing him tomorrow.

I had so many questions, but during this cat and mouse game with the Harlequin goons really wasn't the time, so I let JJ tug me along as he pushed the door wide and fresh air finally greeted me.

Mutt scampered after us as we jogged up a set of concrete steps and we soon found ourselves back on ground level in the parking lot at the back of the Dollhouse.

"Fox will be losing his shit if they've told him they lost you already," JJ groaned as he led me over to his orange Mustang.

"So let's go where he least expects to find me then," I suggested. "Harlequin House."

JJ chuckled as he opened my door for me and I slid inside while Mutt hopped into the footwell.

But by the time JJ dropped down behind the driver's seat and we were heading back along the streets towards his home, silence fell heavily between us again.

"What?" he asked eventually and I cast about for a reasonable thing to be pissed at, settling on one without overthinking it.

"Did you steal the keys I had hidden in my trailer?" I blurted.

I counted to three, wondering if he'd be honest or not and when he finally replied, I was pleased that he at least gave me that much credit and didn't try to bullshit me.

"I did," he agreed darkly. "How did you know it was me?"

"Because I know it wasn't Chase and I realised that Fox would have already gone all Badger on me if he knew. He'd have tried to spank my ass raw and make me repent. But not you. You're the thinker, J. You don't do anything without going over all of the possible outcomes and then aiming for the best results. So I'm guessing you realised Fox would freak out if he knew and that Chase would try and use it as ammo to get rid of me for good, so you decided that you were the best keeper of that little secret for now."

"What do you want me to say, pretty girl? I wasn't just going to leave them there for anyone to find. And I'm not going to let you use them against us either."

"I'd need all five to do anything with them and you know it. You have no right to keep them from me."

I ground my teeth as I fought the urge to yell and JJ scowled out at the road which was lit up with his headlights before us.

"Well I'm not giving them back," he replied.

"Why not?"

"Because I don't know if I can trust you."

"You trusted me enough to fuck me though, right? Although you moved on fast enough, so I don't know why I'm even wondering about that."

"Is that hurt I hear in your tone, pretty girl?" JJ asked and I could have sworn there was a touch of hope in there.

"No," I said quickly. "It's not like I thought I was special to you. I was just one in a list of many, right?"

JJ pushed his tongue into his cheek as he stared at the road and I swear the silence was so loud it hurt my damn ears.

"Well it's not like you waited around for me either, is it? You were quick enough to jump into Maverick's bed the moment I was out of sight."

"That's different," I shot back, my cheeks flushing.

"How?"

"Because it's Rick," I replied lamely. "He was one of us once."

JJ frowned in thought. "So does that mean you're gonna hook up with Chase and Fox too?"

"What if I did?" I asked instead of just saying no for some insane reason. "Would it change us?"

"No," I said instantly, knowing it was true.

"Maybe it is different then," he muttered. "But only with the five of us." He gave me a hard look and I nodded in agreement.

He seemed to accept the ridiculous logic of that for some reason and let it drop.

We turned off of the road and I ducked low in my chair as the Harlequins on duty at the gate let us in. JJ drove straight down into the underground garage and quickly shut off his engine. The lights died and we were plunged into darkness, just me and him alone in his car with nothing but the night air to hear us.

"You know that's bullshit though, don't you?" he asked me in a low tone, his gaze still forward.

"What is?"

"The part about me going straight back out on the game the second I'd had you. You don't seriously believe that, do you?"

"I literally just found you doing some kind of funky fetish thing for a group of admirers while they jacked themselves off and smooshed you."

"*Sploshed.* And I wasn't fucking any of them, was I? In fact, none of them were touching my cock, were they? And I wasn't even letting them look at it either."

"So...what? You expect me to believe that you aren't fucking for cash anymore? Even though the others were literally calling you out on it in front of me a few days ago?"

"They don't know," he said angrily and I arched a brow. JJ rarely got angry like that, but the acid in his tone said he really was pissed. "Why do you think I was working in the fucking Dollhouse doing fetish performances? I'm not fucking for cash anymore which means my cut is coming in low. Fetish work might be a bit odd, but as it doesn't turn me on in any way and I'm not fucking anyone I just think of it as unusual stripping."

"You're right about that," I snorted. "Covering your lickable body in paint shouldn't turn anyone on. It needs to be bare and free and maybe a little oiled up, but that's it for me. They can keep their paint and shit."

JJ breathed a laugh, his hands curling around the steering wheel in the dark. "Like I said, pretty girl, you probably have some fetishes too. Or at least a few hot fantasies. I bet you're not against being restrained. Or using a few toys. Maybe you'd have a thing for balloons if you gave it a go."

"Erm, no, I don't wanna stuff a balloon animal up my vag. But I guess if you wanna dress up as the Green Power Ranger for me and come save me from the bad guys then I wouldn't mind sucking a cock out of gratitude."

"Okay, so Power Ranger role-play and kidnapping bits turn you on, huh? I'll remember that."

"What are you going to do? Jump me while wearing a ski mask and see if I let you fuck me in the back of your psycho van?"

"Strokes for all folks," he purred, turning my way at last. "But I meant what I said Rogue - Johnny D has been out of action since he got a taste of you. Hell, he'll only even get hard if I'm thinking of you. It's only you."

Suddenly the air in the car was too thick and my chest was rising and falling too heavily. I'd heard those words and the truth in them, and it had lit something blazing inside of me which I didn't dare lay a name to.

"But I know you don't feel the same," he went on. "I get it. I'm the mistake you made. I know you don't feel-"

I leaned forward to stop his words and JJ groaned hungrily as my lips met with his. My hand slid up the back of his neck and my mouth parted for his tongue as his hand found my waist and he tried to tug me closer.

I was giving in. I could feel it. His words and his closeness and this sexy fucking car had me going all dick blinded again and I was about to lose my damn head to this man.

With a wrench of determination, I drew back, panting slightly as I grasped the door handle and damn near fell on my ass out of the car as I pushed it wide and got out.

"You can't keep running from me forever, pretty girl," JJ growled as I began to back up and I wasn't certain if I was insane or horny or just fucking lost over this man and the memories my heart held for him, but the words that passed my lips in reply were entirely of their own making and I was in no way responsible for a single one of them.

"Maybe I'm just waiting for you to catch me."

I turned and ran as I struck him with that challenge and as I raced up the stairs towards the house, a shaky, desperate laugh escaped me because I was almost certain that they might be true.

CHAPTER SIXTEEN

"**W**here are you, man? Answer your fucking phone," I growled into JJ's voicemail then hung up for the tenth time. I'd jacked a car parked at the Dollhouse and we'd taken all the guns from Fox's truck, leaving it for Basset and Eddie to take Rogue home. *Fuck you Basset. Oh, did you get left out of this job? Sucks to suck.*

I made sure all of our guns were loaded and that I had at least a couple of small knives concealed across my body. My adrenaline levels were raging and my bloodlust followed. I had more than a few reasons to despise Shawn Mackenzie even though I'd never met the asshole, but now I had one that overrode them all. And despite all the shit between us and how much I hated the girl, I still wasn't going to let some scum hurt her and get away with it.

Fox drove like a maniac through the streets until we approached Carnival Hill.

Cyril sat in the back seat, quiet and seeming nervous as we approached our destination. I doubted the dude had planned on coming along for the showdown tonight, but it was better to rely on a guy who'd been to Shawn's exact location than being distracted using our phones to try and lock down his trailer in the woods. Once Cyril had done his part, he could fuck off back to

Jolene for all I cared. He directed Fox to park up on a dark road before we got anywhere close enough to the woodland beyond the hill to raise suspicions.

We filed out of the car and an owl hooted close by, but all else was quiet. I strapped two handguns to my hips and placed a bag on my back full of ammo, hoping it would be enough to end this motherfucker for good.

"There's a trail up this way," Cyril said, wiping a line of sweat from his brow. He had a gun at his hip and a knife in his hand, but it was clear the guy's jitteriness meant he'd be no good in a fight.

"Don't be a liability, Cyril," Fox growled and the guy nodded, straightening his spine and marching up the road to lead the way.

Fox checked his phone as we followed then tucked it into the back of his fancy trousers. He'd stolen some guy's sneakers in the Dollhouse and had swapped his white shirt out for a black one. Why had he even been dressed like an asshole? To impress Rogue? Since when had she ever been impressed by that shit? She loved mocking posh twats for their stupid ass clothes and quaffed hair, why would he think she was into that? The dude could pull any girl in town with nothing but a look, but when it came to Rogue Easton he reverted to being an awkward teenager with no game. It was kind of sad to watch, especially knowing JJ had been fucking her right under his nose.

We followed Cyril off of the road as he pushed through some foliage into the trees and we found a narrow animal track beyond it. We hurried along behind him, climbing Carnival Hill and veering deep into the woodland. After a while, Cyril pointed to a dirt road a hundred yards away.

"That's how they get in and out," he whispered. "I tracked one of their trucks this way."

He'd already briefed us on what to expect. Five armed men including Shawn were staying out here, keeping hidden from the world. Fox and I could probably take them alone, but he'd called Luther in anyway and he was bringing reinforcements too just to be on the safe side. He'd told us to scout out Shawn's camp and nothing more, but if I got a good shot at the motherfucker, I wasn't making any promises tonight. This was personal. Maybe not to me, but to Rogue. Punishing the asshole who'd hurt her was my duty. Well, it used to be. Now…everything was fucked. But I still felt that allegiance in me deep down. You hurt one of my own, you die. I wasn't going to overthink it beyond that.

Cyril slowed his pace and we followed suit as he glanced back at us with a look that told us to be quiet. Then we crept slowly after him and voices carried through the trees, men hollering and laughing and the crackle of a fire. I glimpsed the flames as we drew nearer in the shadows, hugging the trees to hide our movements.

When we reached a wide oak tree close to the camp, we huddled against it and cautiously looked around the sides. There was a large trailer at the heart of a clearing, the lights were on in inside and the door was wide open. Four men sat around a fire outside it and beyond that were three parked trucks. I couldn't see Shawn among the chatting Dead Dogs, but a large shadow suddenly blotted out the light of the trailer doorway and the motherfucker in question stepped outside.

Shawn was shirtless, wearing dark jeans and a leather belt with a gleaming silver buckle in the shape of a horseshoe. He had a shotgun in his hand which he casually rested on his shoulder as he moved to join the men by the fire. His body was covered in tattoos, but the one that snagged my attention most was the word *violence* which curved along his collarbone and a large dog skull across his right pec which was the symbol of his gang.

"I'm starting to think Rogue has a type," I murmured to Fox as we ducked back behind the tree and his jaw ticked at those words.

"Yeah, men who are soon to be dead at my hands," he growled and I thought of JJ with a knot in my gut.

Cyril crouched in the shadows beyond Fox, seeming on edge and I was wondering if it was best if we told him to get out of here before he trembled loud enough to give us away. He was obviously just a scout, and this kind of dirty work did not suit guys like him.

"Has he answered yet?" Fox breathed and I checked my phone for any sign of a response from JJ. Nothing.

I shook my head, shoving my phone away with a curse as a roar of booming laughter sounded from the camp, making my teeth clench. *Laugh your last laugh, Shawn. You're on borrowed time.*

"How far away is Luther?" I hissed and Fox checked his watch.

"He should be here in fifteen minutes," he whispered and my muscles coiled with frustration. "Just hang tight," he commanded and though my instincts warred with that order, I managed to force myself to stand there and wait.

After a couple of minutes, Fox's phone rang, the screen flashing but no sound coming out. He answered it, keeping his voice to a whisper. "What?... *Fuck*, find her you idiot. If she's not back at Harlequin House by the time I'm home, you'll pay for it." He hung up and I shuffled closer to him with a question in my eyes, but I'd picked up the gist of what was wrong. Rogue. As per fucking usual.

"She's given them the slip," he muttered, his gaze furious and I tutted under my breath.

"Bring them out here then, boys, I'm getting bored," Shawn's loud voice reached us and I shared a look with Fox, freezing for a moment as I feared he meant *us*.

But as I cast a look around the tree, I saw his men hauling a couple out the back of one of the trucks, a man with sandy hair and a pretty girl with large brown eyes. My heart clenched hard as I recognised the guy as a Harlequin. Ned Dorkins and his girl Hannah.

"*Fox*," I hissed and he moved to look as my heart pounded furiously in my chest.

The couple were thrown to their knees in front of Shawn and the asshole swaggered a step closer to them, swinging his shotgun between them as Hannah screamed and tried to shrink away from the barrel. He rested it against Ned's forehead, his finger slipping onto the trigger.

"Boom," Shawn said loudly, making Ned jerk backwards with a yell of terror and his girlfriend scream in panic. Their hands were tied behind their backs and my throat tightened as I watched.

We had to do something. We couldn't just let them die.

Shawn's men laughed obnoxiously, moving closer to enjoy the show and I twisted around to look at Fox. His eyes were dark with thoughts as he decided what to do, but there wasn't fucking time for that.

"We have to go," I growled, about to move into a better position, but he grabbed my arm, his fingers digging in as he pulled me back.

"Wait," he hissed. "Something's not right."

"You're telling me," I shot back in a whisper. "He's gonna kill them if we don't act now."

"Your girl won't look so pretty when her brains are splattered all over the floor now, will she?" Shawn taunted.

"Please," Ned begged. "Don't hurt her. She's not in the Crew, she's not your enemy. Let her go."

"Nah," Shawn said dismissively. "I'm not gonna do that, sunshine. I'm gonna watch you watch her die."

"*Fox*," I snarled.

Cyril looked ready to take off into the trees and Fox was doing fucking nothing except thinking. But we didn't have time for a plan. Shawn could pull that trigger at any second.

"Say goodbye to your girl," Shawn said as she screamed and Ned started begging. "My camp could use a little splash of colour."

"Please, I'll do anything!" Ned yelled.

"I'll get closer and take the shot," Fox decided. "You stay here."

"No," I growled and his eyes flared with my defiance.

"That's an order," he snarled then slid out from behind the tree and moved away in the direction of our enemies.

I watched as he crept quickly along between the trees like a wraith in the dark as he closed the distance between him and the camp. When he was on the very edge of the circle of light, he raised his gun and my heart beat like a drum as he lined it up with Shawn's head.

"Three," Shawn barked. "Two…"

A gun barrel pressed to my temple and my blood ran cold as I turned just enough to see Cyril's shaking hands around the weapon. "Get up," he growled with more confidence than before and my breaths came furiously as I did as he asked. *Oh fuck.* "Drop your gun and the bag."

I let the weapon slip from my fingers and tossed the bag from my back, my mind reeling and anger spewing through me. He took the other gun from my hip and threw it away into the trees before patting me down and locating the concealed knives across my body.

"You motherfucker," I spat as he tossed my blades away into the undergrowth. "You're one seriously dead piece of shit."

Cyril didn't answer, finishing up his hunt for weapons with shaky hands and keeping the gun levelled at my head.

"One and three quarters," Shawn called as the screams grew louder. "One and a half."

"Move," Cyril commanded.

"This is a bad idea, asshole," I warned.

"Get moving," he snipped.

"One and a quarter," Shawn called as I rounded the tree and all my hope dissolved as I saw Fox being manhandled by two men, dragging him out of the trees with a gun pointed at his head.

My world came crashing down before me as Cyril forced me to move faster and Shawn smoothly lifted the shotgun and rested it on his shoulder, turning to Fox as he was dragged towards him with no hint of surprise in his gaze.

"You ruthless asshole," Shawn laughed at Fox. "You were really gonna let poor Ned die, weren't you?"

Fox said nothing, his eyes going to that dark place as he glared at his enemy and promised him his end.

I walked out into the light before I was shoved to my knees at Fox's side. Cyril tossed my phone at Shawn's feet as one of the men who'd caught Fox threw his phone down alongside it.

Shawn grinned widely, looking between us. "Who's your pretty boyfriend, Foxy?" he asked with a smirk.

"I'm Chase Cohen," I spat. "The guy who's going to slit your fucking throat."

"Oh-ho, this one's got balls, boys." He strode towards me, gazing down his nose and inspecting me. "Look at those big blue eyes," he purred. "They'd look mighty good on my mantlepiece, sunshine." He gripped my chin, looking right at me like I was a sacrifice ready for slaughter. "Mmhm, *very* nice." He stepped towards Fox and fisted a hand in his hair and my brother jerked against his hold, a snarl curling his upper lip. "Don't worry, don't worry, I'm not gonna shoot you yet. We've got miles more fun to have while we wait for Daddy Harlequin to arrive. Now lemme see… where was I? Oh yeah."

He swung around sharply, whipping the shotgun off his shoulder and firing. The bang resounded in my skull as Hannah hit the ground, her chest cleaved wide open as she died in an instant. My head rang with terror, my heart thumping so fast I was sure it was going to detonate.

Ned's screams tangled with the night air as Shawn pumped the shotgun and fired another round into his chest, silencing him for good as he was thrown back onto the ground in a bloody mess beside his girl.

Birds took off from the trees, roused from their sleep and terrified by the noise. My head kept repeating that noise over and over again as Shawn wheeled back towards us with blood speckling his chest and face, licking a line of it off his lips. His gaze flicked to Cyril behind me and his smile vanished like it had never existed.

"You did good, boy. But you look like one good arm twist could spill all your secrets. That's okay though, because I have a solution." He pumped the gun again and Cyril didn't even have a chance to run as Shawn fired and hot wet blood spilled over my back as the shot hit its target. "Dead men tell no tales."

I froze, turning my head as Cyril's body hit the ground with a hard thump and a line of his blood trickled down my forehead into my eye. I wiped it away, dragging in a ragged breath as I stared at his headless body in shock.

Shawn whooped excitedly. "Did you see that, boys? His head exploded like a firework!" He mimed out what had happened to Cyril and his men all laughed loudly, sending a shiver of dread under my skin.

I looked to Fox and he met my gaze, panic twisting in my chest and though he showed no sign of being rattled, I knew my brother well enough to know he was. And that scared me more than the asshole in front of us, because if Fox Harlequin didn't have an answer, there wasn't one.

Shawn ordered his men to bring him a chair and he dropped into it, resting his ankle on his knee as a Dead Dog offered him a cigar and lit it for him. He puffed on the end, resting his shotgun across his lap and I mentally did a count of the men in the camp. Ten total, but who knew if there were more hiding in the woods? We'd been fucking stupid to come here before Luther had shown up. And even more stupid to trust that motherfucker Cyril. And I truly feared we were going to pay for that stupidity in blood.

CHAPTER SEVENTEEN

JJ grinned at me across the kitchen island as I gripped the end of it, waiting for him to make his move. He'd been chasing me all around the house and he finally had me cornered. There was something to that smile now. It was more than just the fun of the game we were playing. There was a hunger to it, a darkness and a whisper of the bad deeds he'd committed in the time we'd been apart. This wasn't a boy playing cat and mouse with me, it was a man used to winning when he embarked upon a hunt.

"You really shouldn't have taunted me, pretty girl," JJ purred, his gaze drinking me in as I blew a lock of lilac hair out of my eyes.

"I'm not afraid of you, Johnny James," I replied, my gaze flicking to the patio doors as I wondered if I could get to them and turn the key in the lock to open them before he caught me. "I still remember that time we saw a shark while we were out on Luther's boat and you damn near screamed like a little girl."

JJ barked a laugh but the second I tried to run for the patio doors, he was right on my heels like he'd already figured out my plan. I darted left instead, circling the table and racing back into the kitchen to put the island between us again. I tried to keep it that way, but JJ leapt up onto it like some kind of freaking monkey.

I gasped as his sneakers hit the counter and in the next breath, he was jumping down right in front of me.

His hand shot out and caught my wrist, yanking me towards him before shoving me back against the fridge and taking my mouth with his. His almond oil scent surrounded me and it was the most appetising thing in the world right then.

He kissed me hard and I moaned softly, my lips parting for his tongue as he teased it inside, his fingers maintaining their hold on my wrist so that I couldn't escape him again.

JJ's free hand found the hem of my pink sun dress and he drew it upwards, the material kissing my sensitised flesh as it skimmed over it and I arched my back, giving him the room to tug it off of me.

He instantly dropped his mouth to my tits, sucking and squeezing them through the thin material of my white bra while I moaned louder in the dim space.

I tipped my head back, my gaze falling on his cell phone which sat on the kitchen island as the screen illuminated and it buzzed with an incoming call.

But as my lips parted to ask JJ if he should answer that, he dropped to his knees and slung my left leg over his broad shoulders.

My fingers wound into his hair as a moan of anticipation escaped me and he tugged my panties aside so that his tongue could dip between my thighs.

JJ growled hungrily as he pressed forward, lapping at my clit and making me gasp and pant with need as his hands gripped my ass to hold me exactly where he wanted me. My hips flexed and I ground against his face, demanding more and more of the sweet torture he was inflicting upon my body until I was screaming his name and coming for him before I'd even realised what was happening.

He stood suddenly, his hand slapping down over my mouth and his eyes dark with a warning.

"If you keep being that loud, pretty girl, the men at the gates are gonna hear you. And I don't want Fox to cut my dick off for fucking his girl."

He met my gaze as I shot him a furious look and the corner of his lips pulled up in amusement as he took his hand from my mouth.

"Don't call me *his*, JJ," I warned him. "I don't belong to anyone."

"Hmm..." JJ stepped back slowly, taking his hands off of me and letting his eyes roam down my body. "Maybe you don't. But I get the feeling you enjoy it when men try to."

I pursed my lips at him then shrugged, tossing my hair over my shoulder and moving to pick up my dress which was still decorating the floor.

I bent down to grab it, but before I could stride away from him like a badass who'd gotten what she wanted and was done playing, JJ stepped up behind me and dragged my wrists back to the base of my spine, locking them there in his grasp and trapping me face down with my ass in the air.

"JJ," I growled, but as I tried to wriggle free, my ass ground against his hard cock through his sweatpants and a wanton moan escaped me.

"Yeah, sweetheart, I got you all figured out," he promised me in a low voice as he transferred both of my hands into one of his where he held them at the base of my spine.

His free hand caught the back of my panties and he shoved them down, leaving me bare and bent over before him as they fell to my ankles, resting against my sneakers.

"Johnny James, I swear to fuck if you don't get on with-" a moan cut my words short as the hot, silky flesh of his cock slid between my thighs and he groaned as he fisted it, using his hand to guide it past my opening until the head of it was riding over my clit.

"Fuck, your skin feels so good against mine," he groaned, rubbing his cock over my clit again as I looked back between my thighs and saw the precum beading the tip of it, making me lick my lips.

He rocked his hips back and forth, grinding his cock against my clit and though I tried to chase the movement with my own, the way he held me stopped me from doing much more than just taking it.

"I want you inside me," I begged as he kept riding his cock against my clit, back and forth almost lazily, but the heady groans that escaped him proved how much he was enjoying it.

"Tell me how much you need it, and you might convince me," he said, rubbing against my clit even harder and making me moan his name.

"I want your cock buried in me Johnny James," I groaned. "I want to feel every rock hard inch filling me up as you show me who's in charge here. I need you stretching me, filling me, pounding into me and making me come for you while I scream your name. Give it to me, JJ, I fucking need it. *Please.*"

"Jesus," he cursed and I smiled to myself because yeah I could beg for cock like a good girl when I needed some, and right now I needed it more than I needed air to breathe.

JJ drew back and I whimpered at the loss of the feeling of his skin against my mine. I was burning for him and my pussy was practically dripping for him and he was starting to drag this out for way too long.

There was a ripping sound and half a second later, a condom wrapper fell to the floor by my feet before JJ impaled me with one hard thrust of his hips.

I cried out, my pussy clamping down around his length as he rearranged his grip on my wrists once more until he was holding one in each of his big hands, keeping me in position bent over in front of him with my hair spilling down all around me.

"Is that what you wanted?" he ground out and I nodded.

"Yes. Fuck me like you mean it, JJ, brand my body with the feeling of your dick destroying me," I panted and he growled hungrily.

"You're so fucking hot, dirty girl."

JJ drew his hips back and started doing exactly what I'd wanted, his cock driving in deep and hard, making me scream for him as the position he held me in gave me no control whatsoever. All I could do was take it and enjoy the fucking ride.

He hit me so fucking deep that I was reduced to nothing but screaming for him, wanting more and more of it as the moment swept me away into its embrace and made me feel alive again just for him.

Blood was rushing to my head and making my skull pound and as my needy pussy clamped tight around JJ's cock and I found my release, I swear my entire body exploded with pins and needles as pleasure crashed through me in a wave.

He only fucked me harder as I came for him, forcing every drop of pleasure from my body that he could find and claiming it all for his own.

Even though my body was shaking and spent, the cock buried deep inside me was still just as hard as ever. And as JJ tugged me upright and started kissing my neck while my spine pressed to his chest, I knew he wasn't even close to done with me. But I had no problems at all with being destroyed by him, because I was going to show him that I could destroy him too.

CHAPTER EIGHTEEN

"**A**lways wondered where it started. Because my mother almost died of a meth overdose or because my father beat me black and blue whenever he bothered to give me his attention? It's fascinating how people are made, ain't it? Put me in another life with a little more love and a little more money in my pocket and I coulda been a high flyer in downtown L.A. Or maybe a movie star, I do have a fondness for drama, don't I boys? And I've got the looks for it, the talent's natural. Yeah, that's what I'd be, don't you think? Shawn Mackenzie starring alongside…oh what's that beautiful bitch called with the big tits and come-fuck-me-eyes?"

Shawn talked like the whole world was eager to listen and my teeth ground in my mouth as I tried to block him out and form a plan. They'd taken my phone, my weapons, I was a sitting duck and worse than that, so was my brother beside me.

Chase spat curses at Shawn who plainly ignored him, continuing on with his stories and casually reloading his shotgun.

"Natalie Portman?" one of Shawn's men offered.

"No, that ain't it. She was in those movies with the super powers, you know the one I mean. Big tits." He feigned holding them against his own chest. "Real nice ass. Looks like she'd suck cock for days. Got some fancy ass European name."

"Scarlett Johannsson?" another guy offered and Shawn snapped his fingers.

"That's the one," he said then his eyes fell on me and he leaned forward in his camp chair, resting his elbows on his knees. "What's your type, sunshine? People around town talk about you and some rainbow haired chick."

I bared my teeth, heat blazing along my spine at the mere mention of Rogue.

"Oh that made you angry," he said with one of his twisted smiles. "Her pussy must be premium, huh? Are her pubes rainbow coloured too, or does she shave 'em all off?"

"Shut your fucking mouth," I snarled and he boomed a laugh.

"Hey maybe I'll go hunt her down later tonight and find out for myself," he taunted and my heart beat fiercely, desperate for me to kill this man. I'd dive at him and risk wrestling that gun from his hands if I wasn't afraid Chase would get shot because of it.

"You're dead," Chase gritted out and Shawn's blue eyes swung onto him.

"What's that, pretty boy?" He took the shotgun from his knees, casually aiming it at my brother and panic sliced through me as I tried to shift closer to him. Shawn watched me make that move and smiled cruelly. "Chase Cohen," he rolled the name over his tongue. "That'll look real nice on a headstone. Here lies Chase Cohen, and over there lies fifty pieces of his head."

His men laughed and I gritted my jaw.

"I'm who you want," I hissed, but Shawn didn't take his gaze off of Chase.

"Oh those pretty blue eyes do captivate me something fierce, sunshine." He looked closely at Chase who sneered at him. "It'd be a real pity to watch them blow up with your brain."

My phone flashed where it had been left by Shawn's feet and he hooked it up, leaning back in his seat and reading the message out loud.

"Hey son, we're two minutes away." Shawn grinned wickedly and jerked his chin at his men in an order and all but two of them moved into the trees, disappearing into the darkness.

My breaths came unevenly as Shawn stubbed out his cigar on the arm of the seat and stood up. "Let's get this party started, eh boys?" he murmured to us, aiming the shotgun at me. "And don't get any ideas about shouting out a warning to Daddy, because my finger might slip on the trigger and someone's head might go bang."

Silence prickled along my skin and I prayed Luther had brought enough men with him to take on Shawn's people. Chase and I just needed a chance to run, give them the opening they required to rain down hell on this asshole and his piece of shit men.

"Drop your gun!" Luther's voice rang through the clearing from somewhere behind me and my gut knotted.

Shawn's gaze lifted to the trees and the two men left with us stepped closer to him.

I caught Chase's eye while they weren't looking, finding determination flaring there. He hadn't given up, and neither had I. I just wasn't sure how the fuck we were going to walk away from this alive.

"I'm not gonna do that, King Harlequin," Shawn called to my dad. "You're surrounded. And if you fire a single shot in my general direction, I'm gonna blast your son's head off."

"You motherfucker," Luther snarled.

"You're gonna walk down here and give yourself up nice and slow and easy," Shawn commanded. "A life for a life, Luther. You die for him, and he can walk free." He etched a cross over his heart. "I swear it on my sweet mommy's grave."

"Your word means shit and your mother's not dead," my father called to him. "Let Fox go and I'll take his place."

Shawn jerked his gun at me, beckoning me to stand up but I didn't move. "I'm not going anywhere without Chase."

"Don't," Chase hissed at me. "Just get out of here."

But there was no way in hell I was leaving him here to die. "No."

"No?" Shawn laughed. "He really is your boyfriend, ain't he? How does that work with the little rainbow girl in the mix then I wonder? Or does she not know about your pretty boy escapades?" He jerked the gun in a command again. "Up, up, up, sunshine. I'm afraid your blue-eyed beau is staying right here."

"No," I snarled, but one of his men strode forward, gripping the back of my shirt to pull me up.

A shot went off and whistled past Shawn's head, slamming into the trailer to my right.

"Hold fire!" Luther roared at the culprit.

"Who the fuck was that?" Shawn bellowed as answering gunfire rattled through the trees and his shotgun moved right back onto me again. "Back on his knees," he growled and his lackie shoved me down beside Chase.

A hiss caught my ear and my gaze flicked to a log close beside me where a rattlesnake was coiled up in its shadow.

Two men appeared from the trees, dragging a bloody Harlequin along between them across the ground. His name was Gordon, he was one of the elders, his hair grey and his body covered in age old scars from countless fights. He spat at Shawn's feet and the asshole booted him in the face.

"Did you shoot at me, sunshine?" he demanded. "And ignore your fine leader's orders? Put his son at risk of having his head blown off by this very shotgun?" He held a hand to his heart like he was so shocked and Gordon spat curses at him in answer.

"Luther!" Shawn shouted. "Your man just betrayed you, are you comin' down here to deal with him or am I doing it for you?"

"Let Fox go and I'll come out there, motherfucker," Luther barked.

Shawn moved forward to get me up himself this time and I did the only logical thing I could think of right then. I grabbed hold of that fucking rattlesnake and as he dragged me to my feet, I threw it in his goddamn face. He yelled in alarm, knocking it away from him and it landed on the guy to my right's foot, immediately sinking its fangs in to his leg. The guy's gun went off as he screamed and Shawn threw himself to the ground, narrowly missing the bullet as his shotgun tumbled across the dirt.

I grabbed Chase's arm, hauling him away from them and running for our lives as Luther shouted, "Cover them!" and a storm of bullets rained down around us.

I shoved Chase under the trailer, following him beneath it as we started army crawling towards the other side through the dry mud. My heart pounded madly and adrenaline skittered through my veins as we moved as fast as possible. But then booted feet came in to view on the other side and shots rang out all around us.

Gunfire ripped through the trailer and Chase lurched towards me, covering my body with his. I tried to fight him off as bullets tore the world to shit around us, but he wouldn't fucking move. He grunted sharply and I felt the impact of the bullet as it hit him.

"*Chase*," I growled in alarm, crushed to the fucking ground by his bulk as pieces of the trailer were torn off and shouts clamoured all around us in an endless cacophony of war.

He jerked again as another bullet struck him and panic rushed through me as I fought harder to move. He wasn't going to die for me. Fuck that. He was my brother. And we were in this together.

"Stay down, asshole," he snapped, wrestling with me as I arched my back and tried to move.

A body hit the ground just beyond the trailer ahead of us and lifeless eyes stared in at us from one of my Harlequins. Worry spiralled through me over my dad and I prayed he'd brought enough men with him to win this fight.

"Hey!" a guy barked behind us and Chase lifted his weight enough for me to turn my head.

One of Shawn's men was there, crawling under the trailer and tucking a knife between his teeth. Chase kicked at him then groaned in pain from his wounds and I forced him off of me at last, kicking at the asshole myself as he came for us. He took the knife from his mouth, slashing it at my leg and I narrowly avoided it, scrambling towards the way out as Chase tugged my arm to get me moving.

The psycho kept following us as we frantically scrambled out the other side of the trailer and Chase swore as the bastard got hold of him. I jumped to my feet, grabbing his arm and wrenching him up beside me as the guy tried to crawl out after him. I kicked and kicked him like a wild man until his neck broke and the motherfucker fell still.

I turned, finding Chase looking pale with blood washing down his left arm while he clutched his ass.

"It's fine," he answered my frantic look and I spun him around, finding his right ass cheek bleeding like hell. *Jesus Christ.*

I grabbed a couple of guns from the dead Harlequin on the ground and passed one to my brother, his fingers slick with blood from his wounds as he took it.

I still had Shawn's death to deliver and I pressed my back to the obliterated trailer, keeping Chase close to my side as I moved to the edge of it and threw a look around it. Shawn was climbing into one of the trucks as Harlequins swept through the clearing and finished off his men.

I roared out in anger, sprinting from my hiding place and unleashing hellfire on the vehicle as he accelerated off down a dirt track into the woods. I released every bullet I had until the gun rang empty and fury crashed through my chest as the truck disappeared into the darkness.

Luther ran into view, colliding with me and hugging me tighter than he had since I was a kid. He checked me over for bullet wounds as Chase made it to my side, clutching his bleeding arm with one hand and his ass with the other as he limped along.

"You okay, kid?" Luther asked him as his brows drew together.

"Just a couple of flesh wounds," he gritted out and I pulled up his shirt sleeve to find the chunk taken out of his arm. I tore off a piece of my own shirt and tied it tight around the wound to stem the bleeding, but there wasn't much I could about his ass right now.

"You shouldn't have done what you did," I snarled at him.

"What did he do?" Luther demanded.

"Laid on top of me when the bullets started flying," I spat then whipped my eyes onto Chase. "Don't ever do that again."

Chase stared at me with a look that said he had no regrets and he'd do it time and again regardless of what I ordered him. I made a mental note to forcibly change his mind on that, but right now we needed to get out of here.

Luther clapped his uninjured arm. "Good man. You two head home. And get those wounds taken care of, Chase. I'm taking my men after Shawn." He nodded to me then strode away to where Gordon was standing by the fire, looking around at the devastation. Luther raised his gun and shot him twice in the chest then once in the head, a cold detachment in his eyes as the man who'd betrayed his order slumped dead to the ground.

"Move out!" Luther ordered the Crew and I helped Chase walk as we headed back the way we'd come and left them to hound after Shawn.

I didn't think he'd have much luck though, Shawn was long gone already and he'd go to ground the second he got out of the woods.

I picked up mine and Chase's phones by Shawn's seat, passing Chase his before trying to call JJ once more. There was still no answer, and my pulse beat unevenly as I shared a look with Chase then tried to call Rogue. Nothing.

I was in one foul bitch of a mood, and I'd be damn well giving Rogue hell for giving my guys the slip tonight of all nights.

You'd better hide from me well, hummingbird, because if I find you tonight, your ass is gonna be as sore as Chase's by the time I'm done punishing you.

CHAPTER NINETEEN

My ass was pressed to the cold counter of the kitchen island while JJ claimed a punishing kiss from my lips and drove his cock deep inside me and I dug my heels into his back demanding more. I was still wearing my freaking sneakers and my bra had only been yanked down to expose my tits, but the two of us were too into what we were doing to do any more about getting rid of our remaining clothes and JJ's pants were still bunched around his ankles too.

We were both panting and moaning, lost in each other as we moved closer and closer to our final release. JJ was close to finishing now, I could feel it in the tension of his muscles and the desperate way he was kissing me and there was no fucking way I was letting him pull back from the edge this time.

His cock drove into me harder and harder, his hand grabbing my ass as he encouraged my movements and my thighs squeezed his waist in a clear demand.

The sound of a car engine rumbled somewhere nearby, but I couldn't spare a thought for it because JJ's cock was thickening inside me and I was coming apart at the seams. My fingers tugged on his hair and I kissed him even harder as with a final thrust, my pussy locked tight around his thick shaft and the two of us free-fell into ecstasy together.

I slumped back onto the counter, tugging JJ with me as his mouth moved to trail kisses against my neck and I lay there trying to catch my breath while my heart raced to a rampant tune.

The sound of someone cursing and feet moving up the stairs from the garage made JJ jerk upright suddenly and I gasped in alarm as I recognised Fox's voice.

"Just lean on me, I've got you, brother."

"Shit," JJ hissed, jerking his cock back out of me and yanking his sweatpants up without even removing the full condom from his dick.

I scrambled to get off of the kitchen island, catching my pink sundress as JJ tossed it into my face and throwing it on.

The footsteps were getting closer and Chase's pained groan caught my ear. I hunted around for any sign of my panties as I yanked my bra up to cover my nipples again with my fingers shaking from a mixture of the fear of being caught and the high of what we'd just done.

JJ found my panties by the fridge, but before he could toss them to me, the door to the garage swung open and I hopped down from the counter as he just shoved them into the pocket of his sweats with the condom wrapper instead of trying to give them back to me.

Chase and Fox stumbled through the door together and I sucked in a sharp breath as I spotted the blood covering the two of them, a curse escaping JJ as we hurried towards them to try and help.

"What happened?" I demanded, stopping between the two of them, looking from one to the other as I cupped both of their cheeks in my hands and forced them to look at me so that I knew they were okay.

Fox's green gaze was fixed in concern, but Chase's blue eyes were written in pain.

"Where the fuck were you?" Fox shot at JJ as he moved closer behind me and I looked around at him in alarm as I dropped my hold on the two men before me.

"Working, dude. You know that. What the fuck happened to the two of you?" JJ asked.

"Shawn," Chase growled and I looked around at him again as my heart

leapt in fear at that name. Fucking Shawn?

"Why didn't you tell me you were going to deal with him?" I demanded furiously as I realised they'd ditched me specifically to go find him. Even after knowing that I wanted a shot at him myself for what he'd done to me.

There's a good girl, sugarpie. I swear for a moment I heard his voice in my ears and a shiver raced down my spine at the mere idea of it.

"Because you would have wanted to come and there's no fucking way I was going to let you near him," Fox bit out. "And I suggest you hold back on any ideas you might have about shooting your mouth off at me right now, hummingbird, because I know you fucking ran off again tonight and I'm already more than pissed at you."

"You're pissed at *me*?" I demanded incredulously. "You are such an overbearing, controlling asshole. Where the fuck do you get off giving me babysitters and keeping me away from a fight which I had every right to take part in?"

"I have a fucking bullet lodged in my ass cheek, so can we focus on that for a minute?" Chase snarled and I threw a poisonous look at Fox as JJ grabbed Chase and started helping him over to the couch.

Fox let them go and snatched my wrist into his grasp, shoving me back against the wall and placing his hands either side of my head as he leaned down to speak right in my face.

"You are not and never will be going anywhere near Shawn Mackenzie ever again," he snarled. "I don't give a fuck if you want to be the one to end him. I'm sure there are more than a few survivors of his fucking tyranny who want to claim his head for their own, but I can promise you, you won't be the one to take it. And yeah, I'll happily assign you babysitters and lock you up and do whatever the fuck I have to to keep you safe from him and I don't give a shit if you hate me for it either. You're *mine*, hummingbird. And the thought of him ever laying his filthy fucking hands on you makes my skin crawl. I can promise you that he won't ever lay so much as his eyes on you again, let alone anything else."

"You're fucking insane if you think that I-"

"For once in your fucking life, just do as you're told!" Fox roared at me and I flinched back against the wall, my heart thundering in my chest. "Do you have any idea how close the two of us came to death tonight at the hands of the man you used to spend your free time fucking? And then I find out that you've run off again to fuck knows where and I have to worry about you too! So no, I don't care if you hate me for it and no, I don't give a shit if you want to curse me out or call me insane or any fucking name you like. You. Are. Mine. And you'll figure that out sooner or later, but either way, you're going to start doing as you're fucking told."

Fox's fist slammed into the wall beside my head and I jerked aside in fright. But he was already storming away from me, ripping off his bloody shirt and throwing it towards the trash before taking the stairs two at a time and disappearing. His bedroom door slammed hard enough to make the walls shudder a moment later and I had to blink a few times to clear my eyes of the tears that had sprung to life in them. There was no fucking way I'd be crying for him.

I found Chase and JJ looking at me from across the room where Chase was lying on the couch on his front and JJ held a first aid kit in his fist beside him.

"Pretty girl," JJ murmured softly, a hand reaching out towards me like he thought I might bolt. And maybe I wanted to, but as my gaze fell to the blood soaking its way through Chase's pants and the tourniquet on his arm, I blinked the tears away and raised my chin.

"I can help," I said, ignoring Fox's outburst and striding towards them. "I learned more than a few things about patching people up over the years - my healthcare plan was shit in my last job."

JJ tried to smile at me but couldn't quite pull it off and Chase just swore as he shifted his position on the couch.

"I need a piss," JJ said, his gaze meeting mine and I was willing to bet the condom he'd left hanging from his dick was causing him some issues.

I didn't need him to say a word about keeping my lips shut over what we'd been doing here tonight. Fuck knew what Fox would do if he found out and I wasn't going to risk him hurting the only man in this house who actually gave a shit about me and what I wanted. Fox just wanted to control me, force me into a pretty little cage and take me out to play with him whenever it suited him. But he didn't care about what I wanted. That didn't matter to him at all.

I was a possession to him and that was it. And Chase...well, Chase had been happy to destroy my life and send me to prison to rot for fuck knew how long rather than have me in this house.

So I had no fucking idea why I dropped to my knees beside him and picked up the first aid kit to help him out.

JJ walked away and the moment he was gone, Chase spoke.

"Your dress is on backwards," he muttered and I raised my eyes to meet his, finding pain there that went beyond the wounds he was sporting.

I glanced down at myself, finding he was right and clearing my throat uncomfortably.

"It will destroy Fox when he finds out about you two. And then it will destroy the rest of us in turn," he added.

"I guess you wish your plan had worked and I was tucked away in a nice supermax somewhere right about now then," I replied bitterly, tugging my arms out of the straps of my dress as I twisted it around so that it was on properly again.

"That wasn't my plan," Chase grunted, his eyes shifting from mine to watch as I pushed my arms back through the straps of my dress again. "I had a lawyer who was supposed to come and offer you a deal. The cops were paid off, it was all set up. It shouldn't have gone to shit like it did - they brought you to the wrong fucking precinct. Then my guy told me that you'd taken the deal, took the pay off and the car and had fucked all the way off again. I thought it was done, you were free to start up somewhere new and we could go on being happy without you getting the chance to destroy us. By the time I realised he'd given the money to the wrong fucking girl, Maverick had already come to snap you up and everything had gone about as wrong as it possibly could have."

Chase glanced towards the stairs in case either of the others were on their way back and I tutted.

"What makes you think I would have taken your fucking deal?" I hissed. "You wanted rid of me before then, so why would I refuse until that moment then suddenly change my mind and grab the cash?"

"I was offering you a lot of money," he growled. "And I would have offered more. Everybody has a price, little one. I just wanted you in a tight spot while we made the negotiations. You would have taken the deal rather than end up in fucking prison and we both know it."

"No we don't," I said, grabbing the back of his pants and yanking them down to expose his bleeding ass cheek. Chase grunted in pain, but I just smirked at him as I slapped a wad of gauze down over the wound. "I don't and never have wanted any of your filthy money, Chase Cohen. There isn't a price that you can place on what I want from you, and I would have preferred to rot than take a pay out from some asshole who thinks he can decide my fate for me. That being the case, I have to assume you would have let me go down for it when I refused."

"No," he snapped fiercely, catching my hand and making me pause as his eyes flared with emotion. "I never would have let you go to prison, little one. I just...wanted you gone. I wanted it to hurt now so that it didn't hurt worse later because we both know that's how this story ends. Look at Fox - he's losing his goddamn mind over you and he hasn't even fucked you yet. He's barely holding it together knowing about you and Shawn, not to mention Maverick and now JJ is involved and the whole thing is going to blow up in all of our faces if we don't stop it now. Or then. Because I can see that the time has already passed. You're like a splinter that's worked its way back beneath the skin of my family and I don't see any way to get you back out again without cutting a lump of flesh off now."

"Or maybe I'm a limb that was missing for ten long years. You learned how to limp along without me but now I'm growing back, and the process is making you itch."

Footsteps on the stairs made us drop our glare off and I quickly unscrewed a bottle of iodine before pulling the bloody gauze from Chase's ass cheek and tipping it over the wound.

"Motherfucker!" Chase roared and I gave him a sweet smile just as Fox and JJ made it back into the room. Fox was dressed in clean clothes and his damp hair made it clear he'd rinsed off too.

He didn't say a word to me, striding forward to grasp Chase's shoulders to keep him still while I picked up the pair of big, metal tweezers and eyed the glint of metal lodged inside Chase's butt cheek.

JJ strode around us, his fingertips brushing against my shoulder for the briefest moment before he moved to straddle Chase's legs to pin him down.

"Can I at least get a shot of rum first?" Chase snarled as he fisted the cushions and his muscles flexed in preparation of our home surgery.

"No," Fox snapped. "You're off the booze and you brought this on yourself by shielding me with your damn body. Maybe next time you decide to throw your life away for mine, the memory of this pain will make you reconsider."

My eyebrows arched at that revelation and I could hear the underlying fear in Fox's tone despite the way he tried to deliver those words with anger.

"I'm sorry I wasn't there," JJ muttered and Fox growled irritably.

"Next time, keep your fucking phone on you."

I tried not to feel guilty about the fact that I'd been distracting JJ at the time of the attack, but realistically he had left his phone here while he was at the Dollhouse and I doubted he would have made it out there in time to help anyway. I, on the other hand, could have easily been there to back them up, but I wasn't deemed worthy.

I mopped up the excess blood with some more gauze then quickly plunged the tweezers into the bullet hole.

Chase cursed like a sailor, his body tensing beneath the guys' hold on him and I gritted my teeth as I manoeuvred the metal instrument until I managed to grab the bullet and yank it out.

"Fuck!" Chase roared and I quickly slapped more gauze down over the wound to staunch the bleeding again.

JJ climbed off of him just as Fox's phone started ringing and the big man snatched it out of his pocket with a curse. "What is it, Kenny?"

We all looked at him as he shot a fearful look my way and a second later he cut the call without so much as a goodbye.

"Luther is on his way back here. We have about five minutes to get Rogue hidden. He couldn't catch up to Shawn so he'll probably wanna stay all night and talk tactics," Fox said, swiping a hand down his face.

"I'm not staying in this house with him here all night," I balked.

"She's right, dude," JJ added before Fox could start screaming at me again. "We can't risk your old man spotting her. There's been enough blood spilled tonight as it is."

Chase pushed himself up onto his elbows, his fearful gaze falling on me as he panted through the pain of his bullet extraction. "She's not safe here," he grunted.

"Fine," Fox snapped. "Fucking...fine. JJ you take her back to her trailer. But I want you on top of her all fucking night, do you understand me? She doesn't so much as piss without you there. I don't fucking trust her not to try and run off again so you ride her ass no matter what she tries to pull. Got it?"

"I'm all over it, boss," JJ agreed, winking at me from behind Fox's back as he turned his badger glare on me.

"I don't need a babysitter," I spat. Not that I was opposed to the idea of JJ riding my ass all night if I was being entirely honest.

"Yes you fucking do," Fox disagreed. "And I'm warning you, Rogue, don't push me on this tonight, because if you think I've been an overbearing asshole up until this point, I can promise you, you haven't seen a fucking thing yet."

I glared at him but he ignored me, turning away and striding towards the kitchen where he snatched a box of dog treats out of the cupboard then whistled to Mutt who scampered over to see him.

"JJ, go pack whatever you need for a sleepover and make sure you're packing plenty of heat too. I want you up all night with a weapon in hand in case that motherfucker catches wind of where she's staying. Maybe we should just shave her fucking hair off so he doesn't have any way of recognising her while we're at it."

"If you come anywhere near my hair with a razor, I will personally take a pair of scissors to your balls," I snarled in warning.

"At least put a fucking hoody on and cover yourself up then," he shot back.

JJ made his escape while I scowled at Fox, clearly sensing the oncoming storm of yet another screaming match blowing in from the east.

"Give me my dog," I said as Fox fed him a treat then scooped him up.

"No. You won't cut town without the little fucker and my dad thinks he belongs to me anyway. So he's staying here as insurance against you running off again. And if you don't like it, I'll just gag and hogtie you in JJ's car and let him deal with your bullshit when he unloads you at the other end." Fox strode out of the room and I picked up a potted plant and hurled it after him. It smashed against the wall, the sound of it exploding mostly cutting out the vile names I was screaming after him too. I was pretty sure he must have heard me calling him an ass-eating control freak with a midget cock though, so I was satisfied I'd won that little back and forth.

"The two of you are fucking toxic," Chase muttered as I was left alone with him and I spun his way, ready to hurl Hurricane Rogue in his face next, but as I took in the concern in his eyes, I blew out an angry breath instead.

I moved back over to him and dropped to my knees in front of him, looking at him over the arm of the couch while he lay there, ass up and feeling sorry for himself.

"Does it hurt?" I murmured and he narrowed his eyes at me.

"Like a bitch. Which I'm sure you'll be glad to hear."

My heart twisted at his words and I frowned because they were wrong. I might have been angry with him, might have even hated him, but I'd seen him in pain more times than I could count when he was a boy and his dad had been knocking him about. So no, I didn't enjoy seeing him hurting now.

I reached out hesitantly and pushed my fingers into his dark curls, smoothing them away from his face and sighing as I looked into his blue eyes. That was the one thing about him which hadn't changed at all in all those years and I still felt like he could look right upon my soul when I met his gaze like this.

"When I close my eyes, I don't hate you," I breathed so low that I wasn't sure he'd even fully be able to hear my words. I leaned closer as he watched me, my forehead touching his before I let my eyes fall closed and breathed in the scent of sea salt that had always clung to his skin. "I'm glad you didn't die tonight, Ace."

His breath hitched at my words and I slid my fingers from his hair to his rough jaw. His hand moved over mine to keep it there and I leaned forward, touching my lips to the corner of his mouth as my heart pattered wildly and a whole ocean of heartache welled up inside me, threatening to wash me away.

Chase turned his head towards me the tiniest amount, the scratch of his stubble making my skin prickle as I opened my eyes and found him looking right at me.

"Rogue," he breathed, my name sounding so heavy on his tongue as his lips brushed against my skin and I was flooded with the weirdest temptation to just turn a little more, steal a taste of something poisonous and let it burn me from the inside.

"You ready, Rogue?" JJ's voice made me flinch back and I shoved to my feet again as I whirled around to face him with a fake ass smile on my confused bitch face.

"Yep. Let's get the fuck out of here before I have to lay eyes on the badger again."

JJ looked from me to Chase slowly before nodding, holding a hand out to me in offering. I stepped forward and took it, wetting my suddenly dry mouth and glancing back at Chase as he watched me walk away.

"Feel better, dude," JJ said to him and Chase nodded.

"Just keep her safe," he replied before seeming to think better of being a decent human being and adding, "I don't wanna have to listen to Fox bitching about it for years if she runs off and lets that psycho ex-boyfriend of hers kill her dumb ass."

I flipped him off as JJ rolled his eyes and tugged me towards the exit.

A muffled bark drew my attention and the sound of Fox swearing followed as I looked back and spotted Mutt racing after us, the bag of treats clamped in his jaws and victory shining in his little eyes.

"Run, JJ!" I commanded, yanking on his arm and taking off down the stairs with Mutt racing between our legs.

To his credit, JJ did as instructed and he sprinted downstairs to his car while Fox swore and yelled after us to bring my dog back. But that would be a hell fucking no to that, so I ripped the car door open and let Mutt jump in ahead of me before dropping inside too. JJ hit the gas with a laugh just as Fox appeared yelling curses at us and I waved to the angry badger as we tore up the ramp, locked inside the orange GT speeding away from Harlequin House.

My laughter fell away and I tugged Mutt close as I looked out at the dark streets, wondering if the man who had tried to kill me really was lurking nearby, ready to jump out like the boogie man and finish me off at any second.

"You wanna talk about it?" JJ asked when I stayed silent too long, my gaze on the dark shadows of the landscape beyond the windows. "Shawn, I mean."

I shifted in my seat as the memories I'd been working so hard to block out poured in on me and I chewed on my bottom lip.

"*Not that one, sugarpie,*" *Shawn growled, moving to stand behind me in the mirror as I braided my dark hair over my shoulder. His fingers curled around the straps of my black dress and I met his icy eyes in the mirror, my pulse quickening as I gave him a smile.*

"*You don't like it?*" *I asked as his mouth moved to my neck and he bit down, dragging the straps lower until my tits spilled out of the top of it and he was squeezing them roughly, watching the show as it was reflected back to us.*

"*I said,* not that one,*" he replied firmly, his hand moving to the hem of my dress before he yanked it up so hard that I heard the material rip.*

My hand slammed against the mirror just in time to stop my face from smacking into it and I gasped as he yanked my panties aside and drove his cock into me a moment later.

He grunted as he fucked me and I bit my cheek against the sting of pain from his sudden entrance while his tattooed hands moved to grip my ass.

A moan escaped me as his cock started hitting me just right and I angled my hips to chase that pleasure, but with a curse and a groan, he buried himself inside me one final time and came with a dark chuckle before I could even get close to joining him in bliss.

"*See, sugarpie? You look too goddamn fuckable in that dress,*" *he said, slapping my ass lightly as he tugged his cock out of me and took the condom off. "Don't want anyone else laying eyes on my girl looking this damn good.*"

I turned to look at him as he put his dick away and zipped his fly up again. "So what should I wear then?"

Shawn cocked his head at me, moving forward and cupping my jaw in his hand, his thumb swiping across my lips so that he smeared my red lipstick.

"*Well now I've got the problem of you looking like a just-fucked slut, don't I, sweetcheeks? So maybe it's best you stay home tonight. You weren't really in the mood to party anyway, were you?*"

"*I can get changed,*" *I began and he arched a brow at me, giving me all the warning I needed about what kind of mood he was in, so I switched lanes. "And wait for you to come home later?*"

"*Like some nice little wifey?*" *he scoffed and I narrowed my eyes. We both knew I wasn't that. "Although now you mention it, I might just be in the mood for some more of your sweet pussy when I get back, so it'd be handy to have you here wet and waiting for me, wouldn't it?"*

I nodded, not because I was aching for more of his dick but because I knew he would get well and truly fucked up tonight and be out for hours. So if I was destined for a night in at home then his place was better than the apartment he'd given me to live in. He had Netflix and a shit load of food here as well as a comfy as fuck couch.

"Alright then, sugarpie," he agreed, smearing more of my lipstick across my face. "But clean yourself up before I get back, yeah? You look like a common whore."

He shoved me back a step roughly and I swallowed as I watched him walk out, the door swinging closed behind him as he started whistling while he walked.

I glanced at myself in the mirror, the dress I'd picked out now torn and ruined and my red lipstick smeared across my cheek. For a moment I considered grabbing my shit and walking out. But where was I supposed to go? This was the best I'd had it in a long time. And yeah, that motherfucker got in strange moods and called me names from time to time. But he could be sweet when he wanted to turn the charm on too. And he'd never hit me. So what was I even complaining about?

I tugged the dress the rest of the way off of me and headed to find something else to wear. It was probably a good thing anyway. The parties he held with his gang were always full of assholes getting fucked up on their own product and all I'd really wanted was to dance. I could just do that here. Alone.

So I pulled on another dress, cleaned my face and found a bottle of vodka to keep me company as I used Shawn's speakers to play Empty by Olivia O'Brien, closed my eyes and pretended I was somewhere else while I danced to it. Somewhere where the sun shone and people really knew me. But that wasn't my reality and it never would be again, so I let the lyrics sink into my soul and ignored the tears on my cheeks as I just let the drink steal my pain away and tried not to think about how fucking vacant I was inside.

"Shawn and me were convenient," I said to JJ as I blinked the memories away. "He was hot and I was...better off with him than alone."

"Pretty girl," he murmured and the way he said it cracked something open inside me.

I turned to look at him as he pulled into the parking lot at Rejects Park and cut the engine.

"Do you still wanna rescue me, J?" I whispered, not sure where that even came from but he nodded, offering me his hand and putting something back into place in my heart as I took it. "Then spend tonight rescuing me. Because I need to pretend I'm not the girl I was with him. I need to believe it wasn't real for tonight at least."

"Maybe you can rescue me too then," JJ murmured roughly. "Because I think I've been drowning ever since the day we sent you away and if I don't cling onto you now, I get the feeling I might go under for good."

I nodded, taking my hand back from his and getting out of the car.

We walked side by side back to my trailer, an inch of distance separating us and tension coiling though the air in the most nerve wracking way.

I opened the door and Mutt scurried ahead as I stepped inside, leaving the lights off as JJ followed me. The little space seemed even smaller as I turned to look at him in the dark, his huge body filling it up and dominating everything right down to the air I was breathing.

I backed up slowly towards my bedroom while JJ locked the door, tugging on the hem of my dress and pulling it over my head as I made it into my room.

JJ followed me in silence, the heavy thud of his bag hitting the floor the only thing to disturb the air before he pushed the bedroom door closed too.

Then his lips were on mine and I was in his arms, my ass hitting the mattress as I stripped his shirt off of him and he moved on top of me.

"This should have been our first time," he breathed against my mouth as he dragged my panties down my thighs achingly slowly and my whole body buzzed in anticipation of him. "And it should have been a long, long time ago, pretty girl."

I moaned as he kissed me again, the last of our clothes disappearing as our hands moved over each other's bodies until he was pressing me down into the mattress and sliding his cock inside me so achingly slowly that I could hardly even draw breath.

He kissed me deeply, our bodies saying all the things we wouldn't give words to and I pulled him closer to me, wanting more, needing more and giving myself up to him completely as we spent the night in the bliss of each other's bodies and let the rest of the world fade away.

CHAPTER TWENTY

I woke in a sea of coconut with a seriously satisfied dick and the most beautiful girl in the world in my arms. Though apparently my dick wasn't *entirely* satisfied as it rose with the sun and songbirds seemed to sing its name.

Rogue was like a dead girl beside me as I ran my hands down the length of her back and she didn't stir at all. I pushed her hair off of her face and pressed my mouth to hers, teasing her lower lip between my teeth. Nothing. Girl could sleep through a bomb raid.

Mutt whined by the bed and I rolled over as he scratched at the door and gave me a desperate look that said *if I have to wait for Rogue to wake up, I'll piss myself!*

I reluctantly let go of Rogue and slipped out of bed, naked and yawning as I opened the door and followed him through the trailer to the exit where he yapped impatiently.

"Alright, alright." I unlocked the door and he flew outside, charging down a seagull which took off into the air with a furious squawk before he peed right where it had been standing. *Territorial little beast.*

I waited for him to be done but he went trotting off on some mission and

I shrugged, shutting the door and moving to make coffee.

I kept bumping into shit, this trailer was more like it was designed for a Polly Pocket than a full grown man and his hard cock. Johnny D switched the oven on more than once before I had two cups of coffee poured, and he was not best pleased at whacking into shit instead of sinking back into his favourite pussy. He hadn't gotten hard for a single girl since I'd first had her - barring Rogue obviously. It had cost me all of my private clients and now I was an escort with no one to escort. Though, I couldn't say I was really pissed at Johnny D for that.

I'd wanted that girl my whole life and now she finally wanted me back in some way, I was a goner. But I wasn't sure what the long-term plan was. I wasn't her boyfriend, and I knew well enough that she'd slept with Maverick out on his island. But here we were again, so maybe that meant she wasn't his girl either. *I should probably just talk to her about it.*

I was definitely being a coward. I didn't wanna face the truth because the fact was, I wasn't sure I could handle it. I wanted this thing between us to be more than just sex, but what if she didn't? My dick could do plenty of tricks, but it was useless at making a girl fall in love with me. Especially a girl like her. And if I cut off my dick tomorrow, then what would I have to offer her? Nothing.

But then again, the way we'd been together last night in her tiny bed hadn't seemed like it was just about fucking. I'd never been with a girl the way I'd been with her then, tender and loving and taking my time because I never wanted it to end. And it had seemed like she was right there with me feeling the exact same way.

I stepped back into the room, placing down our coffees on the nightstand before moving into bed. She'd rolled over onto my pillow, her face buried in it and her hair spread out around her everywhere. I grinned at her, lifting her so she lay against my chest instead and raising her hand to inspect the shark tooth bracelet she wore which I'd made for her like a Captain Douchenugget ten years ago. Man, I'd been a sap. But I had to admit, it made me feel like a king seeing her wearing it now. It was just some stupid trinket, but it represented me and she wanted it on her. So maybe that meant something, or maybe I was just living in a dream world. I liked it here though, the clouds were fluffier, the sun

298

brighter and my pretty girl was in my arms. I couldn't really ask for more than that considering I'd have paid every penny I had and given up all non-essential organs to secure that reality once. Alright fuck it, I would have thrown in a few essential ones too. Just not my heart, or my dick. Was a dick an organ? It sure throbbed as often as my heart did whenever she was around, so I was gonna say yes. So I'd have sold everything except those two things so she could have them both. Like, not in a jar or anything, I'd keep them attached to my body obviously.

I released her hand and it slapped down against my chest. I would have checked her pulse if she hadn't been so warm and her breath wasn't fanning over my skin.

I shut my eyes and just enjoyed the weight of her and the pure peace that surrounded me because of it. I was pretty sure I was still in disbelief that she was actually back. My brain couldn't quite catch up with having her here, especially after we'd almost lost her again to Maverick.

I tightened my hold on her, wishing I could keep her, but as much as I wanted to, I didn't really think she'd ever be mine. Not truly. I mean, what the hell was I supposed to do about Fox? Would he ever accept us being together if Rogue even *did* want me? I couldn't see it. My brother was so in love with her, it blinded him to all else. Did his infatuation with her outweigh his loyalty to me? Would this ruin us?

She's not gonna choose you anyway, idiot.

I sighed, running my fingers through her hair. I was a good lay, and I knew I was relying on that to keep her coming back to me, but beyond that, what was I? The local stripper/escort whose cock had seen more action than a movie clapperboard.

"Coffee," she murmured as she woke, sniffing the air with her eyes still closed.

I smirked at her, reaching out for her mug and placing it in her hand. She propped herself up on my chest as she guzzled it down like a thirsty bird, her eyes remaining closed the whole time. Then she vaguely reached for the nightstand, missed and the mug dropped onto the floor as she snuggled back down against my chest with a contented sigh.

"Morning, pretty girl," I murmured and her eyes fluttered open, my heart racing as those beautiful ocean blues fell on me.

"Morning, Johnny James," she said huskily and we just stared at each other for a few seconds before she smirked at me. She twisted the shark tooth on her bracelet between her fingers, slowly tasting her lips.

"Can't believe you kept it," I said and her eyes flicked up to me again.

"It's special," she said and my brows arched.

"Is it?"

"Yeah," she said, smiling at it. "But…wait." She leaned in, pressing her ear to the shark tooth. "Oh, it says you owe me a speech, JJ."

I snorted, tugging on a lock of her hair. "No chance."

"But I want it." She pouted and fuck her for looking so cute and hot at the same time. "I'm *owed* it." She grinned mischievously, tiptoeing her fingers up my chest, my neck then pausing on my lips and I nibbled the ends of them, making her laugh. "Come on, give it to me."

I gave her a dark smirk. "Oh you want it?"

"Yes," she groaned. "Give it to me, Johnny James."

I pulled her fully on top of me, grinding her down over my hard cock and her lips popped open. I reached for my discarded jeans on the floor, hunting for a condom and coming up short. *Oh shit.*

Rogue checked her nightstand drawer but I specifically remembered raiding that too last night now I thought about it.

"Did we go through all the condoms?" she asked in surprise and I gaped at her.

"I don't think that's ever happened to me before. I always come overprepared," I said in disbelief. Jesus, how many times did I fuck her?

At least three times in the bed, then against that wall over there, and that wall over there…the kitchen stove, the little couch…that table…the shower, the bed again…*wow, that's gotta be some kind of a record.*

"I've got some in my car," I said, moving to get up, but she pressed her hand down on my chest, shaking her head at me with a frown.

"Don't go." She lay back down, cuddling me and it felt so good I didn't even care about the sex. "I'll just suck your cock once you give me that speech."

I laughed, skimming my fingers down her back toward her ass. Damn, that was good motivation. "Fine," I gave in. "If you really want it that much."

"I do." She looked down at me with a grin that was all Rogue, and I leaned in to taste it, cupping her face in my hands.

When she broke away I grabbed a pillow from beside me and shoved it over my face.

"What are you doing?" she laughed.

"I'm not looking at you while I say it. It's the words of a pathetic little kid, just remember that, okay?"

"Sure, sure," she said dismissively. "Go on then."

I huffed out a breath then thought back on the speech I'd gone over a thousand times in my head, the one I swore I'd say to her just the moment I found her again.

Well this was going to be the cringe fest of the century. I was literally the most pathetic kid back then. And this was the kind of speech worthy of a low budget holiday romance movie.

"Rogue, wonderful Rogue," I said with a weary sigh at how terrible this was already and Rogue snorted. I pinched her thigh. "Quiet or you won't get any more."

She stifled her giggles and I continued making a home in cringe city. "Your eyes are like the sea on a warm summer's day, your hair as soft as the sand in the cool shade, your lips are two seashells balanced on your face and your skin as shiny as a freshly waxed surfboard."

She lost it again and I lifted the pillow, narrowing my eyes at her. "Silence pretty girl or you're not getting the end."

She cupped her hand over her mouth, smothering her laugh and I dropped the pillow back over my face with a groan. I was the lamest kid. If I could get a do-over with the knowledge I had now, I could have been way cooler.

"Rogue, I missed you like the shore misses the waves when the tide is out, my heart is a dry waterfall waiting for the rains to come and now I have you back, there's a deluge."

"A deluge," she echoed, laughing again and I shoved the pillow off my face and dove at her, pinning her beneath my weight.

"That's it," I growled through a demonic smile. "You've asked for it." I shoved up her top, leaned down and blew a furious raspberry on her flesh, making her laugh, wriggle and squeal. I planted another one on her and she tugged my hair, trying to make me stop, but she was out of luck.

Mutt started barking beyond the trailer and the sound of Fox's voice reached us, both of us falling statue still.

"Ah you little asshole, don't you bite me," Fox growled. "Here, have a treat. Hey, not the whole packet - give that back!"

I flew out of bed as Rogue stared at me in horror. "Pretend you're asleep," I hissed and she nodded, but reached for the trash can full of condoms first, tying a knot in the bag to hide them before throwing on an oversized shirt and diving back into bed.

Meanwhile, I grabbed a bottle of water from her nightstand, undid the cap and poured it all over me, whipped a towel off of the hook on the back of the door along with all of my clothes from the floor then stepped out of her room, tying the towel around my waist and tugging the door shut behind me just before Fox let himself into the trailer with the key he'd gotten made.

"Oh, hey bro," I said casually and he nodded to me, striding up to the sink and washing blood off his hand from a little dog bite. I spotted Mutt beyond the trailer ripping into a bag of chicken treats and wagging his tail.

Shit that was close.

"Is Rogue up?" he asked.

"Nah, she's still sleeping," I said. "I'll just…get dressed."

I looked around for anywhere private I could go, but the bathroom was as tiny as a gnat's asscrack so I figured fuck it and dropped my towel, pulling on my stuff while Fox poured himself a coffee. A couple of girls' giggles carried from beyond the trailer and I realised I probably should have closed the door before I got butt naked.

When I was fully clothed, Fox stepped past me and pushed Rogue's door open to check on her. She was sprawled out in the bed, looking dead to the world and I wouldn't have been entirely surprised if she really had fallen back asleep.

Fox shut the door again, his gaze moving to a drawing of an angry badger on the wall. He lifted it up, finding a hole beneath it and I arched a brow as he turned to me with a scowl and folded his arms.

"How's Chase?" I asked.

"How would you be if you got shot in the ass?" he said with a smirk.

"Fair point," I laughed then his features darkened.

"I can't believe he threw himself on me, fucking protecting me," he said angrily and my heart squeezed. *Oh Chase, I fucking love you, but I hate how much you disregard yourself.*

I made myself another coffee and we moved to sit side by side on the steps that led into Rogue's trailer, the morning sun painting everything gold and already starting to warm the day up.

"I need to talk to him about what he did, but I dunno how to stop him from doing it again," Fox said in concern then turned to me. "You guys know that me being your boss doesn't mean I would ever want you to put yourselves in harm's way for me, right?" His eyes burned into me with worry over that and I pressed a hand to his back.

"I know, man, I just think Chase wants to prove he's useful. He's never really valued himself and I think he'd die happy if it was for one of us. I fucking hate that though. If it helps, I don't think he did it because you're his boss – he did it because you're you."

He frowned as he considered that. "I don't know how to fix the scars his dad left on him," he said gravely. "How can we show him he's important to us if on some underlying level he just thinks of himself as a piece of shit?"

I thought on that for a moment, swigging my coffee. "Honestly? The only one of us who ever made a difference to him in that sense was Rogue."

"And now they despise each other," Fox said with a sigh, pushing his fingers into his messy blonde hair.

"Yeah," I breathed. "They still care about each other though. Hate is just love that caught fire."

"Mmm," Fox sounded his agreement. "Then how do we put out the flames?"

I shook my head, having no idea about that. "Lock them in a room together and refuse Rogue food and Chase cigarettes until they make up?" I joked.

"Don't give me ideas," Fox chuckled, a dark glint in his eyes saying he'd definitely do it if he thought it would work.

"I think they'd tear each other to pieces if we did that," I laughed.

"Ain't that the truth."

"My ears are burning. I think a Badger is talking about me," Rogue said sharply, coming up behind us and squeezing herself between the two of us. The gap was so tight, she was basically on our laps and I didn't really mind that at all, especially as she mostly just sat on me and ignored Fox. "Did Chase die of his ass wound?" she asked lightly like she didn't care if he had, but I could see she genuinely wanted news on how he was under the facade.

"Nah, he's currently propped up on a doughnut cushion playing video games, hummingbird," Fox said and he reached for her but she shifted away, still pissed with him from last night.

I had to side with Fox on that though, we couldn't risk Rogue getting anywhere near Shawn Mackenzie so he was going to keep eyes on her at all times. And I was more than happy to be those eyes. I didn't think screaming at her and threatening her were the best ways to gain her cooperation though, but that was Fox.

Mutt came running over, jumping onto Rogue's lap and licking her cheek. She stroked his head and I reached out to tickle his chin. He shot a glare at Fox when he didn't join in with the fuss and Fox rolled his eyes before scratching his back and Mutt wagged his tail like crazy as he became the centre of attention.

"Get dressed." Fox patted Rogue's thigh and my hackles raised as I fought the urge to slap his hand off of her, but thankfully she did it herself.

"How about no?" she tossed back.

"I thought you wanted to be involved in hunting down Shawn?" Fox said, arching a brow and her eyes narrowed on him sharply.

"You said I couldn't be involved," she accused.

"Maybe I changed my mind." He shrugged.

"Seriously?" she asked, hope sparkling in her eyes and I tried to catch Fox's gaze to ask what the fuck he was playing at.

He nodded, avoiding my eye and she jumped up, placing Mutt in my lap before she ran back inside to get dressed with a squeal.

"You're not really gonna let her help go after Shawn, are you?" I asked in horror.

"Nope," he agreed. "But I'd rather I didn't have to drag her kicking and screaming into my truck this morning."

"You're an asshole," I pointed out.

"I never claimed to be a saint, J." He smirked, standing up and I did too.

Rogue soon reappeared in a little denim dungaree dress with a lacy white crop top underneath it that showed off a lot of side tit. She wore flip-flops and my pink sunglasses which she must have stolen from my car last night. *Little sneak.*

I reached out to take her hand, then did a swerve in the air as I stopped myself and shut the door behind her instead. Thankfully Fox didn't catch it and we followed him to his truck which he'd driven down to Rogue's trailer even though he definitely wasn't supposed to.

We climbed in with Rogue in the middle and Mutt sat on her lap as she used Fox's phone to put on People I Don't Like by Upsahl as we sailed through town.

Fox drove to the Dollhouse and parked up in the shade of a palm tree outside it just as an SUV full of Harlequins spilled out of their vehicle a few feet away.

Fox directed them towards his truck as he stepped out, shutting the door behind him and as I got out too, he moved to shut my door and trap Rogue inside before locking it tight.

"Hey!" she shouted at him, but he ignored her, directing the small army of Harlequins to surround the truck and tossing one of them the keys.

"Crack a window for her, Pedro," he commanded then jerked his head at me in an order to follow and led me toward the huge white building. I threw an apologetic look back at Rogue and she scowled furiously at us before turning the music up so loud that it made the truck vibrate, and would likely flatten Fox's battery in no time too.

"She's gonna hate you for that," I told Fox.

"I don't give a shit. She's in trouble," he growled. "She slipped away from my men last night and if it wasn't for you finding her, who knows what could have happened? What if Shawn had found her wandering around town after the shoot out?" Worry lined his brow. "If she won't stay under the protection of my people willingly, then this is what she gets. I can't afford to be nice right now when Shawn and his men are out for blood. What if they took her JJ? I'd never forgive myself," he bit out and my chest crushed at the thought, making me a whole lot less upset about her being forcibly protected. I knew what she was like; she would be furious about being watched twenty-four seven. But it would be worth it if it kept Shawn from finding her.

In the stark light of day, the Dollhouse showed its signs of wear far more than when darkness cloaked its imperfections. Cracks ran up the walls and one side of the roof looked in desperate need of repair.

Two men manned the doors, letting us inside as they recognised us and we found Jolene in the bar upstairs counting cash at a table.

"Oh Fox," she gasped, getting to her feet with wide eyes. "Are you alright? When I didn't hear from my man again last night, I was so worried. And when I called Luther and he told me what had happened, it just didn't make sense."

"Your man was paid off by Shawn to hand us to him," Fox supplied, eyeing Jolene closely as she gaped at him.

"Jesus, Fox, I'm so sorry," she said, holding a hand against her heart. "Is he-"

"Dead," he said. "Shawn shot him."

She swallowed hard as she nodded satisfactorily. "Why would Shawn kill him if he was working for him?"

"To save himself the money," I guessed.

"Yeah, that or he didn't want any witnesses to all the murders he had planned last night," Fox said, his gaze sharp on his aunt. "Or...he wanted to make sure Cyril's secrets died with him."

"Secrets?" Jolene frowned.

"I wanna question your men," Fox announced. "Anyone who had contact with Cyril, if there's more rats among your people, Aunt, I am going to weed them out."

She nodded, her expression serious. "I'll have them come here for questioning."

"Good." Fox grabbed a chair, sitting down and Jolene's eyebrows rose.

"Oh you want to question them right now?" she asked.

"Evidently," he confirmed and she stood up.

"Okay, I'll make sure they're here as soon as possible - Chester!" she bellowed and he came running into the room a moment later in a bright green shirt.

"Yes, my sweet?" he asked.

"Call all of our men in for a meeting with Fox Harlequin. And don't keep him waiting," Jolene commanded.

Chester nodded to us then scampered away again. I dropped down into the seat beside Fox, stretching out my legs and cracking my knuckles. I had the feeling today was going to be a long ass day and my shirt wasn't going to stay clean for long.

Rogue didn't talk to either of us when we finally returned to the truck later in the afternoon. Fox had ordered one of the Harlequins to fetch her any food and drink she wanted and the car was now littered with Subway wrappers and the steering wheel was smeared with mayonnaise.

Both of our knuckles were bruised and flecked with blood, but we hadn't exposed any more rats among Jolene's people, so we had to hope Cyril had been the only one.

Rogue eyed the blood on us as Fox drove back to town, but kept her lips sealed tight. Fox didn't even make a comment on the mess she'd made of his truck, his gaze swirling with thoughts as he fell into a reverie, trying to think up a way to get to Shawn.

Mutt seemed pissed at us too, his eyes shut as he slept in Rogue's lap, but I could tell he was awake from the way his ears kept twitching.

We arrived back at Harlequin House and I noted the extra security on the gates as we drove inside then parked up in the garage.

I got out of the truck, holding the door open for Rogue as I tried to catch her eye, but she just swept past me, not sparing me a glance as Fox led the way up into the house.

"Hello?" Chase called, his voice sounding muffled. "That you Fox? I need help."

Fox broke into a run and I did too, even fucking Rogue did before we burst into the lounge together and found Chase had fallen off the couch and was wedged between it and the coffee table, his doughnut cushion stuffed tightly in behind him.

"Oh great," he growled as he saw us all there. "I'm so glad you're all here for the show."

"What happened?" I asked through a laugh.

"Fell, didn't I?" he huffed. "And every time I try to move, a shooting pain goes through me like that bullet wound opened up a gateway to hell in my ass."

I hurried forward with Fox to lift him back onto the couch and rearrange the butt cushion beneath him. His neck reddened and he wouldn't look anywhere in the direction of Rogue as he gritted his teeth against the pain.

"Why haven't you taken your painkillers?" Fox demanded and Chase shrugged.

"He hates taking anything strong since that time I got him some codeine from Jim Peeves for his broken fingers," Rogue supplied. "It made his head so fuzzy that he couldn't do anything to fight back against his dad when he was in a drunken rage that night," she added and I glanced back at her in surprise.

She shrugged like the knowledge was common, but I didn't remember that. I guessed Chase had decided not to mention it to me or Fox.

I knew Chase hated painkillers, but I'd never known why. He'd suffered through gunshot wounds before, and I always thought he was just trying to prove he was a big man. Now I felt like a dickwad for not knowing better.

"Take something lighter then," I urged. "There's some over the counter stuff in the cupboard."

Chase shook his head, his aversion to all painkillers clear. For someone who was used to regularly drinking himself into a coma, it was kinda stupid. But I guessed he had a shitty association with the stuff. I was pretty sure he'd drank his way through his last gunshot wounds come to think of it, but Fox had banned him from alcohol so now he was just stuck here suffering. How long had he been on the floor for? We'd been gone all fucking day.

"I need a piss," Chase said gruffly and I helped him up immediately.

He moved stiffly along, limping on his bad side while refusing to look at Rogue again, his jaw ticking furiously.

I helped him upstairs to the bathroom and he refused to let me help him any further as he shut the door in my face, but I leaned against the wall in case he got into any trouble. He cursed a lot, but soon emerged from the room victorious, propping himself against the wall beside me.

"I had an interesting call this morning, brother," he said mysteriously.

"Oh yeah?" I questioned.

"Texas was looking for you, said you weren't answering your phone," he explained and I frowned. *Shit.*

"What did he want?" I asked, sensing this wasn't going to be good.

"He said your client was looking for you. She was waiting at the club this morning, all dressed up for your breakfast date. Mrs Coolings."

Fuuuuck. I'd totally forgotten about Mrs Coolings. She booked in with me once a month for a morning of pastries in the upper quarter followed by fucking in her glitzy apartment.

"Oh woops," I said, trying to play it off, but Chase narrowed his gaze, seeing right through me.

"You don't ever let clients down," he said in a low voice which wouldn't carry back to the others. "And I'm guessing you missed this one because you were deep inside Rogue this morning when he called." Bitterness laced his tone. "How are you going to make up your cut to Luther if you skip jobs like that?"

I cursed, grabbing his arm and helping him down the hall into my room where we could have this conversation in private. My heart pounded harder as he looked at me with a frown and I sighed, pacing in front of him and scraping a hand through my hair.

"I can't do it, dude," I admitted heavily. Chase knew about me and Rogue anyway so what was the point in lying to him? "I haven't fucked a single client since I first got with Rogue. My dick's gone monogamous and I can't change its mind. I don't want to either. I want her, Chase. Only her." I looked to him and his brow furrowed as I bared my truth to him. "I want her so fucking much and if I dip my dick in some paying pussy again, it's gonna break the only pieces of me that are even remotely good enough for her."

Chase's jaw went slack. "Do you love her?" he demanded, his eyes dark and empty and so fucking hollow that it made me hurt for how damaged my best friend was inside. I could see it so plainly in him, how much these past ten years had shattered him. I could never say it though, he'd just deny it, tell me I was losing my mind. But I knew my brothers and he was as lost as I was. Only now…now, I had this glimmer of sunlight in my life and I wanted to cage it, keep it, refuse to ever let it go again.

"Yes," I rasped. "I don't think I ever stopped loving her, Ace. And actually, I don't even remember a time I didn't love her. I think I was born with a heart that already belonged to her and there's no changing it, it beats for that girl and I'm its slave."

His throat bobbed as he nodded, his face twisting with concern. "What about Fox?" he asked, his eyes flickering with pain, and I was sure he also wanted to ask *what about me?* Only he'd never thought himself worthy of Rogue, even now, he wouldn't expect himself to ever be in the running. But he had no fucking idea how much he meant to her.

"I don't know," I said tightly. "I don't wanna hurt him, I don't want this to break us. But I can't let go of her. Once she said she wanted me, there was nothing I could do. I've loved her my whole life, how was I supposed to refuse her?"

"She'll break us, J," Chase growled, his eyes flaring. "I knew it the second she returned. This was exactly what I was terrified of. What's going to happen to us if Fox finds out?"

"I don't know," I said again, hating this, but what could I do now? I was already in too deep, swimming miles under the ocean with her. "Maybe I can talk to him, maybe he'll understand." But those words sounded flat and useless. Of course he wouldn't. We both knew Fox. He would lose his mind if he found out, he could turn on me, kill me for all I knew.

Chase released a heavy breath. "Just be careful, don't take stupid risks. I'll cover for you when I can, but J…" He shook his head. "I hate lying to him. Don't you see what she's done to us already? There's cracks appearing in our family, and I don't know who's going to survive when the roof comes crashing down."

"I'll figure it out," I swore, though it was clear neither of us believed I could. But we were on this path now and I couldn't let Rogue go, it wasn't possible. "And look, while we're on the subject of Rogue, could you ever stop giving her such a hard time?"

Chase's lips pressed hard together for a moment. "No."

"That's it? No?" I growled at him and he shrugged. "She deserves better, Ace. I know you're angry, but I don't think you're really angry at her. I think you're angry at yourself."

"For what?" he scoffed.

"You're angry you let her get away the first time, you're angry you fucked up, angry you let her down, and you can't forgive yourself for it, so you just take it out on her and blame all of your problems on her too. And you know what that makes you, Ace?"

"What?" he grunted.

"Your father," I said, not wanting to hurt him, but it had to be said. I was sick of him snapping at Rogue and treating her like shit. She'd been through hell, and yeah so had we, but wasn't that more reason to show her some goddamn compassion?

Chase's face paled and I regretted the way I'd delivered those words. I just wanted him to see the truth. I knew he didn't wanna be like his dad, but this destructive path he was on with her was only going to end with one or both of them hurt badly. And I couldn't bear to see either of them broken by the other.

Silence settled between us and Chase shifted his weight, wincing in pain before schooling his features. He'd been dealt far too much pain in his life already and I hated how natural it was to him to just get on and face it.

"I didn't mean…" I sighed, dropping my gaze. "I just think she deserves to be cut a little slack by you, brother."

His jaw worked for a moment then he nodded stiffly, though I didn't know if he was really going to be any nicer to her because of it.

"How are you making up Luther's cut without the escort jobs?" he changed the subject.

I hung my head. "I'm taking fetish jobs at the Dollhouse, strictly no sexual contact but dude…*dude*, it's so messed up what some people like. I mean, I thought I was kinky, but now I'm thinking I was vanilla all along."

"You're working for Jolene?" he hissed and I nodded, ashamed.

"No, fuck that. Quit today. I'll help make up your cut until we can figure this out, I have some savings from the Maserati I stole and sold on last month."

"You don't have to-" I started but he cut over me.

"I do," he said fiercely. "You've always said to me you'll sell your body for so long as it never leaves a permanent mark on your soul. But I can see it leaving its mark now, J, and I'm not letting you do something you can't recover from."

My chest swelled and I strode forward, hugging my brother tight. "Thank you," I said heavily. "I just can't tickle another man's balls with an alien tentacle again. Not again."

Chase gripped me with his good arm. "Hang up your space hat, bro. Your ball tickling days are over."

I laughed in relief, stepping back from him as he smirked at me. "Well I dunno about that. If you ever need a ball or two tickling, I'll be there, Ace. You just say the word."

He snorted, swinging a punch at me, but I danced away with a chuckle.

"Fuck you, asshat!" Rogue shouted from downstairs and I sighed as a loud smash sounded.

"Hey, that was my favourite mug," Fox barked.

"Good," she snapped and another smash sounded.

"Oh no," I gasped, yanking the door open. She'd better not be going on a mug massacre. My collection of Pokémon mugs were down there.

Another smash sounded and I upped my pace. *I'm coming, Pikachu!*

CHAPTER TWENTY ONE

Three weeks. Three long fucking weeks shut up in this goddamn house with nobody for company aside from the three amigos and their bullshit.

I was even getting bored of Alexander the Great Big Dildo. Though as I leaned back and ran my thumb over the button which would switch it on, I had to admit a little surge of adrenaline ran through me. This was going to be good. So. Fucking. Good. My breaths were coming heavier already in anticipation, and I just had to hope I could get enough time to do this without Fox creeping up on me like a stalker and ruining my fun like last time. Because I needed this, the rush and the release. It was one of the few things I could truly enjoy in this fucking house and as there didn't seem to be much chance of me getting out of here any time soon, I needed to claim every bit of pleasure that I could as often as I could.

I bit my lip as I prepared to switch the huge vibrator on, knowing how fucking good this was going to feel already.

I tipped my head to the side, biting back a noise of excitement as I spotted Chase there, sitting on one of the sun loungers, his doughnut cushion finally gone. Though the way he leaned to his right suggesting his ass was still a little tender. *Come to momma.*

He had music playing out there, Cradles by Sub Urban colouring the air and giving me the perfect cover to use the vibrator without him even knowing I was right here, my eyes on him and my heart thrashing with excitement.

A cool breeze swept in from outside, making my nipples pebble inside my tie dye dress and I knew I couldn't wait a second longer. I needed this. I'd been holding back for too fucking long and if I didn't get this release, I was going to lose my goddamn mind.

I slipped out of my hiding place and began creeping across the main living area of the house, skirting the stools at the breakfast bar before circling the couch. He thought he was so shit hot that no one could ever get close to him, but here I was, proving myself yet again. I may not have been a big, tough Harlequin gangster, but I was a badass bitch with a weapon of mass destruction in my fist.

My bare foot made it out onto the tiles and I was as silent as the fucking wind - on a not too windy day obvs. I was basically one of those sexy assassin types like Black Widow or the chick from Naruto with the pink hair or maybe even a Green Power Ranger with tits. Maybe Chase was my arch nemesis and we were about to embark upon an illicit affair where he buried his rod of evil inside my... shield of justice. Damn. Why was I so bad at these recently? I used to think up sexy porn scenarios for myself all the damn time and yet these days I was getting stuck wondering how long it would take to get out of a catsuit for a romp with a villain. Seemed like hard work though, so I was pretty sure I had a point.

But right now, none of that mattered because I was only a few feet away from my prey and he hadn't even fucking noticed.

With a battle cry, I flicked Alexander the Great Big Dildo onto its highest setting and leapt at Chase from behind, ramming the plastic cock into his ear and making him cry out in alarm.

A hand came over the back of my head and he wrenched me off of my feet, flipping me right over his head so that the two of us went crashing to the ground and the sun lounger fell over.

My ass impacted with the tiles and his stupid muscular body crushed me as I lost my grip on Alexander and he vibrated away from me loudly. The icy kiss of a blade pressed to my throat and I blinked up at Chase in surprise as he ground me down into the tiles with his weight settled between my thighs.

"Gah! What the fuck are you doing?" he snarled, his eyes a mixture of confusion, relief and fury.

"Vanquishing you, duh. And if you didn't get the memo, you just got dicked to death. Pretty sure that makes it five times now."

Chase's frown deepened and he looked to his right where the incessant vibrations of my mighty hero still rang out. I followed his gaze just in time to see my beloved rattle its way right over the edge of the pool and I gasped at the splash which followed.

"I don't think that was a waterproof model," I cried, wriggling beneath my captor to try and escape him.

Chase grunted uncomfortably as I ground against his crotch, but he didn't let me up.

"Why the fuck do you keep attacking me with that thing, ghost?" he demanded, pressing his weight down on me harder and refusing to remove that blade from my throat. "I could have fucking killed you. We're all on high alert with Shawn still lurking in the shadows and apparently you have nothing better to do than to play childish fucking pranks."

"So do it then, Ace," I dared, tipping my chin back and pressing my neck to the blade even more firmly. "Call it an accident and blame it on me for jabbing you in the ear with a vibrator. I'm sure Fox would understand."

"Don't say shit like that," Chase muttered, tugging the knife away from me and pocketing it.

"What the fuck is going on out here?" Fox asked loudly as he yanked the sun lounger back upright and slammed it down on its feet to reveal us.

"Whoops, you caught us," I gasped. "I love getting Chase to pin me to the ground and dry hump me. If I line my cooch up with his hip bone I can even pretend his dick might be big enough to satisfy me. But obviously I had to insist he keeps his clothes on so as not to ruin my fantasies with the reality of his midget peen. And of course I have to keep my eyes shut so that I can picture him being absolutely anybody else in the world, otherwise my pussy can't get wet - it's a lot of work but I'm locked up here with you assholes twenty-four seven and a girl has needs."

"Fuck you," Chase grunted, moving to climb off of me but flexing his hips as he did so that his not-so-midget-not-so-flaccid cock ground down against my not-so-dry pussy, making sure I knew I was full of shit.

Whatever. So maybe I'd considered hate fucking him from time to time but only in an imagine-the-worst-most-unappealing-and-yet-filthily-hot-thing-I-could-get-up-to-in-this-fucking-house kind of way. Not seriously.

Besides, JJ and me had a pretty damn flawless secret fuck sessions thing of our own going on, so I had no need of Chase's douchebag dick. Of course, I was still pissed at Johnny James for going along with the prisoner bullshit that I was being subjected to in this house, so I'd only let him fuck me like eighteen or so times during my incarceration and I'd taken to slapping him when we were done to remind him that I was still mad.

The moment Chase was upright, Fox manhandled me back to my feet, his hands all lingery and making my skin tingle as I smacked them away. Officially I wasn't talking to him. But I also wasn't very good at that, so mostly I was being a snarky bitch and he was playing the grumpy badger role to perfection. It was kinda like being an old married couple who had been stuck in a fight for so long that they couldn't quite remember what had started it anymore.

"Explain," Fox growled, his gaze on Chase while I eyed the privacy screen I'd forced them to buy me so that I could sunbathe naked without any of them looking at me. I was pretty sure Fox had only gone along with it to stop the others from looking, which had almost tempted me into just going commando around the pool at all times just to piss him off. But not quite.

"She's a fucking psycho. She crept up on me and stabbed me in the ear with a dildo. *Again.* So obviously I reacted like I was under attack and tossed her over my shoulder - she's fucking lucky I didn't stab her."

"I actually think a stab wound would have broken up the monotony of my life," I said casually. "Or better yet, ended it all together. Either way, hell can't be worse than this place, am I right?"

Chase muttered some kind of insult or exasperated expression of my being an ungrateful little bitch and I flipped him off as he took a seat back on his lounger and sparked up a smoke.

"You know I can't let you out of here while Shawn is still-"

I reached up and placed a hand over Fox's mouth to silence those words because by fuck I couldn't hear them one more time without my head imploding.

"I can't do this again," I said, looking into his green eyes and wondering if he even gave a fuck about that. What even was I to him? Just some little doll he could lock up in his castle and play with when he was home? Something to keep and use and look pretty for him?

"Stop looking at me like that," Fox growled, peeling my hand from his mouth like he could read my mind and I shrugged, turning away from him.

Of course he didn't just let me go, catching my wrist and whirling me around to face him again. His lips were parted but I got there first, sick of this shit and just wanting to own my fucking destiny for once.

"When I was Shawn's girl," I began, shutting him up fast because I never spoke about this, and I knew he had a thousand questions burning through his head about it. Even Chase perked up, his glacial eyes on me as he waited for me to go on. "He used to like me looking nice for him, but not for other men. He used to get me all dressed up then keep me home so no one else could see me. He'd call me his good little slut and use my body before closing the doors and leaving me there all alone or sending me back to the apartment he leant me to be alone there instead. And sometimes I'd look out the window and wonder if I could have it better somewhere else. But the reality was that I knew I couldn't. So I stayed and I stayed and I'd probably still be there now if he hadn't decided I'd stayed too long. And that's what being trapped in here feels like all over again. Except here the doors aren't just closed, they're locked up tight too. I'm just someone else's dolly now, aren't I?"

"Jesus, Rogue," Fox groaned, his grip on my wrist tightening and I jerked my hand back to make him release me. "You know I'm just doing this for your protection, right?"

"Well in that case, would you like me to suck your cock now or save it until we don't have an audience?"

"Stop it," he growled.

"She's a brat, she won't stop," Chase added and I sneered at him.

"I'm not a brat," I replied. "I'm a grown ass woman who has spent years doing whatever I fucking had to to survive. I was pinned down and almost raped by a man four times the size of me when I was sixteen and I managed to kill him *myself*. I lived on the streets and in all the shittiest kinds of places, escaped the cops more times than I could count and yeah, I fucked some seriously questionable men. But I'm still kicking, so I think I got it handled. I never asked for any of you to rescue me. The only thing I did ask for was the right to finish Shawn off myself because *I'm* the one he tried to murder and left buried in a shallow fucking grave wrapped in a potato sack. But that's the one thing you refuse to give me. And yeah, I get the concept of it being safe for me here and maybe if you'd *asked* me to stay instead of locking the doors I would have agreed to that because I'm not a fucking moron. But all I want in return is a bit of fucking respect and for you to keep me in the loop about the shit that's going on with *my* ex-boyfriend."

"It's not that simple," Fox sighed. "You're not a Harlequin. I can't just tell you whatever you want to know about the Crew."

"You can actually. You and your stupid *no girls allowed* rules are just an example of the same kind of sexist bullshit you've let your daddy drum into you your whole life. When we were kids you never treated me like I couldn't do things because I was a girl. But now that you've figured out what my pussy is good for you've decided the rest of me has no further use. So excuse me if I'm unhappy locked up here and kept in the dark all the damn time. No doubt if this goes on long enough, I'll learn to shut my mouth and spread my legs like you want and it'll all be good."

I shoulder checked him as I strode away but as his fucking body was built like a battering ram, that mostly just hurt like a bitch. But he was forced to move aside so I took the minor win and headed back into the house.

I flinched as I found JJ there, lurking by the patio doors and hidden in the shadows. The look on his face said he'd heard all of that and I bit my lip against the desire to run from him too. He held out a hand to me where Fox couldn't see him and I moved to him, letting him pull me into his arms behind the curtain.

"I'll talk to him," he murmured. "See about getting him to let you come to the club with me sometimes. The girls have been asking about you nonstop and I can tell you need some time out of this place."

"I'm not an idiot, JJ," I said. "I know I have to be careful with Shawn hanging around, but this is fucking insane."

JJ's hand pushed into my freshly dyed hair and I sighed as a little of the tension escaped me. The one and only time I'd seen anyone aside from the three Harlequin boys and the members of the Crew who were on watch around this place was a few days ago when Lucy had come over here to do my hair for me. I knew I had JJ to thank for that little slice of normal, but it hadn't come close to being free.

"I miss the surf," I groaned. "And the sand in my toes and a breeze that's not blocked off by stupid walls. I miss my trailer and my bed and my friends. And partying. I miss my fucking life, J. I made a decision not to be the girl Shawn had been turning me into ever again and now I'm not getting any kind of choice in that."

JJ started to say something, but he stiffened and I knew instantly that there was a fucking badger at my back.

"Get your hands off of her," Fox growled and my heart lurched because I was so sick of sneaking around him and tiptoeing past his fucking feelings all the damn time. I wasn't his girl which meant I hadn't agreed to any of the terms and conditions he'd decided to place upon my goddamn body.

I gritted my teeth, whirling around in JJ's arms, the truth of what he was to me sitting primed and ready on my tongue because fuck knew he was the only bit of freedom I could claim at the moment. But before I could do anything stupid like tell Fox that I was addicted to JJ's cock and he was gonna have to learn to live with it, the sound of the front door opening interrupted us.

"Hello?" Luther called and my heart leapt up into my chest. It was always the damn same. Any time he came over here, I was shoved in a room, up the stairs, into a fucking closet, anywhere they could put me quick enough to keep me out of sight and then I was stuck there until the motherfucker left.

JJ wrapped an arm around my waist and herded me back out of the patio doors while Fox threw me a panicked look before striding away to meet his dad.

"I'll talk to Fox for you, I promise, pretty girl," JJ whispered as we hurried across the patio and I was directed behind the privacy screen to my sun lounger and table - which meant I was stuck here until further notice.

JJ turned to leave already and I caught a fistful of his shirt, yanking him back around and kissing him hard. He caught my face between his hands, kissing me frantically before groaning in frustration as he forced himself to pull away and I watched him leave with my heart sinking, wondering how long I'd be left waiting out here now.

I peeked out between the little gap in the hinges of my privacy screen and watched as Chase and JJ headed inside. Luther was right fucking there, my dog in his arms and licking his freaking face in greeting. What the fuck was that about, Mutt?

JJ closed the patio doors behind them and I scowled. Well wasn't this just peachy?

I huffed out a breath and looked at my sun lounger, but it was late in the day and the sun had already moved so that it was sat in the shade. They hadn't even left me with a phone or something to listen to some music on.

Fuck this.

I glanced at the table beside me and up at the wall beyond it. Yeah, it was time to make like the Green Power Ranger and disappear. Not that I'd be coming back all dressed in white or any of that shit, but I was gonna spend the rest of my day doing something much better than hiding behind a fucking screen in the corner.

My heart leapt as an even better idea occurred to me and I thought about calling Maverick. I had his number memorised, but I knew Fox was still monitoring my phone and I just hadn't been able to risk calling him while I was locked up here. I hoped he hadn't given up on me and knew I hadn't abandoned him.

I climbed up onto the table then jumped for the top of the white wall, heaving myself up and onto it before dropping down on the other side in the bushes. I hated leaving Mutt behind, but I knew I'd have to come back eventually anyway. I still hadn't made any progress getting those damn keys and my life was too entangled with the assholes inside that house for me to just cut and run now.

But for today, I was gonna claim back my freedom. I wouldn't be a dumbass about it. I knew Shawn was still hanging around. But realistically I would have to be damn unlucky to run into him at random when the Harlequins hadn't been able to find so much as a sniff of him in weeks.

I crept away from Harlequin House on silent feet, being careful not to alert any of their guys who were watching the house before I managed to slip off of the property and was running down the street.

It didn't take me long to find a car to boost - some silly duck had left their front door wide open to combat the heat and the keys had been right freaking there on a little hook. So within no time I was dumping the car a few blocks from Rejects Park and jogging back to my trailer.

"Rogue! Where have you been, dude?" Lyla hollered as I ran up the path with my bare feet and wild hair. It was hot as a clam's asshole today and I was sweating from my jog down here, but the sun was starting its descent towards the horizon so I was looking forward to it cooling down a little.

I turned to grin at my blonde friend as she swung out of her trailer door, completely topless with her impressive tits bouncing as she shooed some random guy out the door and beckoned me closer.

"Oh my god, you have no idea how much I've missed your face," I groaned as I bounded up the steps to her trailer and she threw her arms around me.

"Don't worry, he jizzed on his own chest - he only wanted to pay for a private lap dance while he got off. Dude is clearly building up to paying for the full deal, but I think he somehow convinces himself its more innocent if he's just staring at me and jerking himself off. Plus he tipped big - easiest fifty bucks I've made all week."

I laughed as she released me and we headed into her trailer.

"Tell me your lives have been boring as fuck while I was locked away," I pleaded. "Tell me it's just not the same without me and maybe I can deal."

"Well we haven't had much time for partying if that makes you feel any better? JJ has had everyone pulling extra shifts and he's run a bunch of events too. He said he needs to get the place earning bigger and if I'm honest most of us are all for it. More waitressing and stripping gigs means I can at least be fussy about which Ds I allow to buy entrance to my body. I turned down janky Joel the other night and it felt awesome."

I snorted and she tossed me a beer.

"Sounds like we all need a night out," I said. "But I will let it be known that I am likely to be hunted by Harlequins the moment they realise I'm missing. In fact, this is probably the first place they'll look. So we need to head out fast and we need to go somewhere they won't be able to follow...like maybe The Dungeon?"

Lyla let out a low whistle, sank her beer in four huge gulps then slammed the bottle down on the counter. "Okay. I'm in. Let's go over to Di's trailer to get ready - it's on the far side of the site so even if they show up here before we head out they might not find us."

"Sounds like a plan," I agreed. "Let me head to my trailer and grab some clothes-"

"Wait!" Lyla turned and ran for her bedroom and I followed her, intrigued as she squealed with excitement. "One of my johns bought me this the other week, and don't worry because it's still brand new, not a cum stain in sight, but the second I saw it I just knew you needed to wear it."

"Okay, but I've been locked up in that house for weeks so I wanna go all out tonight. That means slutty as fuck, I'm up for nipple holes, transparency, the whole shebang," I teased and Lyla laughed.

"Unfortunately there won't be any nip on show, but I think I got you covered." She whirled around, holding out a dress on a hanger and I looked it over. It was covered in white sequins which glimmered with a range of pastel rainbow colours to match my hair. It was strappy, low cut, tight and looked like it would barely cover my ass.

"Hell yes," I agreed, grinning big.

"You'll look like an all out unicorn wet dream," Lyla sighed. "I read this book once called Zodiac Academy where a dude had a unicorn fetish...or, well he tried to hump an inflatable unicorn sex toy and then a bunch of people saw him and he was all 'I'm not horny for the horn!' but he totally would have been if he saw you, in fact *everyone* will be horny for you in this."

"Okay, give me three minutes to get changed and we can head over to Di's to figure out hair and makeup then get the fuck out of here before the badger comes looking for me."

"Sounds good."

I made a move to leave as Lyla started rummaging for her own outfit then paused as I thought of something else.

"Hey, could I actually borrow your phone? Long story short, Fox is monitoring mine plus I left it back at his house and the person I wanna call wouldn't exactly make it onto his friends list, so I'd prefer he didn't know I was calling him..."

"Shit, you're gonna get me killed by the Harlequin Crew," Lyla chastised, but she tossed me her phone and didn't ask me anything else, clearly realising she was better off not knowing.

I grinned at her and jogged out of the room, skipping down the steps of her trailer before hurrying over to mine.

I located my key then let myself in, knocking the door closed with my ass before draping the dress over the little table then dialling Maverick.

I headed through into my little bathroom as I listened to it ringing, peeling off my dress and dropping it in a heap as I set some cool water running in the shower.

"Yeah?" Maverick's deep growl sent a shiver down my spine and I bit on my bottom lip as that one word got me all hot for a whole new reason.

"Hey, baby," I purred, teasing him and wondering if he'd been as anxious to talk to me as I had been to talk to him.

"Where are you?" he asked, no fucking about and I smirked to myself as I answered.

"I escaped for a bit. Me and some friends are gonna go out partying at The Dungeon tonight and I was thinking that maybe I'd see you there?"

"I'm there tonight anyway. Got some business that needs dealing with."

I pouted at his lack of enthusiasm and licked my lips as I decided to play him at his own game.

"Maybe I'll see you there then. Some of the boys are talking about hitting somewhere cooler though, so I guess we'll see."

There was silence for a beat then he spoke in a voice that made the hairs stand on end along the back of my neck and my nipples harden.

"Nah, beautiful. That's not gonna work for me. I'll tell you what you're gonna do. You're gonna get that fine ass of yours all dolled up for me in the hottest fucking thing you own. You're gonna wear a nice, bright shade of lipstick that'll look damn good smeared all over my cock if I decide to feed you it and you're not gonna bother with the panties. Because when I get to you, my hello will be given from my fingers as they push right into that wet cunt of yours."

"Christ," I muttered, my toes curling as I fought the flood of desire his deep voice was sending through my damn body.

"And I'll give you fair warning now - don't bring a single fucking dude with you when you come. You wanna show up with some girlfriends, that's fine by me. But if I see some asshole panting all over my girl, I'm gonna snap his fucking neck. You got that?"

"I got it," I replied, some snarky, witty reply building on the tip of my tongue even though it seemed like I'd lost track of it on account of my entire freaking body melting into a puddle at his words.

"Good. Then hurry the fuck up. I've been waiting too damn long for you already." Maverick cut the call.

I stared at Lyla's phone for several heartbeats before pulling myself together and stripping my underwear off so that I could have that cold shower because now I needed it more than ever and I really did have to hurry the fuck up.

I moaned as I washed between my thighs for several minutes, biting down on my bottom lip for no reason at all as my pussy gave in to my demands all too fucking quickly thanks to Maverick's motivation and pleasure tumbled through me in a blissful wave.

I frowned as I thought about JJ, wondering what the fuck I was doing. I'd literally been fucking him this morning, stealing time in his arms while Fox was out running, and gasping his name like he gave me breath and now my skin was prickling in anticipation of seeing Rick.

But we'd talked about this exact thing. The weird bond the five of us had and the way it defied all logic. Even the anger and hatred, the hurts and betrayal that marred our relationships hadn't done anything to dampen the bonds we all held for one another. So maybe it was insane, but somehow I couldn't believe it was wrong. And I was done living my life to standards laid out by other people. I'd made a vow to be free and steal happiness wherever I could claim it, so I wasn't going to overthink any of this. I was embracing life and living for the good stuff and all I could do was hope that if I stole enough of it, I might be able to start filling up some of the empty pieces of my soul along the way.

I stumbled out of the shower again, a little less hot and not really any less worked up as I made quick work of pulling on the sparkling dress with the pair of chunky white heels JJ had bought me and following that up with my Green Power Ranger panties. I was well aware that Maverick had told me not to wear any, but I was also not gonna be a good little sub for him, so he was gonna have to deal with it, because fuck him. But also fuck him in the good way because I was fairly certain that the night was headed that way and I was just a dick blinded girl stumbling down cock alley to destination orgasm.

But what else was a dead girl to do?

CHAPTER TWENTY TWO

I'd been bored shitless since Rogue had left. And it made me realise that I'd been bored for years before she came back into my life. The kind of bored that led to me murdering someone just so I could feel the rush of life leaving their body and claim a piece of it for my own in the wake of their death. It never lasted though. I always circled back around to the numbing nothingness of my life with only a head full of dark memories for company.

I hadn't played my little Russian roulette game since Rogue had thrown my revolver away, but then one of my men had shown up with it at my door tonight. Once it was in my grip and the nightmares started circling in my mind, the temptation was too great to ignore.

So I'd stood on my balcony just hours ago, pressed the revolver to my skull with one bullet loaded in the cylinder and pulled the trigger, but for the first time since I'd started that tradition, I'd hesitated. Just a moment of madness in a lake of deathly calm. My mad moment had belonged to Rogue, a thought of her mouth on mine, her smile against my lips. But I'd pulled the trigger anyway to see if death was thirsty for me yet. I guessed it had other business tonight though, and I was once again left on this earth to see the Harlequins dead.

Rogue's call had been one I'd been quietly hoping for ever since she'd left. I'd expected a text that had never come. I'd even considered reaching out to her before I realised I not only didn't have her number, but I would be a fool to risk one of the Harlequins finding a message from me if they happened to be beside her.

I'd pictured each of them fucking her in great detail followed by me slitting their throats and stabbing until they bled out once they were done with my girl. The fantasy always seemed to go that way. It would play out in full, them owning the girl we'd all loved once while I just watched the show until my fingers got twitchy and I needed to watch them die instead. I'd finally shaken myself out of it at last though. My mind was rife with her and she was getting her hooks in me. But I wasn't going to let her affect me anymore.

Rogue Easton was a distraction which had taken my eye off the prize, but my gaze was focused once more and I wouldn't let it stray again. It was my duty to destroy the Harlequins and she would assist me in that endeavour. If she was fucking every one of them to get the job done it made no difference to me whatsoever.

I sat in a low-lit booth in The Dungeon across from Kaiser Rosewood with his stepdaughter beside me, her hand on my knee under the table. I had no appetite but was forcing myself to eat a meal with him as I nudged the conversation in the direction of the Rosewood manor.

"How are the renovations coming along?" I asked as Kaiser took a large bite out of his burrito.

He was constantly distracted by talking to the people in this place, apparently knowing half the clientele. He was a socialite who liked poker, whiskey and guns. I was yet to be invited to one of the illegal poker nights he held at his manor, but I was angling for an invite tonight. As soon as I got into the grounds of that place, I could get a lay of the land, figure out how much work he'd had done, if he'd done anything to the crypt, maybe even get myself a tour.

"Slow," Kaiser said with a sigh. "You can't get good labourers these days. Bring slavery back I say, it's the only way to get a job done right."

I fought against my lip curling back in distaste. This motherfucker needed a good couple of bullets between the eyes to brighten up his piece of shit face. He resembled a well-oiled old motorcycle with his shining black hair, his voice like the deep, drone of an engine. He wore a maroon shirt under a black blazer with the buttons undone down to his chest, revealing a gold chain with the Rosewood crest on it nestled amongst the dark hair there. His outfit would have been embarrassing on anyone else, but Kaiser had a lot of friends around town and no one dared piss him off by pointing out his unfortunate sense of fashion. Including me.

He hosted a bunch of underground gambling nights across my territory and I took a small cut to turn a blind eye to it all, but I was well aware that Kaiser was using the Rosewood Manor as a sort of private casino for the rich assholes in town and it wasn't just me whose pocket he was keeping fat. He had cops in his inner circle too, cops who – according to Mia - dined at his house and no doubt gambled while they were there too. The amount of power Kaiser was quietly accruing in Sunset Cove might have worried me if I was Fox Harlequin, and I vaguely wondered if he was aware of how fast this asshole was building a network of his own gangsters right under his nose. *Lucky I'm not Fox Harlequin then.*

"Daddy," Mia scolded with a pout. "That's not nice."

"Oh I'm just joking, Mi-Mi," he cooed, reaching over the table to boop her on the nose. What was she, a fucking eight-year-old?

"If you need good labourers, I could lend you some of my men. For the right price of course," I offered, taking Mia's hand from my knee and kissing the back of it, pretending I was all lovestruck and shit.

"Hmm." Kaiser finished his burrito and licked his fingers. "I'll think on that, Mav. Thanks for the offer."

I despised that he called me Mav.

He pinched a waitress's ass to get her attention and I glared at the smarmy motherfucker as he pulled her closer to the table by the back of her bare thigh. She looked like she was about to punch him in the face, but then she saw who'd grabbed her and schooled her expression. Powerful men who used their position to abuse people made me trigger happy. By the time I was done getting what I wanted from this asshole, I might just shoot him. So long as I'd taken the stash from the crypt and made sure Fox and his boys were run out of town, I could risk the wrath of Kaiser's empire for the sake of ending him. Because I didn't give a fuck about anything after that; I'd follow the Harlequins to wherever they might run and finish them off for good.

"Get us a round of tequila shots, will you love?" Kaiser asked her, his hand travelling higher up her thigh.

She nodded and ran away before his fingers disappeared up the back of her skirt and my blood turned icy. Mia leaned in to kiss my cheek, tugging at my shirt to try and make me turn towards her mouth. I indulged her as Kaiser's eyes flicked our way, pecking her lips as she tried to full on thrust her tongue into my mouth in front of her stepfather. *Jesus fucking Christ.*

I pulled away, getting to my feet and jerking my head at her to let me out of the booth.

"I need a piss," I lied, wanting some space.

Kaiser spread his arms across the back of his booth seat, his eyes now on a couple of scantily dressed girls dancing and grinding up against one another in the crowd of people beyond the balcony beside us.

Mia let me out of the booth, but got closer as I stood up, running her hand over my cock as she covered the movement with her body. I hadn't fucked her since before Rogue had come to Dead Man's Isle, and she was getting needy as fuck. I wasn't sure I could put it off much longer, but my cock was like a dead weight between my thighs as she tried to stir it into action.

"You wanna meet me out back in the alley?" she spoke in my ear, her teeth grazing the lobe which did absolutely nothing for me. "I'm so horny."

My gaze hooked on a flash of colourful hair by the bar and my heart thrashed in my chest, my ears going deaf to Mia as she started to purr all the filthy things I could do to her if I had the mind to.

"Uhuh," I said vaguely, my gaze sliding down Rogue's back to her ass as she bounced up and down in her heels, trying to get the barman's attention. She was dressed in a sparkly little number which glittered and caught the light, making her look like a fantasy creature tailored exactly to my desires. A lot of guys behind her noticed her bouncy ass and a growl left me that made Mia shiver and press closer to me.

"Oh hello, big boy," she purred, rubbing her hand over my cock again which was now almost full mast.

Ah shit.

I grunted, pulling her hand off my dick and covering the move by kissing her lips hard to keep her quiet. When I pulled away from her, I found Rogue's gaze slamming into mine as she held two beers in her hands, looking like a savage as she glared at me. Then she turned casually away like I meant nothing to her and headed off through the crowd. *Oh no you don't.*

"So, five minutes?" Mia asked as I stepped past her.

"Yeah, sure," I agreed to who knew what and shoved my way through the crowd, hounding after my little unicorn as she tried to do a disappearing trick on me. But her hair was a dead giveaway and I caught sight of it once more as I pushed past some tall motherfucker and found her closing in on a group of her friends.

Before I could get close, she reached them and I cursed under my breath, moving to stand in the shadows near a couple who were making out. She placed one of the beers in the hand of a blonde girl in a red dress then glanced back over her shoulder curiously, though she couldn't spot me.

I'm right here, baby girl, hunting you in the dark.

My cock had been inactive for days, but apparently now it was making up for lost time as it strained against the inside of my jeans and begged me to plough it into the rainbow haired chick I was staring at.

Rogue finally broke off from the group again, heading straight past me toward a restroom twenty yards away. I moved back into the crowd, following close behind her as my gaze dragged down the length of her body, taking in her tanned legs and the tight dress which showed off all my favourite parts of her body. Barring one of course.

She stepped into the restroom and I didn't think as I walked straight in after her. She slipped into a cubicle and locked the door just as the women by the sinks spotted me with parted lips and widening eyes.

I pointed them out the door and they all fled like my finger was a gun, leaving me and Rogue alone in the restroom. Though she didn't know that yet.

I slid the lock across on the main door, folded my arms and leaned back against it. There was music playing through some speakers in the ceiling and Rogue sang along with Not Your Barbie Girl by Ava Max as she peed, making a smirk pull at my lips.

The toilet flushed and she walked out, heading straight to the sink without noticing me as she washed her hands, rocking her hips to the song. She finally looked up and her eyes snagged on mine in the mirror, a gasp escaping her before she swung around to stare at me.

"Were you listening to me pee like a creeper?" she demanded.

"I wouldn't use the word creeper." I kicked off of the door, walking slowly towards my prey as every drop of blood in my body rushed towards my throbbing cock.

"What else do you call a guy who sneaks into girls' restrooms?" she asked coolly.

"Why are you so angry?" I taunted. "Didn't you miss me, beautiful?"

She tossed her hair lightly. "I've had plenty to distract me, looks like you've had plenty of Mia to distract you too."

A dark, teasing smile pulled at my lips. "Jealous little thing, aren't you?"

She started backing up, looking for a place to run as I closed in on her, but I had her cornered and she'd have to go through me if she wanted to escape.

"I'm not jealous, Rick," she scoffed. "We're not a thing, never have been. Your dick is a free agent just like my pussy."

"You'd sound so much more convincing if you weren't currently creaming your panties for me."

"Fuck off," she growled.

"Oh but you aren't wearing panties are you?" My smiled widened. "Because you're desperate for me."

"Ha," she laughed hollowly. "As if."

"Let me check then," I said, smirking cruelly. "If you're not wet and bare for me, I'll leave you to your night."

She tasted her lips, considering that then shrugged like she didn't give any shits about it. Her back hit the wall, perfectly timed for me to rush forward and strike, pinning her to it with my hips.

"Prepare to lose," she said boldly and I laughed like an asshole, kicking her feet wide and sliding a hand between us.

I dragged my fingers up her inner thigh in a slow path, her silken skin making my cock throb even harder and she could definitely feel every inch of it grinding into her. Her eyes become hooded as she tried to keep her hard mask in place and I ran my fingers higher, taking my sweet time before I hooked her dress over her hips and looked down.

She wore a large, bright pair of Green Power Ranger panties and a laugh got stuck in my throat at her ridiculous defiance.

"Well you're not bare for me, but are you wet?" I leaned in close, so hungry for her I realised she was the exact reason I hadn't wanted to eat my meal with Kaiser tonight. I'd wanted the taste of this wild thing on my tongue and nothing else could even come close to sating that kind of appetite.

I dipped my hand into her panties, waiting for her to crack as I dragged my thumb over her clit and she bit down on her lip as she fought her reaction. My fingers slid between her thighs then onto her soaking pussy and her slender throat bobbed as she stared up at me.

"Bone dry," she panted as I circled my fingers in her wetness and I growled my approval.

"You ever been to a desert, baby girl?" I asked, grazing my slick fingers up to her clit and making her suck in a gasp as I massaged it with my thumb.

She nodded at my question. "It was just like this. Not a drop of water in sight."

I laughed deeply and she raised a hand to grip my bicep as I continued to tease her needy clit between my fingers.

"Mine," I told her plain and clear.

"I'm not yours," she growled at me, apparently still pissed about Mia.

"Are you sure about that, Rogue?" I shoved two fingers inside her and she moaned filthily, her head tipping back against the wall as I pumped them in and out of her. "Who's been here since I last claimed you?" I demanded. "Did you think of me like you promised?"

"I didn't promise...shit," she said through heavy breaths.

I gripped her chin, not letting her look away from me as I fucked her harder with my hand, anger coating my insides at the thought of someone else having her while I couldn't.

"Did you crawl back into bed with Johnny James?" I demanded as she moaned again and her pussy clenched on my fingers as she got closer and closer to coming. "Or was it Fox who you gave into this time?"

"Fuck...you," she gasped.

"Chase?" I guessed. "Did the broken boy throw you around like his daddy did to him?"

Her nails dug into my arm as she bared her teeth at me. "Shut up."

"I guess it doesn't matter," I decided, unzipping my fly and freeing my ragingly hard cock as I pulled my hand free of her tight hole. "By the time I'm done with you, your pussy won't remember anyone but me."

I grabbed the backs of her thighs, hoisting her up and she wrapped them around me. The moment I tugged her panties to one side, I thrust into her in one furious drive of my hips.

She cried out and the repetitive thump of the music in the club hid away the sound of us as I showed her no mercy and fucked her furiously against the wall. My cock practically hummed with how happy it was to be back inside her and she swore under her breath as she took every inch of me, the chunky heels of her shoes, driving into my back and spurring me on.

She felt like heaven around my cock, the hot, wet tightness of her so perfect I was already close to blowing my load. Her mouth collided with mine and we kissed like we were gonna die and the only chance of life was each other. I hated that about her almost as much as I loved it. She was the breath of fresh air I'd been gasping for my whole life, and how dare she come back here and remind me of the good times when I was on the verge of burning the world down?

I pounded her against the wall until she fell apart in my arms, coming so hard, her pussy clamped around my cock and forced me to follow her into her release. I slammed my hand to the wall above her head, pulling out of her and pumping my cock in my hand as I came all over her thighs and panties while she watched me make a dirty mess of her with wide eyes. I gave her every last drop of me before I let her fall to the floor and she hiked her dress higher to save it from the mess as I laughed.

"You asshole," she snarled.

"Hey, I'm just saving you from getting knocked up, beautiful," I said then grabbed her panties and ripped them off of her.

"Rick!" she snapped, but I just used them to mop my cum off of her legs then tossed them in the trash with a shrug before pulling her dress back down.

"There," I announced with a crooked smile and she slapped me hard enough to leave a mark.

"Those were my G.P.R.Ps!" she yelled.

"What?" I balked.

"My Green Power Ranger Panties. My *favourite* panties," she hissed venomously.

I saluted the ruined panties in the trash. "R.I.P. G.P.R.Ps." I snorted and she scowled at me.

"Bring a condom next time," she growled.

"So there will be a next time?" I smirked and her eyes narrowed to slits.

"Not if you're gonna disrespect me there isn't," she snarled and my gut tugged as she stalked past me to try and leave. I twisted around, grabbing her hand and pulling her back against me.

"Wait," I commanded through my teeth as she tried to pull her hand free. "What progress have you made with the keys?"

"Is that all you care about?" she hissed. "No, hi how you doing, Rogue? How's it been living with your enemies? Did you find out anything interesting about the night they abandoned you?"

"Well yeah, those things too." I scrambled for the right thing to say but came up short.

She yanked her hand away with a cold look. "I got another key, and I'll get the rest soon. See ya, Rick." She tossed me her middle finger and walked to the door, casually checking her hair in the mirror and wiping her smudged lipstick from the corner of her mouth before stepping out of the room and leaving me there.

My heart beat painfully in my chest and I had the feeling I'd just royally fucked up, but I wasn't sure how to deal with it. I swallowed down the discomfort in me, knowing I just had to concentrate on what I was planning. Rogue was my weakness and if I let myself get lost in her, I wouldn't finish what I'd started. The Harlequin empire needed to burn, and I had to be ready to strike the match.

Rejects Park

ROGUE

CHAPTER TWENTY THREE

I was pissed. No. In fact pissed didn't cover it. I was fucking fuming and my lady bits were hurting (in all the right ways but that wasn't the point) and now my buzz was waning and I was ready to call the night quits.

Di had gotten lucky and ditched an hour ago and as I looked across the room, wondering if I should go and try to talk to Rick again, I saw him heading for his special little Damned Men exit. With fucking Mia in tow. Mia the clam vag. Ergh. She looked kinda angry at him, but it was hard to tell from this distance and the way his hand was firmly stamped to her back made me fear they were heading straight off for a make-up fuck.

I was angry dancing now. There were elbows and fists and maybe I was actually more moshing than dancing and some guy yelled at me because I slammed into him, but I didn't fucking care. I was basically head banging to Acapella by Karmin as it was blasted through the speakers, the band long since retired for the night.

I pushed my fingers into my hair and closed my eyes and just gave into this anger in me. It wasn't even all for Maverick. It was for so much shit in my life and I kept it locked up tight inside way too often.

Lyla and Bella told me they had a ride waiting for us at some point, but I insisted they go without me. Because I couldn't head back to my trailer now. It wouldn't be empty. It wouldn't be a sanctuary. No. When I left here, I had to go back to the Harlequins because they wouldn't give me a choice in that anyway.

I just kept dancing and dancing and telling anyone who got too close to fuck off as I lost my shit and screamed to the ceiling. And when I was finally done and my limbs were shaking with fatigue and even the booze was fading so that the room didn't spin anymore I just stood there and breathed.

I was finished.

Fucked up and fucking insane, but that was okay. I'd never really given a shit about that.

There was a wide space around me on the dance floor and in all honesty that was exactly how I wanted it to be. I always felt like that. Like there was a void of space around me which people either couldn't cross or which they didn't want to.

I headed into the dwindling crowd, lifted a cell phone from some dude's back pocket and strode towards the exit as I dialled Fox's number. I knew all of their numbers by heart now. One of the many boring as fuck things I'd done during my incarceration at their stupid house.

I strode up the stairs, ignoring the bouncers as they watched me go. I gave no shits. I was walking straight and my heels still held me even if they hurt like a bitch right about now. I'd stopped bothering with the booze hours ago, so I was only like a quarter past drunk.

The call only rang once before he answered. "Is it you?"

"Can you come get me?" I asked, taking a deep breath of cool, night air and looking up at the stars.

"Always. Where are you?"

"The Dungeon."

Silence. Then, "You crossed the fucking Divide? Do you know what could happen if I'm seen driving out there while this war is raging between-"

"Forget it. I'll make my own way back." I went to cut the call, but he spoke before I could.

"I'm already in my truck. Look for me. I can't hang around when I get there."

"Okay."

"Hummingbird?" his tone softened and I released a breath. "Are you okay?"

"No," I breathed. "But I haven't been for a long time, Fox."

I cut the call and started walking down the street in the direction I knew he'd come from.

Some guys cat called me and I paused, bummed a smoke then told them Fox Harlequin was my boyfriend to scare them off before continuing on my way.

After a couple of blocks, I stopped to tug my shoes off and toss the half smoked cigarette, my feet burning as I spiralled.

Headlights lit me up and the familiar rumble of Fox's truck told me it was him before he even pulled up.

I got in, tossed my shoes in the footwell and stared at my lap as he started driving again right away, checking his mirrors like he expected an attack any second.

The time on the dash said it was almost five in the morning. Wow, I really had lost my shit in there. I must have been dancing alone for hours.

"Are you hurt?" he asked. "Did something happen?"

Like That by Bea Miller came on through the speakers and I sighed as I leaned back in my seat and turned to look at him.

"I know it's not all on you," I said to him, ignoring his questions and letting the word vomit out. It was long overdue anyway. "I know that I'm... difficult."

He snorted a humourless laugh. "Understatement."

I looked out of the windows again as I went on, not wanting to see the look on his face as I gave him this truth.

"I'm broken, Fox. And I might want to blame that on you and the others for sending me away, but I know that's not the real reason. I was born to walk this path. I had a junkie mom who I can't remember, and I wasn't even cute enough for anyone to wanna adopt me, so I just bounced around in foster homes. I never had anyone apart from the four of you and I never had anything even when I had you. I was just a nothing kid from nowhere with no prospects and even less hope. Fact is, I was always destined to be the way I am. This girl who blows in on the wind and hangs around for a while before I twist away

341

again. No one has ever wanted to keep me long term - not even me."

"Rogue," he said roughly, but I shook my head, needing to say this, to get it out there and let the universe have it.

"It's okay. Some people just aren't...enough. And that's me. But I can't just blame everyone else for that. I don't have a lot to give so I don't offer it up. There are walls around my heart which even I don't know how to peek beyond. And I'm holding onto the pain of the past because it's the only thing I've been able to cling to for a seriously long time. It's one of the truest things I own. The way I know I felt about all of you once. The love I took a taste of but didn't understand. You were my boys and I thought I was your girl, but we were really just dumb kids, and I was never your responsibility. So, I'm sorry I'm an asshole all the fucking time. I'm sorry I'm not the girl you wanted when you found me and I'm sorry that I made some shitty life choices which have put you in shitty positions now. But all I can say is that every choice I've made in my life has purely been to ensure my own survival. And if I hurt anyone along the way...hurt you along the way, I didn't mean to."

"You are the girl I wanted," Fox growled. "You're the girl I *want*."

"I'm not," I denied because I knew that was true more deeply than I knew most other things. "There isn't enough of me to be that. I'm empty. I'm not even broken really because there are pieces of me which are just missing entirely. There's no putting them back and I'm not certain they were ever there in the first place."

Fox undid his seatbelt and I only realised we were parked up in his garage because he leaned over to cup my cheek in his large hand and we didn't veer off of the road.

"You think if you tell me this or you show me the parts of you which are hurting then somehow that'll change my opinion of you, but it's bullshit. I want the broken pieces just as much as the ones that are whole. And if there's parts missing then I want to help you fill them up again. I want you to smile and mean it. I want you to laugh and feel joy. But most of all, Rogue, I just want *you*. No matter which version of you I get. Because your heart races for me the way it did when we were kids. That's why I call you hummingbird, remember? Because your heart feels like the wings of that little creature whenever we're together. Your pupils dilate and your lips part and I know that I own you already, even if you aren't ready to admit that yet. But I'm not afraid to tell you that you own me. You have from the first moment I laid eyes on you in freaking elementary school. You were just this little thing all lost and unsure and I told the boys right then that you needed us. I saw you and I just fucking knew it."

I blinked up at him as I remembered that day. I'd been placed in a new foster home and bundled off to a new school so fucking fast that I'd barely had a second to figure out what way was up before I was being dumped in the middle of the school yard.

I'd been unsure and a little scared and then these four boys were suddenly there, smiling and asking me if I'd like to play ball with them. Fox had offered me a piece of candy and my stomach had rumbled because there hadn't been time for me to eat breakfast in the rush to get there that morning.

JJ had called me the prettiest girl he'd ever seen to Chase even though I hadn't been meant to hear that and he hadn't stopped calling me pretty girl since that day. Even Rick had smiled, challenging me to wrestle with them and I'd grinned as I promised to grind them into the dirt. And just like that it had been us. Inseparable. Me and my boys. Until it wasn't anymore.

I leaned forward and closed the distance between us and Fox stiffened as I took him off guard, my lips meeting his and his grip on me tightening as his fingers slipped into my hair.

There was so much in that kiss, so much want and need and endless possibilities but there was truth too. Because I wasn't the girl he thought I was and I couldn't give him what he wanted from me. He wanted me to love him and *only* him but that was impossible. I didn't even think I *could* love now. But I had once, with all my heart and it had been divided equally between all four of them. In fact, no it hadn't. There hadn't been any division. Each of them had owned it entirely and that was just the way it was. All in. All of us.

I pulled back and he groaned, knowing I was drawing a line again. But with him I had to. With him it was all or nothing and I didn't have an all to offer.

"Ceasefire?" I breathed, cupping the back of his neck with my hand and keeping him close.

"Deal," he agreed softly.

He took my hand and led me out of the truck and I stayed quiet as I let him.

The house was dark as we made it inside, but Fox told me the others knew I was alright. He'd called them on his way to get me and texted again once I was in the car. I hadn't noticed that, but I was sure it was true.

He paused to pour me a large glass of water then led me on through the house and up to his room. I didn't protest as he drew me inside, but my gaze slid across the corridor to JJ's room where I noticed the door crack open.

Johnny James gave me a small smile which made my heart twist and relief filled his eyes before he closed his door again and I was tugged into Fox's room.

Fox didn't switch the lights on as we entered and I let him tug my dress off of me before he offered me his shirt which was still warm from him wearing it.

I pulled it on and he lifted me from my feet, carrying me to his bed and wrapping me in his arms as he buried his face in my hair.

"You're back where you belong now, hummingbird," he murmured as my eyes drifted closed. "The rest of it is just us figuring out the details."

I woke up wrapped in safety with this heavy sense of peace laying over me alongside the body wrapped around mine.

"You sleep like the fucking dead," Fox murmured, nuzzling his face into my hair and squeezing me as I yawned.

"And you wake up way too perky," I muttered, scrubbing sleep from my eyes.

"I could perk you up too if you wanna just give in to us already?"

"And giving in to 'us' would mean what exactly?" I asked.

Fox rolled me onto my back and propped himself up on his elbow as he looked down at me. My gaze fell to his bare chest and the Ferris wheel tattoo over his left pec, the whole of Sinners' playground inked around it in a circle. Then I looked at the Harlequin symbol of a skull wearing a jester's hat

344

which covered his left bicep and my gut twisted uncomfortably. I hated that fucking thing no matter how unreasonable it might have seemed. But to me, the addition of that tattoo to his flesh - and to JJ and Chase's too - was a literal representation of the divide between me and them. They were Harlequins and I wasn't. They were on the in and I was on the out. Story of my life.

"Well first off it would mean me spending the rest of today, tonight and likely the entire week buried between your thighs."

"What, no pee breaks?" I teased, even though I could feel the blush rising in my cheeks at his words.

"Pee breaks would be acceptable as well as snack breaks because you're a fucking heathen when you're hangry," he agreed.

"So aside from all the fucking, what else would it mean?" I asked, trying to ignore how fucking edible he looked right then, blonde hair tussled from sleep and those inky muscles all poised for action on his huge torso.

"Well aside from that you'd be mine for real. Which means I'd be keeping you all to myself."

"So you want me exclusively?" I arched a brow, wondering when he'd gotten so caught on the idea of monogamy. Was it an *us* thing or his usual go to? Because guys like him were usually pretty hard to tie down, so I was struggling to understand how he could be so certain about someone he only thought he knew through memories.

"Yes," he demanded, his eyes running over me. "Mine."

"Well, what if I'm not done with other D? I'm still pretty thirsty you know, and I don't think I'm ready to embark on a cockdown."

"A what?"

"A lockdown with one cock, duh."

Fox rolled his eyes and pushed himself up and out of the bed in a fluid motion. "Well when you are you know where I am. I trust it won't take you too long to realise that that's what you need. We're destined, hummingbird. If I have to wait for you to realise that too then I will. For now."

"What about after now?" I asked curiously and he looked back over his shoulder at me.

"Then I'll have to force your hand."

Wow, that sent a shot of *own me, Daddy* right to my vagina, but I had to slap that bitch down. She couldn't just go making life choices for me based on an insatiable thirst for bad decisions. This was all gonna hurt bad enough in the end anyway. I wasn't dumb enough to fall for the idea of a happily ever after for me. That wasn't how the story of a dead girl would play out.

I decided not to venture down that minefield and slipped out of his bed before heading down the corridor to my room to grab a shower and get changed.

I emerged downstairs half an hour later with wet hair, wearing my 'I hate everyone' tank and a pair of booty shorts which did not contain my booty at all. But it was hot as fuck and I was good with that.

I made it downstairs and found a plate of sandwiches waiting for me beneath a post-it with a stick drawing of two people fucking on it and grinned at the little gift from JJ.

I guessed that meant he wasn't pissed about my sleepover with Fox at least, but I really needed to speak to him properly about this whole hook up thing we had going on because between his cock and Maverick's and Fox's cockdown request, things were getting sticky and I didn't want any kind of awkward shit between us. I liked him. No, fuck that, I needed him and I cared about him way more than I ever wanted to let myself when I came back here. But I was starting to think the Harlequin boys were like dicksand for me and I was only gonna keep sinking deeper inch by delicious inch until I was trapped for good. But that was tomorrow's problem. Right now, I needed to demolish my food.

"Must you prance about the place half naked all the fucking time?" Chase's voice came from behind me as I leaned over the counter and moaned around a mouthful of sandwich. No doubt he was getting an eyeful of my peachy round ass and he was salty because his had a bullet wound in it now.

"Can you see a hole anywhere on my body?" I asked him without swallowing. "Or a nipple? Because I fail to see which half of my body is naked if you can't."

He rolled his eyes and took a step to walk away from me, but I snatched his arm to stop him before he could head out to the pool where I could hear Fox and JJ laughing together.

"Where are my keys, Ace?" I asked him, giving him a narrow-eyed look that let him know I was done fucking around.

"I dunno what you want me to say, ghost," he sniped. "How am I supposed to figure out where they hid them?"

"Not my problem," I tossed back. "But if you don't hurry up, my lips might get all loose in my boredom."

He jerked a nod in understanding then snatched his own lunch and strode away while muttering insults at me beneath his breath.

I stayed where I was to eat my food, too hungry to want to waste the time it would take walking outside before filling my face.

I decided my sandwich needed chips to go with it and started on a hunt, finding some OJ in the fridge too and pouring a tall glass to help with my hangover.

"We have to go out, pretty girl," JJ said behind me and I turned to find all three of them there, watching me shake my ass as I rummaged in the fridge to add to my feast.

"Where are we going?" I perked up even though I already knew by the set of Badger's jaw that I was taking a trip to nowheresville.

"Some of my guys will be protecting you all day, but you have to stay-"

"Got it," I cut him off. "Same shit, different day, right?" I turned my back on them and went back to my food hunt. I couldn't even be bothered to be any snarkier than that. I just wanted all the food then I'd probably crash in front of the tv until they came back.

Fox knocked his knuckles against the worktop in some kind of awkward goodbye which I guessed acknowledged both that I was pissed and that he wasn't gonna change his mind and Chase strode out beside him without a word.

JJ lingered and I turned to him as he moved up close to me.

I glanced towards the garage door, making sure the others were gone before whispering to him.

"JJ, about me and Fox last night-"

"We don't have time for all that now, pretty girl," he said, brushing his knuckles across my cheek. "Just tell me one thing. Are you sure nothing with him or…any of them change stuff between you and me? Are you sure you're not gearing up to choose one of us?"

I shook my head, looking into his honey brown eyes and begging him to see how much I meant that.

"No. It's not like that. It's not about picking or favourites or anything. It's just me and you…and them. Like it always was and yet not like that at all, and I know it's all fucked up but I just-"

He kissed me to cut me off and I melted into it, fisting his shirt and tugging him closer still, hoping he could feel everything I felt in that kiss and knew I wasn't bullshitting him.

"I get it," he said in a low voice. "The five of us are something…I don't even know what it is but we are. We can talk about it more later but for now I'm good so long as the you and me portion of it is still good?"

I nodded and he kissed me again briefly as Fox yelled at him to hurry up. He jogged away from me, locking the door as he went and I gave in to the call of the food awaiting me.

Mutt yipped excitedly and hopped up just as I was licking the last of the mayo from my fingers and I looked around in confusion as he scampered out of the room with his tail wagging furiously.

Curiosity sank its claws into me and I followed him, calling his name and wondering what had him so hyped up.

By the time I caught up to him, he was at the front door and my heart lurched violently as it swung open suddenly, revealing Luther fucking Harlequin in all his super psycho glory smiling at me like we were old friends. Or maybe like he was going to eat me for fucking breakfast. *Shit.*

"Good afternoon, Rogue," he said casually, levelling a pistol at my forehead. "Looks like you broke our deal then?"

I swallowed a lump in my throat, wondering if I should scream or run or just piss myself in fear and be done with it.

"Come on, don't be shy. You and I have a date, sweetheart. So I think we should go for a ride, don't you?" he offered, his tone as cold as I knew his heart was.

He indicated for me to follow him with a jerk of that gun and fear ran down my spine like fingers of ice. I didn't have a choice, but as I glanced at the dark van he had waiting for us, I knew I was looking at my death inside it. The glass was all blacked out and there was a duffle bag that just screamed 'murder bag' to me. If I got in there, then that would be it. I'd be done and all of it, us, me, them, would have been for nothing.

Fuck.

Luther clearly grew tired of waiting for me to move and caught my arm, the gun pressing right up against my heart as he tugged me out into the sunshine and made me start walking.

The door was kicked shut behind me and that was it. My boys didn't even know I was missing. And yet my death had come calling at the door, dressed in ink and with a dark kind of mayhem dancing in his eyes. Luther Harlequin was a man of his word and I'd made a deal with this devil a long time ago. He'd made it clear that if I set foot back in this town then I was dead.

He gave me a push so that I climbed into the back of the van then followed me inside it before sliding the door closed and plunging us into darkness.

Someone started it up and drove us away, my last shot at rescue from the Harlequin boys staying behind while my destiny finally caught up to me.

Fear took hold of my chest in a vice so tight I couldn't breathe around it as I grasped exactly what was happening to me.

Fuck, my life had sucked so much. I really had been a miserable bitch for so goddamn much of it, but for some reason I'd always held on to this idea of the sun shining somewhere in the distance of my future. But now that future was drifting away from me before I'd even gotten a chance to take a peek at it.

And I might have been a dead girl walking, but I found I really didn't want to die.

CHAPTER TWENTY FOUR

JJ and Fox were having a meeting together at The Oasis clubhouse while I was banished from joining in and left outside like a naughty kid. The huge wooden building towered up to my left, a large balcony swinging around the second level and a flag hanging over the railings with the Harlequin symbol of a skull in a jester's hat printed on it red, blue and yellow.

Apparently three weeks in ass wound recovery hadn't counted towards my time left out of Harlequin business and Fox wanted me to continue to prove my worth to the gang so he could decide whether or not I could officially reclaim my position.

Luther was running late so they'd headed inside to discuss shit, no longer holding meetings at home while Rogue was there. Fox didn't want any more reasons for his dad to come to the house than he already had, or for Rogue to start spying on conversations related to Shawn. So I guessed I was just here to work on my tan and be fully reminded that I wasn't invited to the party.

Fox's attitude toward me was bullshit, but I guessed my head was clearer for the lack of alcohol, and I was sort of getting used to the daily discomfort of being around Rogue. On a fucked up level, I was kind of glad she was punishing my ass for what I'd done and that I didn't have to lie to at least one person about it, but on another, I hated the bitch for what she was plotting. She was fucking JJ, leading him on and snaring his heart in her grip, all the while planning to open the Rosewood crypt and unleash a secret that could destroy him along with the rest of us.

A couple of days ago I'd been in the house when JJ had dragged her into the laundry room while Fox went for his morning run. I was pretty sure she hadn't known I was there, but when I'd gone into the kitchen for a drink I'd heard the two of them and while a part of me had been furious, jealous and just fucking enraged over it, I'd stayed there listening. She'd been moaning his name and begging for more and I'd soaked in every word, but the ones which had been playing on repeat in my head since then were what she'd panted as they'd finished. *You make me feel alive again, J. It doesn't hurt when I'm with you.*

He'd started telling her something about him not being able to get enough of her and hating them sneaking about and I'd left them to it while my gut twisted up, my heart shredded apart and I was left torn.

I didn't want to wish away my brother's happiness and a small part of me couldn't bear to wish hers away either. But then I thought of Fox and how much this was going to hurt him when it came out and I was angry again. So fucking angry on his behalf. And maybe I was angry on mine too. Because this whole thing was messed up and unfair and just so fucking aggravating and I didn't know what to do about it or how to deal with it. So mostly I was just forcing my thoughts and feelings about it aside. But those words of hers kept slipping through my mind and they were a whole lot harder to forget somehow. *It doesn't hurt when I'm with you.* So how much did it hurt when she was alone then?

I'd been putting off something for days, and figured now was the time to deal with it as I got on my motorcycle and rode it down to my old home by the beach. The wooden building looked like it needed some serious repairs done, but while my dear Daddy was rotting inside it, I wouldn't be putting so much as a lick of paint on the property. Frankly, I was waiting for the day he died so I could come down here and set the whole place alight. But all the while my dad lingered on like a cockroach and he suffered from his bad leg and dodgy lungs, I was happy to let the place rot with him until he finally croaked.

I parked up my bike outside, gazing at the weed infested garden that momma would have been horrified by and the old porch where my dad's old rocking chair sat facing the sea. The ghosts of my past clung to every inch of this place and they crept over me like cold fingers, holding onto me and not letting go.

From the outside, the house looked kinda peaceful. I could see the potential it had once had to be a cosy home where I could have played on the beach as a kid in peace and not have feared the shadow lurking just behind me everywhere I went. I guessed some people could make any place hell if they tried hard enough. My dad's wretched soul had coloured this place black and tainted all the good about it, and now every memory I had here was black too, living on forever in my mind to haunt me.

I headed through the creaky gate with my gun tucked into the back of my jeans and spotted my old bike on the ground by the porch, rust biting into the metal frame and weeds wrapped around it, never to let go. That bike had given me a quick escape from this place countless times and I guessed I owed it a lot for that.

I pulled it out of the grass, fighting back the ivy that was determined to hold onto it as I stood it upright and ran my fingers over the flaking green paint. I leaned it against the porch and headed up to the front door, pushing my way inside as a chill washed along my spine.

Dad was in his mouldy armchair facing the window, smoke coiling up around him and trailing along the ceiling as he puffed on a cigarette. A PBR beer can was clamped in his hand and the familiarity of the scene made my pulse quicken and my body feel smaller, like that of a child's.

I cleared my throat and he turned his head to try and see me, a sneer pulling at his lips.

"That you, boy?" he growled, his voice throaty and tainted by years of smoking.

"Yeah, I'm here," I said, the floorboards creaking under my feet as I walked over to him where the light filtered in through the dusty window. I kinda hated that he could gaze out at the ocean and steal some peace from it.

"Come 'ere into the light so I can see ya," he croaked and I indulged him, blocking his view of the sea as I gazed down at him with my arms folded over my chest. His grizzled hair was pushed back from his face and his eyes were heavy with bags, speaking of long nights of unrest. *That's the least you deserve, you piece of shit.*

"You got a look of me about you these days. I never thought you were mine but looks like I drew the short stick," he said and my upper lip curled back.

"That's unfortunate," I muttered.

"Don't gimme that lip," he snapped, then reached for a piece of paper sitting beside him on a side table, an ashtray next to it crammed to the brim with cigarette butts. "Here." He passed the paper to me and I took it. He'd been going on and on about some document he wanted me to look at for weeks, but if he wanted me to sign him over to a care home or some shit, it wasn't going to happen. He was going to die in this house where he broke my momma and made my childhood hell. That was non-negotiable.

I let my eyes fall onto the page and read the printed words, frowning at what this document was. "You wanna give your boat to someone?" I asked.

"Not just someone, boy, I want *you* to have it," he said firmly.

I released a dry laugh. "No thanks."

"I ain't askin'," he snarled like he held any authority with me anymore. "I owe some docking fees and the Forks boys are gonna seize the boat from me if it ain't moved by the end of the week. Don't be a little prick about it, you can keep it, I just don't want the Forks to get their greasy hands on it. That boat's the only thing that's ever been good to me in this life. But you need proof of ownership or they won't let ya take it."

"Don't you talk like that, old man," I spat. "My momma kept food in your belly and beer in your fridge."

"Your momma was lucky I took her in, no man woulda put up with the shit I had to put up with from her."

I gripped his stained checked shirt, yanking him half out of his seat and was satisfied when fear flickered in his eyes. The roles had truly changed now. I was the shadow in his home, the reason he feared noises in the night. Any time I liked, I could come down here and drive a knife into his chest and be done with him. And he knew it.

"You don't speak about her like that, Dylan, in fact you don't speak about her period," I snarled.

"Get your hands off me, boy," he growled, shoving at my arm.

I let him drop back into his seat, knocking his bad leg with my foot and he wailed like a dying animal, his eyes closing in agony as he rode out the wave. It didn't feel as good as I'd have liked it to. Seeing him suffer here didn't make me sleep any easier at night, but I knew it was what he deserved regardless, so it was what he was going to get.

I snatched up a pen from the table as I made a decision, scribbling my signature at the bottom of the document where he'd already signed his name.

"There. It's mine. Where's the keys?" I folded up the document and slid it into my back pocket as he pointed to a drawer in a dresser across the room.

I headed over there, pulling it out and finding the key to the Josephine-Rose – which he'd named after a fucking porn star not his own wife, a fact he'd loved to taunt her over whenever they argued. It had a keyring with a photo of momma and Dylan on their wedding day and I frowned, wondering if she'd had dreams of sailing on this boat with her husband and child. He sure as shit had never taken me out on it and he hadn't taken Momma out during my lifetime so far as I knew. The boat had offered us some peace sometimes though whenever he'd gone out on it for work or at the weekends to drink beer with his fisherman friends, leaving us at home to make the most of his absence.

"Enjoy the silence," I called to my father before heading out of the house and letting the door swing shut behind me with a loud bang.

A string of abuse followed me from him, but I gave no shits, picking up my rusted bicycle as I left and carrying it out of the gate. I couldn't bring it home today, but I rested it up beside the fence with a promise to come back for it, though I didn't know what I was planning to do with it. The thing needed to go in the trash in all honesty, but I didn't think it deserved that and maybe I was still kind of attached to it.

I headed off down the beach in the direction of the small boatyard where Dad kept the Josephine-Rose, jogging up onto the jetty. A couple of security guards were there and I showed them the papers for my new boat before they let me by and I headed down to the shitty little fishing boat that now belonged to me. It could have been a nice vessel once, but its white paint was flaking off and it was rusted to shit in places.

I climbed onto it, starting her up, surprised when the engine stuttered to life and I drove her out into the water as the sun beat down on me. I pulled my shirt off to enjoy the kiss of it and headed for the horizon, sailing her around a rocky outcrop where fish were swimming in the clear water.

I remembered a time we'd taken Fox's dad's boat out here as kids and we'd taken turns climbing to the top of the rock and jumping off of it. We used to be able to spend a whole day doing shit like that, enjoying each other's company and soaking in the sun. What had happened to all that? Those days had just slipped away between our fingers like sand, leaving us with nothing but regret and fading memories.

I drove her off in the direction of my father's house, cutting the engine when I was parallel to it and certain he could see me from his seat by the window.

My phone buzzed in my pocket and I found a text from Fox as I pulled it out.

Fox:

Photo.

I'd left the breathalyser back on my bike so I tucked my phone away, figuring he was gonna have to wait until I was finished here.

I pulled my clothes off and when I was down to my boxers, I rolled them all up and put them in carrier bag abandoned on the deck which had had a bunch of old cans in it. Then I lit up a cigarette and picked up my gun, aiming it at the hull of the boat as I puffed on the smoke in the corner of my mouth.

"Fuck you and your boat, asshole. This one's for mom." I fired the gun, blasting a hole in the bottom of it and water spurted through the hole, making my heart rate pick up.

I grinned around my cigarette. I needed a little carnage in my life. It had been far too long since I'd had a chance to just be free and fucking wild. I fired another shot, picturing my daddy's face as he saw me destroy his pride and joy. I kept shooting until the bottom of the boat looked like swiss cheese and water was pouring in at an alarming rate. I picked up the carrier bag with my shit in it, tossing my gun, phone and cigarettes in there too before knotting it up tight and tying it to my wrist. I laughed as the water rushed in up to my knees, adrenaline coursing through my veins and making me feel alive.

I dove off of the boat before it went under, watching as it disappeared beneath the surface oh so tragically and sank down into the blue, blue sea.

I swam for the shore, enjoying the cool caress of the water as I went and made a mental note to go surfing soon. Me and the boys never had fun lately. Everything was always so serious and since I'd been shot in the ass, I'd been locked up in Harlequin House for what felt like an eternity. I made it onto the beach, walking up to my old house and smirking at my dad through the window. The look he gave me was pure evil and he shouted furiously, shaking his cane at me as he tried to get up.

I casually walked around to my motorcycle, took the key out of the carrier bag and got on, not giving a single shit as I drove it off up the road in nothing but my wet boxers and the smug grin on my lips.

I drove back to The Oasis and was soon laying outside on one of the picnic benches, gazing up at the fluffy white clouds with a cigarette perched between my lips and the warm air drying me off.

"Chase?" Rosie's high pitched voice cut through my rare moment of peace and a scowl pulled at my features.

I ignored her, wondering if she'd just get the hint and go away as I continued to puff on my cigarette.

"Chasey?" Rosie called and her shadow suddenly blotted out the sun as she leaned over me to look down at my face. Her bleach blonde hair swung forward around her and I could see right up her nose as she glared at me. "What the hell?"

"What?" I asked around my cigarette, releasing a line of smoke from my lips that engulfed her. She coughed and spluttered, backing away and moving to perch her ass beside me instead.

"You haven't answered my calls, my texts, that email I sent you – the *letter*," she whined, sounding tearful.

I propped myself up on my elbows to look at her and she licked her lips as her gaze dipped to my chest then flicked back up to my eyes.

"Did you even read it?" she asked.

"What?" I asked in confusion.

"The letter!" she snarled, smacking my leg.

"I didn't get any letter," I said with a shrug. Oh wait…there was that pink envelope Eddie gave me that I used to mop up some spilled coffee on my nightstand that time. *Oops.*

She pouted at me, her hand falling to my thigh and squeezing. "I miss you. I heard you got shot, I was so worried. Is your phone broken or something?"

"No," I grunted. I always treated her like this, like she meant nothing, like her mouth was good for one thing and to be honest it wasn't even that good at it. If I really analysed it, I guessed it was because I was an asshole. And if I really, *really* analysed it, it went even deeper than that. Rosie Morgan had given Rogue hell when they lived together in their group home as kids. Frankly, I didn't like the bitch, and fucking her whilst treating her like shit had felt kind of cathartic. I'd never promised her shit though, so she really only had herself to blame every time she came crawling back into my life for more punishment. I'd never once been nice to her, so what did that say about her? It wasn't anything good, that was for sure. Was I responsible for her pining over me and begging for my cock even when I never made any attempt to make her come? Nope. Maybe she knew deep down she deserved this shit, because Rosie was a bitch plain and simple for all the world to see. She used to rat out Rogue to their group home carer Mary-Beth for all kinds of shit, plus she'd make out Rogue hit or called her names to make sure she got given priority in the TV room – and yeah okay, sometimes Rogue did those things when Rosie was being a twat, but most of the time she didn't.

But my girl's name got blackened so Mary-Beth always sided against her, meaning she lost out on her privileges more often than not and Rosie took the few comforts away from her that her shitty life had to offer.

Rosie reached out to run her fingers over the reddened flesh left by the gunshot wound on my arm which was scarring up nicely. "Poor baby."

I finished my cigarette and flicked the butt away. Not at her, well okay I didn't exactly *not* aim at her because she had to swerve it with a squeak of fright. I felt extra pissed at her today, with her too easy life and her days spent here in Sunset Cove while my girl had been lost far, far away from town. I'd once have handed Rosie right into the hands of the Devil if it would have brought Rogue back. Maybe I'd still do it just to see if it might fix things anyway.

"How'd you even find me here?" I took out my cigarettes, lighting up another one and she stole one from my packet too, slipping it into her mouth and trying to look sexy as she took my lighter from beside me and lit the end.

I was pretty sure she was trying to impress me, but I'd stopped thinking smoking was cool years ago, now I was just an addict who needed nicotine lacing his blood and soothing his worries. Not that it lasted that long, hence the chain smoking.

"You passed my car on your motorcycle," she said with a smirk.

"So you followed me?" I asked in a growl and she shrugged innocently, batting her lashes like I might think it was cute. I didn't.

Her hand dropped to my thigh again and I jerked it up to knock it off. She frowned, going all moody faced.

"What's going on with you?" she demanded. "I'm your girlfriend, you can't just ignore me for weeks and not even see me when you get shot, Chase. It's not okay."

"Firstly, you're not my girlfriend," I said as I sucked on my cancer stick. "And secondly, I can do whatever the fuck I like because of the first reason. I can draw you a negative feedback diagram if you like."

She rolled her eyes. "You're so blind. I know you wanna keep up this tough guy act in front of your friends, but you always come back to me. Your heart wants me, Chase, just admit it."

"My heart's got better things to do than want you, Rosie. Like beating blood around my body." *And being eternally broken over Rogue.*

Instead of being insulted by that, her eyes just moved to my damp boxers and the outline of my cock within them. She licked her lips again and my dick recoiled. How had I ever even let her put those lips on my cock before now? Oh yeah, rum. Maybe there really was something to be said for this sober bullshit. My mind was as clear as a blue sky and there wasn't a single thought in my head dedicated to Rosie. Nope, they were all reserved for Rogue just like they always used to be. Rogue my nemesis, Rogue my downfall, Rogue my forbidden desire. Nah, changed my mind. I missed the rum, just not the pussy I chose when I was drinking it.

My phone buzzed angrily and I took it out of the carrier bag, finding a couple of messages from Fox.

Fox:

Now, Chase.

Fox:

Are you fucking with me?

Fox:

You don't wanna play this game. I want a sober reading right now, Chase Cohen.

I can't believe he full named me. What an asshole.

I sighed, getting up and grabbing the breathalyser from the box under the seat of my motorcycle and Rosie watched in confusion as I breathed into it until it beeped then sent Fox a photo of it with me putting my middle finger up in the background.

"What's with the breathalyser?" Rosie demanded, seeming infuriated for some reason.

"Fox is making me go sober because apparently I'm a liability," I told her.

"Is that why you're never at parties anymore?" She frowned like this was the end of her whole world.

"I guess." I shrugged.

"Ergh, fuck Fox, why's he got to be such a bore?"

"Probably because I was gonna die choking on my own vomit if he didn't ban me from the shit," I said taking my clothes out of the carrier bag and pulling them on. She watched me closely, her eyes roaming over my body and making my skin prickle. I may not have had sex in a long fucking time, but I wasn't remotely interested in getting my end away with her again. Being sober meant she looked as appealing as a toad in a bonnet to me. I mean, all props to the toad for dressing up nice, but I just wasn't into amphibians.

"That's ridiculous," she muttered then her eyes sparkled with an idea.

"Hey, I could get us some weed? There's a party on the beach tonight, we could get silly and you could do that butt thing to me again with-"

"No thanks," I cut her off. "Sober means sober."

"Yeah, but weed won't show up on that breath thingy. Fox won't know," she implored.

"My position in the Harlequins is up for question, Rosie, do you not get that? I'm not smoking pot, I'm not drinking rum, I'm staying as sober as a priest so long as Fox tells me to because I'd rather die than lose my brothers."

She sighed disappointedly. "Fine. But come to the party anyway."

"He said no," Fox's deep voice resounded from behind me and Rosie paled as her eyes whipped over my shoulder.

I turned as he and JJ moved either side of me and Fox folded his arms, glaring down his nose at Rosie with dislike in his gaze.

Rosie bowed her head like a shamed dog. "I just think it's a bit extreme to stop him from having any fun," she muttered.

"If you think fun looks like Chase half killing himself every night, then you've got a fucked up idea of it," Fox bit at her. "But feel free to go ahead and continue to have as much fun as you like on your own, Rosie."

She kept her eyes downcast, her cheeks turning pink then she huffed, giving me a longing look before heading back to her car.

Relief filled me as JJ clapped a hand on my shoulder and I looked to him with a half smile. "Why's your hair wet? Tell me you didn't go muff diving in Rosie's reef?"

"Ergh," I laughed, shoving him away and he started wrestling me. Fox scruffed my hair and the three of us started tussling like kids until we all fell on our asses on the grass beside the bench. I smiled as I lay among my brothers, knowing it was where I belonged, even if some pieces of us were carved off and missing. I just had to hold on tight to what was left and never let go.

"Luther was a no show, so we'll have to have that meeting with him some other time," Fox said and I nodded.

"So come on, what's with the wet hair?" JJ pressed.

"My dad gave me his boat," I told them as I gazed up at the endless sky.

"Seriously?" Fox questioned.

"Uhuh. I drove it out to sea and sank it by Falcon Rock where he could watch." I grinned. "You should have seen his face when I swam back to shore."

They laughed and JJ threw an arm around me. "Did he shake his cane at you?"

"Yeah," I snorted.

"Make me a promise, Ace," Fox said. "If you ever destroy any of his property again, bring me with you."

"And me," JJ said excitedly.

"Deal," I chuckled. "So are you guys all ready for your next job?"

"Yup," JJ said. "It's gonna be a good one."

"You sure you don't need a decent getaway driver?" I asked with longing in my voice.

"Basset's semi-decent," Fox mocked and I punched him in the arm in frustration.

"Come on, man," I begged.

"No," he said simply then got up, pulling me after him. "But maybe next time." He smiled at me, clapping my cheek. "I really am proud of you for staying off the booze, Ace."

"Shut up." I shoved his chest but he just grinned at me.

"He's a good boy, isn't he J?" Fox teased.

"He's a real good boy." JJ pinched my cheek and I threw a punch at him that he danced away from. I couldn't stop smiling though, because dammit I loved these boys. And nothing and no one was ever going to take them away from me.

CHAPTER TWENTY FIVE

If I closed my eyes then the dark was my own choice. It had nothing to do with the man who had taken me captive and everything to do with control over my own destiny.

We'd driven through town in the murder van in silence and had finally pulled up somewhere. But then Luther's phone had started ringing and I'd been left to wait. And wait. And wait.

Seriously. I was starting to wish he'd just come back and fucking finish it at this point because all of this waiting to die was going to give me a heart attack.

Luckily the van wasn't hot. The engine was still idling and whoever was in the front clearly had the A/C pumping so at least I hadn't been left in here to cook to death. Though on second thoughts that might have been a kinder fate than what Luther had planned for me. His style was well known –two to the chest and one to the head, unless he wanted to make an example out of someone and then the stories of the torture and bloodshed I'd heard were more than enough to have given me nightmares ever since he'd first placed this threat over my head. And it seemed pretty damn likely to me that he'd want to make an example of someone who went back on a deal they'd made with him like I had. Not that I'd ever been given any choice in the matter. Either way I was done with this waiting.

I was ready to face this fate, get the fuck on with it and just die.

The sound of the van door rolling open sent a spike of fear through me and my eyes snapped open as I found two big motherfuckers there, covered in tattoos and looking like an evil version of Tweedle Dum and Tweedle Dee.

Oh fuck. I don't wanna die. Ignore my last statement universe, because I'm not done with this life no matter how fucking miserable it might have been. My ass is too peachy to end up rotting in some grave in the woods and my tits need more of the good stuff in life. I never even really looked after them all that well but I could wear bras more often, be a more supportive owner of my body if I was just allowed to keep on living in it.

A meaty hand reached for me while the other dude pointed a big fat shotgun right at my head.

I moved, fighting down the urge to scream and taking stock of the things I had going in my favour. I wasn't tied up. And I was fast. If I could just figure out some kind of escape plan then I could run for it. I was good at running. Damn good at it. So that was what I was going to have to do.

I squinted against the brightness of the light outside the van, raising a hand to shield my eyes as a sweaty palm closed around my wrist and began tugging me along. The shotgun jabbed me in the lower back and I sucked in a shaky breath as I tried to get my bearings.

Shit.

We were up high on a cliff, the sea air billowing over the bluff and blowing my hair to my left as we walked. My heart began to beat even faster as I recognised our destination.

We were up on Devil's Pass. The same cliff where my boys had stood over me after becoming Harlequins and had shoved me down in the mud. The same place where they'd broken my heart and sent me away from them. The same place where my once perfectly imperfect life had come to an end right before I'd been cast adrift.

The shotgun was prodded into my back a little harder and I wasn't surprised to find myself herded towards the little shack which stood just inside the tree line.

My pulse was pounding even more furiously now because I didn't want to go in there. Not because I was certain my death lay waiting for me inside, but because there was a ghost lurking in there too. The last piece of the girl I'd been. That place held the memories of me waiting for my boys when I'd believed with all my heart that they would come back for me. The last time I'd been so certain of their love that the idea of what had come next never would have even occurred to me.

This grass I stepped across held a taste of the last time the five of us all been together. And no doubt my tears had watered it and become a part of the cliff itself. I'd already died here once, and it looked like Luther had decided to haul the rest of me back here to finish the job.

I stepped into the little shack, remembering the way the rain had leaked through the roof and dripped onto me. Ten years had weathered the place even more and the scent of damp clung to everything.

Luther sat on a stool which I guessed he'd brought with him because it looked new, solid and clean unlike everything else in here.

Before him another stool sat in the centre of a clear tarp and my throat closed up as I was forced to walk my ass over to it.

The plastic crinkled beneath my bare feet and I wondered if it would really be enough to capture every drop of blood in my body? Maybe Luther would torch this place once he was done carving me up too. Just to make certain no piece of me remained.

My ass hit the stool and a wave of calm suddenly washed over me. I wasn't sure what it was or why, but my fear just melted away. I guessed my body had accepted my fate. This was it. I was here at his mercy and there was no way I could do anything other than accept it and I wanted to go out strong if this really was the end.

I raised my chin as the two goons turned and left and Luther remained silent until the door closed behind them.

"It seems you and I are overdue a chat, Rogue Easton," he said slowly, reaching down to his murder bag which sat by his feet and forcing my gaze to follow his movements. My brow furrowed as he pulled two cans from the bag and tossed one to me.

I caught it automatically, looking down at the cold can of still lemonade in confusion before glancing back up at him.

"I figure we can try and do this the nice way," Luther explained, cracking his own drink open. "But if that doesn't work out then I assume you know how this will go."

"You're saying you might not kill me?" I asked, running my finger around the top of the cold can.

"Maybe is a powerful word in this kind of situation, don't you think?"

I nodded because fuck yeah it was. I had been deader than dead three seconds ago and now I had a lemonade and a maybe. So I was all ears.

I cracked the can open and took a hit of sugar to try and help calm my nerves. The drink was cold and sweet and I would have sighed in satisfaction had I not been sitting here prepped for death.

"So," Luther began, his gaze running over me in an assessing way. "You're back."

"Seems like it."

"And Fox is in love with you. Even after all these years." He said it as a statement and I couldn't be sure if that was true or not. Fox certainly made it seem that way sometimes, but he also reminded me of the man sitting before me often enough too. He'd seen something he wanted and was determined to claim it. Was that love? Hard to say. Maybe of the toxic kind.

"What about the other two? Johnny James and Chase?" I opened my mouth to reply but he held up an inked finger. "It might be worth adding here that I'm not a fool. You showed up in town and the three of them banded together to hide you from me. They chose you again just like they did all of those years ago and it seems damn clear to me that this time apart hasn't dulled the infatuation they all held for you. So I can only assume they all want to claim you for their own."

My open mouth fell wider and my heart thrashed. What the fuck was I supposed to say to that? He'd just told me he thought his son was in love with me and now he was saying he thought his two best friends wanted me too. That sounded a whole lot like a problem to me. This didn't seem good. Not at all.

"How's Maverick?" Luther asked, changing lanes again and I just blinked at him. "I know you were out in his compound for more than a week and if the information I was given was correct then it seems he's still quite fixed on you too."

"I...don't know what to say to all of that," I admitted eventually because what the fuck was I supposed to say?

Luther watched me closely and I couldn't help but see so much of Fox in him. He was a powerful man, built tall and broad like his son though his skin was marked with more ink and a scar crossed one side of his jaw. There was a coldness to him which I'd seen in Fox too, a brutality which his son seemed to switch on and off as required but which seemed to live more permanently in this creature. Though maybe that was just because he was looking at me.

"I'm gonna tell you a story," Luther said, readjusting himself so that his ankle rested across his knee. He held his can of lemonade loose between his fingertips as he leaned towards me to tell me whatever the fuck it was. I felt like a mouse in the paws of a lion but there wasn't anything I could do other than wait for him to stop toying with me. "I assume you know the basic facts about Fox's mother being out of the picture. But perhaps if you hear the full extent of what she did to me, you might be more inclined to understand why I sent you away ten years ago."

"Sure," I muttered because I didn't have any other words for him, but I couldn't understand what this had to do with anything either.

Luther ran a tattooed hand across his jaw, hesitating before he began and then pinning me in his gaze. He looked so like Fox in so many ways, but his eyes were a world of their own, this dark and chilling void which spoke of some deep hurt in him as well as reeking of the screams of his victims. I was no fool. I knew this man's reputation and I knew that he would have no qualms at all about adding another body to the list. What I did have to wonder about though was why the fuck he hadn't done it already, and I found I was really damn curious about that.

"Adriana was a beautiful woman," he began. "Sexy, funny and ambitious. She was the kind of woman no man could take his eyes from and that was how it was for me. I was...enraptured. But so was my brother Deke. Back then, the Harlequin Crew were little more than a ragtag band of assholes, but I was making something of them. I was smart and ruthless and piece by piece, I was carving out a place for us right here in Sunset Cove. Adriana saw that, she saw me and she wanted a taste of my power. What else can I say? We were young and we fucked a lot, it wasn't a surprise she ended up pregnant. So she had the baby and all the while, I kept building my empire, working tirelessly to claim more and more power for her, for Fox, for all of us. I wanted to provide everything, and I wanted to have it all. But Deke had set his gaze on a prize closer to home and I suppose that with me gone so much, he found a way to convince Adriana that he might be a better choice for her."

"They had an affair?" I breathed, the idea of that making so much sense. Because he fucking hated women. Fox had told me his dad said she was the worst mistake he'd ever made and warned him not to trust women. So if she'd broken his heart with his own brother then a lot of that hatred was understandable.

"I gave that woman everything," Luther snarled and I had to fight a flinch. "And I made sacrifices for her which she clearly never appreciated. Because while I was out, risking my fucking life and building her an empire, she was in my bed with my brother's dick between her thighs."

My pulse was racing at his words because he clearly wasn't over that betrayal, and he'd literally just accused me of being something to all of my boys while telling me Fox loved me. Did he think I was going to hurt his son like he'd been hurt? But it wasn't like that with us. I didn't know how to explain it, but it wasn't.

"I found out of course," Luther went on. "And I told her to choose. Me and Fox or *him*. I told her that if she chose my brother then they had to leave that night and never return. Or she could choose me and I'd banish Deke instead. That was it. Simple."

"So they left?" I asked, my heart twisting with pain for Fox as I realised that his mom had chosen a life with some other man over her own son. But Luther was shaking his head, his gaze darkening and I got the feeling it got a whole lot worse than that.

"Turns out, Deke had only wanted a taste of what was mine. He'd enjoyed the thrill of fucking my woman, but he had no intention of keeping her. It was all just a game to him. I'd grown more powerful in Sunset Cove than him with my gang and though I'd offered him a place at my side, he hadn't liked his little brother claiming more power than he owned. So he thought he could take a piece back from me by fucking Adriana. But when she went to him and told him he had to leave and that she wanted to stay with me, he didn't like that. And I guess he decided that she was the problem between us and took it upon himself to get rid of her."

I was chewing my bottom lip as my heart hurt for Fox and I tried to deny the truth of what Luther was saying.

"She called me and told me she loved me," he said. "She told me she was sorry and that she was going to tell Deke to leave. But when I didn't hear back from her again for hours, I went looking for her. It doesn't matter how much blood I may have spilled in the years since that day, I swear I've never seen as much as there was in that room."

"Deke killed her?" I breathed and Luther nodded, his eyes haunted as he remembered the moment.

"He was standing there, covered in blood, her body still beneath him and he turned to me with a fucking smile. Told me it was done and that we didn't have to worry about the bitch coming between us again. I put two bullets in his chest and one between his eyes. My own brother. A man I'd believed would stand by my side through thick and thin, no matter what. But that was the cost of us wanting the same woman."

"I'm sorry," I whispered, feeling his hurt over that even after all these years. He'd lost so much and I could see that his heart hadn't healed from it no matter how much time had passed since.

He blew out a breath, took a long drink from his can then sat back, eying me with interest.

"So I assume you understand now why I thought sending you away was the best choice ten years ago? I could see the way my boys looked at you, hungered for you, and I could see it all ending in tears one way or another. I didn't want that for my boys. I wanted them to be together, a unit, unbreakable. But ten years later they're broken anyway. There hasn't been a single thing that I could do or a plan I could form which has had any hope of uniting them. Or at least there wasn't - until you came back."

"Me?"

"They should have forgotten all about you - sorry to be crass, sweetheart, but teenage boys hunger for pussy and I assumed that once yours was out of mind they'd move on to another. Each find girls of their own and forget about you. But they didn't, did they?"

"The five of us were something special once," I said, running my thumb up and down the lemonade can in my grasp. "I don't know what we are now, but that bond...it's still there."

Luther nodded. "Then I think we can come to a new arrangement. I want you to help me reunite my family. Fox and Maverick have been caught in this spat for too fucking long and I want my boys back in harmony with one another."

"Spat? Maverick despises them - you especially. He literally hungers for your death and-"

Luther waved a hand dismissively and I arched a brow. "That boy has always had a hot head. He throws a fit when things don't go his way and acts out. He's just pissed because I stopped him from chasing after you all those years ago, but now you're back. So he needs to stop spitting his pacifier out like a baby and come home."

"He formed a rival gang," I said in disbelief and Luther chuckled.

"I think we can all agree that The Damned Men are more of a sub-sector to The Harlequin Crew than a rival gang. Besides, gang politics are my domain, so you don't need to worry about that. All you need to concentrate on is getting my boys back together. I'll give you whatever you require to achieve that and in return, I won't blow your brains out."

"I do prefer my brains in their current position," I agreed, while I turned over what he was asking. "What about Chase and JJ?"

Luther shrugged. "They're not my kids but I know that they're important to Fox and Maverick just as you are. And they're good soldiers. So I'm willing to allow them to be a part of this truce you'll form."

I opened and closed my mouth at a fucking loss. How the hell was I supposed to do what he was asking of me? On the other hand, I really wasn't keen on the whole idea of him shooting me as an alternative, so I was willing to bet I didn't exactly have a choice in the matter.

"I have no idea how I'm going to do what you want," I said slowly and Luther raised an eyebrow. "But, I guess I can try and figure it out. Somehow."

I didn't sound in any way convinced but Luther beamed like I'd just made him a promise.

"Good. I want Maverick home. It's long overdue and we need to unite his people and mine against the fucking Dead Dogs. You can report back to me on your progress as you go. I don't care what it takes for you to bring them all together again, Rogue, but you'll figure out a way."

"Err-"

"Come on. This place is a shithole. Let's get back to civilisation." Luther stood and motioned for me to join him so I got up too, walking at his side as he headed for the exit.

He was all smiles now, acting like everything in the world was great and I had to wonder if he was a little unhinged. But as I took a breath of fresh air, I decided that shit didn't matter because this dead girl was still kicking and today was looking like a particularly beautiful day.

CHAPTER TWENTY SIX

We arrived back at Harlequin House and my men were all looking sheepish as I drove past them at the gate. By the time I was parked in the garage, my instincts were burning and I jumped out of the truck, leaving the door wide open as I ran up into the house.

"Rogue?" I called and Mutt came running down the hall with a frantic bark. My heart hammered in my chest as I got no answer. "Rogue!" I tore down the corridor and up the stairs, racing to her room and shoving the door open as Mutt ran at my heels. Empty.

I ran back down to the ground floor as JJ and Chase appeared with frowns on their faces.

"Has she escaped again?" JJ asked, looking kind of impressed and if I hadn't been so busy hunting for her, I'd have punched him for it.

I made it into the kitchen as the guys jogged after me, unlocking the patio door and hunting the area. Nothing.

Mutt whined like he was trying to tell me something, looking anxious as hell and I didn't like that one bit.

"I swear she *wants* to get caught by Shawn," Chase growled as we made it back inside and I swung around, shoving him back against the kitchen island as I knotted my fist in his shirt.

"Well maybe if you weren't such an asshole to her all the time, she'd prefer staying here over that shitty trailer," I snapped, then left him there with a snarl on his lips as I marched past JJ back towards the garage, preparing to rip the town apart again to find her. But before I made it outside, a loud knocking came at the door and I practically sprinted to answer it. *Please be you.*

I swung it open, finding Basset there with red ears and a guilty expression. "Sorry, boss. Luther came home and er-"

I didn't hear much else of what he said as my whole universe imploded and the breath in my lungs was strangled out of existence.

"No," I gasped.

"Luther took her?!" JJ bellowed from behind me, his voice sharpening my thoughts in an instant.

"How long ago?" I roared at Basset and he stumbled backwards in alarm as he scrambled to come up with an answer.

"Er, um, I, er," he stammered and I lunged at him, locking my hand around his throat.

"Answer me!" I bellowed.

"A few hours?" he guessed and I released him, my ears ringing, my heart fighting with my ribs to get out and find her.

Mutt was barking with all the fury I felt in my soul and panic seized me more fiercely than it ever had in my life. I knew in that moment that if my father had killed her, I would never, ever recover.

JJ tugged on my arm, dragging me back into the house and grabbing my face between his hands as he forced me to look at him.

"I need you to focus," he demanded as Chase started loading a gun behind him, his features twisted with terror. "Where would Luther take her, Fox?"

I tried to drag in breaths as my brother held onto me and gazed into my eyes with the most desperate, urgent need of his life staring back at me.

"I don't know. Maybe the woods," I forced out. "Where Luther made us kill to initiate into the Harlequins."

JJ nodded, his face pale and fear pouring from his gaze.

"Come on," Chase snapped. "We have to hurry."

We rushed to the garage, tearing down the stairs together and diving into my truck. My mind was a haze of bloodshed and terror, swirling into this raging storm that blinded me. If he'd laid a finger on her, I would kill my own father today, and I would not make it quick.

I slammed my foot on the gas as the garage door opened, speeding outside and racing for the gates. But they were already opening and as a black van drove in, I spotted my father in the passenger seat and slammed on the brakes, diving out of the car and raising my gun at him.

"Where is she?!" I roared so loud it shredded my throat and as if answering my rage, the heavens boomed with an oncoming storm.

Luther jumped out of the van, holding his hands up, his eyes wide as he grabbed hold of the side door to the van and yanked it open. Rogue stepped out and my heart thumped two furious beats before I ran to her, falling to my knees on the drive and wrapping my arms around her waist.

"Fox," she gasped, her hands gripping my hair as I shut my eyes and pressed my forehead to her stomach, just feeling the reality of her still being here with me.

JJ and Chase were suddenly upon us, slamming into her until we were all on the ground, fighting to hug her tightest. Mutt dove between us, licking her like mad and she hugged him along with us.

"You guys," she half laughed, half sobbed as we clung to her and my father's shadow fell over us all.

I looked up at the man who'd threatened her life all those years ago as the dark clouds drew in behind him in the sky. My fingers were still tight on the gun as I raised it, but he knocked it aside and dragged me out of the dogpile, hugging me firmly against him, the scent of coffee and earth hanging around him like always.

"You and me need to talk," he said in my ear.

My emotions were shot to shit and I was still in a daze as I looked for Rogue over my shoulder. She was pulled to her feet by JJ and Chase got up, brushing off his knees and looking awkward as he stepped away from her. Fucking idiot would never admit he cared about her even now.

Luther tugged me toward the house, his arm remaining firm around my shoulders and I wondered if he was just reminding our men of our solidarity seeing as I'd pointed a gun at him two minutes ago.

I looked back at Rogue again as she offered a small smile and my dad shoved my face to make me look forward as we stepped into the house. He pulled the gun from my grip when we were all inside, taking the bullets out as he placed it on a table in the hallway and gave me a pointed look.

"It's never a good idea to have an argument with a loaded gun in hand, kid," he warned.

"Is that what we're about to have?" I growled.

"Your face says so."

We moved into the kitchen just as the first droplets of rain plinked against the patio doors and Luther took a seat at the island.

JJ, Chase and Rogue appeared and Luther eyed us all with intent.

"Sit," he commanded and though I didn't wanna obey the asshole right then, I knew I wasn't going to get an explanation unless I did.

I moved to sit beside Rogue with JJ next to her and Chase on my other side. We were a unit, the four of us - okay five if you counted Mutt on Rogue's lap - gazing across the island at my father who casually flexed his inked hands and rested them on the surface.

"Where'd you take her?" I snarled.

"Why is she still alive?" JJ demanded, shifting closer to her.

I looked at Rogue and pushed a lock of hair behind her ear, needing to touch her and finding my hand was still shaking over the fear of almost losing her. She leaned into my touch, meeting my gaze with those astounding eyes of hers which held my entire soul in their grip.

"It's okay," she breathed and I nodded, dropping my hand and taking her fingers into my grasp, thankful when she didn't pull away. I would have died if I couldn't touch her then.

I looked to my father for the answer to those questions, finding him regarding us with satisfaction in his eyes. What the fuck was going on?

"I've known Rogue was here for a while now," he said, making my heart stumble. "Your men are my men, Fox, and I'm afraid when it comes down to it, they will always be more loyal to me than you until I die."

My jaw ticked at that and my grip tightened on Rogue's hand.

"So why didn't you say something?" I demanded.

"I was trying to decide what to do, kid," Luther said, scratching at the tribal tattoo covering his throat. "Do you think this shit is easy for me? You think I wanna be the asshole who takes your girl from you?"

"I'm not his girl," Rogue offered unhelpfully and I practically growled at her like an animal, making her eyebrows arch in surprise.

"Well, he thinks you are," my dad chuckled like this was fucking hilarious and Rogue fucking laughed too.

"Excuse me," Chase interjected. "But have I stepped into an alternate reality or something because you're the one who sent Rogue away, boss, and now what? You're just laughing with her, letting her sit there like it never happened?"

Luther frowned as me and my boys stared at him, desperate for the answer to his change of heart on all of this shit. The shit that defined our entire lives. It didn't make any sense.

He sighed, looking to me. "All I ever asked was that you were loyal to me, Fox. But when Rogue killed Axel for trying to rape her all those years ago, you went down there and took it into your own hands, bundled his body off on my fucking boat and dumped him in the water."

"And?" I snarled.

"And you fucked everything, didn't you?" Luther growled, his features twisting in anger. "You lied to me. And tried to cover the whole thing up. Then the body washed up and every Harlequin in town knew one of our own had been murdered, so I had to be seen to take action too, didn't I?"

"So you're saying if I'd come to you, you wouldn't have sent Rogue away?" I scoffed.

"Yeah, that's what I'm saying," Luther said with no hint of a lie in his gaze. "If you'd been honest from the start, I would have dealt with it. You think I care about avenging some piece of shit rapist in my gang?" He sneered. "It wasn't about that. The fact was, you betrayed me, son. So did Maverick. And you almost shot to hell any chance of Chase and JJ joining the Harlequins too."

"There's no reality that exists where we wouldn't have shown up to help Rogue that night," JJ said icily. "And who said we wanted to be Harlequins back then anyway? You forced our hands."

Luther shook his head at him. "Showing up for her could have looked a whole lot different if you'd gotten me involved. And you might not have wanted to be a Harlequin, Johnny James, but joining the Crew is the only chance you kids ever had of making something of yourselves." He turned his gaze on Chase. "Where do you think you would have ended up if you didn't have this home handed to you?"

"I'd have figured it out," Chase muttered, shrugging his shoulders.

"At least the five of us would have still been together," I bit out and Rogue squeezed my fingers. She was unusually quiet and I guessed my father had had a lot to say to her, I just wondered exactly what that was. If he'd known she was here, why hadn't he shown up while we were here too, why had he snatched her away from my goddamn house and scared the life out of me? *Oh right, because he's an asshole.*

"Bullshit," Luther hissed. "You all lived in a fantasy world back then, and I let ya because you were young. But you had to grow up sometime and face reality. And the fact is, kids in this town end up one of two ways; broke and miserable or broke and dead. You think I wanted either of those things for you? For *any* of you? Being a Harlequin is about more than just about being in a gang, it's security, safety, family. You will always have a home so long as you're one of us, and you have people who'll watch your back, help you out when shit gets rough. There ain't no price you can put on that in this life."

"But you didn't have to send Rogue away," I said bitterly, resentment clinging to my heart. "You say there was nothing for us out in the world, but you still sent her off into it alone, didn't you?"

"I was the sacrifice, right?" Rogue guessed with disdain. "Get rid of me and you could save the rest of them."

Luther nodded in admission and my hackles rose. "That's the long and short of it, yeah. It didn't have to be that way, but you made your beds when you tried to pull the wool over my eyes. I'm a reasonable man, but I'm still the king of this crew and there are things I have to do even if I don't like 'em all that much at the time."

"You're full of shit." I shoved out of my seat and pointed to the door. "And I'd like you to get out of my goddamn house."

Luther gazed at me with a hint of pain in his eyes as he slowly got up and I stared him down, not flinching from that penetrating gaze of his which used to cause me so much fear.

"Son..." he tried. "You need to let go of the past."

"I'm fine holding onto it thanks," I ground out. "And you may be the king of the Crew, the king of me and the king of the whole fucking world for all I care, but you gave me this house and said it was mine, so I think I'm within my rights to ask you to leave it."

Everyone's eyes swung between us as tension made the air thick.

"Fine, I'll leave," Luther conceded. "You can have today to process all this, but tomorrow there's work to be done and I won't stand for any subordinance, kid."

"I'm not a kid," I bit at him and his eyes moved over me for a long moment.

"Yeah, yeah, I know," he sighed like he was sad about that, then nodded to the others in goodbye and headed for the front door. I didn't move until it clicked shut, then I snatched Chase's cigarettes off the island and strode out of the room, heading for the back door.

I unlocked it, stepping onto the wooden porch that overlooked our private stretch of sandy beach. Rain hammered down on the roof of it and the sea churned and roiled like an angry beast as I lit up a cigarette and stared into its murky depths. The boat out on the jetty rocked and bounced on the furious waves that were rolling in to shore, looking exactly like the turmoil of my life right now.

The others spilled out onto the porch then gathered around me and we all just smoked and watched the storm in silence, taking some peace in the closeness of each other.

I dropped my arm around Rogue's shoulders as she stood at my side, and she leaned into me with her arm around my back, her rainbow hair dancing in the wind.

"Fuck your dad," Chase muttered on my other side, releasing a line of smoke from his lips.

"Fuck him up the butt with a coconut," Rogue added.

"Fuck him sideways with a spiky dildo," JJ offered from beside Rogue and I finally cracked a smile.

"Fuck you!" I hollered into the wind and they all started shouting it too, our voices dragged away into the storm.

After a while it didn't even feel like we were saying it to Luther anymore, we were saying it to the world, our fate, to fucking Shawn, and to Rosie Morgan and every other fucker who wasn't one of us. I wanted everyone and everything to just fuck off and leave the four of us here together, to give us time to heal our wounds and find a new way to love each other.

For a moment, it was just like it always had been, though I couldn't ignore the carved out chunk of my heart where Maverick had existed. I'd missed him every day for the past ten years, but I knew that feeling didn't relate to the Maverick who lived out on Dead Man's Isle.

I missed the brother I'd grown up with, the boy I'd learned to surf with, the one who'd punched me when I did stupid shit and laughed with me over nothing until our stomachs hurt.

I remembered him out on this very porch when we were kids, carving our names into one of the wooden posts with the new penknives Luther had given to each of us. He'd accidentally given me the one with Maverick's name etched into it and my one to him. But we hadn't switched them back, we'd decided we liked the idea of stabbing our enemies with a blade marked with our brother's name, because back then, we would have killed for one another. But now…we only wanted to kill each other.

We took a couple of days of downtime and no one said it, but I was pretty sure we all just wanted to be around each other. We ate every meal together, even when we didn't say much and my heart finally started to settle over what had happened. I was far from forgiving my dad for his bullshit, but I had to admit I was fucking relieved to know he wasn't out for my girl's blood anymore. It was a heavy relief after an endless stretch of fear. She was home, and she could stay. And that was the only thing I'd ever truly wanted in ten years.

I headed into JJ's room in the morning while he was sleeping, trying not to disturb him as I sought out book two of the Twilight Saga. I'd been trying to implement more of the Edward Cullen tactics, but I was pretty sure it wasn't working.

The click of a gun sounded and I wheeled around, finding JJ squinting at me from his bed as he pointed his handgun at my head.

"Da fuck are you doing?" he asked sleepily as he placed the gun on his nightstand.

I waved Twilight at him. "Looking for book two. And by the way, I don't really understand what you expect me to learn from these books. I do everything Edward does from the following her around, to the protecting, even the watching her sleep and Rogue still doesn't want me."

"You still watch her sleep?" JJ growled and I shrugged, shoving Twilight back on the shelf.

JJ jumped out of bed, grabbing it from where I'd put it with a scowl. "It doesn't go there, it goes here with the others. And dude, you're totally missing the point. If you wanna learn from these books, you should've asked me for guidance."

"Well what am I doing wrong?" I growled. "You said these stories are what women want and shit, so why am I failing so hard with her?" I folded my arms and he shook his head at me.

"Edward Cullen is a fantasy, but you don't wanna *be* Edward Cullen," he said like that made perfect sense. Definitely didn't.

"I'm confused," I said and he sighed.

"Edward's like the ultimate wet dream, he'll be obsessively in love with you, protect you from all evil, die for you yada, yada, and that's great as a concept, but in real life? Not so much." He looked through his books, considering each one. "You wanna have elements of Edward, but you also need to be Jacob with a little sprinkling of Charlie."

"Bella's dad?" I wrinkled my nose, confused as fuck.

"Yeah," he said. "And forget Bella, we're talking about Rogue, and also about any girl reading Twilight, see?"

"No, but go on," I encouraged.

"Edward's love is obsessive and he's sexy as fuck, but Jacob is her best friend and Charlie's the mature one who knows when to step back and give a woman her space. So you gotta be all three as and when Rogue needs you to be."

"And how do I know when to be Jacob over Edward?" I frowned.

"Look, it's not about being anyone else. You're great, dude," JJ said in exasperation.

"But you just said-"

He grabbed a book with a gasp then rounded on me and slammed it into my chest with a huge grin. "Holy shit, I've got the answer."

"To what?"

"Just read this," he commanded in a growl and I looked down at the book as I took it in my hands. The cover had a lilac haired girl on it wearing a black dress, looking all mysterious and shit. The title was *Dark Fae.*

"Is this fantasy?"

"Yeah, the sexy kind. It's like Twilight if everyone was fucking and killing each other all the time. It's got gangs and enemies to lovers and you'll get a boner every other chapter."

"Um, okay," I agreed. "And this will help with Rogue?"

"Definitely," he said. "Just focus on Leon's character. He's got the answers." He looked seriously excited about something, but I had no idea what it was.

"Alright," I said, my mood brightening a little as I hoped this could really help me out with Rogue. I was determined to make her happy and maybe this book could be the one to up my game. Because seriously, it was embarrassing how useless I was with her. Was I always this bad with women or was it just because it was Rogue Easton and she made me want to tie her to my back and carry her around everywhere I went just so I could be sure she'd never leave town again?

JJ clapped me around the face. "Now fuck off, bro, I wanna go back to sleep."

I laughed, heading out of the room and moving across the hall to jimmy Rogue's lock. I was soon into her bedroom and I sat down in the chair by her bed as I tossed Mutt some treats and started reading, my gaze flicking from the pages to her peaceful face as she slept. It was very fucking distracting.

After a couple of hours, I was firmly on team Gabriel in the book and didn't know what JJ had been talking about when he said to take notes from

Leon. Gabriel was the girl's one true mate and he knew it, sure he was acting like an asshole, but I was guessing he'd figure it out sooner or later.

I left the book in my room while I showered and came up with a plan to spend some time with Rogue this morning. I dressed in some swim shorts and packed a bag for us before heading down to the kitchen and preparing some fruit and muesli for when the boys got up. Then I packed up Rogue's Jeep with our surfboards, put my bag in the front and headed back upstairs to get her.

She hadn't appreciated the kidnap move before so this time I'd try something else…

Mutt yapped as I entered the room and I didn't bother to shush him with treats as I walked up to the bed and waited to see if she might stir. Nope.

I grabbed hold of her comforter and whipped it off of her in one fluid movement, throwing it on the floor. She tucked her legs to her chest, but didn't wake and I snorted a breath of amusement. She was wearing a Rolling Stones t-shirt which I was pretty sure belonged to JJ and I wondered if I should start leaving my own shirts around for her to steal. I'd sure like to see her walking around in my things, but she probably wouldn't do it just to spite me.

"Morning, hummingbird," I called, but she didn't respond. I stepped up onto the bed, standing either side of her then started jumping, making her bounce on the mattress.

"Earthquake," she murmured. "Run, Mutt."

I dropped to my knees and sat on her, making her wheeze out a breath as her eyes fluttered open.

"Badger," she croaked. "Why are you sitting on me?"

"Because we're going out."

"Nooo," she groaned, covering her eyes with her hand dramatically.

"I have pastries," I said. "And if we don't go now, we'll miss the tide. Don't you wanna surf?" I said temptingly in her ear and she shivered beneath me.

"I want an ice cream sundae, with sprinkles, and chocolate sauce," she murmured, keeping her eyes shut as I peeled her hand away from her face.

"It's eight in the morning." I frowned.

"And this girl doesn't get out of bed before nine for anything less than three scoops of ice cream, Badger."

I snorted. "Fine. We'll pick one up on the way. Get dressed." I kissed her forehead then stepped off the bed and waited for her to get up.

She immediately started breathing softly as she fell back asleep and I shook my head at her, grabbing the edge of the mattress and flipping it up so she went tumbling onto the carpet. The t-shirt she was sleeping in slipped up to reveal her bright pink panties and she growled as she crawled her way to the closet, grabbed some clothes and kept crawling into the bathroom, kicking the door shut behind her.

I smirked, picking up Mutt and heading downstairs with him to wait for her while I gave him his breakfast.

She eventually appeared in a lemon sundress with a hot pink bikini peeking out from underneath it and JJ's sunglasses on her face. Her hair was twisted up into a knot on her head and little tendrils of coloured locks tickled her neck. A neck I wanted to kiss and bite and mark and – *focus*.

I smiled, offering her my hand, but she just walked past me toward the garage.

"Ice cream," she said like a zombie and I smirked, following her closely, happy to enjoy the view of her ass as her sexy little dress swung around her tanned thighs. We walked downstairs and I led the way to her Jeep, tossing her the keys.

"I'm driving?" she asked in surprise.

"That a problem?" She hadn't used her car for ages and I hadn't gotten it for her just so it could sit here and rot. I mean, I hadn't been letting her out of the house so that might have had something to do with it, but that wasn't the point.

She snatched the keys, jogging around to the driver's side and leaping in, apparently more awake now. I got in the passenger's side with Mutt on my lap, putting on Rogue's seatbelt for her as she started up the car. My fingers brushed her waist and she looked at me as I remained close to her, the heat of her body drawing me in.

"We could always skip the surfing and you could ride me instead of the waves?" I offered with a dirty grin and she smacked my arm, shoving me back, but a smile played around her mouth.

"I'll take the waves, Badge. I won't owe them anything after I'm done with them."

"You won't owe me shit," I said as she drove out of the garage and I waved at my men as we approached the gate so they let us out.

"Wrong," she sang. "If we fuck, you'll think I really am your girl."

"You are anyway," I pointed out.

"Don't piss me off, Badger, I might become a flight risk again," she warned and I rolled my eyes, rubbing Mutt's head as the road sailed by outside the window.

We stopped off at a café to get Rogue's ice cream and I bought myself a chocolate sundae too because why the fuck not for once? After our sugar-filled breakfast Rogue drove us down to the beach near the cove where the best surfing waves were found and as we stepped out of the Jeep, Mutt went running off toward the water, snapping at the waves and barking happily.

I pulled my shirt off and tossed it onto my seat, my gaze hooking on Rogue on the other side of the Jeep as she pulled her sundress over her head and dropped it onto the driver's seat. She adjusted her little pink bikini bottoms over her hips while I took in every perfect inch of her body, a possessive need to be closer making my heart thump erratically.

I moved to unload the surfboards and she grabbed her own from me when I tried to carry it for her.

"I'm just trying to be a gentleman," I said.

"Well try being a gentleman somewhere else." She wafted her hand in the vague direction of a seagull. "I'm busy being a badass and your grandad vibe is killing the mood."

Grandad vibe?

She kicked off her sandals and went running down the beach towards the sea as the morning light made her tan glow. I locked up the Jeep and followed her like a hound on a scent, catching up as she waded out into the waves. Mutt watched us from the shore, wagging his tail before heading off to sniff his way along the sand.

We paddled out beyond the break and Rogue's eyes sparkled with excitement as we turned our boards around and eyed the waves rolling in behind us. There were a few other surfers out and they were all bobbing in the water on their boards as they waited for a big wave to catch.

The water started swelling behind us and I shared a grin with Rogue before we began paddling our arms hard to pick up speed, the once familiar feel of surfing with her sending a rush through my body. We'd done it thousands of times when we were kids, and yet the high never lessened. The look in Rogue's eyes reminded me I needed to let her come down here more often. It wasn't like I wanted to lock her up, but with Shawn in town all I wanted to do was put her in a tower and bolt up the doors. I wasn't saying I was on the side of dragons who guarded princesses in towers or anything, but yeah, okay I was.

The water rose beneath my board and I paddled harder before jumping up and riding the wave as it hurtled towards the shore.

Rogue whooped as she popped up too, bending low as her board cut diagonally along the wave and I followed her with my eyes on her ass and my mind well and truly distracted. And because I was distracted, I didn't see the asshole coming directly for her on his surfboard, the guy shouting for her to get out of his way instead of just dropping into the water.

My gaze narrowed and she screamed as he collided with her, the two of them tumbling into the water and crashing under the waves. I dove off of my board, swimming for her as a snarl tore from my lips.

She came up for air, rubbing her shoulder and I pulled her close, inspecting the skin as a red mark started to blossom already.

"Asshole," she growled. "Come on, let's get back out there, I wanna do that a million times before we're done."

The guy who'd hit her bobbed up out of the water and I lunged past her, throwing my fist into his face. He cried out as he realised who I was, trying to turn and swim away but I dove on him, grabbing his head and shoving my weight down so he went underwater.

"Fox!" Rogue gasped as I kept the motherfucker down and he started thrashing beneath the water.

She dove onto my back, trying to pull me off of him but I wasn't letting go. The piece of shit needed the point driven home. He'd hurt my fucking girl when he could have prevented it, and that shit was not going to go unpunished.

"Fox, you'll kill him!" Rogue cried and it was only the feel of her skin on mine that gave me any sense at all to stop.

I reluctantly let go and the guy broke through the surface with a desperate gasp, his eyes full of terror as they landed on me. "I'm sorry, man, I didn't realise it was your girl."

"Get out of my fucking sight," I snapped and he nodded, swimming away and his surfboard went after him, towed along by his leg strap.

I glared at him until he was out of the water and running up the beach to his car, dragging the surfboard all the way behind him through the sand.

Rogue swam around in front of me, cupping my face as my muscles bunched and my breathing came too heavy.

"Dude, you need to chill," she said, flicking me between the eyes and making me blink.

She wound her legs around me as I treaded water and my breathing settled as her body pressed flush to mine. I was instantly captivated by her, my arms winding around her and my hands pressing firmly to her back to keep her there. All the heat in the world seemed to live between us and I wished she'd just lean into it to find how good it felt to burn.

"You're cuckoo," she whispered. "You're missing all the marbles."

I smirked at her. "I think you took them with you when you left, baby."

"Mhmm, then I gave them to a pirate," she said through a grin. "You know how I love a pirate. That sexy eyepatch and peg leg, mmmm. I couldn't resist him when he came after your marbles. I gave them to him just so I could have a night in his pirate arms." She licked her lips and I wanted to lick them too, resisting the urge.

"I'm afraid I hunted that pirate down and killed him, hummingbird."

"Sometimes I don't know if you're joking about murdering all my exes, but I really hope you are."

"I'm not," I said easily and she swatted my shoulder.

"Psycho."

"At least I'm an honest one," I taunted.

"You're not always honest, Fox. You like keeping things from me. You think I can't handle the big wide world, but I've got tougher skin than even you."

"I think I'm starting to realise that," I said, resting my forehead to hers and her lips parted, her gaze dipping to my mouth. But before I could try and steal a kiss, she wriggled out of my arms, dove under the water and splashed me as she kicked her way deeper.

I followed my little rainbow dolphin under the waves, our boards trailing behind us on our leg straps as we swam for the horizon.

After an hour of surfing, we headed back onto the beach and I set up a parasol and towels on the sand, taking the cooler box from the Jeep and popping it open to tempt Rogue closer with the pastries and watermelon juice hiding inside it.

"One thing I like about you, Badge, you know good food," she said, drying her hair off as she approached me and dropped down onto the towel at my side. Mutt sat next to me, wagging and giving me the big eyes as he looked from the cooler box to me. I poured him out a dish of cold water and tossed some chicken treats onto the towel at my feet, making him yap appreciatively as he snatched them and lapped at the water.

"Is that the only thing you like about me?" I grabbed a bottle of sun lotion I'd stashed in the cooler box, beckoning her closer and she rolled her eyes, but indulged me as she moved to sit between my legs and face the sea.

"Yep, that's about it, the rest of your personality is clouded in possessive macho bullshit these days."

I squirted the lotion onto my hands and rubbed it over her back, making goosebumps rush across her skin from the cold liquid.

"What did you used to like about me then?" I pushed, wondering if the answer to capturing her heart lay in my past. But I'd just been some idiot kid back then, and if she thought I hadn't been possessive as a fifteen-year-old then I guessed I'd hidden it better than I realised. Of course, as a kid I hadn't really known what to do with those feelings, though I wasn't sure I'd figured it out as an adult yet either. But I'd always spent plenty of time scaring other guys away from her whether she knew it or not.

"Hmm." She tipped her head forward as I rubbed the lotion over her shoulder blades and I studied every detail of the angel wings inked there, running all the way down her back. I guessed they were meant to be ironic, because she hadn't been a good girl a day in her life. "I liked how free you were, how you'd have some spontaneous idea for us to all pile onto a boat and go search for dolphins or head down to the cliffs and explore all the old smuggler's caves. You didn't answer to anyone, especially your dad."

I frowned, squeezing more lotion onto my palm. "It's not that easy being spontaneous these days when I have a whole gang to run."

"I know," she sighed. "I just wish we knew how good we had it back then. There's only a few years in life where you get to just…be. No one asks anything of you, no one expects anything of you. Even if you fuck up, people just say 'oh she's just a kid' or 'she'll grow out of it.' But I don't think I did, Fox. I think I'm still trying to be a kid in a world full of adults and no one wants to play anymore."

My heart twisted and I caught her waist, pulling her back against me. "I'll play with you," I said in her ear and she shivered as my lotion slick palms slid over her waist. "When my father's not here, I'm the king of this town and if I wanna play with my girl, I will."

She turned her head to look at me, her eyes a dark sea of emotion and unmet needs. Needs I wanted to fulfil again and again until she didn't look so empty.

"That's the problem," she breathed. "Luther rules your life these days, but you never let him before."

Her skin against mine created a flaming kind of ache in me that was desperate to be answered.

I traced my finger over the sea turtle inked on her shoulder. "Because he took the one thing from me that I can't risk him ever taking again. He may say he's fine with you staying in town, but I don't trust him. He's up to something."

Her brow creased and she turned her head to gaze at the sea again. "Maybe he just wants you to be happy, Badger."

I released a hollow laugh. "That's the last thing he wants, or he wouldn't have sent you away in the first place."

"I think Luther maybe realised he fucked up," she said and I tsked.

"Is that what he said to you?"

She shrugged one shoulder. Whatever they'd talked about when he took her, she didn't seem inclined to tell any of us, but I knew my father. He couldn't be trusted. The faith I'd once had in him as a boy had been firmly eradicated the moment he ripped Rogue out of my life and forced me to join the Harlequins. He may have done it under some bullshit guise of protecting me, but I knew better. He just needed a protégé for his gang, his empire. He wouldn't die a satisfied man unless he knew I was there to take his crown. And I couldn't say I wouldn't be anymore. The Harlequins had become a part of my life which I needed. The Crew gave me purpose, gave me the opportunity to provide for my boys. But it had also stolen away two of the people I loved most in the world.

"He said a lot of things," she said eventually. "He mentioned your mom…" She eyed me for a reaction and a trickle of ice ran through my blood. "Did you know about-"

"Don't," I cut her off sharply. "I don't wanna know. Whatever he told you about her, I don't care."

"What do you mean? Surely you know-"

"I don't. My dad has tried to tell me plenty of times since I turned eighteen and he deemed me 'old enough to know the details,' but I don't want to hear it, hummingbird. She's not a part of my life."

Rogue frowned, chewing on her lip. "I think you should talk to him about it."

"Would you wanna know?" I growled. "Whatever he said to you, would you care to know it if it was about *your* mom?"

Her features darkened. We'd always shared this in common; the two of us motherless and abandoned. That was the stories we knew, the only ones we had. I was well aware there was more to my mother's story, but I also knew it wouldn't change shit. She'd broken my dad's heart and the rest didn't matter. Because she was gone and the details would only taint the small piece of bliss that ignorance provided me on the subject.

"Maybe not," she breathed. "But I learned to face reality a long time ago, stare it in the eye and tell it that it doesn't own me."

I leaned in and kissed her neck, the taste of sea salt, coconut and sun lotion flooding my senses. "It's not because I'm afraid of the truth, it's because the truth will take away the one image in my mind I have of her. When I was a kid, I imagined up this woman who loved me, who built sandcastles with me on the beach and walked me out for my first ever steps in the sea. I don't know if it's true, Rogue, but I need it to be. Maybe what my dad told you was a better image than that, or maybe it was far worse. Either way, I'm happy with the image I have and I want to keep it."

"Oh Fox," she sighed, leaning back against me as I wrapped one arm around her shoulders. "Your mind paints prettier pictures than mine. When I think of my mom, all I see is a dark silhouette turning her back on me. I think that's why I fear the rest of the world doing it too, why I expect it from everyone."

"It breaks me to think of you believing I turned my back on you," I said in a deep tone, my grip on her tightening. "Are you ever going to trust me again?"

"I don't know," she admitted. "Trust is like a whole kingdom falling to ruin, sometimes the stones are chipped away bit by bit and other times an army destroys it all in one fell swoop."

"Kingdoms can be rebuilt," I said fiercely, swearing that I would work tirelessly to do so, even if I had to do it one brick at a time.

"I guess," she whispered. "Do you think you'll ever trust your dad again?"

My shoulders tensed and a frown furrowed my brow. "Some kingdoms are best left fallen," I muttered. "And don't let your guard down with, Luther, hummingbird," I warned. "He's delusional. He even thinks Maverick will just arrive home one day ready to offer everyone warm hugs."

"Would that be so terrible?" she asked and I growled, closing my arms tighter around her.

"If you think that's a possibility you're as crazy as my father," I snipped.

"Don't you miss him?" she asked in a whisper, not biting back, trying to tease the truth out of me. And I never wanted to lie to her again, so I tried to give her the honest answer.

"Yes, of course I do," I said. "But I miss the brother I grew up with, not the person who lives on Dead Man's Isle. They're two entirely different people."

"Yes and no," she said thoughtfully and I bit back a stream of curses, not wanting her to shut down on me, but the tension in my muscles was probably a dead giveaway on how close I was to losing my shit. Every time I thought of his hands on her, I wanted to murder someone.

"He went through hell in prison, I don't even know all of it and what I do know isn't my place to tell you, but..." She dipped her head. "It's left its mark on him and frankly I'm not surprised he hates the Harlequins."

"I know I failed him," I forced out, my chest almost too tight to breathe. "But that doesn't excuse him turning on us like he did. We could have worked it out…but then he decided to try and kill us and I had to protect Chase and JJ. It wasn't a choice I ever wanted to make but he forced my hand, baby, so here we are."

Her shoulders rose and fell and she pulled out of my arms, taking the lotion from beside me and starting to coat her legs.

I watched with a hunger rising in me that could only be sated by her and I lay down, gazing up at the inside of the parasol to distract myself. When she was finished she stood up, moving to place one foot either side of my hips and holding the bottle of lotion like a dick between her legs.

I snorted a laugh. "No dicks allowed out on the beach, sir."

"I couldn't help myself when I saw those perky tits, baby," she put on a stupid man voice and I laughed harder.

She groaned loudly and squirted a load of lotion on my chest and I lunged for her, knocking her legs out from beneath her so she fell down on top me. Her hands slipped in the lotion on my body as she tried to push herself up and her forehead collided with mine.

"Ah motherfucker," she swore, pressing her hands to my shoulders and managing to sit up on my dick. Which was definitely hard and definitely obvious.

Her eyebrows arched and her hips rocked in a way I wasn't sure was accidental, making me suck in a breath.

"*Rogue*," I gritted out and she bit her lip which only made my problem worse.

She leaned down so she was nose to nose with me, her damp hair creating a curtain around us and my breathing all but stopped as I considered fucking her right here on the beach. That'd be one way to prove to the world that she was mine, on the other hand I didn't want a single fucker in the vicinity seeing her naked flesh. But so long as I was thoroughly inside her, maybe I could make an exception.

"Do you have any money, Badger?" she purred.

"What?" I murmured through the fog of lust in my head, my hands falling to her waist and gripping tight.

"I need a couple of dollars," she said huskily.

"Sure, whatever, my wallet's under the cooler."

She reached over to get it, grinding her tits over my face and making me groan into her flesh. Then she got up with the dollars between her fingers, running off up the beach towards a vendor to grab a drink.

I stared after her, abandoned and fucking desperate. When Rogue was done guzzling her lemonade, she ran back toward me, tossed the bottle down beside me then jogged off towards the surfboards.

"I'm going back in the water, Badge! Byeee!" She waved vaguely at me and I growled in frustration, shoving myself up to sit and watch her as Mutt gave me a dry look.

"Yeah, I get it," I shot at him. "I'm whipped."

I watched Rogue out in the sea, not giving one shit about that. I'd been whipped since the moment I met her and that was fine by me. She could toy with me all she liked, but I'd be spanking her ass red for toying with me eventually, then she'd realise who owned her. If Rogue Easton wanted someone to play with, she'd better get used to the darker versions of the games we used to enjoy when we were kids. I wasn't her teammate anymore though, I was the opposition. And she was going down.

It was another half hour before she emerged from the ocean and I watched the water streaming down her toned body with only sin filled thoughts in my mind.

I'd packed everything into the Jeep and was waiting for her by the car, my arms folded as I watched her. Mutt was off creeping up on a toddler whose ice cream was melting and dripping onto the towel beneath her.

Rogue smiled at me as she approached, looking flushed with life from her time out on the waves. I took her board from her, loading it in the back of the Jeep as she jogged away to use the outdoor shower at the edge of the beach and I enjoyed the show as she washed, glaring at any asshole who so much as glanced her way.

But the beach had mysteriously cleared around us. I guessed that wasn't so mysterious when I remembered how violent I could be over her though. Word had no doubt spread about what had happened to her little friend Carter when he'd recorded her out surfing. And he'd turned into a ghost ever since I'd left my last message to back off. One more strike and we both knew I'd be dragging him into the woods to drive the message home permanently.

I hooked a towel out of the Jeep as Rogue jogged back over to me, holding it out as a screen against the side of the car so she could get changed.

"Shut your eyes," she commanded and I complied, though I didn't really see the point considering every inch of her bare pussy and tits were gonna be mine one day soon.

When she was done, she spammed me on the forehead and I growled, capturing her hand as I tossed the towel into the passenger seat. She was back in her little lemon dress and a turquoise bikini peeked out from underneath it.

"Lemme go." She tugged at her fingers, but I crowded her against the Jeep, shaking my head.

"You think you got away with that little stunt you pulled earlier?" I growled and her eyes widened.

"What stunt?" she played dumb.

"You know exactly what I mean. Being a little cock tease."

"I think you're delusional like your daddy, Badge," she said lightly, but I could see the hint of mischief in her eyes.

"Yeah? Well I'm violent like my daddy too." I grabbed her waist, twisting her around and throwing her across the passenger seat so her legs hung out the car. Then I flipped her skirt off of her ass and spanked her so hard she squeaked. The reddened print of my palm lay over her tanned flesh and I got high on the feeling of owning her like that.

"Fox," she gasped breathily with a hint of a moan in her voice.

"Yeah, baby?" I asked casually, but as she went to answer, I clapped my hand down on her ass again in the very same spot, making her yelp. I leaned over her, my hard cock grinding into her sore ass as I made my long term intentions towards her very fucking clear.

"You got something to say, hummingbird?" I growled.

She wriggled beneath me, only serving to getting me harder as I pinned her in place.

"You're an asshole and I hate you," she snarled.

"And you're a liar." I smirked, shifting my weight and squeezing her spanked ass cheek in one hand. "You lie to me, but mostly you lie to yourself, baby. Because if you don't want me right here putting you in your place, then why don't you ever tell me to stop?"

She panted, trying to wriggle free again, but she wasn't going anywhere. "Fuck you."

"Big words, but I still don't hear any objections," I taunted her then fisted one hand in her hair, tugging her head up so my mouth was aligned with her ear. "You ever disrespect me again and I'll show you what happens to bad girls in Sunset Cove. This is my kingdom and everyone follows my rules, but I know you're not like the rest of them. You're a queen in your own right and you've come for a war. But if you lose, you'd better be prepared to get on your knees, baby, because the loser will have to bow."

"Then you'd better bring your kneepads, Badger, because it's gonna hurt when you hit the ground," she laughed wildly.

I released her with a wicked grin, standing upright and whistling for Mutt as Rogue climbed across into the driver's seat and rearranged her dress. Mutt gave up licking the melted ice cream dripping onto the toddler's towel, instead snatching the whole cone from her hand, turning and running away like his ass was on fire. The little girl wailed and I directed Mutt into the footwell of the Jeep where he chomped down the ice cream in two bites. I climbed in after him and Rogue high tailed it out of there like we were in on the heist. *Even the dog's a fucking criminal.*

Rogue turned the music up as This Life by Vampire Weekend started on the radio, her free hand hanging out the window as her fingers twisted in the wind. She threw me a challenging look as she sang along and I threw one right back, my heart pounding furiously in my chest. She could handle everything I dished out and more and I just wanted to keep pushing her to see how far she could go. Every other woman in this town feared me, but Rogue held a power over me like no other. Nothing fazed her. It was one of the things I was in love with her for, but if I named them all I'd be there until my dying breath listing them. To me, she was perfect, a creature hewn by the gods of the sea, placed on this earth to lure me into the depths of the ocean. And I'd go gladly into the deep for her and never look back.

My phone rang as we closed in on home and I took it out of my pocket, finding my dad calling. My mood soured as I answered, turning the music down so I could hear him.

"Yeah?" I grunted.

"Still angry with me then?" he asked. "I would have thought you'd be grateful for me pardoning your girl."

"I would have been grateful ten years ago," I said coolly and he sighed.

"Look, I need you on form with your head straight. Some asshole Dead Dog just showed up at the clubhouse with a message from Shawn Mackenzie."

I sat upright in my chair, my pulse roaring in my skull. "What message?" I demanded.

"He wants a meeting to discuss a peace deal, no weapons, four men only," Luther said and my mind sharpened like a blade. "I figured as he's on your turf, I'd take you and your boys."

My free hand locked in a fist and I sensed Rogue's eyes flicking onto me. "You sure this isn't a trap? I don't trust that piece of shit."

"We'll be meeting out on the cliffs, open land, no one's allowed to wear anything but their underwear," Luther said.

"Great, and who says we want peace anyway?" I growled.

"I do," he said fiercely. "I want him dead as much as you do, kid, but if it comes to a war, I can't say for sure we'll win it. His gang is as big as the Harlequins and if he decides to move in on Sunset Cove, well…it won't be pretty. There'll be a lot of bloodshed and he already came too close to killing you, son, I'm not risking your life for anything."

My breaths came unevenly as I considered those words, weighing them up and knowing he was right. If peace could be brokered, we had to try, because I didn't want to lay my boys' lives on the line in a war. I couldn't risk Chase or JJ, and now Rogue was back in town, the idea of her getting caught up in all that was unthinkable.

"Alright, what time?"

"An hour. Meet at the top of the Ventosa Cliffs," Luther said. "And kid," he growled in that dominating father tone of his that I hated. "You check your boys closely for weapons, ass cracks and all, I'm not gonna stand for a single Harlequin fucking this up."

"Got it," I said and hung up, pushing my phone back into my pocket.

I caught Rogue looking at me and arched a brow at her, but she just tossed her hair and looked back at the road. "Who was that?" she asked lightly.

"My dad."

"Did he have anything interesting to say?"

"Depends what you mean by interesting." I shrugged and she narrowed her eyes on me for a moment.

"Anything about Shawn?" she demanded.

I considered my words, feeling assessed by her and not wanting to lie.

I sighed, figuring she could know this much, it didn't matter if she went crazy at me for not letting her be involved. She knew my stance on the situation. "He wants to discuss a peace deal. I'll be going to see him with the boys in an hour."

Her upper lip curled back. "Peace?" she spat. "The motherfucker has moved in on your land, he's killed your men, and you're gonna discuss *peace*?"

"Yes, Rogue," I growled in warning. "Because if we don't, it means there's going to be a war. And if war comes to this town, it puts everyone I love at risk."

She frowned, thinking on something. "So just shoot him when you get there. Bang. Job done," she insisted.

"We have to go without weapons and wear nothing but our boxers," I said. "Where do you suggest I stash a gun, baby?"

"I dunno, you must have a lot of room up there in your big head," she tossed at me. "You certainly aren't using the extra space for brain power."

"What do you expect me to do?" I snapped. "This is what's best for the Crew, I can't take risks that put my family in jeopardy."

"He deserves to fucking die," she snarled, and I could see the hurt in her eyes over what he'd done to her. I felt it too, right down to the pit of my soul.

I reached out, squeezing her leg. "I swear to you, I will kill Shawn Mackenzie, hummingbird. But not today. Not in any way that can be connected back to me, because if he dies, some other asshole will take his place as king of The Dead Dogs and declare war on the Cove, and I simply can't risk that."

"I want to be the one to kill him," she snarled furiously.

"Well that's not gonna happen," I said firmly. "You think I'm gonna let you anywhere near that asshole?"

"I'm not asking for permission," she hissed.

"I'm afraid you have to in this town, baby, and I'll never grant it."

She fell quiet, chewing angrily on her lip and I hoped that meant she got the message.

We arrived back at Harlequin House and she parked up in the garage. I led her inside with Mutt and she stalked up to her room without another word to me. She'd get over it. At least I'd been honest with her, so that was something, right?

I found the boys out on the patio; Chase was swimming in the pool and JJ was sunning himself butt naked and face down on one of the loungers. He was as bad as Rogue for that shit. His eyes were closed and he had headphones on so he didn't notice my arrival.

I beckoned Chase out of the pool and he moved over to JJ, whipping the headphones from his head and turning them off. His phone connected to the poolside Bluetooth speakers instead and a gravelly male voice spoke over them, "-ploughed into her steamy, wet pussy while she begged for my cock and-" JJ turned it off on his phone, standing up and baring his dick to the world before pulling his shorts on like it was nothing.

"Jesus, what the fuck were you listening to?" Chase asked.

"A book," JJ said with a shrug. "I'm cultured like that."

"What's the culture? I think I wanna join up," Chase said with a smirk and JJ laughed.

"Romance books. Side note, I'm an expert on satisfying women so I'm thinking of becoming a dating coach, what do you reckon?" JJ said with a grin. "You could be my Guinea pig, Ace."

Chase opened his mouth, looking like he was about to tell him to get fucked, but I spoke before he could.

"Shawn's called a meeting," I announced, grabbing their full attention before explaining how it was all gonna go down. We needed to get our shit together and leave.

"Holy fuck," Chase breathed.

"Yeah, so get moving," I commanded and JJ and Chase headed off to the garage while I jogged upstairs to tell Rogue we were going.

I knocked on her door, but she didn't answer and I sighed, leaning my forehead against it. "Don't hate me, hummingbird. I'm just trying to do the right thing and keep everyone safe. You understand that, right?"

Silence.

"There's cold pizza in the fridge if you get hungry. We'll be back in a while and I'll tell you what happens, okay?"

Nothing.

I ground my teeth, fighting against the frustration rising in me before forcing myself to walk away downstairs. I headed into the garage, climbing into my truck where Chase and JJ were already waiting inside in their boxers. I didn't need to 'check their ass cracks' as my dad had so sweetly suggested, I trusted both of them to do as I asked. And though Chase was still on probation, I was sure he wasn't going to let me down on this. I wanted him there today, because whatever happened was going to change the fate of the Cove. Either we'd find a way to make peace with Shawn and he'd get the fuck out of my town, or he'd declare war once and for all. Either way, the asshole was still a dead man. Today just determined whether I was going to sneak into his home in the night and slide a knife into the back of his skull, or if he died at the end of my gun in plain sight of the whole world in a war.

We drove up onto the Ventosa Cliffs, heading onto an off-road track that wound along towards the highest point.

We soon drove onto the flat, grassy expanse of land at the peak of the cliff then parked up and assessed the area. My father was there in his blue truck and he nodded to us through the window.

On the horizon, a white SUV appeared, spewing up dust as it sped along the dirt road on the other side of this cliff. It pulled to a halt and Shawn stepped out in his boxers with his hands raised in the air. Three of his men followed and Luther got out of his truck too, nodding to us in a direction to follow. I stepped out onto the grass, the sun beating down on my bare skin as JJ and Chase flanked me while Luther moved to lead the way across the plane. My dad's body was pure muscle and pretty much entirely covered with tattoos. The word Harlequin arched over his shoulder blades and a tattoo of his spine ran down the length of his back.

"Hey there, boys," Shawn called like we were old friends meeting for a drink and hatred rippled under my flesh. "Aren't you all a sight to behold?"

We closed in until only five feet parted us and Shawn did a little twirl as if to prove he was completely unarmed. His men followed then Shawn spun his finger in the air to encourage us to prove we weren't hiding any weapons and we took it in turns to spin around so he could make sure there was nothing strapped to our backs or legs.

"Beautiful," Shawn said with a smirk. "Shame no one brought a camera, huh? We'd make one hell of a porno right now. It'd sell out in five minutes flat. Come to think of it, I'd like being in movies even more if I got my cock sucked twelve times a day, I think I need a change of career." He laughed and his men laughed louder like good little cronies.

I scowled coldly at him as I moved to my dad's side and JJ and Chase kept close.

"You called us here, Shawn," Luther said in his booming voice. "So why don't you use your mouth for something worthwhile and tell us what you want."

"Alright, King Harlequin, calm down, don't bust a hip," Shawn mocked, though my father wasn't that much older than him. Which was just another reason to make my skin crawl over Rogue dating him. It took everything I had not to just attack him here and now with my bare hands, choke the life out of his worthless body and make him pay for laying a finger on my girl.

"Watch your mouth," I snarled and Shawn's blue gaze slid onto me.

"Oh he's got fire in his belly today, boys. Last I saw of you, you were crawling under my trailer like a coward," Shawn said through a dark grin.

"Well the last I saw of you, you were running for your life like a deer at the end of a hunter's gun," I spat and he chuckled.

"Touché," he said. "Now listen up." The smile dropped dramatically from his face. "I got some terms I wanna put to ya, and if you can't meet them, well…I think I'll enjoy shattering your skulls in the coming days."

"What are your terms?" Luther demanded.

"I want Sunset Cove," Shawn announced, raising his arms and gesturing to the place and my hackles rose. "It's real beaut down here. The women are… *mmm*." He kissed his fingers. "And the beach is mighty pretty. I think I can see me living here, lording it up in that shiny house of yours. You give me this town and I'll back off, no more fighting, no more war. Simple. So what d'ya say?"

"No," I snarled before my father could get a word out. "No fucking way."

Luther took longer to consider it and I gave him a look that said I'd fight him to hell and back on this. Shawn was not going to take this place from my family. It was our home, the land we grew up on, and I'd die for it here today if I had to.

"I think your daddy gets the final say, boy," Shawn taunted, looking to Luther as Chase and JJ shifted around me, looking ready to go to battle for the Cove too. "So what'll it be, Daddy? A bloody war? Or one eency weency town?"

"This is Fox's domain," Luther said at last. "If he says no, that's your answer."

Shawn ran his tongue across his teeth in anger, his eyes flashing back onto me. "That's what you want then, is it sunshine?" There was a deadly undercurrent to his tone. "Because lemme tell you, if you make an enemy outa me, you make an enemy outa the Devil himself. I'll have your pretty town running red with blood, I'll have kiddies screaming in their beds terrified of the monsters crawling in their front doors, I'll have your women on their backs and taking Dead Dog cocks in every hole they fancy, showing 'em what real men feel like inside them." He took a step toward me, all swagger and cockiness and my fingers itched for a blade to drive into him. "If you want war, you're asking for hell to come pay you a visit. So are you sure you wanna extend the invite, boy?"

I squared my shoulders at this arrogant piece of shit, taking a step towards him to show him he didn't scare me. There wasn't a flicker of fear in my heart over Shawn Mackenzie. I was a monster in my own right, and one who could deliver death as brutally and painfully as he could imagine. And I knew what I had to do, because it was my only chance to save my town from this dog.

"Face me here. No weapons. We fight, and whoever's still breathing by the end of it takes Sunset Cove. If you win, you let my family pack up and leave town and if I win, your men get out of my hometown and never come back," I snarled.

"Fox," Chase hissed urgently at those words, but I shot him a look that told him to back down. This was my decision. If Shawn was going to shoot his mouth at me like a big man, then I was going to call his bluff.

Shawn sized me up, getting closer until his chest brushed mine. We were the same height pretty much dead on, his eyes like the palest blue sky gazing into the forest green of mine. I wanted blood for Rogue and I was happy to take it from him right here, right now with nothing but the strength of our bodies to decide the victor. And I would win, there was no doubt in my mind.

"Tempting, little Fox," Shawn purred, devouring my breathing space as he tried to intimidate me. "I'd just love to see you on the ground choking out your last breath."

"Then fight me," I challenged.

He cocked his head from one side to the other, pretending to consider that but I could see the decision in his eyes. "Nah." He stepped back to re-join his men. "I've always been fonder of war. I think I'll invade your town like an olden day pirate and let my men pillage, rape and murder their way through your people."

"Coward," Luther hissed at him.

"Oh no, I assure you, King Harlequin, I am no coward," Shawn said with a wide smile. "I just wanna prolong your fall from grace, make sure you're there to see your boys die one by one by one by one." He aimed a finger gun at each of us pretending to fire it as he spoke those words, his eyes glittering wickedly.

"I'm your death, Shawn," I warned as we started backing up towards the trucks. "My face will be the last thing you ever see."

"We'll see about that, sunshine," he laughed, remaining there as he watched us go, but as we made it back to the truck, a flash of colour caught my eye and my heart lurched.

Rogue leapt up from under a tarp in the bed of my truck, springing onto the roof with a handgun in her grip and her yellow sundress whipping around her thighs in the wind.

"Die you motherfucking dickweed!" she screamed as she fired at Shawn.

I gasped, twisting around as one of Shawn's men hit the ground with a shot to the leg and Shawn dragged another one in front of him as a shield as

404

he ran the fuck away. Most of Rogue's bullets went wide though one hit the human shield in the arm and Shawn roared a laugh as her gun rang empty.

"Hey, sugarpie!" he shouted as he made it back to his SUV. "I wondered when you were gonna show your face. Keep that pussy wet for when I reclaim it!"

I dove onto the hood of my truck with a shout of rage, grabbing Rogue and leaping off of the other side as Shawn took a gun out of his car.

I leapt into the driver's seat with her in my arms and as JJ and Chase got in, I threw her over their laps. Shawn returned fire and my dad drove his truck into the path of the bullets as he ducked low, giving us a chance to turn and drive the fuck away. Luther gunned it down the track after us, but Shawn didn't follow.

JJ shifted Rogue upright on his lap as she fought with him like she was desperate to get out and go after that asshole.

I spanked her thigh to snap her out of it and she gasped, glaring at me and slapping me hard across the face. The truck veered and JJ caught the wheel to stop me careering off the dirt road and I growled at Rogue.

"What the fuck were you thinking?" I barked at her.

"I was thinking Shawn was gonna fucking die at my hands while he was exposed," she snarled. "Seemed like a damn good opportunity to me."

I shook my head, though I couldn't even fucking argue with that. She almost took him out, and her plan might have really worked if she could actually fire a gun for shit. That didn't make me any less angry though.

"That was badass, pretty girl," JJ chuckled and I shot him a glare, finding Chase fighting a grin at her too. *Assholes.*

"Well I hope you enjoyed the field trip, baby," I snarled in fury. "Because we're officially at war with The Dead Dogs and that means you're not leaving the house until Shawn's head is full of bullet holes."

CHAPTER TWENTY SEVEN

I leaned back in the La-Z-Boy chair Shawn liked to use as a throne whenever he was here and sighed. He'd texted me, asking me to stop by. Well, asking *was a little soft for the 'come over' text message I'd received but still, he'd told me to come so here I was, wearing a red dress because he liked that colour on me and sitting on my own.*

It had been almost an hour, but I didn't bother shooting him another message because this wasn't that unusual. He'd be here when he got here and if he changed his mind about wanting me to wait for him then he'd just text me again. And as pathetic as I knew that made me, I just didn't care enough to argue over it. Apathy was my new favourite flavour and I was finding it easy to swallow most of the time.

A knock came at the door to the big apartment and I looked towards it with a slight frown. Shawn had men hanging around downstairs - this entire apartment building was full of his gang members and there was always someone watching the comings and goings. So people didn't just come knocking on the door at random.

"It's Travis," a voice came from outside and I pushed to my feet at the sound of Shawn's number two calling out a greeting. Or was he number three?

Maybe four? Whatever, he was one of the gang banger elite as far as The Dead Dogs went and that meant he was cool. Or it meant Shawn said he was cool. I never really got to know many of his people so I couldn't say I'd formed my own opinion on him.

"Shawn's not here," I called back, keeping my ass in my chair.

"No worries, sweetheart, I can wait with you until he is. I need a word with him when he gets back."

I considered my options then shrugged. I was bored as fuck and Travis was one of Shawn's men, so I couldn't see the problem in having some company while I waited around.

I got up and opened the door, smiling up at Travis and stepping aside to let him in. He was a big fucker, some combination of muscle and plenty of food filling him out, his skin dark and smile used to breaking hearts. He tipped an imaginary hat to me, my gaze catching on the skull he had tattooed on the back of his hand as I smirked.

"Oh, I didn't realise The Dead Dogs employed gentlemen in their ranks," I teased, closing the door behind him and heading over to the fridge. Shawn always kept it well stocked, so I grabbed a couple of beers out and tossed one to Travis as he dropped down on the couch.

"Well, you wouldn't would you, secret girl?" he asked, smirking at me over the top of his bottle as he took a swig. "Shawn likes to keep you hidden away as if the rest of us won't even realise you're here just because he keeps you to himself most of the time."

"I don't have any interest in The Dead Dogs," I said as I dropped into my seat and took a drink of my own beer. "So there's not a lot of point in me spending time with them too often."

Not that I'd have minded really. I was bored a lot. And kinda lonely too. In fact, I couldn't remember the last time I'd had someone to sit and drink a beer with.

"We don't have to talk gang bullshit then," Travis replied. "You can tell me all about your day. Are you into knitting or some shit? Is that why you're sitting around up here when the sun is shining? You got some cardigan you're tryna finish for my boy to wear on a chilly evening?"

I laughed loudly at the idea of Shawn in knitwear and Travis grinned at me.

The sound of the front door slamming against the wall made me flinch and I whipped around as Shawn strode in, his gaze moving from me to Travis and back again as a sneer pulled at his top lip.

"Well doesn't this look like a cosy little gathering?" he asked with a wide smile, that dangerous look falling from his face as if it had never been there. But it had.

"Your girl was kind enough to let me come in and wait for you, boss," Travis explained, standing his beer on the coffee table and getting to his feet. "She was just being hospitable."

"Oh yeah, my little woman is always supremely hospitable," Shawn agreed, throwing me a look that made my stomach clench. "What are you doing here, Travis?"

"I found that asshole you were looking for. The one who stole the-"

"Where is he then?" Shawn asked with a wide smile which didn't reach his blue eyes and my gut knotted.

"Got him in the warehouse. You want me to deal with it, or-"

"Nah. I'm feeling all kinds of het up right now. I think I could use a workout."

Travis nodded and headed towards the door while I remained where I was, hoping to escape that look Shawn was giving me, but I knew that wasn't going to happen.

"Come on, sugarpie," Shawn said, holding a hand out to me. "I think it might be fun for you to see what I do to men who touch things that belong to me. Don't you?"

"Sure," I agreed like I didn't have a care in the world, getting to my feet and taking his hand. He squeezed my fingers tightly and towed me along as we took off after Travis, following him to the elevator and riding it down to the ground floor.

Shawn cracked jokes with him and I tried to relax too, smiling along, but the knot of unease in my gut was only tightening and I couldn't figure out why. Shawn never wanted me anywhere near any of his work and I never wanted to get near to it either. So why the fuck was I being brought along for the ride?

Travis hopped into his car and Shawn nudged me towards the back seats as he rode shotgun and I listened to the two of them laughing and talking shit on the drive. But more than once, Travis caught my gaze in the rear view mirror and the looks he shot me were more than enough to set my anxiety on edge. He was worried about something and considering his line of work, I was inclined to be pretty worried in response to that myself.

We drove away from town to an old industrial estate and Shawn opened my door for me, taking my hand once more with a crocodile's smile before leading me into a dark warehouse. It was empty, abandoned, more than a few of the windows busted and puddles of water coating the concrete floor.

I spotted a few lower ranking members of The Dead Dogs hanging about the place, but they moved out of sight as we passed them. When we walked through to the main part of the warehouse, we found a shivering, shirtless man tied to a chair, his face bloody and body beaten.

He wheezed in a breath and raised his head to look at us as we entered and fear filled his swollen eyes as he caught sight of Shawn.

Shawn gave him a look like a feral beast who was starving for a meal before leaning down to speak in my ear.

"I catch you playing whore for one of my men again, and we're gonna have a problem, sugarpie. Got it?"

Objections coated my tongue, but one look into his blue eyes told me to keep silent so I just nodded and he leaned in to press a rough kiss to my mouth which bruised my lips and made my pulse scatter.

When he strode away from me, I found Travis watching us, looking a little uncomfortable, but not saying a word. He was a soldier after all and Shawn was the one in command. There were no white knights in stories like mine.

The guy who was tied to the chair started screaming as Shawn turned towards the wall where a bunch of tools and knives were laid out and I got the feeling that this place saw this kind of thing a lot.

I didn't flinch as he picked up a hatchet and began spinning it in his hand, his smile widening while the guy screamed and thrashed against his chair. Death had brought me to this place after all and I'd seen enough blood when I killed Axel to know I didn't need to fear it unless it was mine.

Shawn circled his prey, a shark in the water with an injured seal at his

410

mercy and I just watched as he taunted him. I didn't know if this man deserved his death or not but there wasn't anything I could do about it. So as Shawn began making a song and dance out of asking the guy if he'd seriously believed he could get away with stealing from him, I just retreated to that place in my head where the sun was shining and the waves crashed against the golden sand. I heard gulls calling and tasted salt on my tongue and could almost remember what it was like to truly smile as bright as that sun.

Shawn began swinging the hatchet and the guy stopped screaming long before he was done with it. I watched the massacre without a flicker of emotion crossing my face, feeling Travis's gaze moving to me more than once but it didn't really matter what he thought of me or my reaction. It had been nice to have a friend for a little while there. But I doubted we'd be hanging out again any time soon.

Shawn tossed the bloody hatchet to the ground with a loud clatter as the metal hit the concrete and he turned back to us, grinning wildly, his face and body splattered with blood. Travis held his ground as he approached him, not even flinching when Shawn's fist collided with his face.

"I see you making moves on my girl again then this asshole's death will seem like a daydream in comparison."

"Yes, boss," Travis agreed, spitting a wad of blood from his mouth and cutting me a look before dropping his gaze again.

Yeah, my friend count had definitely just dropped back to zero.

I remembered an episode of The Power Rangers where the Green Ranger had been held captive by Rita Repulsa and he'd been all sad and powerless and shit. It had worked out okay for him. Then again, I didn't have any other Power Rangers to come help me out, so I was probably just gonna have to figure this one out for myself.

Shawn took my hand and tugged me back out of the warehouse, the blood of the man he'd just killed still wet on his skin.

"You know why it's so important I gave that motherfucker a death by my own hand, sweetcheeks?" he asked me casually and I shrugged.

"So everyone knows what happens to anyone who crosses you," I guessed.

I probably should have been afraid, screaming, running, I didn't even know what, but when I considered running from here, from Shawn and from all of it I could just see more of the same. On and on and on forever. One shitty town to the next, one group of assholes after another. I used to run in hopes of finding a home. Or just because I'd figured out that the place I was at wasn't it. But I didn't see the point anymore. Unwanted things didn't find homes because we didn't belong anywhere. And at least Shawn wanted me. For now. That was better than the alternative of heading back out on the streets. Besides, better was an elusive concept. And one that didn't apply to people like me and the lives we got to pick.

"Come on then, sugarpie," Shawn growled. "I'll let you remind me why I like keeping you around and then we can forget this little mix up."

"Already forgotten," I agreed as we made it back outside.

Shawn grinned then shoved me to my knees beside Travis's car and I realised he meant right now, while he was still covered in the blood of that guy and feeling the high of the kill. I hesitated and he cocked his head at me as he looked down, waiting for my next move. Maybe I should have run. But my heart was thumping again and despite how fucked up a little part of me knew this was, I was actually feeling something for once. A little fear and shock, but that was okay because it was better than the endless empty abyss I usually existed in.

So I gave Shawn a sultry smile, let my gaze run over his muscular body then hitched my skirt up so that I could get off on this too.

I rolled his fly down and took his cock like a good girl as I started to touch myself and in my head the sun was shining and the waves were crashing and I could almost taste happiness too.

I wanted to scream as I remembered that girl. Her false smiles and empty heart and her vacant fucking life.

The longer I spent away from her, the clearer I saw her and I fucking hated that. Shawn used to laugh at how broken I was. And I used to smile with him because I was beyond caring about it. But now I cared. I cared and it was too late to fix her. But that didn't mean I was going to keep on being her either. She was my shameful little secret that I never wanted anyone to see. But Shawn knew, that was who he thought I was, but he was wrong. And I was determined to show him that at long last when he met his end at my hand.

Fox was still yelling upstairs and occasionally JJ or Chase would pitch in, but mostly it was Luther who was going back and forth with him. I couldn't understand all that much of it, thanks to the fact that I'd been locked down in the freaking basement while they decided what to do with me.

But I'd told Fox. I'd told all of them. Shawn was mine. He'd owned me for too fucking long and I wanted to take that piece of me back from him myself. They'd had no right to try and keep me away from him and I was just as determined as ever to be the one to pull the trigger on him in the end. I was probably going to need a few more lessons with a gun before then though because point and shoot hadn't worked out the way I'd hoped.

"Enough!" Luther bellowed. "That girl has been a problem to you your whole fucking life and I'm done with it."

The door banged open at the top of the stairs and I fought a flinch as Luther pounded down them towards me with Fox and the others right on his heels.

"You keep away from her," Fox warned and my eyes widened as he pulled a fucking gun, levelling it at his dad's head with nothing but cold malice in his eyes. "I'm not some kid you can just force into line anymore. Ten years ago you took her from me but that won't be happening again. I'll do whatever I have to to ensure that."

JJ and Chase looked stuck for words, but their postures said they had Fox's back on this. If he pulled that trigger, they'd be right there with him.

Luther arched an eyebrow at his son then slowly turned to look at me again.

"This girl is gonna be the death of you," he said in a low voice that sent a shiver down my spine. "If you keep up this back and forth, tryna force her into line and make her conform to your idea of what's best for her then I can already see what way that'll play out. You can't keep her if you keep trying to control her, son."

"I'm trying to *protect* her," Fox snarled and Luther nodded.

"Yeah. But I don't think she wants protecting. Do ya?" He nodded his chin at me and I set my jaw, wondering if my answer might be my death but giving it anyway.

"I'm sick of being forced to dance to someone else's tune," I replied. "I want to control my own fate for once in my fucking life beyond just running away."

"You hear that, Fox?" Luther asked, looking back to his son who looked damn close to pulling the trigger. "Are you listening to the girl when she speaks?"

"Me and Rogue can sort our own-"

"*No*," Luther barked so suddenly that I was pretty sure all of us flinched and it must have been a miracle that Fox didn't pull that damn trigger. "Your way ain't working. And I get the feeling this needs to work if I'm ever gonna get my boys back. So here's what I'm gonna offer. You want Shawn Mackenzie's head, wildcat?"

His question was for me and I couldn't help but arch a brow in surprise, but my answer came quick enough. "Yes," I said firmly.

"Well, the Harlequins owe him a death. So I can't just let you have it." My upper lip peeled back, but he wasn't done. "Not unless you're one of us."

"What?" Chase gasped while JJ breathed, "No," and Fox just wheeled his furious eyes from his father to me while still pointing that fucking gun at his dad's head.

"You boys are gonna need to hush up if you don't want me taking action against you. It was your truck the girl snuck into today, Fox, and that means the failure of that shit show is on all of you. Now let the girl talk. I wanna hear how much killing that fucker means to her."

"I want his death more than I want damn near anything else," I said without needing further prompting. "I'm owed it. Hell, I'm owed a lot of freaking things, but revenge is pretty fucking high on my list and right now, he's the asshole I most wanna serve it up to. So I'll do whatever I have to to give it to him, no matter what you say."

"Good," Luther replied, clapping his hands together like we'd just sorted something out, but I still wasn't certain what. "Then you can become one of us right now. That means my son can't go on locking you up in this house, because I can order you out of it. The Harlequins report to me, not him, so if you're in, you're no longer subject to his *protection*. You'll be a member of my army and under my command, not his. Then maybe the two of you will have a shot at figuring your shit out without his fucking fury colouring the air."

I gaped at him, unsure what the fuck to say. I hated the Harlequins. I'd never wanted to be a part of any gang and I still had every intention of running from this place just as soon as I could get my hands on the rest of the keys to that fucking crypt. Though as my gaze moved to JJ's honey brown eyes, my heart snagged on that idea and I had to fight against the desire to forget about it. Forget about all of it. And just…stay.

Fuck. These boys were beneath my skin again already and I didn't even know how to begin untangling myself from them. Or whether I even wanted to anymore.

But what I *did* know was that I wanted fucking Shawn dead, and I was sick of Fox locking me up in this fucking house. And it sounded like Luther was willing to offer me an alternative.

"It's blood in," I said, unsure why that was the first thing that came to mind, but it did. And I wasn't up for killing some random asshole just to gain membership to their stupid club.

"I already know you got the killer in ya," Luther replied, a smile tugging at the corner of his lips. "The way you did Axel in ten years ago proved that. And if you want an official body to swear in on then Shawn can be your hit."

"No," Fox snarled, but both Luther and I ignored him. This was between me and Fox's father right now, and it was my decision to make.

"I'm not gonna start hurting random people for you. Or dealing drugs or any of that shit," I said. "I'm in this because I want Shawn dead. I can pull my own weight as far as money goes, but I'll pick my own jobs."

Luther shrugged. "I don't need any more grunts to add to the ranks. You have free rein to pursue that asshole however you see fit. Besides, you know what I really want from you. You give me that and I won't ever ask another thing of you again."

"Why the fuck are you discussing this like it's happening? And what the fuck do you want from her?" Fox demanded angrily, still brandishing that gun but no one was paying it any attention anymore. And neither I nor Luther answered his questions.

"There's no girls in the Harlequins," JJ tossed in, his fearful gaze catching mine and I knew he didn't want this for me. But that wasn't his choice. It wasn't any of theirs. Besides, Luther's deal was sounding pretty damn sweet to me. And I had bigger balls than a lot of the men I'd met, so I was fairly certain my lack of dick wouldn't hold me back.

Chase looked about ready to burst that throbbing vein in his temple and I was willing to bet his teeth were getting ground down to dust in his jaw with how hard he was biting back his words

"Those are your terms?" I asked, my gaze meeting Luther's as I ignored the other three assholes in the room. "You aren't gonna try and pull a bunch of rank shit on me and start handing out orders as soon as Shawn is dead and I've given you what you want?"

"You have my word," Luther said with a predatory smile which said I'd just walked straight into his trap, but I didn't care. He was offering me Shawn's head on a platter as well as freedom from this house. The only string attached was the impossible reality where he believed I could reunite Fox and Maverick, but I wasn't gonna worry about that. Me calling myself a Harlequin wouldn't affect my ability to run and Luther's reach might be long, but I could run further and faster than he'd ever be able to catch up to if I had to. So all in all, this seemed like a deal I'd be an idiot to refuse.

"Then I'm in," I agreed as Fox shouted, "No!" and Chase had to grab his arm to stop him from lunging between me and his father.

But neither of us cared what the badger had to say on the matter.

"Sounds to me like you need some new ink then," Luther purred.

"What the fuck have you promised him?" Fox begged of me, his eyes burning with fear.

"That's between me and him," I said, raising my chin and his brows pulled together as he realised I was never going to tell him. He'd only refuse it as a possibility anyway and if I was being totally honest, I wasn't certain it was one. But that wasn't the point.

He turned his furious gaze on his dad, his upper lip peeling back with hatred. "I knew you'd never just let her stay here," he spat. "Luther Harlequin always has to get his pound of flesh, doesn't he?" He turned his back on his father and Luther gazed after him with a taut expression and longing in his gaze.

He turned those eyes on me and I could see him resting his hopes for fixing his family on my shoulders. I felt the weight of them pressing down on me like a thousand tons.

Did I get the feeling I'd just made a dumb ass decision? Maybe. Was I going to be going back on it now? That would be a hell no. Even the Green Ranger had been forced to join the dark side for a while and it had worked out okay for him. So I was gonna assume I'd be fine too. And I'd just deal with the furious look in Badger's eyes after I got myself a shiny new Harlequin tattoo – it wasn't like he'd be able to change shit about it after that anyway.

CHAPTER TWENTY EIGHT

"This is bullshit!" Fox shouted.

Luther had left the house and taken Rogue with him over an hour ago and Fox still hadn't calmed down. I wanted to go after them as much as he did, but our boss had us by the balls. What were we supposed to do? It was Luther Harlequin we were up against for fuck's sake, and it wasn't even like Rogue had refused this initiation. I'd always said it was stupid that girls couldn't join the Crew, but *her*? Of all the girls in all the fucking world, *she* was the one he chose to make an exception for?

It wasn't like she didn't have the fighting spirit required of the Harlequins, hell she'd make a better member than most, but it was Rogue. She wasn't meant to be a part of this life. She would never have chosen it. She was meant to be unchained and unbeholden to anyone.

Now she was going to be shackled to Luther just like the rest of us, and it was worse than that, far fucking worse. The things I'd done as a part of the Crew had changed me, left scars on my soul. I didn't want her subjected to the same life we'd been moulded for. I didn't want blood on her hands or enemies hunting her in the night. Becoming a Harlequin meant inheriting the hatred of every Damned Man and every Dead Dog in the state plus plenty more besides.

Fuck…and Maverick. What the hell was he gonna think? Not that I cared. Only, fuck me, he was gonna lose his shit. What if he tarred her with the same brush now, hunted her like he did us?

I scraped my fingers through my hair, following Fox as he stormed around the house and broke things. It was frustrating as hell considering we'd only just replaced half this shit after his last meltdown. I kept close to him mostly just to make sure he didn't pack up a bag of guns and chase down his dad on a suicide mission. Because if Fox turned on him, the Crew would turn right back on Fox. Luther held too much respect among our people – especially the elders - and I knew for a fact at least half of them would avenge him with a bloody wrath.

Chase sat at the kitchen island with his head in his hands and a cigarette between his lips. I threw him a look every time Fox made a passage through the room and destroyed something. We were going to have no furniture left by the time he was done. Mutt ran at my heels, yapping angrily at Fox for all the good it did.

"I'm sick of him ruling our lives," Fox snarled, kicking a trash can and sending it flying out onto the patio.

I grabbed his shoulder, pulling him around to face me. "Stop," I demanded and he almost shoved me away before he met my gaze and found something to hold onto there. "You can't change it. So we need to figure out how to handle it."

"J," he rasped. "Her being in the Crew means she's gonna have do whatever he says. I don't care what kind of deal she thinks she's just made with him to protect herself from that – I know him. I know what he's like. And I'm willing to bet this task he's set her is damn near impossible. Which means that as soon as she fails at it, all of his pretty promises will fade away to nothing and he'll use her in any and every way he wants."

I nodded, warring with that truth myself. "I know, man, I know."

"We could take her out of town," Chase suggested. "Say she ran. Just put her somewhere she can't come back."

"Is that your answer to fucking everything these days?" Fox snapped at him and Chase shoved out of his seat, moving toward us.

"If we'd just done that in the first place, we wouldn't be in this position,"

Chase said in a low tone.

Fox lunged at him and I got between them, pressing my hands to each of their chests.

"Enough," I commanded. "We've got enough shit to deal with without you two falling out too. Keep your fucking heads together."

"I'm just saying, if we went with my original plan then she'd be somewhere far away from here, safe. And Shawn wouldn't even know she was alive," Chase snapped.

"I am so sick of you acting like you don't even want her here," Fox hissed, forcing his weight against me as he tried to reach him. "Grow up and own your fucking feelings. You think I don't see how much you care about her? She was one of your best friends once."

"Yeah, keyword *once*," Chase growled, shoving against me from the other side so I was trapped in a muscle sandwich.

"He's right, Chase," I chipped in, but I kept my voice level, not rising to this argument. "Besides, she isn't going anywhere now and we were never going to let her go anyway, so your point is moot."

"My point is always fucking moot with you two," Chase snarled. "But I'm the only one around here who isn't dick dazzled by that girl."

My throat tightened and Fox tsked.

"What the fuck does that mean?" Fox demanded. "JJ's dick doesn't come into the equation with her, does it J?"

I glanced at Chase over my shoulder as my heart thrashed with panic.

"Oh you know what I mean," Chase said dismissively, trying to cover for what he'd said. "JJ's her little bestie friend."

I shoved the two of them apart at last, moving away to get some air. "This conversation is pointless. What's done is done, so we need to figure out a way to protect her from the worst this crew has to offer."

Mutt jumped up at Fox's legs and he lifted the dog into his arms, stroking his head like a bond villain as he narrowed his eyes at Chase and Mutt joined him in the scowl off. Chase leaned back against the kitchen island with an equally cutting glare and I sighed.

"Luther said he just wants one thing from her, so maybe she'll succeed at it, and he won't ask her to do the shit we've done," I went on when no one else had anything to say.

Fox's head snapped towards me at last. "I want to know what it is, then I'll personally deliver it to him myself, so she doesn't have to."

"If it's something Luther has asked of her, then it's something only she can give him, idiot," Chase bit at him.

"Well it ain't money," I said with a frown.

"What's she got that none of us have?" Fox questioned as he tried to focus.

"A pussy?" Chase suggested.

"How's that fucking relevant?" Fox demanded.

"I dunno, man, maybe the fact that she's the first girl to ever be initiated to the Harlequins?" Chase threw back at him. "And she isn't just any girl, is she? So I'd say it's very much to do with the fact that she's got a pussy, and likely to do with the fact that pussy has *you* on a tight leash."

"What more can my dad make me do that I haven't already done?" Fox shook his head.

"Well...maybe it's more about the practicalities," Chase went on with a dark shadow in his eyes and I frowned, wondering where he was going with this. "You want Rogue, and only Rogue."

"And?" Fox pressed.

"*And* if Luther's figured out that you're never gonna settle down with any girl but her then..." Chase shrugged like it was obvious but Fox and I weren't any clearer. My heart was thrashing though and I didn't like the way my stomach was churning either. Chase rolled his eyes at us like we were being dumb. "Heirs," he announced. "Where's Luther gonna get heirs from if you're never gonna marry anyone else?"

I fell unnaturally still and my heart sank like the Titanic and took every hope and dream in my chest down with the ship. Fox fell quiet too and darkness seemed to cloak him. I knew his stance on kids and it was a hell to the fucking no. He didn't wanna bring up children destined for the very same life he'd been forced into, and it wouldn't be the first time Luther had tried to make him settle down. He'd even suggested Fox knock up a whore if he didn't want to do the marriage and happy families thing. It was fucking insane. But Fox had shut him down about it, saying he'd die before he brought kids into this world.

Now Luther might be playing another angle and it made me fear so fucking much, because I knew for a fact that Rogue had agreed to whatever he'd asked.

It's not that. It's not fucking that.

"No," Fox rejected the idea in one cutting word and I couldn't deny how relieved I felt for it. "Rogue would never agree to that, she won't even fuck me let alone-" He cut himself off, his jaw tightening.

"She might soon. It's pretty obvious she's the one girl you might have a different opinion on making a family with," Chase said, his eyes flicking to me as a glimmer of his shattered soul peered from his eyes. My hope vanished again just like that as I pictured Rogue fucking Fox, trying to get herself pregnant with his child. Rage billowed up inside me like gasoline catching light and I fought with everything I had to keep it contained.

The front door sounded and Mutt yapped excitedly, writhing madly in Fox's arms as he tried to get free. He put him down and the tapping of his claws against the floorboards filled the air as he ran out of the room and down the hall.

Rogue stepped into the kitchen a minute later and we all shifted around her, drawn closer like she was a magnet.

"Where'd he take you?" Fox demanded, reaching for her hand and she let him hold it, making my head spin with anxiety.

Chase had planted the seed of doubt in my mind and it was growing shoots already. Rogue hadn't committed to me, she could choose him if she wanted to. She might have agreed to give Luther an heir if she wanted to kill Shawn badly enough. I mean yeah it was fucking extreme, but my pretty girl was fucking extreme, and I was suddenly so caught up in the fear of it that I was losing my mind.

"To mark me," she said a little bitterly, then tugged her hand from Fox's and turned around, pointing to the covering on the back of her right thigh that was concealing a new tattoo.

Fox dropped to his knees with a curse, peeling it off to see and Chase's shoulder butted against mine as we leaned over him to get a look. The symbol of the Harlequins stared back at us, the skull seeming to mock me from beneath its jester's hat and my world felt crushingly small for several long seconds. I remembered the day I'd gotten my own tattoo on my inner wrist, branding me, owning me, making me Luther's and forever a part of this crew right down to my bones.

I couldn't take it anymore. It was all too fucking much and I just had to get the fuck away from here.

I stepped past her, striding down the hall and shoving through the door into the garage.

"JJ!" Rogue called after me, but I didn't stop, jogging downstairs and getting in my car.

My head was a haze of anger, jealousy and regret. I didn't know what the answer to all of this shit was anymore. I didn't even wanna go back in time and run for the hills with Rogue and the boys. I just wanted there to be a now that didn't look so fucking fucked. A life where I could have her without losing my family. One where I didn't have to bow my head to Fox over Rogue because of the vows I'd taken as a Harlequin. One where Chase didn't look at me like I was going to rip our family apart. Because I knew he was right, in the depths of my heart. Me fucking Rogue was going to end up fucking our whole lives up if I didn't stop. And maybe now I'd have to. Maybe now I'd be forced to swallow down my love for her and watch as Fox staked his claim on her and she let him because of some deal she'd made with Luther. Or maybe she wanted him anyway and I was just delusional to think she ever could have wanted me.

Before I could drive out of the garage, Rogue appeared, dragging the passenger door open and ducking her head in the car. "Wait," she said breathlessly.

"I have to get out of here," I muttered, not looking at her.

She dropped onto the seat and pulled the door closed. "Then go."

I sighed then revved the engine as the garage door opened, tearing away from the house and out of the gates.

I didn't stop until we made it to the beach and gazed out at our old sanctuary of Sinners' Playground.

I pushed the door open, stepping out of the car and striding off down the sand, not waiting for Rogue as I went. I knew I was being an asshole, but I didn't give a shit. I just needed to return to the one place in this town where I could pretend I didn't have any responsibilities.

I climbed up the roughly hewn ladder, jumping over the fence at the top of the strut into the amusement park and Rogue soon appeared behind me, following me as I strode at a furious pace along the boards.

I made it to the far end of the pier as the wind picked up and whipped around us, gazing down at the deep blue water as I leaned against the wooden railing there. How many times had I stood here, gazing at the horizon and wondering if a better life awaited us beyond it when I was a kid? There were days we'd been tempted to hop in a boat and see how far we could go, but we never had. The problem was, Sunset Cove called to us like our souls were bound to it, and I knew deep down we could never truly leave. It was our home, and we were tethered here by blood and memories and each other. I should have known Rogue would come back one day, her life was too deeply linked to this place, and eventually it had summoned her home.

Rogue moved to my side, her arm brushing mine. "Talk to me, J," she urged.

"I have nothing to say," I muttered.

"I think you have a lot to say," she said quietly. "Are you angry at me?"

I thought on that question for a long moment then finally shook my head. "No," I admitted. "I know you came back to this town for your own reasons. I'm not fool enough to think I was one of them. Luther's giving you Shawn, so I guess you did what you felt you had to do."

"JJ…" She rested a hand on my shoulder and I shrugged it off.

"Don't," I warned in a growl. "Don't pity me, pretty girl."

"I don't," she said seriously. "Look I know you're angry, but this choice isn't about you, or Fox, or Chase. It's between me and Luther. I need to do this."

"I get it," I muttered. "You wanna kill Shawn for what he did to you, and you'll pay whatever price you need to for your revenge."

"Yeah," she said.

I nodded stiffly as my gut knotted. "So what's the price?"

"I can't say," she sighed.

I twisted sharply towards her, staring down at her as I invaded her personal space. "Fine, don't say. But tell me this, is it going to cost me you?"

She frowned, her eyes full of some internal battle I couldn't decipher. "I can't promise it won't."

I nodded, my lips twisting in a bitter smile. "Well I guess that's it then. Because I'm not gonna sit around waiting to get my heart broken." *Not again.*

I moved to leave, but she caught my arm, pulling me toward her and her mouth clashed with mine. I resisted for all of two seconds before I kissed her back, weak for her as always.

"Please, wait," she begged, her hand knotting in the back of my shirt and I did because I was pretty much in shock that this girl was begging me for anything. "You don't understand."

"Then make me understand," I commanded, my lips grazing hers again and tasting so fucking sweet that I wanted to die here and now just so I didn't have to face the loss of her again. "Because I'm starting to fear that what Luther asked of you is going to mean I'll end up watching you choose Fox. And I'm not sure I can do that, pretty girl. I think it'll kill me."

She shook her head. "I'm not choosing anyone," she insisted and I hoped that meant Chase had been wrong about what Luther wanted.

"You're not? You swear it?"

She nodded, her eyes full of honesty. "I swear, J."

Silence pooled between us and the tension in my chest eased, letting me breathe again. And everything became clearer than it had in a long time. I'd wanted Rogue my whole life, and I knew I'd never deserve her, but I had to try and make her mine or I'd regret it forever.

"Well what if I asked you to choose," I said in tight voice, terrified of what this conversation was going to do to me. But I'd put it off too long and now I was faced with losing her and if I dragged out the inevitable any longer, it was only going to destroy me more deeply. So fuck it, I'd ask and I'd take my refusal now like a big boy if that was my fate.

My brows stitched together and she gripped my cheek as she looked intently into my eyes. Tears welled in her ocean blues until I felt like I was gazing into the shallow waters of Sunset Cove. She was this town embodied, beautiful enough to bring a man to his knees and dangerous enough to tear his heart from his chest.

"You wouldn't want me if you didn't know me from before, J," she breathed. "We're bound in this fucked up way by our childhood, but you don't know me anymore. You don't know who I've been or how I've changed. I'm not the whole girl you want, I'm full of broken pieces."

I gripped her hand, placing it firmly against my thundering heart. "You think I'm whole? I've twisted up my soul so bad that it'll never be undone. But just because life tries to break us, doesn't mean it changes who we are deep down. I see you, Rogue. I'd see you if I was blind and buried at the bottom of the ocean. And I want you more fiercely now than I ever did before because this girl is a warrior, she's fought every day of her life and survived. She's faced pain and loss and she's still here fighting for that free life we all dreamed about so long ago. The rest of us lost that, Rogue, but you didn't." I knotted my fingers in her hair. "And when we're together you make me think that maybe it's possible again. That maybe all we ever wanted is just waiting for us if we dare to try and get there."

She gazed at me like she wanted to dive into that dream with me and never let go, but then her eyes fell from mine and my hopes fell with them.

"I built a wall around my heart a long time ago, JJ," she said sadly. "And as much as I want to give it to you, I'm afraid I lost the key to get inside."

Pain burned a hole in my chest at those words, but not for me, for her. I was broken over the fact that this girl had been hurt so deeply that she couldn't trust her heart with anyone anymore. And I knew I was partly responsible for that. It was something I couldn't forgive myself for, and maybe the right thing to do was to let her go. Because who was I anyway to think I could capture her heart? I didn't deserve this girl. I was the town's whore and had sold off pieces of my soul to anyone who wanted them for years. I'd tried to keep some part of me whole for her, but when I looked closely, I wasn't sure I'd really managed that. So why should I expect what was left to be enough?

I took a step back, but she moved with me, not letting me go.

"Wait," she croaked as a tear slipped from her eye. "I still want you. And I want you to have me too. But I can't promise forever because I don't know what forever looks like anymore. All I know is I can't let go of you. Not yet. So please don't go."

"Rogue…" I said heavily.

"I'm just afraid, JJ," she said as another tear ran down her cheek and the wind sent her hair flying around her shoulders. "I'm so fucking afraid. You broke my heart once whether you intended to or not and I want to trust you, but it's not that easy. Everything's so fucked, but when I'm with you it feels a whole lot less fucked, and I love that. And maybe, hopefully, I can figure out how to give you everything because that's how it feels when I'm with you. Like I'm just so full of…everything."

She turned to clutch onto the railing and look out over the sea to hide her tears from me. I moved up behind her, swiping her hair away from her face and turning her to look at me as I held her and found I couldn't let go either.

Of course walking away was impossible. It was Rogue. She owned me and I was just fine with that so long as I knew she wasn't going to tear my heart from my chest and leave this town again. But maybe she just needed someone to stand beside her, be her rock and refuse to let her leave. I could do that. I'd prove to her that the rug wasn't going to be pulled from under her feet again, and even if it was, she'd have me to hold onto to weather any storm that came her way.

I ran my thumb over her lower lip, wiping her tears across it as more spilled down her cheeks.

"Sometimes you look so fucking alone it breaks me," I murmured then leaned in to kiss her lips and taste the saltiness of her pain. "I'm here though, pretty girl. And I'm not going anywhere. I promise. So long as you want me, you'll never be alone again."

She tiptoed into my kiss with a sigh of longing, her tongue pressing between my lips and we sealed that promise to each other there and then. It was a commitment of some kind, maybe not the one I'd hoped for, but one that was possibly far more meaningful than anything I'd ever experienced. I'd seen the wounds in her more clearly than before and knew this was what she needed. Time.

So no matter what happened in the future, I'd find a way to be there for her, I'd be the man I'd wanted to be when I was a boy. And maybe someday she'd see that even if it took eternity for her to heal, I'd still be standing there at the end of time, waiting for her to love me.

A tense week ticked by in which every day we expected an attack that didn't come. We may have been at war and Shawn's men could strike at any moment, but it was still business as usual while we waited for him to make his first move. And I had to return to work and get as much cash as I could to make up my monthly cut, plus make sure everything at Afterlife didn't go to shit while I was juggling Harlequin commitments.

Chase may have been helping me out so I didn't have to work at the Dollhouse anymore, but there was only so much charity I was willing to accept and the rest I'd damn well work my ass off to earn right on the stage of my club. He couldn't afford to be spread too thin himself and I wasn't going to put him in danger of being unable to make his own cut.

Tonight was the debut of my troupe's new show and we'd sold out tickets in less than an hour for the event. I'd snagged one for Rogue when she'd asked to come and watch and I was kind of nervous for the performance for the first time since I'd begun dancing. Now she was a Harlequin, Fox couldn't stop her from leaving the house, but he also gave me direct orders to keep my eyes on her at all times. Which I didn't mind one bit because most of the time it was more difficult for me to take my eyes off of her anyway. Especially since we'd decided to officially be...something. We were forgoing labels, but I didn't need to call her my girlfriend to know she was mine. We were just living for the now, and so long as she was in town, in my arms and in my fucking life, I was counting my damn blessings every day.

I raced along the roads in my GT toward Afterlife with Rogue beside me and my phone started ringing loudly. I hit the button to connect it through the Bluetooth just before my mom's panicked voice filled my car.

"Johnny James," she sobbed.

"What?" I demanded in fright, my heart jack-hammering in my chest as I thought of fucking Shawn and the threats he'd made on our town.

"It's Greg," she choked out.

"The moustache?" I growled.

"Yes, he turned up at the house and he…he," she choked on her words.

"What Mom?" I pushed as Rogue gave me a worried look from her seat.

"He robbed me," she rasped and my blood turned icily cold. "I don't wanna cause a fuss, but I can't make my rent and the landlord's been onto me, and now I don't know what to do and-"

"What's his address?" I snarled ferociously and she told me before making me promise I wouldn't kill him and hanging up the phone.

"You don't mind a quick detour, do you pretty girl?" I asked, my grip tightening on the steering wheel.

"Nope. Go get him, J," she said firmly and I hit the gas, taking the next right turn and tearing through the town towards Sandy Lane. Greg was just walking out of his house as I pulled up and his eyes widened in fright as he saw me stepping out of my car.

"Ah!" he wailed, making a run for it, but it was more of a waddle as he fled down the street in the direction of the beach. I let him go, moving to the trunk of my car and popping it open before taking out a baseball bat. When I shut it, Rogue was there, her eyes all twinkly as her gaze raked over me like she was enjoying the show.

"Shit, Johnny James, you make terrifying look real good," she said and I couldn't say I hated the tone to her voice.

She was wearing a baby pink dress that hugged her curves and had a cut out over her tits which showed off her cleavage, the outfit paired with little white sneakers. Point being, she looked hot as fuck and if she was down for watching me play psycho, I was here for it.

"Come on, I'm going moustache hunting." I smirked and she grinned, hurrying along at my side as I strode down the street onto the beach in search of my prey.

Greg was running along the sand, but he hadn't gotten all that far and I upped my pace as I stalked him, twirling the bat in my hand.

"You're not gonna kill him, are you?" Rogue breathed and I laughed darkly.

"Why do you sound disappointed?" I teased, then jogged forward after Greg, catching him in a few seconds and whipping my bat through the air.

It crashed into his ass and he fell down onto the sand with a scream, rolling over and holding a can of pepper spray up in defence. I hit it with my bat and he wailed as I broke some fingers and the can went sailing away into the sea with a distant splash.

"Hello, Greg," I said calmly, placing my foot on his chest so he couldn't get up. "Now help me out here, buddy, because I'm having a memory blip. Wasn't there something I told you I'd do to you if you went near my mom again?" I toyed with the prick, making him cringe beneath me and start to cry.

"I d-don't know," he sobbed.

"Oh yes you do, Greg," I pushed, stabbing my bat in the sand by his head and he flinched. "Tell me now before I get bored and decide to shove my baseball bat up your ass. It's a real nice baseball bat, Greg, I don't want to do it. But so help me, I will."

"My m-m-m-moustache," he forced out.

"What about your m-m-m-moustache?" I taunted him.

"Y-you said you'd…you'd…"

"I'd what?" I demanded.

"R-rip it off and f-feed it to a s-starfish," he cried, full on fat tears running down his face now. I knew this piece of shit was no good for my momma.

"That's it, there, there," I mock comforted him, dropping the bat as I knelt down and patted his arm.

His lower lip wobbled as he gazed at me, looking hopeful that I might not be about to attack him. But he was a fool with a moustache, soon to just be a fool. "Now tell me where you stashed the money you took from my mom."

His throat bobbed as he swallowed and he took in a shaky breath. "I…I spent it," he croaked.

I shook my head sadly. "Oh Greg…Greg, Greg, Greg."

"I'll get it back, Mr Brooks, I swear it."

"I believe you," I said. "And I'm going to need it by the end of the week, Greg, or I'm going to have to rip off more than your moustache. It'll be double by then though mind, to account for interest." *May as well take what I can get while I'm short on cash.*

He released a fearful noise.

"Yeah," I said with a sad smile. "That's what I was thinking too. Your tiny cock will be next."

He whimpered as I reached for his face. "P-please."

"Shh, shh," I hushed him, then moved to press my knee down on his chest and took a switch knife from my pocket. With a sharp cut and a firm yank, I tore his ugly moustache from his face and he screamed like a baby as I stood up and held it between my forefinger and thumb.

"Here you go, J." Rogue appeared beside me, taking a doggy poo bag out of her sparkly purse and I smirked as I grabbed it, dropping the moustache inside and tying it up.

"Thanks, pretty girl." I wiped the blood off my hand onto my jeans while Greg cupped his face with his good hand, rocking back and forth and crying in agony.

"End of the week, Greg, or I'm gonna ruin a perfectly happy starfish's day when it has to swallow down your tiny cock."

"What's with the starfish?" Rogue muttered as I dropped my arm around her shoulders and guided her away from Greg back towards my car.

I shrugged. "No one wants their body parts eaten by an invertebrate. It's a man's worst nightmare."

She snorted a laugh and I grinned at her as we made it back to my car and dropped inside. I tossed the doggy bag into the cupholder and made a mental note to get myself a starfish after work tonight. Yep, I'd be going down into the sea outside Harlequin House and yep I'd be using a lamp to find one, because yep, I always made good on my promises.

Rogue took my hand as I sped up the road and that feeling made me feel like an invincible god. My eyes kept sliding off the street onto her and all I wanted to do was pull over and kiss her until our lungs collapsed. But as I was already late and my troupe were probably losing their shit over where I was, I couldn't afford the distraction.

I soon pulled up in the parking lot and Rogue squeezed my fingers in goodbye. "Good luck, I'll be watching."

I glanced around the lot, not finding anyone there before I lunged at her, stealing a kiss as I pushed my hand under her dress and rubbed her clit through her panties.

"I'm gonna dance for you," I said against her mouth as she parted her thighs for me and released a ragged breath. "So you'd better remember that every girl in there will go to bed tonight wishing I was fucking them raw and bending their bodies to my will, but it's you I want. Only you. And when the show's over, the only fantasies I'm gonna fulfil are yours, sweetheart."

I took my hand from between her thighs and leaned over her, opening her door and pushing it wide with a dirty smirk. I withdrew from her and she sucked the taste of me from her lower lip before stepping out of the car and straightening her dress.

I watched her walk inside, my gaze on her ass and a groan of longing leaving me as Johnny D throbbed in my pants and told me Viagra was not gonna be needed for the show tonight. I didn't like taking the stuff anyway, but JD wasn't always up for playtime, especially now he was trying his hardest to make an honest man of himself over Rogue. But he was my performing monkey, and sometimes monkey needed to dance to bring home the cash. He didn't have to play hide the banana anymore with private clients, so I didn't know what he was complaining about.

Being a sex god was hard work, and it was even harder work now that I was only relying on stripping to make ends meet. I'd upped the prices for this show and promised it would make even the straightest of men rock hard. I'd been training every hour I could and whipping my dancers' asses into shape. They were ready, so if we pulled this off tonight, it was gonna rain dollars.

I headed in the back door, pulling off my clothes as Texas came jogging over with some oil in his hands. "Cutting it close, eh boss?" He squirted a load into his palms, helping me oil up and Adam jogged over to help too until I was shining.

I dropped to the floor, doing push-ups naked until I had a good pump on then pulling on my ripped jeans for the first dance of the night. I was opening with Di and she came jogging over in her sparkly silver leotard and high heels as she pushed a black purge mask onto my face.

"Two minutes, JJ," she warned as she sprayed water in my hair and slicked it back before pushing a woodcutter's axe into my hand. This dance was a club favourite, but I'd changed it up tonight, swapping an axe in for the usual umbrella and adding the mask, plus changing out a few moves for some more risqué shit. I was calling it the psychodelic waltz and it was gonna blow minds and soak pussies.

Lyla's voice carried from out on stage, telling dirty jokes which had the club roaring with laughter. My heart beat with adrenaline as I thought of Rogue out there and I took a breath to calm my nerves. *You do this every fucking week. Buck up, idiot.*

Di towed me to the stage door, smiling excitedly at me. "Ready?" she breathed.

"Ready."

"Let the show begin!" Lyla cried and Di winked at me before running out onto the stage as white laser lights fell on her and the rest of the bar went dark. An *ooh* sounded as she started up a sexy dance to Eyes on Fire by Blue Foundation and I waited for my moment.

The lights went off, plunging everyone into darkness and I smirked as I switched on my mask so a frightening face lit up in red with Xs for eyes and a stitched, smiling mouth.

I swung the axe in time with the beat as the music changed and Twisted by MISSIO cut in instead. I strode out onto the stage, standing with the light at my back so everyone could see me as Di continued to dance in front of me. Gasps rang out as I stalked up on Di in time with the pounding beat then she twirled around mid-pirouette and I caught hold of her, twirling her under one arm before yanking her back against my chest.

She fought me dance style and I locked the axe around her as she bent over backwards and flipped over it to escape me. I caught her again, my hand on her throat this time as I rolled my hips and the music thundered in my ears as we moved to a fluid, warring beat, and she struggled against me before I threw her to the floor.

The lights started flashing and I fell over her, resting the axe on the stage and she dragged her hand down my chest like she was trying to stop me. It was filthy and wrong and made every girl in here scream in excitement because it was exactly what all of them wanted from me. The strobe lights started up and I rolled sideways, flipping Di up over my lap and she rolled her body over me, running her hand down her own chest with an expression that said she was in turmoil over what she was doing.

I whipped the axe around and held it behind her, pulling her down by it before flipping us over again. Then I got to my feet, leaving the axe on the floor and dragging her after me, spinning her around before throwing her over my shoulder to a round of cheers. I let go of her legs and she dropped to the floor and rolled, getting to her feet again before diving onto my back, her arm locking around my throat and making the crowd whoop excitedly.

When she released me, I swung around and we danced in a furious push and pull that was sexy as hell and had girls reaching for me from beside the stage.

I lined Di up for the finale of the song, gripping her head in my hands and pretending to snap her neck just as the lights turned off. The crowd called out for more and I felt the movement of my troupe behind me as they joined us on stage.

When the lights came back on, Di was wearing a mask, standing at the front of my boys as we all fell into a synchronised dance and the crowd went crazy. My boys dropped down with me to grind on the stage while Di moved to grab the axe and swing it around her head, moving into her final pose as all of us guys reached for her from the ground, placing our hands on her body. The final note rang out and the crowd screamed as the song ended and applause poured into my ears as dollar bills were thrown onto the stage in a rain that never seemed to end.

I found Rogue's gaze near the stage as my breaths came heavier and exhilaration tore through me at her expression. She looked captivated by me in the exact way I always felt around her. And I wanted her to look at me like that every day of my life for the rest of forever.

I sat backstage after the show counting out my money and laughing my ass off from the amount of cash I'd earned tonight. Adam sat beside me counting his own tips and I scruffed his hair, pulling him in for a tight hug.

"You killed it," I laughed as I released him. "I knew you'd be a star, Adam. You're fucking made for this gig."

"One of those old gals I pulled on stage stuffed two fifties in my ass crack." He grinned.

"You're living the dream, man," I told him. "This is it. Can you taste it?" I slapped him around the face with the wad of cash in my hand and he laughed.

"Heads up, J, Tom Collins wants a word," Texas called to me and I looked over at him with a frown, finding the middle aged dude who loved attending all of my shows there. He had a shy sort of smile on his face and I pushed to my feet, smiling at him. He tipped me bigger than some of the highflying upper quarter women that blew in here on the weekends. I swear he'd practically kept my whole club afloat when we'd had a dry spell last fall. But I'd never seen him backstage and he barely said two words to me whenever I tried to engage him. The guy was possibly missing a few shillings, but he was a sweet dude and I didn't really care if he went home and jacked off over me because that was the name of the game.

"How are you, Tom?" I asked. "Did you enjoy the show?"

"Yes, I er…" He cleared his throat, looking a little sweaty. "I just wanted to personally congratulate you. It really was a marvellous show tonight."

I beamed, my chest swelling. "Well thank you, why don't you stay and have a drink back here? I'll get Estelle to bring you a Tom Collins."

"No, no." he waved a hand. "I just want to give you this." He held out a hand full of cash and I gaped at it. Jesus. How fucking much was that? He placed it into my palm, squeezing my fingers and I suddenly had the fear he was going to ask for some compensation for that money.

I lowered my voice, leaning in so as not to embarrass him as I purred in his ear, "I'm not taking those kinds of jobs anymore, but thanks for the compliment, big boy." I placed the cash back in his hand, but he immediately pushed it back into mine.

"Oh that's not, um, no I didn't mean that. It's just a tip for the show, JJ," he stumbled over his words then suddenly he was running away as fast as Sonic the Hedgehog and he slipped back out the door into the bar in a flash.

I ran a hand down the back of my neck. Poor, poor sad balls Tom. He probably hadn't gotten laid in years. I didn't usually take on male clients but if I hadn't been hung up on Rogue, I probably would have given him a freebie handjob for all the cash he'd injected into my club.

Rogue appeared and all my thoughts scattered as I watched her running over to Di and Lyla to congratulate them on the show. Her eyes wandered to me, a sexy hunger burning within them that my dick held the answer to. She started walking over to me and I felt like I was the only person in the room with a front row seat to the best show of my life.

I had a dark, dark craving for my girl tonight, and it looked like she had one for me too.

CHAPTER TWENTY NINE

I leaned back against JJ's dressing table as he finished counting out his cash and he fixed me with a look as he began to walk away. "I need to put this in the safe and I'll be right back. Stay," he commanded.

"No promises," I tossed after him, my eyes roaming over the room as the other dancers moved around it, coming back from showers and getting themselves dressed without paying me much attention.

I was getting an eyeful from pretty much every direction as they just strode about with their cocks out, laughing and joking amongst each other and I snorted to myself as I picked up JJ's phone for a dickstraction. I found some music and hit play on MONTERO (Call Me By Your Name) by Lil Nas X, accidentally sending it through the room's speaker system which he must have had hooked up.

Lyla and Di whooped in excitement, grabbing my arm to yank me up to dance and I laughed as I joined in with them.

The strippers all started cheering and dancing too and a huge guy leapt up onto his chair and started grinding against a clothes rail wearing nothing but a leather thong. I was pretty certain that hadn't been a part of the set though... were they his day to day underwear choice? Wow. I was impressed. He caught me looking and leapt from his makeshift stage, prowling over to me with a grin.

"Hey, gorgeous, I'm Texas," he said, offering me a hand which I took with a smile.

"Rogue," I replied.

"We know who you are," a blonde guy sitting at the dressing table beside JJ's said, glancing my way with a smile. "JJ mentions you from time to time."

"Time to time?" Texas boomed a laugh. "More like *all* the time. You have that boy so whipped I keep expecting him to retire. He's all 'Rogue's so funny' and 'Rogue and me did the cutest thing this morning' and 'I'm so hard for Rogue my balls might explode.' So put us out of our misery, are you gonna lock him down or what?"

"Leave her alone," Di commanded, waving Texas back. "You can't ask her shit like that. JJ would have to ask her about that himself and none of you assholes would be hanging out to listen in on that conversation, so drop it."

Texas raised his hands in surrender and backed up, allowing me to escape answering him, but I could feel my cheeks heating a little from his words. My mouth was all dry and I couldn't help but think about how hot JJ had looked out on that stage tonight. Did I like knowing he was all mine? Err, yeah, yeah I did.

Shit. I needed to pull myself together or I was gonna have to put my vagina in jail.

I moved back to JJ's dressing table and dropped down, opening the top drawer and looking amongst the tubs of almond oil and tubes of army paint, glitter, fifteen million condoms and a bunch of other random shit for a stick of gum or something.

I pouted when I failed to find anything edible and shoved my hand to the back of the drawer, feeling around just in case but sighing when all I felt was more condoms. I pulled my hand back, but the drawer was so full that I knocked my fist against the top of it and through a pause in the music, I heard something metal fall down somewhere in the back of the unit.

I drew back and looked at the dressing table curiously before closing the top drawer and opening the bottom one. This drawer was much bigger and held a bunch of props like whips and handcuffs, a ball gag and some bunny ears.

I swiped the bunny ears and put them on then grabbed the sides of the drawer and yanked until it came out of the unit.

The dude beside me was watching me and I flashed him a grin before carrying on with my business.

I dropped down onto my knees and looked into the back of the dark space, my heart thumping faster as I spotted what I'd been too afraid to hope for. There sat my necklace, key intact with Maverick's right beside it.

I snatched the two of them with my pulse thundering and quickly threaded Maverick's key onto the necklace and clasped it around my neck again, sighing at the feeling of the metal against my skin. I'd worn that damn thing every freaking day for ten years and it was sad how much I'd missed the familiar weight around my neck, though it was a little heavier now with the two keys.

I leaned back and shoved the drawer into place once more, standing up and giving it a kick when it didn't slot back onto the runners right. When I was done it was like eighty percent back the way I'd found it and the dude beside me was looking more inclined to tell tales than ever.

I didn't bother to hide the necklace. It wasn't really possible in this dress and a part of me wanted to call JJ out and see what happened anyway.

"We should hit up Bessie's," Di suggested with a groan. "I'd kill for a short stack right about now."

There was a lot of agreement from around the room about taking a drive out to the twenty-four-hour diner on the far side of town and by the time JJ made it back to us, pretty much all the strippers had agreed to go.

"Are you hungry, J?" I asked, beaming at him as he strode towards me with the kind of intent that made me feel like the only girl in the room.

JJ began to smile as he plucked the bunny ears from my head, but it slipped as his gaze fell to my neck and the keys hanging there, his jaw ticking as he took in what I'd found.

"I was meant to move those somewhere harder to find," he said in a low voice as the rest of the group began to head for the door, laughing and chatting amongst themselves as they discussed what food they wanted at the diner.

"Yeah, well I tried that, and they still ended up stolen."

JJ leaned in until he was right in my personal space and I was forced to take a step away so the backs of my thighs were pressed against the edge of his dressing table.

He reached out and wrapped his fingers around the keys, his gaze meeting mine and a frown lining his brow.

"You can't really think I'm going to let you take these, do you?"

"Well, that depends," I replied, raising my chin and holding his gaze.

"On?"

"Whether or not you're full of shit, Johnny James."

"What do these have to do with that?"

We were alone in the dressing room now, the others having gone ahead to their cars and I wondered if I was about to find out exactly how little I meant to him or not.

"Because you told me you want me. You told me I mean something to you and I'm wondering if that's true or not. Because if you really think you know me well enough to want me now, then that must mean you think you know me well enough to trust me too. So that's what I wanna know, do you trust me, JJ? Or are all of your pretty words limited?" I watched him as he processed that, his frown deepening while I just waited. I wasn't going to try and fight for them. This was up to him. If he really meant the things he'd said then he'd prove it.

"Trust is a big thing to offer out, pretty girl," he said slowly.

"Yeah," I agreed. "I know. I remember how it felt to have my trust broken. So I guess it's up to you. Either you want me, or you want the *idea* of me. If you think you know me so well then you should be able to decide whether or not I can be trusted with these. So tell me, JJ, will I use them to break all of you? Or do you believe I'm all in?"

JJ wetted his lips, his free hand moving to my thigh and his fingertips brushing the back of it where my Harlequin tattoo now lay.

"I believe you think you'll use them," he said slowly, his fingers uncurling from the keys. "But in the end, you'll realise you can't."

His mouth found mine before I could reply to that and I kissed him openly, bending to his will as he pushed me back, lifting my legs and stepping between my thighs as my ass landed on his dressing table.

He even tasted of almonds tonight, the scent clinging to him and making me groan as I tugged him closer and his hard cock rutted between my thighs, causing the most amazing friction between my panties and his jeans.

JJ pulled back with a groan, glancing over his shoulder before looking back to me. "This is too risky here," he said. "I could take you to the supply closet, but that doesn't seem good enough for tonight. So shall we just get out of here?"

"Are we going to the diner?" I asked hopefully, licking the taste of him from my bottom lip as he forced himself to step back, leaving the keys around my neck.

"You're hungry?" he asked in surprise and I gave him a flat look which made him laugh. "Okay, dumb question. Hurry up then because they won't be waiting for us."

I grinned and hopped up, taking his hand in mine and tugging him towards the door.

JJ looked between our clasped hands and my face then the smirk on his lips grew to all kinds of smug proportions.

"What?" I challenged as we made it outside.

The parking lot was empty as JJ had predicted but I was willing to bet that in his car we'd catch up to the others just fine.

"Sometimes I don't think you're real," he replied. "Like I must have been in an accident and now I'm just living inside my head in a coma because that's the only reality in which I could have predicted this."

"Wow," I said, moving closer to him and slipping my arms around his waist. "You're so freaking cheesy, J."

He laughed and shoved me back playfully and I grinned as I retreated, fisting the key to his Mustang in my hand and backing up.

JJ hounded after me until we were at his car and while he wasted a few seconds hunting his pockets for his keys, I unlocked it and leapt in behind the wheel.

"No," JJ commanded, but I just locked my door and shrugged up at him.

"Get in, Johnny James, or I'll leave you behind."

"Rogue," he growled and I started the engine, driving forward a few feet before stopping again. JJ tried to make it to my door, so I did it again and he growled.

"Last chance or I'm getting food without you," I called.

JJ cursed me as he was forced to move around and get in the passenger side and I hit the gas before he'd even managed to close his door.

Neither of us mentioned the doggy bag in the cup holder as I made it to the road and I hit the gas hard as I turned us towards the highway and started speeding in the direction of food.

I began listing all the things I wanted to eat, groaning between each option and JJ soon ditched the scowl as he laughed at me and just enjoyed the ride. I considered mentioning the fact that I didn't officially have a driver's licence but figured it wasn't the best time. All the best drivers learned by boosting cars anyway.

We sped out of town and I let the engine fly as we raced down the highway towards the food.

The diner was just close enough to town to be an option but also close enough to the highway to grab the attention of the passing traffic, so when we pulled up outside it, I wasn't surprised to find the lot busy with customers.

I parked up and got out, my eyes on the brightly lit windows where I could see my girls and a bunch of the other strippers already ordering their food and I began to walk toward them with my stomach growling impatiently.

JJ made it to my side, but before I could get to the diner, he caught my hand and pointed off towards the trees to the left of the building.

"Do you reckon the old train car is still there?" he asked me and I paused, remembering the time we'd all jacked a car and driven it out here. The cops had shown up, looking for their own food but they'd clearly had a call about the car already so they came in asking questions. We all ran, dove into the trees and kept going until we found the old train car abandoned out there. We'd hidden inside it and slept in there too, all of us crammed together on the floor to gain some body heat while laughing about stupid shit and calling the cops all kinds of names.

My gaze slipped from the trees to the diner and my stomach protested a little as my gaze got caught on the mischief in JJ's eyes.

"Only one way to find out," I hedged and he grinned, winding his fingers between mine and tugging me towards the trees.

I laughed as I followed, ignoring the shiver that ran down my spine as we stepped beneath the leafy canopy and were enveloped by the dark. I could have sworn there were eyes on us as we walked, but I was pretty sure that was just because of the creepy woodland and my overactive imagination.

Despite JJ dressing this up to seem like he'd had no idea if the train car was still out here, he seemed to know exactly where to go while I was confused by the dark and the trees. He tugged me along, cutting a direct path through the foliage and before I knew it, we were stepping into the little clearing where the train car lay abandoned just like it had been all those years ago.

JJ led me right up to the door and tugged it open, drawing me inside the dim space and illuminating the flashlight on his cell phone so that we could see.

I looked around at the train car with a giggle escaping me, feeling like those naughty kids again, sneaking in here and trying to stay silent while the cops yelled out for us to come back.

I took in the old, red cushions lining the chairs and the wooden tables with metal detailing. There was even a fancy glass light fitting overhead. This thing had been nice once, designed for people with money to travel in style before it was abandoned to the miscreants who lived out here when they stopped using the old tracks that ran through these woods.

I moved further into the space and JJ set his cell phone down before following me, leaving the light on so that we could see a little in the darkness.

His hands came around my waist and my skin tingled where he touched me. As his mouth lowered against my neck, a sigh escaped me and when he bit down, a shot of pleasure surged through my body, making my nipples harden and ache.

JJ turned me around and captured my lips with his, not wasting any time as he backed me up until my ass was perched on one of the little dining tables and he was unzipping the back of my dress.

I raised my arms so that he could peel it off of me and he groaned desperately as he found me in nothing but my panties beneath it, his mouth lowering to suck my nipple hard as I arched my back and moaned for him.

I kicked my sneakers off as JJ gripped the edge of my panties in his fists and lifted my ass for him as he tugged them off of me, dropping to his knees before me as he went.

JJ yanked his shirt off, tossing it aside then gripped my knees in his large hands and forced them wide, bearing me to him as I gripped the sides of the table and whimpered, biting down on my lip as I fought off the desire to beg him to hurry up.

When his tongue finally found my core, a loud and wanton moan escaped me and I hooked my legs around his neck, tipping my head back against the glass window and closing my eyes as I concentrated on the feeling of him bringing me to ruin.

JJ cursed, murmuring my name between devouring me and I cried out as he moved two fingers up to join the party too, pushing them deep inside me and making my pussy clamp down tight around them.

"Fuck, Johnny James," I gasped, grinding my hips against his mouth as I chased the pleasure which was dancing around the edges of my body, waiting to tear me apart and bring me to ruin for him.

But just as I was about to fall crashing from the cliff, JJ fell entirely still, his body locking up and giving me half a second of warning before a cruel voice filled the air.

"Well, well, well, what would Foxy boy think if he knew his girl was fucking his boy behind his back like this?"

I gasped, my eyes flying open as I found Maverick standing there right behind JJ, his revolver pressed to the back of JJ's head as he forced him to stay where he was on his knees between my thighs.

"Rick," I squeaked in alarm and he arched an eyebrow at me, his gaze unreadable in the dark. He had a pair of black jeans and a black shirt on which I guessed were to match up to his heart. "What are you-"

"Please, don't stop on my account," he said in a rough, demanding voice. "I want to see why Johnny James charges so fucking much for his time."

"Let Rogue go," JJ growled, drawing back just enough to be able to speak, though his fingers were still very much inside me and my pussy was gripping him like a vice as a mixture of need and fear immobilised me.

"She looks plenty comfortable there," Maverick reasoned. "But she also looks like she's in need of a release and it's damn rude to leave a girl wanting, JJ. So how about you make her come like you were about to or I'll have to blow your head off for letting her down."

446

JJ's eyes met mine and I licked my lips as my heart pounded. This was so fucked up. So, so, fucked up. But...it was also hot. Like, crazy, serial killer on the edge, fucked up kind of hot. And my pussy was practically dripping as I looked from JJ to Maverick and back again.

"Look at her, Johnny James. You've gotten her all worked up. Look how much she wants it. I bet she'll be coming all over your face within thirty seconds. Don't let me being here steal her pleasure from her." Maverick pressed the gun to the back of JJ's skull a little harder like he might actually shove his face back down and I held my breath.

JJ drew his hand back like he was going to pull his fingers out of me and a whimper escaped me, but that was nothing on the word that left my lips. Because I was going to hell for that word. All the way to the deepest, darkest pits of hell. But I was hoping I'd be stopping by heaven on the way.

"Please," I begged and yeah, that really was a beg because my whole body was tingling and I was so fucking close and this was definitely fucked up, but something about it was so, so hot and I wanted him touching me. Shit, I was fairly certain I wanted Rick to be touching me too. But I wasn't gonna broker that issue right now because most importantly I wanted JJ fucking me with his tongue as soon as he possibly could.

JJ growled, this deep, animal sound and I saw the decision in his eyes half a second before he dropped his head down and resumed his assault on my flesh.

"Fuck," I moaned, my eyes locking with Maverick's as he watched me, the darkness in his gaze making my pussy throb even more than JJ was managing alone.

Yeah, I was going to hell. But it was so fucking worth it.

JJ licked and teased me then sucked on my clit hard and I exploded for him, pleasure cascading through my body as I screamed and arched my back and he kept driving his fingers in and out of me while lapping up every single second of my pleasure.

When I was finally done, he drew back and Maverick directed him to his feet, his gaze unreadable as he looked between the two of us and I just lay there on the freaking table, butt naked, panting and seriously fucking wet.

Rick's gaze travelled down my body hungrily before he looked towards

JJ once more.

"It doesn't really look like the two of you are done yet," he commented, dropping the gun and jamming it into JJ's crotch hard enough to make him hiss a curse.

"What do you want?" JJ demanded. "Whatever it is, you can have it. Just let her go. She isn't part of your hatred for us, so don't drag her into it."

"Christ, that got me right in the fucking heart," Maverick mocked, clutching his chest. "And if I hadn't just found you eating her out like you were starving for it, I might have been inclined to believe you were all noble and shit. But your dick is rock hard and I just can't believe you had no intention of using that on our girl here."

"Rick," I warned, pushing myself upright and moving to grip his arm.

He turned to look down at me, his gun still jammed up tight to JJ's balls and I found myself experiencing a heady mixture of terror and being seriously turned on. It was very, very wrong. But breaking the rules had always gotten me hot.

"Yeah, beautiful?"

"If this is about you being jealous-"

"Oh, so your little fuck buddy here knows about you and me, does he?"

"I know," JJ growled. "And I don't fucking care. Rogue always had something with all of us. The only thing that matters to me is what she has with me."

Maverick arched a brow at him then backed up a few paces, raising the gun again until it was firmly pointed JJ's way then he beckoned me over to him. And of course I wasn't going to go. Except my feet were moving and suddenly his lips were on mine and his free hand was between my legs and I was moaning all over again.

I jerked away again, guilt warring in my gut as I looked back at JJ, but instead of the hurt or fury I expected to find in his gaze, there was only heat and some dangerous thoughts which made my damn toes curl with the want in them.

"Shit. I think you meant it, didn't you?" Rick asked him, barking a laugh.

"In my line of work, I learned fast enough to recognise my own desires. And I'm man enough to admit that watching you with her is hot. Are you trying to tell me you weren't getting off on watching me and her too?"

Maverick licked his lips slowly, his eyes moving back to me and a dangerous smile pulling at his lips.

"It's one thing watching her come for you, Johnny. But I don't think I'd much enjoy seeing her take your cock."

"Only one way to find out," JJ shot back and my eyebrows officially disappeared into my hairline.

"What?" I squeaked and Maverick chuckled.

"Don't you want that, beautiful? Or did you already take all you wanted from him?" Maverick tugged me in front of him and bit down on my neck hard enough to make me suck in a sharp breath, making JJ watch us together as he kept that fucking gun pointed his way. "You can be honest with me, do you want his cock?"

I swallowed thickly, adrenaline thundering through my veins and everything in my body warning me to run, telling me that this was insane, dangerous, quite possibly life threatening. And yet I was nodding, my gaze on JJ's body and my pussy so wet that I was pretty sure I was about to start begging again.

"Show me then," Maverick snarled, his hand cracking down against my ass and making me moan as he pushed me forward a step.

I wasn't going to do it. No fucking way. Except, my feet were moving and my gaze was on JJ's and then it was falling down his sinfully sculpted body to that bulge in his pants and I was dropping to my knees in front of him.

"You don't have to, pretty girl," JJ said, his fingers tangling in my hair as he used his grip on it to make me look back up at him.

"There's no gun being held to my head. And you already know I want you," I replied, my fingers finding his fly. "But if you want me to stop..."

JJ's gaze flicked back to Maverick as I pushed my hand into his jeans, but the moment my fingers found his dick he started groaning.

"I'll never say no to you, pretty girl," he grunted and I smiled at him as I freed his cock and leaned in to lick my way up his shaft.

JJ's grip in my hair tightened and my skin prickled with the feeling of Maverick's eyes on us, but that only spurred me on.

I circled the head of his cock with my tongue then slid my mouth over him, moaning hungrily as I took him between my lips.

JJ cursed as I drew him in deep, his hips beginning to move in time with me as he fucked my mouth and I loved every fucking second of it. My pussy was throbbing desperately and I moaned around his shaft as I upped my pace, taking more from him, wanting to own him, destroy him the same way he had me.

"Up," Maverick barked behind me and I was hauled to my feet before I could really compute that.

JJ snarled something angrily as his release was stolen from him and Maverick chuckled in my ear as his solid body pressed against my back.

"I didn't tell you to stop sucking, beautiful." This time when he spanked me, his hand cracked down on the Harlequin tattoo on the back of my thigh. I sucked in a sharp breath, turning to look over my shoulder at him in alarm as I realised he'd seen it and would have to know what that meant. "You've been a bad girl, haven't you, Rogue?"

"I...it's complicated," I breathed pathetically.

"I'll bet. Are you gonna take your punishment like a good girl then?" He gripped my hip and tugged my ass back into his crotch so that I had no doubt whatsoever about what that meant and I found myself nodding. Fucking nodding. Like I just casually took two cocks under my command all the goddamn time and this was no big deal.

"Jesus," JJ muttered, but he sounded more excited than freaked out and as I looked back to him, he leaned in and placed a demanding kiss on my lips.

Rick gave us about three seconds of that before he pressed the gun to JJ's chest and made him back up. Then he fisted his free hand in my hair and bent me over.

I'd given up any attempt at fighting this because it felt too fucking good and was too fucking hot, so I grasped JJ's hips to balance myself and moaned as I took his cock back into my mouth like a good girl.

Maverick snarled something which I couldn't make out before pushing three fingers deep inside me and giving me what I'd been aching for.

"You're so fucking wet, beautiful. How long have you been fantasising about this?"

I moaned a reply that I knew would have been garbled nonsense even without me choking on JJ's cock because his fingers inside me felt so fucking good that I almost wanted to cry.

But that was nothing, nothing, to the way it felt when he released his dick from his pants and sank it into me with a throaty groan of relief.

I couldn't even be mad about him going without a condom again because the feeling of his flesh against mine, the hot slickness of our bodies colliding and the perfection if his cock deep inside me forced out all other thoughts.

Rick drove in and out of me slowly a couple of times with a growl of satisfaction like he was simply enjoying the feeling of my body claiming his, my pussy gripping him tightly and his dick filling me up. Then he moved to grasp my hips, the cold metal of the gun pressing against my right ass cheek making it even fucking hotter.

I moaned around JJ's cock as he fisted my hair and the two of them began driving into me at once in this brutal, messy, fucking punishingly blissful rhythm and I swear I saw stars as my body was overloaded with the felling of owning the two of them at once.

Rick was rough as always, his hand cracking down on my ass, his thrusts making me take JJ's dick right to the back of my throat and my moans of pleasure filling the air for every animal in the vicinity to hear.

I arched my back a little more and suddenly Rick's cock was slamming right into that magic place deep inside me and my pussy was clamping tight around him demanding more and more and more.

He hit it over and over until I was coming and screaming and my pussy was gripping him so tight that he was swearing and yanking his dick out of me, coming all over my back with a groan.

His hand moved to grip my hair alongside JJ's as I fought to stay on my feet and the two of them forced my head up and down until JJ was coming too, his cum spilling down my throat as he thrust in hard and I swallowed every drop.

Maverick laughed, the dark, dirty noise making my toes curl and JJ cursed as he released his grip on my hair and stroked his fingers through it tenderly instead.

Rick started mopping the cum from my back for me and I stood upright as he finished, finding him using JJ's shirt which he tossed back to him with a dark smile.

"Well, that took a turn," Rick said, backing up a little more as he buckled his pants up and I sagged back against the table.

"Wow," I murmured because apparently, I was still in a dick coma and that was all I could manage.

JJ looked between me and Maverick warily, his own pants still unbuckled though his cock was back in his boxers. He looked even more like a sex god than usual standing there like that in the dim light, his abs slick with sweat and his pupils wide with satisfaction. I'd done that. *Me.* And one look at Rick told me how much he'd enjoyed that too.

I couldn't fucking help it so I gave in and started smirking, feeling all kinds of smug.

"We should do that again," I said, not even caring that they hated each other or any of that shit because holy fuck that had been so good. So, *so* good. I wanted more and I wanted it soon.

JJ blew out a laugh, shaking his head and Maverick just looked between the two of us for a moment before rolling his eyes.

"You and I have things to discuss, beautiful. And I think you're gonna let her come with me, Johnny James. Or I'll be sending the video I took of you eating her sweet pussy to Foxy boy and leaving you to deal with the fallout."

"You're fucking kidding me, right?" JJ growled. "After what the three of us just-"

"Hey, I'm happy to tell him we spit roasted her right after I finished making that video if you think it'll help," Maverick offered. "But it kinda seems like he'd be even more pissed to hear that. Besides, I don't give a fuck that he wants me dead, so it seems like you've got a whole lot more to lose than me in that scenario."

JJ took a step forward angrily, but Rick just raised his gun again and I stepped between them, placing a hand on Johnny's chest.

"It's okay, JJ. Rick won't hurt me and I owe him a conversation." I waited a beat to make sure that he got that then grabbed my clothes and started pulling them back on.

"And what am I supposed to tell Fox when I show up without you?" JJ demanded.

"Keep your panties on, sweetheart. I'll only take her for a few hours. You can hang out in your car until I bring her back and Foxy will be none the wiser."

"And why should I trust that?" JJ hissed, looking like he was going to fight me out of Rick's arms.

"Just trust *me*, JJ," I said to him, sensing the argument brewing between the two of them and cutting it off before it could develop.

JJ sighed, swiping a hand down his face and shaking his head. "Seems like I'm going to have to. But I swear, Maverick, if she comes back with so much as a hair out of place-"

"Yeah, yeah, JJ, I'm sure you'll come fuck me to death or whatever gigolos do to kill people. I'm shaking in my fucking boots. Let's go, Rogue, we have a lot to sort out and not a lot of time to do it."

Maverick turned and strode out of the train car and I kicked my shoes back on as I turned to look at JJ.

"Are you sure about this, pretty girl? If you don't want to go with him, I'll-"

I tiptoed up and pressed a kiss to his lips. "It's Rick, JJ. I know that deep down you understand what that means. I'm just as safe with him as I am with any of you."

JJ's brow furrowed at that but he nodded, following me out and accepting my decision.

The three of us walked back through the trees in silence and Rick tugged me beneath his arm as we reached the parking lot, directing me towards his bike which was parked up well away from JJ's Mustang.

I gave JJ a wave and he watched us go with a concerned expression on his face. The other dancers had all cleared out already and as I looked through the windows into the brightly lit diner, my stomach rumbled.

"Food," I demanded, turning towards the diner and Rick only gave a half-assed complaint as he let me direct us inside.

I ordered a burger and a sub and a vanilla milkshake and some fries and onion rings...and a side of nachos, then I let Maverick order his shit and pay for all of it. When it was bagged up for us, we returned to his bike and he loaded it into the storage box beneath the seat before I climbed on the back and we tore away into the night.

Maverick headed out onto the highway and I just clung on as he raced out of Sunset Cove, following the dark, quiet road for so long that I let my eyes fall closed while I enjoyed the ride.

We finally pulled up in another town which I was vaguely familiar with but couldn't name and he parked the bike up beneath a streetlamp on a deserted street.

I got off the bike so that he could grab the bags of food out then Rick directed me to sit backwards on the saddle, my ass practically on the handlebars as I faced him and he placed the bag of food on the seat between our thighs.

We were quiet while we started eating, though I could feel his gaze on me through every nacho and all of the onion rings too.

"What?" I asked as I prepared to start on my burger and he shrugged.

"You tell me. I've barely seen you since you left the Isle and now you seem more interested in your food than enlightening me on what's been going on."

"Bullshit. I need to eat because it's stupid late and you fucked my energy out of me. Besides, I don't even know what you want to know." I took a big bite of my veggie burger while I waited to hear him out because it was already getting cold and I wasn't leaving that shit for anything.

"All of it. But you might as well start at the beginning. Because for a girl who swore to me she wanted nothing more than vengeance against those pricks for abandoning you on that ferry, you sure were enjoying a taste of JJ's cock."

I sighed, accepting the fact that I had to stop eating to answer and dropped my half-eaten burger in my lap.

"Turns out that didn't go down the way I thought it did," I admitted. "It was actually only Chase who fucked me over. He planned the whole thing. I mean, he swears he had some plan which would have kept me out of prison, but yeah...he's an asshole and my vengeance is now squarely aimed his way. I'm making him help me get the keys and I already have his. The other two are more of an issue though."

"Well maybe you need to put some more pressure on," Maverick said in a low growl and I scowled at him.

"Is that what you tell yourself when you're fucking Mia's ass?" I shot back.

"You really wanna know?"

"No," I hissed. "And don't go thinking that I'm gonna have a three way with you and her just because you and JJ went all power team combo on my ass tonight."

"Oh, baby girl, if we go power team on your *ass* I think you'll know about it," he taunted and I freaking blushed. Fuck. I hadn't considered that. There were mechanics involved there which needed consideration, but I was definitely not opposed to figuring them out and I was pretty sure the way my nipples were pressing through the fabric of my dress was making that clear.

"So you aren't opposed to a repeat of-"

"Tell me why you have a Harlequin tattoo stamped on your thigh, beautiful," Maverick demanded and I swallowed a lump in my throat.

"Right...well, I didn't really get much choice in that. Luther figured out I was back and he actually made some demands of me that I'll need you to help me out with. Plus, I kinda tried to shoot Shawn while they were having this peace meeting thing and then everyone got all pissy and Fox tried to lock me up in the house and Luther was all 'if she's a Harlequin you can't tell her to do shit' and that sounded like a sweet deal. He even promised not to boss me about. I've got two tasks and so long as I achieve them both, I'm basically just a bitch with a tattoo, so it's all good."

"What tasks?"

"Err, I have to kill Shawn - so score for me because that was on my agenda anyway."

"And?"

"Umm...." I grabbed a handful of fries and stuffed them in my mouth while speaking as fast as I could, "I just have to get you to come home, make up with Fox and co and merge The Damned Men with the Harlequins forever."

Maverick stared at me while I chewed and my heart hammered as he took that in before he finally barked a humourless laugh.

"Luther Harlequin still seriously wants peace with me?" he asked, his eyes flaring with disbelief and I shrugged as I swallowed.

"If I'm honest, he seems a bit off his rocker, but he loves you, dude. He wants you home and I believe him. I've got no idea how I'm gonna get you and Fox to make up yet, but I figured I'd focus on killing Shawn and then see where I'm at."

"That man is fucking insane and he's full of shit too. I don't believe for one second that he wants to just welcome me back with open arms even if I did have the slightest inclination to go back - which I fucking don't."

"Don't shoot the messenger," I said, chomping down on more fries. "I'm just telling you what he said. And I agreed to make it happen because it was that or a bullet to my face and I'm pretty fond of my face."

Maverick thought about that while I demolished the rest of my food then he finally seemed to come to some decision.

"That ink on your leg pisses me off, beautiful," he growled. "And I'm thinking that if Luther is so sure that The Damned Men are pretty much a part of his crew already, he wouldn't have an issue with you getting some ink to represent them too."

"You want me to get a Damned Men tattoo? Are you making me a part of your gang as well?"

"Why the fuck not?" he asked with a laugh and I huffed.

"Fine. But only in an honorary way. I'm not doing shit for you. Nada. Nothing. I'm not one of your men to boss about or-"

"I'm good dominating you when we fuck, baby girl. I don't need you playing gangster for me."

"Alright then. But Fox won't like it."

"Good thing I don't give a shit about that then, isn't it? Besides, you always did love riling him up. Don't tell me you aren't getting off on the idea of how pissed he'll be when he sees it."

I couldn't hold my smirk in and Maverick laughed. "Come on then. Shoot Luther a message telling him I'll come see him in a few hours when the sun comes up somewhere neutral to listen to his bullshit. I've got a guy who can give you your ink before then. Oh and I guess you'd better let Johnny James know he doesn't need to wait around in his car for you anymore either."

"Why do I get the feeling you only want me to do any of this because you enjoy getting me in trouble?" I asked as I took a drink of my shake and Maverick's smile darkened.

"Come on, beautiful, you know I've always lived for getting you in trouble. And you've always fucking loved it too."

Man had a damn good point there.

Dead Man's Isle

MAVERICK

CHAPTER THIRTY

A pretty fucking interesting night had turned into what I expected to be a pretty fucking interesting morning. After Rogue had made arrangements with Luther, I'd taken her phone and switched it off, letting Foxy boy stew over where she was and smirking to myself every time I thought of him losing his shit.

We'd checked into a shitty motel for the remainder of the night and instead of the fuckfest I'd had in mind until dawn arrived, I'd gone to the bathroom for a piss and come back to find her passed out spread eagle in the double bed.

I'd slept for a few hours with her in my arms, the nightmares kept at bay by her presence and allowing me a rare bit of peace. When I woke, I bit her ear to try and stir her as the sunlight poured in through the window, but that did nothing, so I moved on top of her, tugged her panties aside and shoved my cock in her.

That did the trick.

"Rick!" she cried, then moaned loudly as I pinned her down and drove myself into her with the pent up fury of a man who'd been waiting on her to phone him for far too long. I was tired of being apart from her and even more tired of fucking my hand.

I locked my fingers around her throat and she instantly came on my dick, writhing and moaning beneath me as I pulled out and finished all over her stomach.

"Gotta stop fucking me without a condom," she panted, her hair a bird's nest and her lips all reddened by the sting of mine.

I smirked, getting up and lifting her into my arms as I carried her into the shower to clean up. "Nah, I'm good."

She punched my arm. "It's not funny, Rick."

"I'm not laughing," I sniggered, turning the water on as I placed her on her feet and watching as my cum was washed down her body.

We had about twenty minutes before we needed to leave to meet Luther, so I made sure I spent every one of them either licking her pussy or deep inside it while she cursed me out and clawed at my back for fucking her bare again. I knew I was an asshole, but so did she, and she couldn't seem to resist my cock enough to actually tell me no. Besides, pulling out was like ninety nine percent effective, right?

We finally got ourselves dressed and I admired the little pink dress and sneakers she'd had on last night, squeezing her ass as I led her to the door. What I admired even more than that was the Damned Man tattoo she now had covering the back of her left thigh to counter the Harlequin one. Before we'd headed to this motel, I'd taken her to meet one of my men to get inked up in his mom's trailer not far from here. She'd laid on the couch and watched Power Rangers while telling his mom stupid stories about us from our childhood. I'd liked listening to those, remembering a time when life had been easy, though I hadn't liked the uncomfortable tugging in my stomach every time a story included Fox, Chase or JJ.

We got on my motorcycle and Rogue's arms and thighs felt so good wrapped around me as I drove towards the park where we'd planned to meet Luther. Was I looking forward to seeing the asshole who'd adopted me? No. Not even a little bit.

I might have been slightly more enthused if I knew I was heading there to blow his brains out, but unfortunately I wasn't going to get my wish on that today. I did need to figure out the lay of the land though, because if he'd made my girl commit to this foolish idea of reuniting me with Fox and his lapdogs, then I needed to make sure she had an out. Even if that out was simply getting her on my bike and driving ten states away from the motherfucker. But I hoped the answer would be more bloody than that.

A bullet in his skull, his son's, JJ's and Chase's seemed like the simple solution to my problem. But that wasn't exactly an easy feat considering I'd been trying to pull that off for years now. And as my mind hooked on JJ and the way Rogue had looked at him last night, I wondered how much she'd like me after I showed her the inside of his skull. Probably wasn't the best way to win her over, but was that what I was trying to do anyway?

I'd made it clear what my intentions were towards those assholes, so she couldn't exactly expect more from me than bloodshed when it came to them. Still…it was something I was going to need to consider if I wanted to keep her. But that wasn't meant to be my plan. She was temporary. My pretty little obsession for a while. I couldn't have her long term. I wasn't sure there even *was* a long term for me. I certainly hadn't planned on there being one. Now, well fuck, she made me think about things that I'd never thought about before. Like where I'd take her once I'd finished the Harlequins to start our new life. That shit needed to stop. Yesterday.

I parked up and we walked through a gate into the park, a large stretch of green running away from us with a stone path down the centre of it flanked by trees. I took Rogue's hand as we walked along the path and felt her eyes on me with a question in them. But I didn't have to explain myself. I wanted to hold onto her, so fucking what? It didn't have shit to do with Luther.

We made it to a bench at the centre of the park which faced a large stone water fountain with mermaids leaping out of its depths, their tits covered with large seashells.

"I think I was a mermaid in another life," Rogue mused, squeezing one of her own tits as if comparing its size to the ones in the fountain.

I snorted. "I think I was a seashell in another life then because I wanna be stuck on your tits all day."

She laughed. "Nah, you would have been like a…hippo."

"I'm not a fucking hippo, lost girl."

She sized me up, cocking her head to one side. "You're the most hippoish thing I've ever seen – apart from a hippo obvi." She tugged her hand free of mine, trying to run away, but I caught her around the waist and dragged her back against me, hauling her towards the water fountain as if I was going to dump her in it.

"Rick!" she laughed then someone cleared their throat and I straightened, catching hold of her hand in mine again and holding on tight as the smile fell from my face and I glared at the motherfucker standing there.

Luther Harlequin was just as I remembered him. Tall with his dark blonde hair messy and ink covering as much of his skin as mine. He was watching us closely, his eyes skipping from Rogue to me with intrigue. What the fuck was he on? Did he really think making some deal with her would be enough to reforge the family he'd raised me in? I'd die before I walked back through the Harlequin House front door.

"Hey, Rick," he said.

"Maverick," I corrected sharply.

"It's good to see you," he said, taking a step closer and I scowled as he smiled at Rogue. The kind of smile that said she was now a part of his little inner circle, and when he got his hooks into you like that, you had to cut them out if you ever wanted to get free. That was something I'd learned the hard way.

"Not the words I'd use," I said coldly. "So tell me, old man, what's this bullshit I hear about you ordering Rogue to reunite me with Fox and his cunt friends?"

Luther folded his arms in that king of the world way of his that his son had inherited and surveyed me closely.

"Watch your mouth, kid," he snarled like he was still anything of a father to me. "And listen closely to me. You've had your fun, thrown your tantrum and killed a bunch of my men while you're at it. And don't think I haven't seen what you've been trying to do with those kills either. I get it. But we haven't got time for games anymore. Shawn Mackenzie has become a substantial threat to our people."

My fingers tightened on Rogue's at his name. She'd told me all about the shit that asshole had been getting up to and I was inclined to hunt him down and bring him to her myself. She could strike the killing blow but not before

I'd made him taste every colour of the agony rainbow.

"Barring Rogue, I think you mean *your* people," I growled. "And by the way, if you're just gonna ink up Rogue's skin and say she's yours, then I guess you have to accept she's mine now too." I flipped her around and she cursed as I held her still, showing him the fresh Damned Man tattoo of a grim reaper on the back of her left thigh exactly in line with the Harlequin jester on her right.

I smirked at Luther, but he just fucking smiled back like he was pleased and I let go of her so she could turn around again. *What the fuck?*

"Good. You're making progress already, sweetheart," Luther said to her and I sneered at him as she laughed at me.

Fucking asshole.

"As I was saying, Shawn has declared war on the Harlequins and Sunset Cove," Luther said, rage spewing from his gaze.

"Uhuh, and?" I pressed in a bored tone.

"And it's your hometown, the land you belong to, and don't feed me some bullshit about you not caring about it because I know you do," Luther pushed.

"The only thing I care about in Sunset Cove is right here beside me," I said simply. "And maybe I fancy taking her off on an extended vacation today. If I'm lucky, when I get back Shawn will have laid you all out like bloody cuts of meat and me and my girl can finish him off together."

Rogue yanked her hand out of my grip, moving a step away from me. "No," she said before Luther could speak. "I'm not going anywhere. You might not care about the Cove anymore, but believe it or not, I do. And that asshole already took enough from me, I'm not letting him have the beach I first learned to surf on, or the streets I know like the back of my hand. It might not mean anything to you anymore, Rick, and maybe it shouldn't to me, but that town is the one place in this world where I was ever happy. And I'm not going to let fucking Shawn have it."

I wasn't going to let it be known, but I was protective over Sunset Cove for those very same reasons. The only difference was, I was exiled from it and everything I'd ever loved there had been blackened and tainted. She was the only thing left intact that I could still lay any kind of claim on.

"The long and short of it is, Rick, we need your help," Luther said frankly. "The Damned Men can join forces with the Harlequins. We'll fight this war together and when it's done, I'm sure we'll find a way to make peace with each other at last and let bygones be by-"

"Are you fucking loopy, old man?" I spat, rage coursing under my skin at him dismissing ten years of the venomous hatred I'd aimed toward him and his family. "I'm not your ally. I'm not fighting a war at your side. If you're worried Shawn's gonna come claim your turf and kill your men, that's really not my fucking problem."

"Come on, son," Luther softened his tone and I stared at this headcase in confusion as he made a move toward me that looked suspiciously like he was angling for a hug.

I backed up, my fingers itching for a gun as I remembered Officer White and his men holding me down, beating me black and blue night after fucking night. I remembered them handing me to Krasinski then laughing when the door shut and he could get his meaty fucking hands on me.

I kept backing up as the world started to get smaller and Luther's eyes seemed to belong to all of those monsters who'd battered and broken me. There was a ringing in my skull and cloying darkness pressing in on my chest that I couldn't escape. His face represented all of the evil in my life. He was the man who'd ordered those Harlequins to try and force me into line. The man who'd allowed me to be endlessly abused in the hopes that I'd break. I'd rather cut my own throat than make a peace deal with him or his fucking prodigy.

"Get the fuck away from me," I warned. "I may not have a gun, but I assure you I don't need one to kill you."

Luther halted in his tracks, his eyes twisting with some furious emotion. "I know I was harsh on you as a boy, but I never wanted to push you away."

"What did you expect?!" I bellowed, years of pent up rage pouring out of me and Rogue stared at me with pain in her eyes. "For me to just bow down like a good little grunt and do whatever you say? Well I'm not like Fox, never was, Luther. That was why you showed me the dirty work, wasn't it? Kept your precious Fox innocent a little longer, prolonged his childhood as much as possible until you couldn't keep the cruel world from him anymore."

"It wasn't like that," Luther growled. "I knew your strengths, you were made for the dirtier work of the Crew, Fox was made to rule. It's who you both are."

"You don't know me!" I bellowed. "You're just a tyrant who wants to dictate his family's whole lives, it's no wonder your wife left you. Who'd wanna lay in your bed night after night? Who'd wanna belong to a man who doesn't allow his people to think for themselves?" I got closer to him, baring my teeth in his face as the poison I'd drunk for so long poured out of me in waves. "And you may have gotten Fox to kneel, but I knew him my whole childhood, grew up under the same roof and you know what Luther? He fucking hated you just like I did. And if you think he holds a scrap of love in his heart for you now, you're even more crazy than you seem. You may have made a little clone out of him, got him to do exactly what you wanted all along, but if you think he's grateful for it, you only have to ask her to find out what he really thinks of you. Because that girl there knows us all better than you ever did." I jerked my head at Rogue and Luther turned his gaze on her as his jaw ticked. "Tell him, beautiful," I encouraged, not taking my eyes off of my enemy. "Has Fox ever spoken a kind word about his dear old daddy to you? Is Fox grateful that he stole you away from him and forced him into a life he never wanted?"

Rogue opened and closed her mouth, glancing at me uncertainly as Luther awaited her answer.

"Well?" Luther prompted.

She swallowed, looking up at the Harlequin king who could so easily destroy her if he wanted to. Initiating her into his gang was just another game, trying to manipulate us all once more now he'd realised the power she held. We were all just pieces on a chessboard for him, but if he thought even Rogue Easton could bring me home to play house with him and his son, he was going to be in real shock when he found himself on the ground beneath me with my knife in his gut instead.

"Yeah, I mean…yeah he hates you," she admitted and Luther swallowed, looking like that was news to him and I relished the way it cut deep into his eyes and made him look weak for the first time in his life.

He nodded stiffly, turning to me. "Well I never claimed to be a good father," he muttered. "But I tried to love you both in the best ways I knew how…I suppose I didn't do such a good job, huh?" He looked to Rogue with a frown carving into his brow. "I guess this ain't going the way I planned, wildcat. We need to return to town. You'll come with me."

She looked like she was going to argue but he raised his chin and anger rippled through me when she nodded. He was not going to own her. I'd be cutting their ties very fucking soon, and he would pay the price for thinking he could chain my girl to him.

"Bye, Rick." She gave me a tight smile and I grabbed her hand before she could leave, yanking her into a rough kiss and not giving a fuck what Luther thought of that as I crushed her against me, and drove my tongue between her lips.

When I let her go, I gave Luther a look over her head that said I'd murder him soon enough and he inclined his head at me.

"Goodbye, son. When you change your mind, let me know," he said and I flipped him my middle finger as he guided my girl away from me.

I headed back to the road where I'd parked, my hands fisting and unfisting as I went. When I reached my bike, I flipped the seat up to the compartment underneath and smirked darkly at Rogue's phone sitting in there. I took it out as rage twisted through my blood and the temptation to ruin Luther's happy little family was far too much to resist.

I called Foxy boy and leaned back against my bike as I prepared to rain down hell on his life. It had been way too long since I'd made him suffer and today I felt like making the whole world scream thanks to Luther.

"Rogue, where are you?" he asked frantically.

"She's just on her way home with your daddy," I said and he swore under his breath.

"What the fuck do you want, Maverick?" he demanded.

"Firstly, I wanna tell you how good Rogue's pussy felt last night when I pounded into it. Oh and then again this morning. God, she can go for gold in the sack, can't she? Woops, sorry, I forgot she hasn't fucked you. Or so she says anyway."

"Fuck off," he snapped furiously. "I'm gonna make you regret ever laying a finger on her."

"I laid four fingers on her actually. That tight pussy can really stretch out when you put your back into it."

"I'm gonna fucking kill you!" he bellowed and I laughed obnoxiously.

"Are you sure there's not someone else you'd rather kill today, Foxy boy? Because I've just found out a very dirty secret about you and your boys..."

"What the hell are you talking about?" he spat.

"A little birdie with rainbow feathers told me you and JJ weren't actually to blame for Rogue getting left on that ferry and being arrested," I said in a calm, measured tone as I enjoyed delivering this news. "But your boy Chase who's so very, fucking loyal to the kingpin apparently isn't so loyal to you after all, Foxy."

"What do you mean?" he growled.

"I mean, once I was finished making Rogue come and she'd taken my cock as many times as I could feed it to her, me and her had a little heart to heart. Turns out, Chase left her on that ferry on purpose. Planned the whole thing, right down to the cops taking her away. He never did want her back apparently. Seems pretty fucked up even by my standards, but some rats hide their little rodent faces really well, don't they?" I tutted.

"You're lying," he said immediately, ever the loyal idiot.

"Am I?" I questioned through a smirk. "Can't see a reason why Rogue would lie about that. Anyway, if you're so sure, why don't you ask him yourself?"

Silence rang out and I could tell he was in turmoil over this news coming from me, having no idea if he could believe it. But he was sure fucking going to. "It's so hard for you to believe one of your precious boys could have turned on you like that, isn't it? But let's not forget how easily you all turned on Rogue and me. So let's find out how tight your little family really is, eh Foxy?"

"Fuck you," he snarled then hung up and I twirled the phone in my hand satisfactorily before bringing up Chase's number and hitting dial. The sun broke through the clouds above and I smiled cruelly. Today was a beautiful fucking day for absolute destruction.

"Rogue?" Chase answered in confusion like she'd never called him once in her life. Probably hadn't since she'd come back to town.

"Wrong," I said.

"Maverick," he growled. "What the fuck do you want?"

"Funny, that's what your boy Foxy said when I called him a second ago."

"So what?" he snapped.

"Well, I thought I'd let you know I just saved you the bother of telling Fox about your little ferry escapades."

A beat of silence. "What?" he asked quietly. Too quietly. *I've got you in my trap, little rat. How does it feel to be at the end of my gun?*

"You know, the time you abandoned Rogue, let the cops arrest her, lied about it to your boys and hoped she'd fuck off out of your life forever?" I said smoothly.

His heavy breaths came down the phone and I laughed wickedly, enjoyed every second of his panic as I bathed in it.

"She told you?" he rasped.

"Yeah, every ugly little detail, Ace. I'd gut you myself if I could be assed, but I think I'll let Foxy boy do the honours. It'll be all the more sweet to know he cut down his own brother in cold blood. Or do you think he might be lenient?"

"You fucking bastard," he growled. "Why? Why would you fucking do this?"

I laughed loudly. "Don't go blaming this on me, you fucking rat, you're the one who left her. I'm just mighty curious to find out how deep Fox's loyalty runs to his so-called brothers, because it seems to me like you're gonna be our old crew's victim number three. So humour me, what are you gonna do? Run for the fucking hills or let Foxy boy gun you down?"

"Jesus fucking Christ, Maverick," he said in a panic. "You really hate me that much?"

"Apparently," I said, my face falling into a scowl. "Now run away like the little coward you are."

"I'm not running anywhere," he hissed and my eyebrows arched. "Guess I'll see you soon in hell, Maverick."

He hung up and I stared at the phone for a long moment, surprised by that and my heart started to beat unevenly. Was he really gonna choose death over getting out of Sunset Cove? I'd given him a fucking heads up for god's sake. Not that I gave a shit, but still. That wasn't the reaction I'd expected.

I got on my bike, my jaw ticking as I felt the weight of what I'd just set in motion falling over me. But Chase had made his bed, so if that was his choice, I was going to let him lay in it and never think of him again.

The problem was, I couldn't get him out of my goddamn head.

Rejects Park

ROGUE

CHAPTER THIRTY ONE

Luther had been silent for most of the drive back but as we started down the familiar streets of Sunset Cove, he spoke up as if we'd been in the middle of a conversation the whole time.

"I tried to be a good father. Not one who was *liked*, but a good one. One who taught my boys the things they needed to know to survive in this life. I wanted them to grow up to be powerful men and they have. But I also wanted them to learn the importance of things like loyalty, honesty and strength of character. I thought that by teaching them the lessons I was they'd come to realise that I was giving them the tools they needed to be men of true power. That's all I wanted."

I looked at him, studying his profile for a moment then deciding to just run with the words that were on the tip of my tongue because fuck it. I was a dead girl walking and toeing the line hadn't done me any favours with Shawn. Men like him and Luther would always be bigger and meaner than me and if Luther was serious about wanting to fix his family, then he was the one who needed to learn a few things. Not that I was convinced that there was any way to fix this shit between him and his boys, but still, my honesty was worth more than me just telling him what he wanted to hear as some kind of ego stroking platitude.

"Life doesn't always go the way we plan," I said, shifting in my seat so that my new tattoo wasn't pressing to the leather. "All I ever wanted was to stay here with my boys and have a less shitty life. Just one simple thing that seemed so easy to keep in my grasp when I was a kid. I knew I'd always be broke and I was never gonna make it big or be someone important. But I was important to them. Or so I thought. But then you hauled me out of my little slice of paradise and made sure I knew my worth and lost any foolish fantasies of having something more than I was born to."

"You might wanna remember who I am before you start mouthing off at me, wildcat," Luther growled, turning his bad temper on me and a prickle of fear ran along my skin, but I wasn't going to back down.

"All I'm saying is shit happens. You think life will turn out one way or you try and orchestrate it to go another but then *bam*, something slaps you like a wet kipper to the face and you're staggering down some other path which you don't know how to traverse. So you can stumble along it and let yourself fall or you can figure out how to navigate the potholes and survive." I shrugged, tugging my hair over my shoulder and starting to braid it.

"Well you found your way back here," Luther pointed out. "So maybe I can find my way back to my boys too."

I held my tongue on that shit show and concentrated on braiding, but he clearly felt my unspoken words filling the space in his fancy ass car anyway.

"Spit it out."

"How about you swear to me that I won't be punished for running my mouth before you start ordering thoughts from my mind which you won't like?" I offered because fuck ending up dead over his hurt feelings on my opinions.

"Fine," Luther huffed. "Speak freely."

"Kay. You just said I found my way back here like that's all good and dandy now. Like I didn't live on the streets and between questionable homes with some more than questionable men. Like I didn't have to force myself to keep breathing through my misery every goddamn day. Like I didn't fall into some seriously fucked up situations and get stuck there for more fucked up reasons than you can imagine. So no, I didn't just rock back up here with a smile on my face all excited to reminisce about the good times. I'm a broken thing now. Even if my boys might claim to want me like this, I know they don't. Not really. Because I'm not the girl they remember. And I'm not capable of being her anymore either. The things I survived in the last ten years left marks on me which won't wash off. Just like the things you've done to or even *for* your boys have left marks on them. So I don't think Rick will just get over the fucked up shit you subjected him to when you sent him to prison for a crime he didn't commit. And no, I don't think Fox will just perk up and suddenly decide the decisions you made for him and the life you forced him into were all for the best. Maybe you can do some shit to try and build something new with them, but that's really not on me to say. Mostly I think you just need to take a look at why they hate you and figure out if there's any way to change that. If not, then..." I shrugged because I had to imagine that if not then nothing would change. His boys would go on hating him just like I would go on being this shell of the girl I once was, trying to cling onto something which wasn't really there anymore.

"If I said I was sorry, would that make any difference to you?" Luther asked as we pulled into the drive at Harlequin House.

"You're not though, are you?" I asked him and his brow furrowed.

"Hindsight makes it easy to look back and consider the ways you might have acted differently. But if I'm honest, then at the time I saw no other way. I needed those boys back in line and you were the thing pulling them out of it. A Harlequin should be loyal to the Crew and to me above all else. I couldn't allow them to just throw all of it away over a girl."

"Well then. It seems to me like fixing this fucking mess is the only option now, and I told you I'd try. Rick came to speak to you today which is something."

"It is." Luther pinned me in his gaze and I had to fight a fidget. "But don't forget what I require from you. I want my family united once more. And with The Dead Dogs pushing into our territory, we don't have an unlimited amount of time to achieve that."

I fought an eye roll and just nodded. "Got it." I had no real plan on how the hell I was supposed to reunite Fox and Maverick though. So far, I was just going with winging it which was my usual go to for all things. I didn't even really believe it would work at all, but I was going to keep playing Luther's game because the alternative didn't sound like much fun.

"Say good morning to Fox for me." Luther unlocked the doors and I got out with a word of agreement, not surprised that he wasn't coming in. He looked like a man on the edge, and I knew that he didn't want to face the reality of Fox's hatred for him right now.

I swung the door closed and he turned the car away before driving off and leaving me there.

The new tattoo on the back of my leg was itching and I sighed in anticipation of the oncoming badger meltdown when he saw it. But as tempting as it was for me to just run off and hide for the rest of the day, I was probably best getting it over and done with.

I strode up to the front door and reached out to ring the doorbell, hesitating when I heard Fox bellowing something furiously from inside.

I couldn't catch the words, but my stomach knotted and I tried the door handle instead of ringing, finding it unlocked and stepping inside. Mutt shot up to me, looking half terrified as he tore away from the sound of Fox roaring something and JJ shouting for him to explain himself.

I gave my little pooch a reassuring scratch around the ears then strode into the house. I wasn't an idiot, but I also wasn't afraid of the rampaging badger. He was probably just pissed about me going missing again anyway so I was likely the only thing that could calm him down right now.

"Honey, I'm home," I called out teasingly, hoping to lighten the mood, but as I stepped into the kitchen, I was almost barrelled right off of my feet as Fox collided with me.

"Tell me it's not true," he demanded, gripping my biceps and shaking me a little.

JJ moved in close behind him and my heart fluttered in fear as I wondered if Fox had found out about us. I hated sneaking around behind his back, but I knew that he wouldn't just accept what me and Johnny had easily either. Fox was the big, bad wolf and I was the lamppost he wanted to piss on. He might have loved his pack, but I knew for a fact he wouldn't love knowing his beta had been pissing on his post.

"What?" I demanded, trying to front him out because I wasn't dumb enough to make a blind confession.

"You and Chase," Fox demanded, throwing me for six.

"Me and Chase what?" I tried to push his hands off of me but he held on tight, his eyes wild with a need I didn't understand.

"I received a phone call from Maverick earlier. He said you told him that Chase fucked you over on that ferry job. That it wasn't an accident - that he left you there on purpose. That he *abandoned* you."

Fury and outrage tangled with shock and fear in my gut as I stared into the desperation in Fox's gaze and I found myself wanting to lie. I didn't know why but I didn't want to do this to him. I didn't want to tear apart the love he held for Chase or make him question the bond they all held. But I couldn't force my tongue to bend to the lie either, so I just opened and closed my mouth uselessly instead while I tried to figure out what the fuck to say.

"We need to know, pretty girl," JJ said firmly, moving up behind me.

"He...had his reasons," I said lamely, not knowing why I was trying to get that asshole off the hook but as Fox's gaze flashed with fury, I knew it hadn't worked.

"I'll fucking kill him!" he roared, releasing me so suddenly that I stumbled back a step as he stalked away with intent.

"Wait," I gasped, hounding after him. "You haven't even heard me out. Maverick had no fucking right to tell you that. I didn't want you to know. It wasn't his place to tell you. Chase was-"

"Don't try and protect that piece of shit!" Fox shouted at me as he ripped a drawer open and yanked a pistol out of it.

"Shit, Fox, wait a second," JJ implored, moving between me and him and I could see why he was trying to get between us. There was nothing of the boy I'd once known in Fox in that moment. A stranger stood there before me now, a machine moulded in the image of his father, a monster carved in the likeness of the Devil. This was the man feared throughout the Cove and beyond. This was the man who had earned the brutal reputation that followed him.

"What do we do to traitors in the Harlequin Crew, Johnny James?" Fox demanded, his eyes so dark in that moment that I couldn't see anything light in him at all.

"This is Chase you're talking about," JJ protested. "He's our brother. You can't just-"

"He's no brother of mine. And believe me when I say I can." Fox took off towards the door and I shoved my way around JJ, diving in front of Fox and placing my palms against his chest.

"Stop," I begged, digging my heels in as I fought to hold him back, but I knew I couldn't really. He was so much bigger than me and if he wanted to push me aside he could do so easily.

Something shattered in Fox's gaze as he met my eyes and my heart lurched as he hesitated there.

"I swore nothing would ever take you from me again, hummingbird," he snarled. "You know I can't let this stand."

"Fox," I breathed, my voice cracking at the darkness in his eyes, the determination, the way he held that fucking gun and exactly what I knew he was planning to do with it. "Don't do this. There's no coming back from it if you do. I know he fucked up, I know he's an asshole, I fucking *know*. But he's also the boy I loved once. He's the boy I know you still love. He's-"

The sound of the front door opening stole Fox's attention from me and a lead weight fell into the pit of my stomach as my chance at stopping this slipped through my fingers. Because there was only one person who would be coming through that door and the look in Fox's eyes said he was about to find his death waiting for him here.

CHAPTER THIRTY TWO

My heart was still catching up with the decision my brain had made. I wouldn't run. I wasn't a coward, and running didn't equal freedom to me anyway. The only place I belonged in this world was here. Harlequin House. Among my family. So if that was no longer an option then I had to face my fate.

I'd done this. I knew that. I'd fucked up, betrayed my brothers. I hadn't meant for it to go like this, but maybe it was always gonna go down this way. I'd just wanted to protect them, to keep us all together, but I'd ended up ripping us all apart instead.

My breaths came heavily as I stepped through the front door and I half expected to die there and then. Fox slammed into me, throwing me against the wall and pinning me in place with his forearm as he pressed a pistol to my jaw. The sound of Mutt barking reached me, but I couldn't see him, all I could focus on was a cloud of my own mistakes falling over me.

My heart thrashed as I stared into his dark green eyes and found my betrayal there like cracked glass. He saw me differently now, saw me as a snake in his home, one who'd tried to get rid of his girl. And that was exactly what I fucking was.

"You know that I know," he snarled in realisation and I nodded.

"Fox, let's just talk about this," JJ begged and I threw a glance down the hall, finding him holding onto Rogue, keeping her back, both of their eyes written in fear.

"How could you?!" Fox bashed his hand against the wall beside my head and for a moment I thought the gun had gone off, my soul trying to leap out of my body.

"I just wanted to protect you and JJ," I said but it sounded so fucking weak now. My plan had been a raft riddled with holes, and every one of them had let the water in and taken me down into the depths of the sea. "It wasn't meant to go like this."

"How was it meant to go then, huh?" Fox demanded through his teeth. "You wanted to send Rogue off to prison, you piece of shit."

"No, I was gonna get her out," I tried, but I didn't know why. My fate was already written, I could see it in his eyes. And what was worse than anything was knowing how much I'd hurt my brothers, hurt Rogue. "I'm sorry, man, I'm so sorry."

He stepped back and shoved me down the hall, pressing the pistol to the back of my head and sending a wave of fear slicing through me.

"Fox, stop it!" Rogue screamed as JJ pulled her out of my way, looking to Fox and knowing he couldn't intervene. Mutt stood beside them, barking furiously and I couldn't tell if he was cheering Fox on or telling him to stop.

JJ shook his head at me, his features full of hurt and I hung my head, marching through the house as Fox guided me past them toward the basement. When I was outside the door, panic reared up in me and I turned back to my brother, my heart lurching as I came eye to eye with the barrel of his gun.

"Please," I said in a low tone. "Not down there. Do it on the beach," I begged.

His jaw ticked and pulsed and his eyes were a chasm of pain that I hated myself for.

"JJ, let go of me!" Rogue yelled from down the hall as she fought to get out of his arms.

"You hold onto her," Fox barked. "That's an order, JJ."

JJ gripped her tighter and I threw her a glance, wondering why she was fighting so hard. I wanted to hate her for this, but it was impossible when my life had just been reduced to a few minutes at most. All I felt in my heart was regret. Over all of it. I'd made bad choices my entire life and it probably shouldn't have come as a shock that one of them was about to finally put me in the ground. But I'd never wanted to hurt my family. They were the only people who'd ever been there for me.

"I know I don't deserve it," I said as Fox still refused me an answer. "But I don't wanna die somewhere I can't see the sky or the sea." My voice came out choked because I had the feeling he wouldn't indulge me on this. I deserved to die in the dark and the cold, between four stone walls and a roof that let in no light.

"Fox, stop, please stop," Rogue begged as tears lined her cheeks and I hated that my little one was crying for me again. Her coming back to town had triggered a fear in me that blinded me. Because the problem was, we all loved her, and we'd all tear the world apart for her, even if that included each other. I'd known that for a long fucking time now. It didn't make it right, or good what I'd done, I'd just hoped it would save my boys from this. But I'd gone and made sure I wrecked us instead. At least they'd all have one less bad thing tainting their lives when I was dead.

Fox jerked the gun to direct me down the hall, a flicker of agreement in his eyes. "Move."

I stepped past him toward the others and met JJ's gaze as desperation filled his eyes.

"Chase, tell him you're sorry. Tell him you didn't really want Rogue gone, that you fucked up," he demanded of me, but I couldn't tell Fox that. Because I had wanted Rogue gone. Maybe only with the darkest pieces of my soul, but they were the sum total of me now. I was destructive like my father, a plague on anyone I was meant to protect. And maybe the world would be better off without me.

My gaze moved to Rogue as she reached for me, grabbing my arm and trying to pull me toward her. Her cheeks were stained with tears and the emotion in her eyes confused me as she tried to pull me out of harm's way. Mutt jumped up at my leg and for once he didn't savage me, he just whined like there was something he wanted from me. But it was far too late for me to give it to him.

"You're sorry, aren't you Chase?" Rogue sobbed. "Tell him, please tell him."

"It's too late for apologies," Fox snarled, yanking my arm out of her grip and shoving me along.

My heart thumped too hard, too painfully. There was a crushing, suffocating sense of fate surrounding me as I walked my final steps to where I'd die. This life had been hard and painful and sometimes unbearable, but there was good in it too. And that was what was hardest to let go of.

As I walked, I thought of all of us as kids, laying down in the cool shade beneath the pier, loving each other with our entire hearts. I saw Rogue's laughing face as she buried JJ's legs in the sand, my cheek still stinging from the impact of my father's fist that morning. She always made the pain hurt less, it was something in her smile, the way she made the shadows withdraw. I used to believe a piece of the sun lived beneath her flesh because every time I looked at her, she seemed to have this glow about her which I couldn't look away from.

I stepped out through the back door and my frantic heart calmed a little at the sight of the waves lapping against the shore. It was a perfect day in Sunset Cove, the wind gentle, the gulls soaring through an azure sky, the water coloured brightest blue. I walked down from the porch onto the beach and drank it all in one last time.

"Fox, I'll do anything, please!" Rogue screamed.

I walked towards the sea and tasted the wind on my lips and felt the sun beating down on my face. Countless times I'd experienced this and yet the sun had never felt so warm and the whole world seemed to shine with this golden shimmer I'd never noticed before. It was the perfect place to die and yet I found I didn't want to gaze into the waves when I went. So I turned back to face my family, focusing on them as Rogue screamed and begged Fox to listen to her.

It's too late, little one.

"You knew I had to do this," Fox spoke to me in a broken tone as he levelled the gun at my head. "You fucking knew it would come to this if I found out."

I nodded, my chest too tight as I gazed at this man I loved with all my heart. "I don't blame you," I said earnestly. "I'd do it too."

His eyes glinted wetly and his jaw tightened in pain as he gestured for me to kneel.

I lowered down and my gaze slid to JJ who was shouting something at Fox which I couldn't hear through the roaring fear in my skull. Then my gaze found Rogue's and my fear fell away like it was nothing. My regrets turned to ash in my chest, because none of it mattered anymore. Wherever I was going was far from here, maybe into a pit of nothingness, or maybe to hell where the Devil would make me pay until the end of time. Either way, I wanted to hold tight onto my favourite pieces of this life and pray I could take some slice of them with me into the dark.

Mutt came running over, biting Fox's ankles and my brother bellowed, "Get back!" at him, sending the little dog scampering away with his tail between his legs to re-join JJ and Rogue. I guessed he didn't like all the confrontation but it was gonna be over soon enough.

I gazed at Rogue for a long moment, wanting her to be the last thing I saw as she screamed my name and battled to get to me. Then I turned my head to the sky and wondered why this world I'd loved so fiercely had never loved me back.

I closed my eyes and waited for the bullet to come, drowning in the memories of my past and remembering a time where we'd all been happy, together and full of hopes of something better.

My pulse pounded in my temple and the waves seemed to steal away the rest of the noise in the world.

"Chase Cohen," Fox growled in a fierce tone that sent a tremor through my bones. "You're no longer a Harlequin. I rid you of your bonds to the Crew. You're banished from Sunset Cove and if you ever come back, I won't hesitate to kill you. You're outcast from my family as punishment for what you've done. And you'll never lay eyes on us or our home ever again."

I opened my eyes, in shock as quiet pressed in on me from all sides. Fox had his gun hanging loosely in his hand, his expression broken. He didn't look at me, he just gestured for me to leave and I looked to JJ and Rogue as I took a breath I hadn't expected to still be able to take. Rogue turned in JJ's arms, sobbing against his shoulder as he hugged her, my brother gazing at me over her head with loss in his features, but utter relief too.

I got to my feet, looking to Fox, but he just turned away and my heart shattered to pieces. I took one last look at them all and walked back into the house, breaking into a run as I headed through the familiar corridors and out the front door where my motorcycle was parked.

I swung my leg over my Suzuki and started her up, my chest cleaving apart as I went, trying to process what had just happened. In the wake of the shock over still being alive, panic set in at what my life was about to look like. I was banished, cursed to live on the outside of this town and I suddenly realised that was a far worse fate than death. My pulse raced frantically as grief closed in around it. Fox had realised death was too kind a punishment for me, that I deserved to be outcasted from the only thing I wanted on this earth. I was as good as dead, but cursed to live on in the wake of everything I'd lost, never able to grasp it between my hands again.

I drove to Raiders' Gym which was closed, parking up in front of it, finding my hands shaking as I headed inside and strode into the office.

I grabbed my spare gym bag by the desk and opened up the safe in the corner of the room, shoving the cash into it which I had stashed there before heading to the locker room and grabbing a bunch of spare clothes and some weapons I had in a locker. When the bag was full, I dropped it to the floor, catching sight of my reflection in the shiny locker as I shut the door.

My upper lip peeled back and I threw my fist into it, again and again as hatred poured through me for myself. My knuckles busted and as I kept punching and denting the metal, blood smeared across it and I didn't stop until I physically couldn't do it anymore.

I dropped my hand as blood dripped steadily to the floor and I focused on the bite of pain radiating through my knuckles, relishing the punishment. I should have been dead, torn from this body and put to rest. But instead I lingered on and my heart battled to get out of my chest and leave me behind. I didn't blame it. I'd disregarded it for too long, the way it beat for Rogue and no other girl, the way it pounded at the sight of her and begged me to do right by her. But I never did. I fought my instincts and made her life more difficult, more impossible, like if I could just be significant to her in some way then it would matter that I existed. Because I knew she could never love me, so I'd decided to make her hate me instead.

I grabbed my bag and unzipped it, taking out the gun I'd put there and stalking into the bathroom at the end of the locker room. The fluorescent lights were blinding as I switched them on and I moved to face my reflection once again in the mirror above the sink. I placed the gun against the underside of my jaw and stared unblinkingly at the failure in the glass.

This is what you get. This is what you deserve.

My father's voice blended with mine inside my head.

Weakling.

Nothing.

No one.

Useless.

Pathetic.

Coward.

Leaving this town was worse than death. So maybe this was what it came down to, dying in a room that stank of piss, staring myself in the eye and owning what a waste of space asshole I was.

My finger kissed the trigger and I didn't look away. I looked at him. The one who'd done this. Who deserved it.

"Chase?" Rogue's frantic voice filled the air and my heart lurched as I lowered the gun.

I stepped out of the bathroom, finding her there, her face still wet with tears and panic in her gaze.

She ran at me, colliding with my chest and wrapping her arms around me, her ear to my heart like she was assuring herself it was still beating.

"I didn't want this to happen," she said breathlessly and I wondered if she'd run all the way here.

"Why do you even care?" I muttered and her grip tightened on me.

I couldn't remember the last time she'd touched me like that and I wondered what fate was up to now, getting high on fucking with my head even further today. I wanted to close my arms around her, but they just hung there leadenly, my hand still locked around the gun.

"Because you're Chase," she croaked. "You're the boy who gave me his sweater whenever I got cold, the boy who carried me three miles to town on his back when his bike got a puncture up on the cliffs, you're the one who managed to smile through all the pain your father threw at you."

"You were the one who made me smile, Rogue," I admitted, tossing my gun onto the nearest bench. Fox was right, death was too sweet a punishment for me.

She looked up at me, her eyes reddened by tears and blazingly blue at the same time. My breathing hitched as I stared at this girl, looking so young right then, just like the Rogue I'd loved when I was a kid. My heart beat to a powerful tune that it reserved just for her and I knew I wasn't strong enough to deny its wants anymore. I was just some nothing boy who had nothing to lose.

"I hate you for what you did," she said in a tight voice and I cupped her face in my palm, my fingers sliding into her hair.

"That makes two of us then," I growled, my fingers twisting into the strands.

"But I also don't hate you," she breathed, her nails tearing into my bicep. "I don't hate you so much it burns me up inside and sets me alight."

"I don't hate you too, little one," I admitted, because what was the point now? I had to leave. It was over for me anyway, all of it. I was still angry at her, angry she'd come back, angry I'd ruined her coming back, angry I'd tried to make her leave, and angry that I'd wanted her to stay all along. She was my real death, this girl, this creature who lived beneath my skin and ate away my strength.

"Ten years, I've held onto a hurt over you that I've never shared with anyone," I admitted in a rough tone. "And I'm done holding onto it, I'm done with it eating at me and reminding me that I never could have had you. Because I realise now that I was never an option anyway. I never could have been enough for you, little one. You're a star shining in a dark sky seeming so close at times, but when I reach for you, I remember I still have my feet firmly planted in the mud and nothing's ever gonna change that."

"What are you talking about?" she croaked, a tear slipping from her eye and rolling down her cheek. This girl did not deserve to cry, especially not over me.

I sighed, feeling like a fool because of this. I should have let it go a long time ago, so it was time to put it to bed. "I saw you and Maverick together the night you killed Axel. My dad had been in a rage and I went to the Rosewood manor, thought I could hang out in the summer house for a while. But when I got there, you and Rick were in there…naked. And I knew you'd finally chosen one of us."

Her lips parted and her brows knitted in confusion. "What? You think me and Rick were together back then?"

"It was pretty obvious from where I was standing. And yeah I've been fucked up over it, but I know it doesn't matter now. You're with JJ anyway, and-"

"You fucking idiot," she growled. "I was never with Maverick back then, we were naked that day because we'd been out spray painting a wall and got paint on our clothes. We were getting changed, and yeah okay we had a little look at each other because I'd been dick curious and he'd been tit curious, but that's about it. No touching, no kissing and definitely no fucking. Mostly it was weird and awkward."

A sharp lump formed in my throat as I stared at her, that knowledge taking hold of me as I saw the truth in her eyes. "You never chose?" I rasped.

"No," she snapped. "And I haven't chosen now either. And I'm not going to. I don't belong to anyone, Chase."

My head spun as I stared at her, my reality shifting and I suddenly felt like a fucking idiot for holding onto so much anger over that for ten years. I guessed it didn't matter though, she'd made her choice in the end. She wanted JJ and Maverick now, probably Fox too on some level. I wasn't stupid enough to think she could want me as well, but the way she was looking at me right then made me wonder if I could steal a single moment in my life where I'd know what it was like to be chosen. It was my last chance, I'd never see her again after today, so why not?

This girl was the end of me, always had been, and now I was facing my downfall at her hands just like I knew I always would. But maybe it didn't all have to taste so bitter.

I tugged on her hair, forcing her to look up at me and her lips parted in surprise.

I'll take all this pain and more if I can have this one kiss. Just one.

I kissed her brutally, my mouth full of demands she didn't want to meet and that made me angrier still. She bit my lower lip then kissed me back savagely and I shoved her up against the lockers behind her, my heart urging me on as my brain yelled at me to stop. But I couldn't, I'd opened Pandora's box and I was letting all of my demons out of it one by one. If this was the end of the world, then why did it feel like all of my goddamn dreams coming true?

But as her mouth moved in time with mine and my cock throbbed furiously in my pants, the good gave way to the bad once more and suddenly the rage in me spilled over. I had to leave and lose her all over again. I had to say goodbye to JJ and Fox and where would I even go?

"Why?" I begged of her, slamming her hands above her and pinning them to the lockers in one of my own. "Why can't I get you out of my head?" I demanded in a growl, kissing her bruisingly as she tugged against my hold.

"Chase," she panted as I used my free hand to pull up her shirt and drag my fingers over her velvet flesh. She was my darkest temptation, the seven sins wrapped up in the perfect body designed to ruin me.

I dragged my mouth along her jaw and bit her neck, marking her roughly and making her buck her hips and gasp. "I knew you'd be the end of us," I growled in her ear.

"You're the one who did it," she snarled back, jerking against my hold and grinding her stomach over my hard cock, drawing a groan from my lips. I desired her so fiercely and I wanted to take and take from her until this furious beast in me was fed. She was my enemy and my end, the love of my fucking life and the only girl I wanted in the world. But I couldn't have her, not really.

"You've ruined everything," I accused, but those words were really for myself. I was the culprit, but I wanted to punish the world and right now the world was her. I dragged my teeth over her ear and she shivered, her back arching and I was lost to the way she reacted to me. Did she really want me? This was a fantasy I'd played out in my head a thousand times, but I'd always expected the reality to look a lot more like her rejecting me.

"Fuck you," she said breathlessly. "You think you're such a victim, Ace, but you do this to yourself. Your dad lives in your head and it's about time you showed him the door."

"Shut up," I growled into her flesh, the scent of coconut everywhere as I pushed my hand into her bra and grazed my thumb over her nipple. She moaned, wanting more and I gave it to her, pinching and tugging and making it hurt because she deserved it. And yet she didn't deserve it at all.

"You're acting just like him," she growled. "You want me to bow to you, but I never will."

"I'm not like him." I shoved her top up, biting her tits and palming them forcefully as I punished her for those words, but she just moaned like she loved it.

"Yes you are," she panted. "And it's about time you grew up."

"Fuck you." I stood upright, letting her top flutter back down as I gripped her jaw in my hand and bared my teeth at her. "You're gonna break my family, ghost. Fox is going to find out about you and JJ and then what are you gonna do?"

"I'll figure it out," she growled, trying to jerk her head out of my grip, but I had her at my mercy now.

"Will you?" I scoffed. "Because you can't just go through life without a plan, little one. You think I should grow up? Then what about you? You still live your life like a leaf on the wind. You don't care who gets hurt by your actions, because little lost Rogue doesn't make plans or decisions, she just waits to see wherever she lands and deals with the consequences when it's done."

"At least I don't plan to destroy people's lives," she hissed and my fingers dug into her jaw as I got up close to her face.

"So it's okay to be destructive so long as you aren't responsible?" I scoffed.

"Let me go," she demanded and I held on for one more second, knowing the moment I let go, that would be it. I'd never touch her again, never be this close, never smell her or breathe her in. I took one last, hard look and released her hands, dropping my hold on her face too.

She rearranged her hair over her shoulders, trying to hide the hurt in her eyes as she looked away and my chest tugged.

"Rogue..." I tried. *Come with me.*

"You should go," she said, her voice level as she continued to avoid my gaze. "Fox might come looking for you."

"But what about us?" I asked, my face burning as those words slipped out.

She turned to look at me at last and I saw every inch of pain I'd caused her in the depths of her gaze.

"Us?" she laughed hollowly. "There's no us. You think I'd actually want you after you tried to get rid of me?"

My heart shrank and I felt myself shrinking with it, heat starting to blaze up the back of my neck. I felt small, and when I felt small I felt cornered. Like my father was standing over me again. A blaring noise went off in my head as the man in me fought back and refused to be seen that way again.

"Then get the fuck out of here!" I bellowed at her, pointing to the door and her expression pinched as she moved to follow my command. But then she lingered there in the doorway and looked back at me with a cold detachment in her beautiful blue eyes.

"Sometimes I wish I'd never met you, Chase Cohen," she hissed then headed out the door and slammed it behind her, leaving me in the wake of those words as my heart shattered into a thousand sharp pieces.

I picked up my bag, shoving the gun into it and pulling on my leather jacket before heading out after her, finding her long gone already. When I had all of my shit together, I locked up Raiders Gym and tossed the key on the doorstep, not giving a fuck what happened to it as I got on my bike and rode for the edge of town.

I didn't look back as I drove up into the cliffs and left the only good things in my life behind.

I gazed at the road as I made a plan of what to do next, seeking out purpose in this godforsaken world, and there was only one thing that came to mind. My life wasn't worth shit now, so I may as well put these flesh and bones to good use while I still stalked this earth. I had a gun and was willing to bleed for those I loved, so I'd hunt down Shawn Mackenzie and end this war before it even began. And if I died in the process, so be it.

Rejects Park

ROGUE

CHAPTER THIRTY THREE

I lay face down on a sun lounger with JJ's headphones on and the music cranked loud as I tried to drown the thoughts in my head which were playing on repeat. Mostly, that Chase had been right about me. Even if I hadn't wanted it or intended it and even if he'd been the one to cause this fracture in their brotherhood, it still came back to me.

Ten years ago I might have had the right to come between them the way I had. Hell, ten *weeks* ago I might have danced for joy seeing Chase take a taste of his own medicine after what he'd done to me on that fucking ferry.

But there was no joy in it for me now. All there was a knot in my stomach and the words Chase had tossed my way over and over again since I'd first come back here.

You're going to destroy us.

He was right about that, wasn't he? But they'd destroyed me first, so wasn't that what I'd wanted?

Maybe vengeance didn't taste as sweet as I'd thought it would.

A hand landed on my shoulder and I cracked an eye open as JJ perched his ass on the side of my lounger.

He offered me half a smile, his fingers slipping along my spine then falling from my skin just as fast as he'd touched me. I was butt naked and ignoring the advice about keeping my new ink out of the sun. The tattoos were healed up now anyway and it wasn't like I cared all that much about a bit of fading. I didn't care all that much about anything recently. Sometimes the void inside me ached and burned around the edges, and sometimes I liked being able to slip into it and forget how to feel because reality hurt too damn much.

"Are you okay?" I asked, tugging my headphones off and letting them hang around my neck, the music loud enough to carry to us from them.

JJ's lips twitched but he didn't bother to answer that.

"Yeah," I agreed, pushing up onto my elbows as I looked at him and his gaze fell to my chest for a moment before he tugged it back up to my face and he picked up the shirt I'd discarded beside me.

I shrugged it on, biting my bottom lip as the black wifebeater covered my body, the outline of a howling wolf splashed across its front. JJ's gaze lingered on it and I knew he recognised it as Chase's but neither of us wanted to question why the fuck I'd chosen to wear it.

I'd slipped into his room more than once since he'd gone, breathing in the scent of him which clung to it and closing my eyes as I imagined him still being there. I wasn't going to torture myself over why, but sometimes that made me feel better. And sometimes sleeping in his stuff, wrapped up in his scent helped too, though it also hurt. But maybe I deserved to hurt.

I guessed I was a glutton for punishment, or maybe I was just fucked in the head, or perhaps I got off on knowing I'd fucked his life up just as thoroughly as he'd tried to fuck up mine and I wanted constant reminders of him for that. Maybe it was a bit of all of it. And maybe my lips still burned with the memory of his kiss when I closed my eyes and I couldn't for the life of me understand why.

"Are you done hiding from me?" I asked curiously because we both knew JJ had been more than a little absent in the few weeks since Chase had been banished. We hadn't been alone together, he hadn't fucked me, hadn't even kissed me actually. And I got the feeling I knew why. "Or have you come to tell me that I'm not the right choice for you again? Because you don't need to spell it out for me, Johnny, I got it loud and clear since Chase left. You saw what might happen to you when Fox finds out about us, and you decided I'm not worth the risk. It's okay. I've been aware of how worthless I am for a long-"

JJ caught the back of my neck and kissed me so hard he stole my breath away. His tongue sank into my mouth and his fingertips dug into my skin and something inside me cracked open and bled for him as relief spilled through me endlessly.

I wound my arms around his neck and drew him closer, climbing into his lap and kissing him like he was my whole reason for existing. I'd been so alone again since Fox had banished Chase. And I'd thought it was him pulling away from me, but maybe it wasn't. Maybe it was me and I was ruining things just like I always did. But I didn't want to ruin what me and JJ had. I needed it. He was my breath of fresh air and my rush of release. He was the smile on my face and the heat in my flesh. And he was kissing me like I was all of that to him and more.

"Never say anything like that to me again," JJ growled, pulling back and holding me in place so that I couldn't escape the fire in his gaze. "Swear it."

"I swear it," I breathed and he kissed me hard enough to bruise.

"I don't know how to deal with this, pretty girl. I don't know and I don't want to fuck it up, but I'm yours. All in. I'll say it a thousand times until you believe it. I just...I'm afraid of what this will do to Fox. He's destroyed over Chase. And I can't let him lose me too. I know he seems strong and unbreakable, but he isn't. He needs us and he needs you. I don't know what that means, and if you pick him I-"

"I've already told you, Johnny James," I growled, punching him in the chest. "I'm not picking. I never have. Never will. Even now. Even with fucking Chase being a royal cunt, he's still here." I touched my heart. "You're all still here. It's the five of us. And it might be fucked up and the sex stuff between you and me and Rick is clearly adding another layer of bullshit to the heap we all have to wade through to remember the people we used to be but...I dunno what else to say. There's never been anyone for me the way there's been the four of you. Never will. We have a bond that goes deeper than our blood and that doesn't go away no matter what. Believe me – I tried to get rid of it more times than I can count when I was gone and I know now that it just isn't possible. We're family. So maybe it is fucked up and maybe we're all destined to keep on hurting each other over and over again, but I'm starting to think that the good might be worth the bad. And you're all good for me, JJ."

"Good?" his lips twitched and he leaned in to take my bottom lip between his teeth, making my skin come alive for him. "Nah, pretty girl. I'm not letting you rate me 'good.'"

I laughed and he kissed me once more, but he pulled back too soon and the hurt in this house fell over us again.

"I need you, Rogue," JJ said softly. "But right now...I think Fox needs you more."

I chewed on the inside of my cheek as I nodded. I knew that. I'd known that every day since Chase had gone. But I was afraid of it too.

"I'm the reason he feels the way he does right now," I whispered. "If I hadn't come back into your lives-"

"Don't. Just don't. Before you came back, we were only treading water. We laughed and joked and ran jobs, but we didn't feel any of it because there was always something missing. *You* were missing. And this shit isn't on you. But he does need you now."

I blew out a breath and nodded, taking JJ's headphones from around my neck and dropping them onto the sun lounger as I got to my feet. I leaned down and pressed a kiss to his cheek before turning and walking back into the house.

I didn't need to ask where Fox was because he'd been sticking to the same moping routine whenever he was home since it had all happened.

Mutt looked up as he spotted me, wagging his tail sleepily while all four paws remained pointed at the ceiling from within the luxury bed that had randomly appeared one day. Fox wouldn't admit it had been him, but I knew it was. He was getting my street pooch addicted to gourmet dog treats and now he was upping his efforts to include luxury living. The world was going mad. But Mutt seemed to be okay with it.

I grabbed a couple of beers from the fridge then padded up the stairs before letting myself into Fox's bedroom.

I kept going, crossing the wide space until I reached the door which led out to the balcony where I found him.

Fox sat in a wide, wicker chair, his gaze on the sea and his posture almost seeming relaxed. He dominated his seat, long legs spread wide and one arm slung over the side of it while the sun shone down on his bare chest and he twisted a key between his fingers thoughtlessly. My gaze snagged on it and my heart skipped a beat as I recognised it. It wasn't just any key. That was his key to the crypt. The one I'd been hunting for all this damn time and had never seen so much as a hint of.

But I found I didn't care right now. I didn't even want to ask why he had it. I just wanted to steal that pain from his eyes and that frown from his brow. I wanted to see his lips turn up in a smile and hear him whisper silly promises in my ears like he used to.

I sat the beers down on the little table beside him and climbed into his lap, his gaze only moving to meet mine once I was straddling him and the agony I found in his green eyes cut me open.

"Maybe I should have just killed him," he muttered, reaching for my cheek and running his thumb over my lips.

"Don't say that."

Fox looked deep into my eyes, searching for something, hunting and scouring and frowning deeper the longer he looked.

"Is it all hate in there?" he asked me, a hopeless tone to his voice which I hadn't heard before.

"No," I replied. "But there is hate too."

Fox set the key down on the arm of the chair, but my gaze stayed on his as he considered me.

"Does hurting me help?" he asked roughly. "Does it make up for how much I hurt you?"

"I don't know what you-"

Fox grabbed my waist and flipped me over so suddenly that I shrieked and I found myself lying face down across his lap as his fingers dragged over the back of my right thigh where the Harlequin Crew tattoo lay.

"This tears me open," he growled before moving his hand to The Damned Men tattoo on the back of my left leg. "But this bleeds me out. So tell me why? Tell me this pain serves some fucking purpose."

I managed to shove his hands off of me and scrambled upright. But when I tried to climb out of his lap, he just snatched my hips in his grasp and forced me to straddle him again.

"Tell me, Rogue," he demanded.

I was breathing deeply. Too deeply to account for the little struggle we'd just had and the feeling of his powerful body controlling mine was making my thoughts scatter.

"It's not the fucking Harlequins or The Damned Men," I snapped, shoving his chest because I needed some outlet for this heat in my veins. "I don't give a fuck about gangs or oaths or any of that shit. Do you seriously think I'd swear my life away into Luther's keeping? Or even Rick's? Fuck that. You know me better than that. I'm not theirs just like I'm not anybody's. Did I have to promise your dad some bullshit to make him spare my life? Yeah. Do I plan on running the fuck away from here and never looking back when I'm done here despite those oaths? Yeah."

"What does that even mean? Done here doing what?" Fox snapped. "What is it that you're so desperate to do before you run off?"

My mouth opened and closed but I didn't have an answer. I'd been planning on revenge but there sat Fox's key and I was making no attempt to claim it. Chase had been run out of town and I fucking despised him, but I was gaining no joy from knowing he'd gotten what he deserved. I still hated him the same. Still hated all of them the same. None of it mattered. So what was I still doing here?

"I don't know," I admitted and some of the tension ran out of Fox's body.

"Yeah you do," he replied, his hands slipping around my back as he tugged me closer. "You're home, baby. That's why you're here. And you're not running off any time soon. If ever."

I swallowed thickly, refusing to give that suggestion any thought because it wasn't true. It couldn't be. I couldn't allow it to be.

"Fine. Don't answer that. But tell me what the tattoos mean then if it's not about the gangs," Fox said.

"It's you, asshole," I snapped at him, gripping his bicep where that fucking mark was branded on him too. "No matter how much I might not like it, or how we might have all wanted to escape it once, you *are* a Harlequin. It's in your blood, your nature, your soul. So that tattoo doesn't mean I'm in some fucking gang. It means I'm yours."

The dark in Fox's eyes lightened at my words and he leaned forward suddenly, his mouth on a path straight for mine but I pressed a hand to his chest to stop him and he frowned in confusion before I went on.

"And The Damned Men tattoo means I'm Maverick's too."

Silence hung between us as he processed that, his eyes bouncing between mine as he drank it in and digested it and realised what I was saying.

"We're not kids anymore, Rogue," he growled eventually. "You have to pick a fucking favourite now. You can't keep on playing us off against each other and claiming you love us all the same. It's bullshit. Fucking bullshit and you know it."

"It's not," I snapped. "And don't be so fucking conceited, I never said I love you."

Fox gaped at me then suddenly he was laughing and I was crying and he was tugging me closer and I didn't want to hold him back anymore.

His hands pushed into my hair and I kissed him when his mouth found mine. It hurt so fucking good that I was almost certain my heart was breaking and re-forming all at once, but I couldn't get enough of it.

He didn't try to push for more for once, instead just kissing me the way I used to wish he would when we were kids. The way I was too afraid to admit I wanted and the way I knew would break me in the end. But sometimes that was what I wanted. To be broken by him and all of my boys and to lay myself at their feet for that destruction. Because being a dead girl got old long before Shawn had tried to kill me. And at least when I was with them, I felt every moment I was in. The good, the bad, the ugly and the damn fucked up alike. And I wasn't ready to let that go yet. So maybe Fox was right, maybe I was full of shit and I wasn't ever going to run again. But I couldn't let myself think about that. I couldn't let hope try and slide its way into my heart. But I could steal a kiss from Fox Harlequin and maybe the two of us could steal a little happiness from each other too.

Fox's cell phone started ringing and he groaned as I pulled back, then he reached for it with a frustrated sigh, answering just before it could cut out.

I watched him as he barked at the person on the other end of the line, tracing the sharp angles of his cheekbones and the solid shape of his jaw. Fuck, this man was edible. I just wished I could take a bite of him without the strings attached.

He cut the call and looked at me, his thumbs tracing over my hips and sending heat beneath my skin. "You wanna go to a party tonight?" he asked unenthusiastically. "Jolene needs me to stop by and she said there's some huge event on at the Dollhouse tonight anyway. I figure it might do us good to get a few drinks."

"And go dancing?" I asked hopefully, making him snort.

"You can dance. I'll watch."

"JJ will dance with me," I assured him and his jaw ticked as he nodded.

"Maybe I'll dance after all."

I rolled my eyes at him and hopped out of his lap. "Well then, I'd better go and make sure I look shit hot. We can't have Fox Harlequin's girl looking like crap when he takes her out."

"You mean that?" he asked me, pushing forward to lean his elbows on his knees. "You're my girl?"

"No," I laughed as I skipped away from him. "Not even a little bit, Badger."

He cursed me out as I headed inside and I grinned to myself as I went in search of something to wear. All that shit with Chase had been bringing us down for too long. We needed this. A night out to just relax and make some fun memories to focus on. Everything could be solved by a good night out.

And I had the feeling this one would be a night to remember.

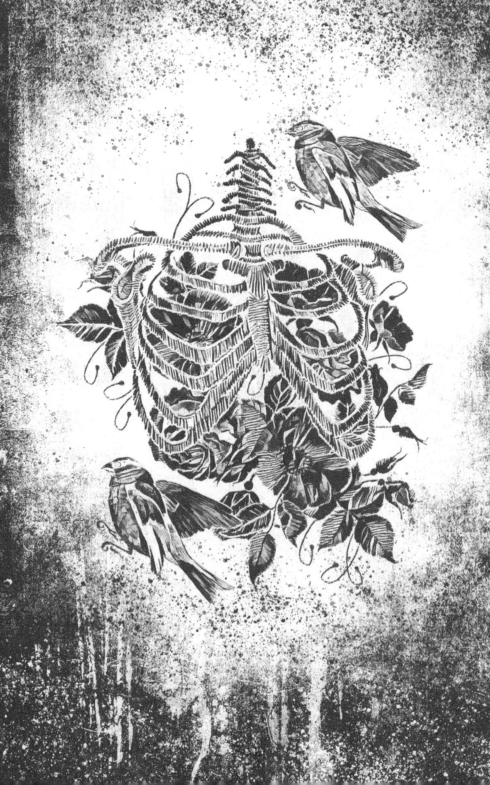

FUCKING SHAWN

The Dead Dogs

CHAPTER THIRTY FOUR

"That's it, boys!" I called. "Dig 'em all up, let's move this along." I swung a metal detector across the ground, squinting at the dark ground to find my way forward. The detector bleeped and I grinned, directing one of my men over to the spot to start digging.

"Nice and easy now, boy." I placed my hand on his back. "Take her out like a new born babe and place her with the others."

I stepped past him, continuing along my path as I whistled, waving the detector back and forth across the ground. The lights of the Dollhouse shone in the distance and my skin tingled with excitement at all the festivities I'd be enjoying later tonight. The firework show was gonna be a real beaut.

Rogue was on my mind. My dirty, bad girl Rogue. Rogue Oliver, or that was how I knew her. But I guessed Rogue Easton had a nice ring to it too. She was the best piece of ass I'd had in a long time, but I'd put that piece of ass in the ground and expected it to stay there. So colour me intrigued, because the bitch had risen from the dead like some sexy ass zombie. I'd dumped her body in Harlequin territory in case it was found and the cops wanted someone to blame, but how that had backfired.

I didn't get surprised all that often, but Rogue had done a number on me and now I knew that Fox Harlequin had claimed her, well, I was determined to get her back and punish her for fraternising with my enemies. Especially as those enemies had recently cost me everything when they'd stolen my shipment of cocaine and set the fucking cartel on me.

Rainbow haired Rogue looked like she had a little more spunk in her than I remembered, though she'd always had a sharp mouth on her. It was one of the reasons I enjoyed plunging my cock into it so much. But women didn't tend to get a grip on me like this. Revenge did though, and I guessed she was now a combination of a hot pussy and vengeance, so that meant I wanted her. And I wanted her bruised and bloody while she cried over her Harlequin boyfriend and I fucked her back into being a good girl.

I'd get her on a tight leash this time, bring her to heel, because it looked like she'd always been harbouring a wild streak in her that I'd missed. But I wouldn't miss it this time. No, when she was back in my hands, I'd crush it out of her for good and watch as she broke like a thoroughbred filly for me. I hadn't fantasised about something this exciting in a while, which was why I'd played the long game since I'd declared war on Luther and his cuddly little family.

Jolene and Chester Granville had been feeding me info on the Harlequins for quite some time now, so imagine my shock when Jolene had told me about seeing my sugarpie right outside her office while she had a meeting with Fox Harlequin himself. Jolene had recognised her on account of Rogue witnessing my arrangement with her and her husband all those months ago. Which was the reason I'd put my steadiest piece of ass in the ground.

Poor dumpling hadn't even known why, but I couldn't risk my little Harlequin spies being exposed before I'd even managed to wield them. No, Rogue had had to go. But maybe my fondness for her tight pussy had meant I hadn't squeezed quite hard enough on her throat to finish her. A fact I was kind of thankful for now, because I sure did love a challenge. And getting her back really presented me with one. It looked like I'd gotten lucky too, because Jolene may have seen Rogue, but Rogue sure as shit hadn't seen Jolene or she would have ratted her out to the Harlequins by now. So I was sitting pretty, and tonight was the night it all paid off. Come dawn and I'd be back inside Rogue's pussy, licking her tears from her cheeks and laughing about the bloody mess

I'd made of the Harlequin boys.

Some people called me a monster, but I liked to think of myself as an opportunist. This life was full of juicy ripe fruits to be squeezed and devoured and I wasn't afraid to pick the ones on the highest branch. I enjoyed the pleasures of the darkest sins because there was no god in the sky and no devil below. There was only me walking this earth with no shackles to tether me to good or evil. I was the in between, a deity of my own making, the freest man in America. No one was coming to smite me, and no punishment awaited me in death, so why not bleed the world dry while I was here and take what I could get?

I gazed out at the Dollhouse with a smile curling up my lips, the metal detector finding another bomb in the earth. Chester had put them all out along the cliffside, surrounding the Dollhouse in some backwards ass idea of a defence against his enemies. The guy was a wannabe fat cat with no money, acting like his business was the monkey's tits and yet he and Jolene always seemed to be strapped for cash. Hence why they took to me lining their pockets and greasing their palms so easily, I guessed. But I'd gotten hold of the blueprints to this here little empire of theirs and I knew exactly where the safe was where they kept every dollar I'd given them.

Jolene's pussy had been half decent admittedly, but not worth the thousands of dollars I'd coughed up for their assistance. No siree, I'd be taking that back pronto and the rest of their savings to boot.

The funny thing about the people I always met was, they all assumed I was a man of my word, but I'd grown up in a place where loyalty was a burden and if you didn't cut loose the dead weight around you quick, you'd end up in the gutter with the rest of the moral kids. So I held loyalty to one person and one person only. Me. And Jolene and Chester had run their course of usefulness. They'd had long enough to hand me Luther and his son, and I was tired of waiting. So tonight, I was a force of nature waiting in the dark, and time was ticking down to the final hour. Tick, tick, tick, *boom*.

Dead Man's Isle

MAVERICK

CHAPTER THIRTY FIVE

I crept through the trees with my gun raised, almost able to scent the blood I was about to spill. I couldn't see the asshole any longer, but he'd definitely gone this way.

I'd been tracking this Dead Dog around the edges of Harlequin territory for hours in the hopes that he'd lead me back to Shawn. But now it looked like he was about to slip off the grid and I got the feeling he knew someone was hunting him. So I had to get to him fast before he could make a break for it.

He'd stolen a car from outside a diner and had abandoned it a mile or so back, walking off into these trees. That could only mean one thing; someone was coming to pick him up from the highway on the other side of them. So I needed to catch him before that happened.

The canopy above only allowed a small amount of moonlight through to the woodland floor and I couldn't see him anywhere close, so I upped my pace as I listened for his movements in the dark.

Where are you, you little shitbag?

I kept very still, a predator ready to pounce and as a twig cracked to my right, I lunged through the foliage, colliding with a hard body. But he was on the crest of a damn hill and we crashed to the ground, rolling down it at speed.

my hand colliding with a tree and my gun going flying. As we hit the bottom of the steep bank, he landed on top of me and his fist crashed into my face just before I delivered a furious blow to his chest and sent him flying off of me.

I lunged at him as he came back at me, the glint of a blade in his hand making my adrenaline surge.

I caught his wrist to stop him driving it into my thigh, punching his jaw and vaguely wondering why he'd gone for a disabling blow instead of a kill shot.

He lunged at me again, the rage in him seeming to match my own as his free fist collided with my jaw and my head hit the dirt. I rolled with a snarl before he could get on top of me again, shoving to my feet and booting him in the side. He swung his legs hard with the skill of someone trained and knocked my feet from under me once more.

I didn't stay down another second, leaping on top of him and grabbing hold of his throat with one hand while I tried to catch the blade he swung at me, but I missed. He held it to my jugular, one moment away from killing me when the clouds shifted above and a little more moonlight fell over us. He recognised me the same moment I recognised him and he eased the knife away from my flesh as a drop of blood ran down my throat.

"Chase," I hissed and I couldn't ignore the rush of relief that took hold of me. So Foxy boy hadn't killed his little traitor friend? Interesting. Not that interesting though.

"Maverick?" he questioned in confusion. "What the fuck are you doing out here?"

"I could ask you the same thing," I growled, my fingers tightening on his throat, but his answer to that was pressing the blade against my own again. *Stalemate.*

"I'm hunting some asshole Dead Dog," he told me just like that and I frowned.

"So am I," I muttered. "Looks like I found myself a Harlequin to kill first though."

"I'm not a Harlequin anymore," he said bitterly. "And one decent slash of this knife will slit your throat, but how long will it take you to choke me out?"

I laughed darkly. "I don't plan on choking you, Ace. I can snap a man's neck easy enough these days."

"Well get on with it then and let's see who comes out the victor." He pressed the knife harder to my throat and I regarded him, finding a dead man gazing back from his eyes. He didn't give a damn if I killed him or not and that rather made the murdering less appealing.

"Nah, I wouldn't wanna end your suffering that easily." I took my hands from his neck, raising my palms in surrender and wondering if Chase was going to be my end as he didn't immediately drop the blade.

Slowly, he withdrew it and I ran my tongue over my teeth as I observed the hollowness in his expression.

I shoved to my feet and offered him my hand which he regarded with disdain, pushing to his feet without my help.

"So Foxy discarded you like yesterday's trash, huh?" I mocked as Chase tucked his knife into his belt and started hunting the ground for something. He didn't answer me, so I went on, enjoying this moment despite the fact that I really should have been going after the bastard I was hunting through the trees. "I suppose I should welcome you to the club - sorry I don't have the t-shirts printed up yet, but I'll be sure to get one with your name on it soon." He continued to hunt the ground and I frowned, his lack of response irritating me. "Three out of five now, huh?"

"Will you shut your mouth?" he snarled at me and I smiled at finally riling him up.

He started walking up the hill we'd fallen down and I followed him as he picked up his phone from the ground followed by his gun.

I spotted mine at the same moment, lunging for it and raising it in the air just as he swung around and we pointed them at each other. I smirked, pressing my shoulders back.

"I suppose JJ will be joining us soon too when Fox finds out he's been taking a taste of the forbidden pussy," I said, dropping that little bomb on him.

"You know about them?" he gasped, his finger sliding onto the trigger of his gun.

"I'm not gonna tell Foxy," I said with a shrug.

"Well maybe I'll make sure of that," he growled.

"Don't be dramatic." I smirked. "If I was going to tell him, don't you think I would have done it by now? Besides, I rather enjoyed being inside Rogue while she sucked JJ's cock the other day, I might do it again before Foxy blows his brains out."

"What?" he gasped, his eyes wide and I released a dark laugh.

"Oh your little bro didn't tell you about that? Lots and lots of secrets in that tight little family of yours, isn't there?"

"JJ wouldn't," he said, but there was a hint of doubt in his voice.

I took my phone from my pocket and showed him the filthy ass photo I had of JJ eating out Rogue, placing my thumb strategically over her tits so Chase didn't get a freebie look at them.

"What the fuck..." Chase breathed.

"Like I was saying, I won't tell Foxy boy about this because I'm enjoying the game too much. JJ will fuck up soon enough anyway and I'd much rather Foxy walked in on him railing our girl and found out that way rather than a boring ass phone call."

"You're sick," he spat.

"Guilty. So how's it feel being an outcast, Ace?" I asked, smoothing my hair back with my free hand.

"Feels like I've got nothing to lose," he said darkly and he raised his gun a little higher so it was levelled on my heart.

"Sure does," I agreed then lowered my gun and shoved it in the back of my jeans. I strode up to him until his gun pressed right to my chest. "Pull it then. Bang goes my heart. And one of your many, many problems will be solved."

He tsked, looking me dead in the eye. "I'm not here for you, Maverick."

He lowered the gun and brought his phone up to look at the screen. I leaned in closer to see what he was doing, finding a marker on a map moving away from us along the highway, but not at a speed that said they were in a car yet.

"Clever little Ace," I chuckled. "Planted a tracker on him, did you?"

"Yup," he said, turning his back on me and heading off into the trees. I jogged after him, taking to his side and he shot me a glare. "You can fuck off now. I'll deal with the asshole."

"I need to ask him some questions," I growled. "So you can give me that phone and fuck off yourself."

He clutched it tighter and gave me a look that said that wasn't gonna happen without a fight. "I have some questions for him myself."

"Well I guess we're hunting him together then, brother," I said with a taunting smirk.

"Why do you do that?" he muttered.

"What?" I asked.

"Always calling us brother or by our nicknames like we're still your family," he said icily.

"Because unlike you and the other assfucks, I don't ignore the past and act like we've always been enemies. I still own a few jagged pieces of your hearts and I like to twist 'em to make you all bleed inside whenever I can."

"Good to know," he sighed, like he didn't care anymore and maybe he didn't. That was what I wanted though, right? To see Foxy throw away another one of his boys like he was nothing, just like he'd thrown me away. And yet it didn't feel so great now I was looking at my old friend. He just looked...empty. The kind of emptiness I'd been a slave to for far too many years. *Way to kill the mood, Ace. You're no fun.*

I decided looking away was the best option and focused on the task at hand. I wasn't gonna cry over him like a little bitch. It was what it was. Chase was now just another casualty in our so-called unbreakable family, a loner with no home, nowhere to go and no one to love him. It was what I'd faced, what Rogue had faced, and now he was burdened with it too. The three rejects. We could start a band. Shame I couldn't play guitar for shit and Rogue's singing voice left a lot to be desired.

"Hurry up then if you're coming," Chase demanded as he quickened his pace. "He's gonna get picked up any minute and I'm tired of this hunt. I'm ready to spill some blood."

"Come on then, Ace." I clapped him on the shoulder, shoving him along so hard he almost fell and I smirked at him as he shot a glare at me.

We ran through the woods side by side and I was reminded of being kids playing in the trees beyond Carnival Hill, having sword fights with sticks and building wigwams in the undergrowth. Good fucking times. Shame they went up in smoke. Or maybe I didn't give two shits.

We made it to the road, but kept within the cover of the trees as we ran up beside the highway and hunted for our mark. My mind sharpened as I readied to take down our prey, my fingers tingling with the need for violence.

When my gaze fell on the guy walking along, eyeing his phone before looking up at the road frantically, a wicked grin pulled at my mouth.

Chase and I moved behind the cover of a large tree a few feet from him and we glanced at each other, forced to work together.

"I'll get his attention, you grab him," he whispered and as I preferred being the grabber in the plan, I didn't complain about being bossed by him.

I nodded and he slipped around the tree in the direction of the road as I crept through the shadows near our target.

Chase whistled sharply and the guy whipped around in his direction raising a gun, but I was already on him from behind, my hand slamming over his mouth and my fingers snaring the weapon from his grip. I tossed it into the woods and dragged him backwards into the dark as he thrashed like an animal.

Chase followed, checking the guy's pockets and taking his wallet and phone from him plus a knife concealed on his leg. He stamped on the phone to make sure any tracer on it was firmly shattered and pocketed the cash in the guy's wallet before tossing it away into the trees. Now it would look like your every day mugging when the cops found the body.

When we were far enough from the road, I held his arms tight behind his back and let him scream all he liked. No one would hear him here, it was a no man's land so we could do whatever we needed to to get our information.

"Where's Shawn Mackenzie?" Chase asked the exact question that I'd had for this piece of shit.

"I don't know," he gasped and Chase's fist slammed into his gut.

I held the guy tighter as Chase laid into him, his eyes filled with a demon's fury as he attacked the Dead Dog.

"Where is Shawn Mackenzie?" Chase growled again as the guy groaned and spat a wad of blood onto the ground.

"I don't know," he said breathlessly.

"Your life for his name," I said in his ear and he took a ragged breath, then shook his head in refusal.

I shoved him to his knees between us, taking the gun from the back of my jeans and pressing it to his head. "Where is he?!"

"Please," he begged and fuck I hated when they begged, it was grating as hell. "Please don't kill me."

"Then give him up," Chase demanded, pacing like a caged animal in front of him.

I pistol whipped the asshole and he hit the ground, trying to scramble away and make a run for it, but Chase strode forward and kicked him in the side, sending him sprawling back in my direction, laying on his back. I pointed the gun down at him with a sneer on my lips.

"Your boss or your life," I growled.

"P-please, you don't know what he'll do to me if I betray him," he stammered, fear glittering in his eyes.

"Don't worry yourself, sweetheart," I said calmly. "I'll be planting ten bullets in his head by the end of the night, he won't be coming for you."

He swallowed hard, glancing around in terror. "I can't," he choked out.

I lowered the gun and shot him in the leg, making him scream like crazy.

"Oh yes you can," I encouraged. "You just need the right motivation." I stepped on the gunshot wound, pressing my weight down and he wailed, rocking back and forth on the ground.

Chase moved closer, just a shadow in the dark as he crouched down beside him, gripping his face and turning him to look at him. "Where. Is. He?"

The mark released a whimper of fear as Chase kept hold of him, murder swirling in his eyes.

"Alright," the guy sobbed at last. "But swear you'll let me go."

"Cross my heart and hope to die, stick a needle in my eye," I said and Chase nodded.

"Shawn's p-planning an attack at the Dollhouse. He's set up a trap for Fox Harlequin and his gang. I don't know the details but – but that's where he is. He said he's gonna k-kill the Harlequins and take back his girl."

Chase's head snapped up to look at me and panic warred in his eyes.

"Rogue," I gritted out.

Chase was on his feet in a flash and the Dead Dog gazed up at me with hope in his gaze. A foolish man's hope. I lifted my gun, pointed it between his eyes and pulled the trigger. I didn't leave canaries alive to sing and I knew Chase hadn't been planning on it either. The Dead Dogs weren't nice people, you didn't even initiate to their crew without wetting your hands in the blood of innocents. So my guiltometer was set at a cosy zero.

Chase started trying to call someone on his phone who was no doubt one of the Harlequins then swore, trying another number then another.

"They've blocked my fucking number," he hissed, shoving his phone into his pocket. "I gotta get there."

He turned and started running back through the trees and I sprinted after him. I didn't have a number for Rogue since I'd taken her phone and as I attempted calling the others, I found myself thoroughly fucking blocked by them too.

"Goddammit," I snarled through my teeth as Chase pulled ahead. "Wait up asshole, I'm coming with you!"

Chase threw a look back over his shoulder at me, then nodded as we tore through the woods together. I didn't give a fuck if this prick was my enemy, if Shawn fucking Mackenzie was out for blood tonight, then I needed to get to the Dollhouse as fast as humanly possible, because I'd heard the stories about that motherfucker, and when he wanted death, he rivalled the grim reaper's reputation. And there was no way I was going to risk him getting anywhere near my girl.

CHAPTER THIRTY SIX

The Dollhouse was buzzing, people partying everywhere, all of them laughing and drinking, dancing and having a good time.

I walked between Fox and JJ as we headed through the crowd, the two of them flanking me like bodyguards and shooting warning looks at any assholes who seemed inclined to cause us any issues.

I was wearing a black halter dress which was backless and drew attention to the angel wings which ran down my spine and Fox's hand was resting lightly against my skin just above my ass.

We strode through the building and into an elevator which was guarded by a couple of dudes in black suit jackets and dark shades like old school bouncers. I wondered why bouncers were supposed to seem more intimidating when they were smartly dressed though. Was it the idea of the guy getting his cuffs dirty? And what were the shades about? It was dark in here. I was sure the dudes couldn't see shit so surely that made them worse at their jobs, not better.

Though as we took up position inside the elevator, I did get the crawling feeling that they were watching me from behind those shades with creepy, clinging eyes. Ew.

A shudder ran down my spine as the doors closed and we began ascending towards the top floor where Fox's aunt kept her office.

"What is it, hummingbird?" Fox murmured in my ear and I shrugged.

"Those bouncer dudes just gave me the creepo vibe."

"Were they doing something to make you feel uncomfortable?"

"Not really. It's just one of those run away feelings, you know? Like when your sixth sense picks up on the creepo vibe and warns you to hightail it before you end up with a direct confrontation with said creepo."

Fox exchanged a look with JJ and shifted a little closer to me. "We'll be with you all night, baby. If anyone else is making you feel weird just say the word and they'll be gone."

JJ flashed me a reassuring smile and I nodded. "What ever did I do before I had two guard dogs with me at all times?" I teased but neither of them seemed inclined to laugh. I guessed they had fair reason to feel on edge with the whole war thing going on with their gang and The Dead Dogs, but I was pretty sure a night out would help them chill.

The doors slid open and we headed down a much emptier corridor. There were a few private party rooms through various doors up here with several more bouncers lining the walls, but Fox just swept past them all, guiding me along with him as we headed for his aunt's office.

He knocked on the door and opened it without waiting for a reply, tugging me in with him just as my gaze snagged on one of the bouncers and something about him made me pause. He seemed familiar somehow, but I couldn't quite place why and between his suit and shades and the dim corridor, it was hard to get a good look. I was nudged into the office before I got the chance to figure it out.

"Evening, Aunt," Fox began, drawing my gaze around to the blonde woman who sat behind the desk in the room, and a large man standing beside her with his hand on her shoulder.

I sucked in a sharp breath, my eyes widening as recognition filled me and a cry of warning escaped my lips half a second before the bitch pulled a gun.

My shout was enough though and Fox had his pistol out first, firing towards the desk half a second before JJ slammed into me and knocked me to the ground.

I tumbled aside as he kicked the door shut and locked it in the face of the bouncer I thought I'd recognised and I suddenly knew who he was. Travis. Shawn's second or third or whatever the fuck in command. And that alongside the fact that Fox's aunt and her husband were the couple I'd seen the night Shawn had tried to kill me made it terrifyingly clear that we'd just walked into a trap.

Gunshots filled the room and people were shouting but I kept my focus on moving my ass out of the damn firing line.

I crawled over to the wall, covering my head with my hands as I went and snatching a wooden chair into my grasp. I shoved myself upright and hurled it towards Fox's aunt and uncle where they were shooting from behind the cover of the desk and I screamed at Fox to run.

He didn't need telling twice as the sound of the guys outside trying to smash through the door filled the room and he yelled at JJ to run too.

JJ grabbed my arm and yanked me towards the back wall of the room, confusing the fuck out of me before he ripped open a secret door that had been hiding there and shoved me through it.

I found myself in a dark corridor and I darted further into it with Fox and JJ right behind me.

"That was them," I gasped as Fox slammed the door behind us, flipping a bolt across to secure it and we began to run, JJ's hand snatching mine as he dragged me along. "The people I saw with Shawn before he tried to kill me. Your aunt and uncle have been working with him for months."

"Fuck," Fox cursed, firing back over his shoulder to hold off the men pursuing us as JJ reached another door and ripped it open.

We found a staircase and raced down it as fast as we could, spilling out into a room full of partygoers at the bottom of it.

The bouncer who had been standing beside the door whirled on us, yanking a gun out of the back of his pants but JJ put a bullet between his eyes before he could aim it our way.

I blinked as blood splattered the right side of my face then shook off the shock and snatched the dead fucker's gun from the floor. I might not have been a great shot, but I'd take a gun over going unarmed right now.

People started screaming at the sound of the gunshot and we were caught in a stampede as they raced for the door.

JJ grabbed my arm as Fox stayed close behind me, the two of them scouring the crowd as they ran, looking for any more of Shawn's men while I just concentrated on not breaking my neck in my fucking heels. I would have taken them off if they hadn't been strapped tightly around my ankles and I couldn't waste the time it would take to remove them now.

A girl almost knocked me from my feet as she slammed into me and I stumbled aside as JJ lost his grip on my arm and I collided with a wall. My gaze caught on Rosie's makeup caked face before she wailed in fright and ran back towards the crowd.

A tide of people surged between me, Fox and JJ and I backed away from the crowd, gripping the gun tightly as I shouted my boys' names.

Gunfire sounded again and I had to fight against a scream as I tried to squint through the dark club and screaming partiers to see what was happening.

"Hello, sugarpie."

I whirled around at the sound of Shawn's voice, raising the gun between us and squeezing the trigger, but he slammed into me before I could finish aiming. The blast of my gun firing cut through the air, but the bullet hit the drywall over his shoulder instead of taking his head from his shoulders.

Shawn grinned at me as he ripped the gun out of my hands before shoving me through an archway into the adjoining room which most of the people had already run from.

"What's the matter? Aren't you pleased to see me?" he taunted as he hounded after me and I backed up, searching behind him desperately for some sign of Fox and JJ while more gunfire rang out beyond the screaming crowd where I'd lost them.

"Keep the fuck away from me," I snarled more bravely than I felt because there was something about this fucking man which always stole my confidence from me, which made me want to submit, agree, give in. But not anymore. Not since he'd dumped me in a shallow grave and I'd begun to get a taste for the girl I used to be. Fuck him.

Shawn grinned at me as he pulled his cell phone from his pocket and my brow furrowed as he jammed his thumb down on it.

A huge boom resounded through the building and I was knocked backwards by the force of it, slamming into a wall as a lump of the ceiling collapsed behind Shawn and dust billowed out in a huge cloud around us.

My eyes widened as I realised he'd just cut me off from my boys, my way out, my fucking freedom. And as he read the panic in my gaze, his smile widened.

"Come on, sweetcheeks. It's time for you to come home. You don't wanna be stuck in here when the whole place falls down, do you?"

Shawn pointed the gun at me and I looked down the barrel at my death. No. It was worse than death. It was my old life. The one I'd been caught in with him. The one I'd escaped via a shallow grave and had sworn I'd never go back to.

He gestured for me to come to him, but I spat at his feet instead then turned tail and ran.

I ripped open a door as a gunshot rang out, but I barely even flinched at the sound of it. I didn't care and I didn't fucking stop. He wasn't going to get his hands on me ever again. I'd gladly take the bullet over that. But mostly, I just needed to fucking run.

CHAPTER THIRTY SEVEN

The crowd surged around me and blocked my view as we were forced along in the tide of panicked people down a curving flight of stairs to the floor below. I'd seen Shawn with Rogue just before the roof collapsed and cut me off from her and my skull was fucking ringing as we tried to fight our way back through the river of bodies flowing against us.

"Hey – someone grab them!" Chester's booming voice caught my ear and I swung my head around, spotting him running along the edge of the balcony at the top of the stairs with a gun in his grip.

I grabbed Fox's shoulder, dragging him away toward a bar beside the bottom of the stairs as Chester lifted the gun and took a fucking pot shot at us while Jolene ran along behind him. Screams filled the air and Fox and I ducked low as more bullets were fired and my heart thrashed in my chest.

Chaos spun a web around us and didn't let go as we dove behind the bar out of sight.

"What do we do?" I demanded of Fox who looked ready to run back into the fray and go after Rogue. I was desperate to go after her too, but that asshole was coming this way with Jolene and we needed to form a fucking plan. Now.

Fox stuck his head out over the bar and ducked back down again just before a bullet struck overhead and smashed a bottle of vodka which had been sitting on it.

"*Rogue*," he growled through his teeth, his focus locked on her. "We have to get to her."

We looked between each other, trying to form a plan and one finally sprang to mind.

"Fire," I said jerking my chin at the bottles above the bar. "Maybe I can cause a distraction."

"Jesus," he gritted out. "Aright, I'll keep them back."

Fox peeked around the bar, firing out at Chester as more bullets whipped through the air above us.

"Give yourself up, Fox!" Jolene's voice rang out before more gunshots cracked through the room.

I lunged toward the bottles of alcohol, grabbing a bunch of them along with a lighter off that had been abandoned alongside some cigarettes and a bar towel. Then I set about making Molotov cocktails as quickly as I fucking could before throwing a look out at the emptying bar. Lights flashed and the music still pounded through the air, Play with Fire by Sam Tinnesz and Yacht Money taking on a whole new fucking meaning as I took in the mayhem in one sweeping look and prepared to burn this place to shit. Most of the crowd were gone already and Jolene and Chester were taking cover behind the DJ booth as they shot at us.

"You fucking traitors!" Fox bellowed at them.

"You wanna know about treachery, Fox?" Jolene snarled between firing her gun. "My asshole brother refuses to allow women into his crew for my entire life but then he initiates some random whore into the fold just like that?"

Fox narrowly avoided a shot to the head as a piece of wood was blasted off the bar and I cursed in alarm, hurrying to get the first cocktail lit. I crawled to the end of the bar as fast as I could, setting my gaze on the long pink curtain running down one wall beside the DJ booth. With one furious swing of my arm, I threw the blazing cocktail at it and it smashed against the curtain. The material went up in flames fast and Jolene shrieked in horror at her bar being destroyed just as a deafening boom sounded somewhere deeper in the building.

"My sugarplum!" Chester wailed to Jolene. "Shawn's bringing the club down."

"Not if I can help it, I'll kill that traitorous little shit," she spat, then dove from her hiding place and I launched a cocktail between her and Chester as her husband tried to follow.

He was forced to dive back into the safety of the DJ booth and Fox stood up, trying to gun down Jolene as she sprinted along on her high heels with far too much speed than should have been possible in the things and turned down a corridor out of sight.

I launched the next cocktail at the DJ booth and it smashed all over the speakers in a blaze as Chester squealed like a pig.

"Come on," Fox commanded and I ran after him, throwing another cocktail to keep Chester down as we sprinted back upstairs and I saved my bullets for Shawn's skull. I didn't wanna reach Rogue and find myself lacking and it looked like Fox agreed as we raced along the balcony in the direction we'd last seen Shawn and Rogue, my heart beating out a frantic tune. We had to take a corridor to the right of where the ceiling had fallen down and I just hoped we could circle around to find her.

"Shawn!" Fox bellowed as we raced down the hallway that was thronging with running people. "You're dead, so fucking dead!"

We battled our way against the tide as scantily dressed women ran past us and drunk idiots stumbled everywhere.

"Get out of my way!" Fox roared, firing a bullet into the ceiling and they all screamed, ducking their heads and parting like the red sea for us.

We picked up our pace, tearing along together and I tried not to fall into a state of terror as I thought of my girl in the hands of Shawn Mackenzie.

She's strong, she can handle herself. She'll be alright.

Another resounding boom made the whole building shake and a crack shot along the wall to my right, making my gut tighten with anxiety.

Just keep going. Find Rogue and get out.

My breaths came unevenly, my instincts telling me to run from this building and get as far away as possible, but I wouldn't do that until Rogue was in my arms and Shawn was laid out dead before me.

We ran through another bar and Fox rammed his shoulder against mine as one of Jolene's men fired at us, knocking me out of harm's way. Fox gunned him down with a snarl on his lips and we kept going as I thanked my brother and didn't stop running.

Our breaths came heavily and I saw the same unending desperation in Fox's eyes to find Rogue as I felt in my own heart. I saw his love for her as clearly as I felt it in my chest, like it was connected somehow, forged of the very same thing.

"We'll find her, brother," I promised through my teeth and he nodded firmly as we ran down another corridor and searched for our girl.

I realised she'd always been ours, even when I wanted her for myself. We all belonged to each other in a way that defied the laws of nature, like we were one soul torn apart at the beginning of our creation and housed in five bodies that could never escape one another. I'd lost too many pieces of that soul already, and tonight I would not lose another. So if I had to face death itself to hold onto her, then I would. Because Rogue Easton belonged to *us*.

Rejects Park

ROGUE

CHAPTER THIRTY EIGHT

The air was coloured with screams as I ran through the Dollhouse, trying to navigate my way past chairs and stages as I sprinted through a performance room in hunt of an exit.

"Come on, sugarpie, don't be like that!" Shawn called after me and adrenaline surged through my body as I ran faster.

An emergency exit sign lit up a door in the corner of the room and I raced for it, slamming against the metal bar securing it and almost sobbing with relief as I found a dimly lit staircase behind it.

I just needed to get outside. I needed to get away from Shawn and find my way back to Fox and JJ. I had to focus on that and nothing else and it would all be okay.

I gripped the railing and started running down the stairs, my stupid heels clicking loudly against the concrete with every step I took and making certain that Shawn would know exactly where to find me. But that didn't matter because I was still ahead of him and he still had to catch me if he wanted to stop me. Every step I took was freedom, each one bringing me closer to escape.

I ran down flight after flight, not paying attention to anything other than making sure I didn't fall and break an ankle in these damn shoes. I tuned out the things Shawn was yelling after me and just focused on running. Only running.

Down and down I went until the stairs ended and I found myself at another door.

I ripped it open, expecting it to lead outside but I recoiled in horror as I realised I'd missed the ground floor. Beyond the door was nothing but a concrete passageway filled with electrical wires and pipes which were clearly for the building above me. I'd run all the way down to the fucking basement in my haste to escape the man hunting me.

I whirled around to turn back but found Shawn there, grinning at me as he leapt down the last few stairs and I screamed as I was forced to turn and flee.

I ran several paces before another explosion rocked the building overhead and dust rained down on me as I stumbled and fell against the wall, looking up at the ceiling in fright. What the fuck was he thinking? He was going to bring this entire place down on our heads.

I started running again but a gunshot ripped through the air and I cried out in fear as I ducked my head, cradling my arms over myself protectively. I still didn't stop, but the pounding of Shawn's footsteps at my back sent panic flooding through me and his weight suddenly collided with me as he hurled me against the wall.

I kicked and punched and he drove his body against me, a laugh escaping him as I tried to fight him off until his hand locked around my throat and the back of my head slammed against the bricks hard enough to steal the energy from my limbs.

"Well, look at you," Shawn purred, cocking his head at me as he jammed the gun into my stomach and held me in place at his mercy. His eyes were alight with excitement and I feared how insane this asshole had to be to blow up a building he was standing inside. "Don't you look good enough to eat?"

"Let me go," I hissed with all the venom I could muster while trying not to lose my shit altogether at the feeling of his hand locked around my throat like that.

"Come now, sweetcheeks, don't be salty with me," he said, eyeing me hungrily like he was planning out where to take his first bite from my flesh. "You know it wasn't personal. And now that my plans have all come together, there's no need for me to finish what I started." His fingers flexed around my throat as he cut off my air for a moment before relaxing them again. "But we might have a few other issues we need to work through before I can claim that sweet ass of yours again."

"Fuck you, Shawn. I'd rather die than let your cock get anywhere near me."

Shawn tutted in disapproval, shaking his head like he didn't believe me for a second.

"See, that's where I know you're lying to me. Because you always did love a good fuck. Always willing and wet for me, touching yourself to take even more pleasure. But that also causes us some problems, because I mighta liked you being *my* whore. But I don't like thinking of you being my enemy's whore. So tell me..." Shawn slid the gun down my stomach until he was pressing it to my pussy through my skirt. "How much making up do you gotta do for me, sugarpie? How often did you let my enemy fuck you, little whore?"

"I'm not a whore," I snarled at him and he laughed in my face, holstering his gun and moving his hand to the hem of my skirt.

"Let's see about that, shall we? What's the betting I can feel the imprint of another man's cock down here?"

My heart hammered as he hitched my skirt up and moved to force his hand between my thighs, his blue eyes shining with amusement like he thought I'd love this, or maybe like he was hoping I wouldn't so he could enjoy doing it even more. He'd never forced me to do anything when we were together but then he'd always been rough and taken without asking. I didn't know what might have happened if I'd tried to say no one time.

I closed my eyes as I froze, the fight falling from my body as he gripped the edge of my panties and yanked them aside. But that movement sent a flood of memories rushing through me. Memories of some asshole trying to do this same fucking thing to me when I was just a kid and he thought he could take whatever the fuck he wanted from me.

But I'd killed that asshole for trying to touch me against my will and there was no way in hell that I was letting fucking Shawn violate me without doing everything in my power to fight him off.

I swung my head forward with a snarl and slammed my forehead down on Shawn's nose, a harsh snap filling the air as he bellowed in pain and stumbled away from me.

I didn't waste another second as I turned and fled into the darkness of the passageway, running as fast as I could while he cursed and swore at me, a few bullets flying after me as he bellowed in pain.

"You'd better run, little whore!" he roared. "Because when I catch you, you're gonna wish I killed you more thoroughly the first time around!"

CHAPTER THIRTY NINE

I drove like a motherfucker on my motorcycle beside Maverick on his, tearing along the cliff roads towards the Dollhouse. The screams carried through the air before we even got close, and tremors ran through the cliffside that had my pulse hammering with terror.

We rode like maniacs towards our destination and finally flew up the drive where a clamouring, panicked crowd of people were gathered outside the massive building.

Dust and smoke was rising into the night air at one end of the huge white house which was half collapsed and the foundations were shaking ominously. *Holy fucking shit.*

"Move!" I bellowed at the crowd, carving a path through them as I got as close as possible to the building, then threw my bike to the ground as I leapt off of it.

Maverick was at my side in a heartbeat, shoving some guy out of his way before leaping on top of a truck parked beyond him and cupping his hands around his mouth as he stared around at the mass of people.

"Rogue!" he shouted and I climbed up too, searching the sea of faces for any sign of her or my boys.

"Fox – JJ!" I cried.

"They're still inside!" Di called to me, forcing her way toward me through the crowd with a terrified looking Bella and Lyla behind her. "They haven't come out. I saw them near the bar on the top floor."

"Fuck," Maverick swore, diving off the hood of the truck and I leapt after him, the two of us shoving our way to the front of the crowd and running for the entrance of the house.

Panic coated my veins and fear daggered through my skull as we made it inside and the floor beneath us trembled violently. I wasn't afraid to go in here because so long as my family were within these walls, I couldn't be anywhere else.

We raced through the entrance hall and up some stairs as a few party goers fled past us in the direction of the exit. At the top of the stairs, we met a fork in our path, one corridor leading left and the other to the right.

"Rogue!" Maverick roared, his voice filling the halls, but no answer came in response.

My breaths became shallow as a huge boom split the air apart and the two of us dove into an alcove as chunks of masonry tumbled down from the torn open ceiling above.

I shared a frantic look with Maverick, my brother from the past, a man I'd once trusted as surely as I trusted the sun to rise. And I didn't have much choice but to place that faith in him once more. "We have to split up, it'll give us more chance to find them."

"Them?" he spat. "I'm here for Rogue."

"Well find her then, Maverick," I demanded. "And get her the fuck out of here no matter what it costs." I shoved him toward the left corridor and he nodded tightly to me before turning and running away.

I took the other corridor, watching the ceiling carefully as a spiderweb of cracks spread across it.

"Fox! JJ! Rogue?!" I called into the rumbling house, upping my pace as I searched room after room.

The building was starting to empty out but as I made it onto a stairway, I found a blonde girl there in a flouncy blue dress, hugging the railings and shaking. A fire was roaring across the room, flames curling around a DJ booth and licking along the walls.

I dragged the girl to her feet, making her look at me and realised it was Rosie fucking Morgan.

"Oh my god, Chasey," she gasped, clinging to my arms. "You came to save me!"

"Have you seen Fox, JJ or Rogue?" I demanded, shaking her and she screamed, clamping her eyes shut. "Look at me for fuck's sake," I barked and she opened her eyes, her lower lip trembling with terror. "Have you seen them?"

"What are you talking about?" she cried, trying to pull me down the stairs as she hobbled along. "We need to go, but I've sprained my ankle. You need to carry me to safety, baby." She clung to my arm and I yanked it free of her.

"Listen to me," I snapped and her face paled. "I'm not leaving without them, so have you seen them or not?"

"I -er, I saw Rogue a while ago," she said with a pout. "She went um, that way." She pointed and I turned my back on her and ran.

"Wait! Come back! What about meeee?" she wailed.

I pushed myself to my limits as I turned the way she'd pointed me, hoping beyond all hope that I was going to find my little one.

When I made it to a dead end, I doubled back and tried to calm my thrashing heart.

Think, just fucking think.

"Rogue!" I cried in desperation.

I'd let her down before and I couldn't bear to do it again. I had to get her out of here because her death would be the end of me if I didn't. That girl might not have been destined for me, but she was destined for life. A good fucking life. She deserved that more than anyone and if I could just give her a chance for it, maybe my soul would be worth something in this wretched fucking world.

Don't take her, she's the best thing this town has ever had. Please don't take her away. I know I fucked up, I know I let her down before, but she and my family need to walk away from this. I'll pay any price, face any fate for that. Just don't let them die.

A scream pierced the air that I would have known anywhere, in any universe and suddenly I had a direction and a vow to save the girl I'd failed.

I'm coming, little one. Just hold on.

CHAPTER FORTY

Jolene and her men were blocking our path to the door beyond this room and I sat with my back to a wall, shooting through a set of open French doors at any chance I got to try and finish her. JJ took shelter on the other side of the doors, his brow gleaming and tension knitting his features.

My gun rang empty again and I cursed as JJ slid a round of ammo across the floorboards to me. I loaded it into my gun and fired again, throwing a look around the wall and counting three dead men on the ground within the large lounge.

Jolene was hiding behind a brick fireplace, firing off shots at me as she shouted in anger while I returned fire. The corridor we'd come from had collapsed and our only way onwards was through this room. My aunt needed to fucking die, and quickly so we could keep moving and looking for Rogue. There'd never been much love lost between Jolene and I, she'd been a pretty absent woman in my life growing up and now she'd turned on us, I would put her down just like she was any other of my enemies.

Another two men ran through the door we needed to get to on the other side of the room followed by Chester who was sporting some pretty ugly burns on one of his arms. He had an Uzi in his hand and I ducked quickly back behind the wall as it went off, bullets rat-tat-tatting through the air as my heart thrashed in my chest. *A fucking Uzi??*

"How many rounds have you got left?" I called to J.

"Three," he said. "And I gave you my last clip."

"Fuck." I counted what I had. "Eight."

The Uzi went quiet and I leaned around the wall, firing true and taking out one of the cronies covering Chester as he reloaded. The guy to his right returned fire and I cursed, ducking back as pain burned across my arm and the bullet grazed me.

JJ fired two of his final shots to take down the asshole with a roar of anger just as Chester got his Uzi firing again and rounds hammered into the wall.

Fuck. This.

I panted as I remained within cover, trying to figure out what the hell to do. We couldn't keep this up much longer. We were down to our final bullets and if we didn't move soon, this whole building could collapse and we'd go down with it.

I had to get to Rogue before that happened and these traitorous motherfuckers were keeping me from finding her.

An ear-splitting boom made me flinch and a crack tore along the floor beneath us, a tremor vibrating through my body which said we needed to fucking move. And right now.

"JJ, run!" I barked and we leapt to our feet, firing off what few shots we had as the floor started to collapse beneath us.

We sped into the room as the floorboards began to split open and Chester and Jolene were forced to stop firing so they could get out of harm's way.

I ran furiously with JJ just ahead, trying to make it to the other side of the room but suddenly the floor was disappearing beneath me and I lost sight of everything as I fell, dropping my gun where it went skittering across the floor.

I threw out my hands with a growl of determination, grabbing onto anything I could, my hand locking around a rug and gripping tight.

I ducked my head as an armchair went tumbling over me and cursed as the rug started dropping inch by inch, the couch it was under slipping down the sloped floor toward me.

I started to climb, panic clawing at the inside of my chest as I fought to hold on. But it wasn't me I was afraid for, it was Rogue and JJ. I needed to save myself so I could get them out of this hell. I was born to look after them, it was in my blood.

One look over my shoulder showed me my death. I was hanging fifty feet above a dancefloor two floors below me.

I growled as I clung on with a feral determination, but the rug kept slipping and the couch was coming closer and closer to falling.

No, come on, come on.

I reached for a broken floorboard above my head which was still attached to the main floor, desperate to get hold of it as I gritted my teeth and worked to climb higher.

"Fox!" JJ shouted from somewhere far away, his panic clear.

Gunshots rang out again, a furious tune of bullets tearing through the room above and JJ called out something I couldn't hear.

The couch came falling down and I lunged for the floorboard with a gasp of alarm, grabbing onto it by the tips of my fingers, the sharp edges slicing into my hand.

I battled to heave myself up as the couch went tumbling down to the floor below with a loud bang and I swore between my teeth, fighting with everything I had to try and get up. For Rogue. JJ. I could do it. I could fucking do it.

Only I couldn't. And my fingers were failing me as they came loose and I saw my death terrifyingly clearly, hating myself for letting them down.

A hand locked around my wrist half a heartbeat before I was a goner and I was wrenched up with a ferocious strength that had me falling against my saviour and knocking them to the ground.

I found myself gazing down at my brother, but not the one I expected to find. Maverick's brows were pulled together and he shoved me off of him, placing my gun in my bloody hand.

"Shut your fucking mouth," he growled, even though I had no goddamn words to say anyway.

He'd flipped a table up to give us cover and I hunted for JJ as I crouched behind it, spotting him behind a couch, trapped on the opposite side of the huge hole in the centre of the room.

Chester and Jolene made a run for the door and the floorboards gave way beneath them as another tremor ran through the house. Chester screamed like a girl as he went through the hole and Jolene fell to her knees, trying to pull him out of it as he latched onto her arms.

"You great, big, wildebeest," she growled through her teeth, clawing at his back as she tried to save him.

"Don't let me go, sugarplum!" he cried, pulling at her arms and half dragging her through the hole with her.

"Stop!" she screamed in panic, slipping forward and I watched as she fell half way through, her skirt ripping up the back and showing off her ass. "No!" She tried to let go, fighting to get free of him but his hand suddenly fisted in her hair and she screamed, trying to push him off.

Chester fell with a roar and he didn't let go, dragging his wife through the hole with him and their screams tangled with the rumbling and shaking of the Dollhouse as they fell.

A hard thwack sounded their fate and silence followed, making satisfaction fill me over their deaths.

It didn't last long though as the ceiling shuddered and I leapt out from behind the table, running to the edge of the hole and ripping a long mirror off the wall, laying it down over the gap parting JJ from me. It only just reached, but I had to hope it would hold long enough for him to get across.

"Come on," I urged JJ and he blindly trusted me, heading over to the mirror while I held it steady.

Maverick moved close beside me as JJ carefully made his way across and cracks spread over the glass. Maverick caught his shirt in his fist, dragging him to safety and I looked at him in confusion, ripping a piece of my shirt off and binding it over my right hand which was bleeding like a motherfucker.

"Don't go getting any ideas about us being besties again, I just need more men hunting this house for Rogue before it falls down," Maverick gritted out, shoving JJ away from him as he released his shirt.

"Fine by me," I hissed and JJ mumbled a shocked thank you at Maverick who pointedly ignored him.

We raced through the door together, finding ourselves in a dark corridor where the lights were flickering and the floor was groaning.

The passage to our right was blocked by debris, so we turned left and soon arrived in a massive room that overlooked one of the balconies outside. Large pillars held up the ceiling and my heart froze in my chest as the house shuddered and one by one the pillars began to fall, bringing the roof, the sky and the whole world down with them.

JJ grabbed my arm and we started racing toward the doors that led out to the balcony, but we were too far away. We weren't going to make it. All I could think of was Rogue as terror rippled through my core and I realised I'd failed her. I was going to die in this house and never see her bright blue eyes ever again or her smile which held the purest kind of power over me.

I love you, hummingbird. And I'm so fucking sorry.

CHAPTER FORTY ONE

I ran and ran down dark hallways, going as fast as I could while hunting for another way back up into the building as the sound of gunfire and screams carried down to me from above.

But it didn't matter what was up there because I was being hunted by my own personal monster down here and there could be no worse fate for me than being caught by him now.

I launched myself around another corner and almost sobbed in relief as I found a set of stairs there, throwing myself onto them and racing up as fast as I could.

Shawn had lost track of me somewhere down in the dark when the walls had been shaking and the roof collapsing in chunks and I was going to take every second of advantage I had to escape him now.

My legs burned and lungs laboured as I raced up to the ground floor and I wrenched the door open, a scream escaping me as I collided with a hard body.

"Rogue?" Chase gasped, pushing me back a step as he looked me up and down and my eyes widened as I found him there before me.

"Chase? What are- no, fuck that. We need to get the hell out of here. Shawn's right behind me and I don't have a gun."

Chase's upper lip peeled back and he drew his own pistol, giving me a shove to put himself between me and the door. "You need to run. The whole fucking building is going to come down. I'll deal with Shawn."

"Wait," I gasped, grabbing his arm and yanking him to a halt as he made a move to leave me and he swung around to face me angrily.

"Just go," he barked, but before I could argue with him over it, another explosion rocked the building somewhere ahead of us and I screamed as I threw my hands up over my head.

Chase grabbed hold of me, throwing me against the wall and pinning me beneath his body as he crossed his arms against the wall above us and tried to shield me from the lumps of falling masonry.

I coughed as I clung to his shirt, fear paralysing me until the building stopped quaking then he grabbed my arm and started hauling me along through the dust that had billowed up around us.

I threw a terrified look at the cracks spiderwebbing through the ceiling and pointed to the far side of the open room we were in where a doorway was looming in the shadows.

Chase threw a conflicted look back towards the stairwell I'd emerged from then caught my hand in his and started running for the exit.

I stumbled over broken pieces of furniture and several lumps of masonry and an awful groaning sound filled the air from overhead, promising us a quick death if we didn't get the fuck out of here sharpish.

A gunshot went off behind us and Chase threw me in front of him to shield me as he returned fire, cursing Shawn as he emerged on the far side of the room, coughing and laughing through the dust.

"You can run, sugarpie, but you know you can't hide forever," he called, making my heart spike with fear.

Motherfucker.

I ripped the door open and dove through it, grabbing a fistful of Chase's shirt to make sure he was following me.

"You don't need to yank me along like a dog," he snapped as we started running down a corridor where another door beckoned us on.

"Well I don't know when I might turn around and find myself alone like last time," I bit back.

But he didn't manage to answer that before an enormous crash sounded again and the entire building rattled around us. I almost fell in my stupid fucking shoes and Chase hurled me off of my feet, throwing me over his shoulder and running flat out towards that door.

He slammed into it with a curse, dropping me back to the ground as he found it locked and shoving the pistol into my hands.

"Point and shoot, little one, it's not rocket science."

"Fuck you," I hissed, raising the gun and trying to aim straight with my nerves shot to shit and the roof trembling overhead like it was going to come crashing down on us at any second.

Another huge crash rocked the building and I flinched as Chase slammed his shoulder into the locked door over and over again, making the hinges rattle while the whole thing trembled.

"I fucking hate you, Chase," I said, my voice raw and my hands shaking where I held the gun as more and more sounds of destruction came from around us and I tasted our death in the air. "I hate you so fucking much, but I love you too. I've always fucking loved you and that's the problem, isn't it?"

The door flew open with an enormous crash and Chase turned to look at me as he righted himself, his dark curls falling in his eyes which were wide with disbelief at my words.

"Did you just tell me you-"

A crash sounded through the roof right above my head and I looked up in time to see a massive beam come tumbling through the ceiling, poised to crush me in one fatal strike.

But before I could be flattened by the harbinger of my death, strong arms banded around my waist and I fell through the open door with Chase on top of me. The gun went flying out of my grip as I was crushed beneath him and a cry of fright escaped my lips as I expected the whole building to come falling down on top of us.

Chase's hands slammed down on the carpet either side of my head and he gritted his teeth as he held himself up like that, shielding me from the bricks which were tumbling down from above. His gaze met mine with this burning, searing kind of desperation and my heart raced with panic as more debris rained down on him and he grunted in pain.

The moment the downpour lessened, he was scrambling upright again, tugging me with him and moving into the room, but we both fell still at the same moment.

The room we were in was small and without windows. There was no way out and the only thing inside it was a tall, metal safe which stood at the back of the space, the door standing open and revealing nothing inside it.

"Shit," I breathed because that was it. Our last chance to get out of here before the whole place came crashing down on our heads and we were crushed.

Chase licked his lips, his chest rising and falling heavily as he looked around in desperation, clearly realising the same thing as I had while more chunks of ceiling fell down around us.

"I'm sorry," I whispered. "I'm sorry I came back here. I'm sorry about Shawn and Fox and coming between-"

"Shut up, ghost," Chase snarled. "You're not fucking dead yet."

He grabbed my wrist and hauled me across the room towards the safe, throwing up an arm as more debris rained down on us and that groaning noise got louder. Any second now and it would all come crashing down. It would crush us here in this fucking place and that would be it. All of it come to this. Nothing. The end to a story that had barely begun.

Chase threw the safe door open wider then started ripping the metal shelves out from inside it.

"Get in," he barked as he hurled the last one aside.

"We won't fit," I protested, realising what he was trying to do but he grabbed me before I could make any more protests and shoved me inside.

"You'll fit, little one. You always were fucking tiny."

My arms pressed to either side of the confined space while my head brushed the top of it and my heart raced with panic as I realised what he was saying. I'd fit, but he wouldn't.

"No," I snarled, making a move to step back out of it but he shoved me again, making me stay inside.

"Don't make me close the fucking door," Chase barked, "Because so help me, Rogue, I'll do it. Just let me be the good guy for one fucking time in my miserable life, alright?"

I shook my head as a crash tore through the room and I caught hold of the front of his shirt, yanking him towards me like I could force him into the tiny space with me if I just wanted it enough.

Chase's broad shoulders jammed in the opening and a sob escaped me as he dropped his forehead to mine and I felt him giving up.

"It's okay," he breathed, his hand skimming my waist as I shook my head in refusal and the building continued to fall apart around us. "It's okay, little one. Don't cry for me. Just go on hating me. I don't want this to make you cry."

"Then get in here with me," I demanded even though it was useless and we both knew it.

I yanked on his shirt harder, trying to force the impossible and suddenly his lips were on mine, the taste of them so bittersweet because I knew what he was saying to me with that kiss and I refused to hear it. I needed him. I needed him like I needed all of them even when I hated them. I'd never stopped needing any of them and I couldn't let this be the end for him.

"Where are you, sugarpie?" Shawn's voice called out over the sounds of destruction and Chase broke away from me, looking back towards the door with his jaw clenching.

"Promise me you'll stay here, little one," he growled.

"You stay," I demanded in return, my grip on his shirt tightening painfully.

"I'm not letting him find you here."

The groaning was getting louder and as I looked up at the ceiling in fear, Chase shoved me hard enough to break my hold on his shirt and knocked me right into the back of the safe again.

I screamed as the roof collapsed above him and saw him diving away from the worst of it moments before the whole thing came crashing down.

Bricks and mortar slammed into the metal safe all around me, the sound deafening as the entire room was filled with it and I was forced to shield my face, cowering in the back while screaming and screaming for the boy I used to love.

But as more and more of the building caved in all around me, I found myself trapped with no one to answer my screams and no way of knowing what had become of the Harlequin boys who owned me heart and soul.

I was trapped in the dark just like I had been for all of those long, lonely years. But this time I couldn't be sure I'd ever find my way back out again.

CHAPTER FORTY TWO

I made it out of the falling wreckage somehow still breathing, still moving, praying my girl would be okay. As I climbed over a pile of debris, I made it to the relatively intact corridor and heard Shawn singing Boom! Shake the Room by DJ Jazzy Jeff and The Fresh Prince under his breath. This guy had some serious issues.

I ran down the corridor with my heart in my throat, hating leaving Rogue behind but I was sure that safe would live up to its name and look after her. I couldn't go back, so all I could do right now was kill fucking Shawn and try to get the hell out of here.

A bullet slammed into the wall beside me and I cursed. *Speaking of the motherfucker.*

"Did your daddy teach you to shoot, shithead!?" I shouted, turning down another hallway which trembled ominously, drawing more of his attention to me in case he even considered searching for Rogue the way I'd come from. "Because I know he wasn't aiming to knock your momma up when they had you."

A bullet tore through a bright pink lamp as I passed it and my heart crashed into my ribcage.

"Don't you talk about my momma, boy!" Shawn shouted.

I ran harder and faster, unsure where I was even going and not giving a damn so long as this asshole was nowhere near Rogue. Life was still somehow clinging to me, refusing to let me out of this world anytime soon so I was sure I had a chance of surviving this yet.

I ducked around the next corner, pressing my back to the wall and my brain yelled at me to move, but my heart rooted my feet in place. This piece of shit needed to die. I had to send him deep, deep into hell where he could never touch my family again, and if I had to go there with him then that was fine by me.

"Come out here, pretty eyes," Shawn called.

I picked up a fallen lump of masonry, weighing it in my hand as Shawn drew closer and the wall against my back shook violently. "Where's my little whore gone? I'm not leaving here without my pound of flesh."

His voice drew closer and I held my breath, ready to end this asshole once and for all. I needed to get that gun from him, turn it on his head and pull the trigger. No fucking pressure or anything.

"Oh, pretty eyes?" Shawn sang, just a few feet away and his boot crunched on some glass just beyond the wall I was using for cover.

I remained entirely still, focused, ready to do what I had to. But I drowned myself in thoughts of Rogue and my boys one last time just in case this was it. The closing curtain, the final fucking bow. But at least the encore would be sweet.

Shawn stepped into view and I swung the lump of masonry at his arm, smacking it so hard that the gun went flying from his grip, banging loudly as it went off.

He roared in pain and his other hand swung at me, his knuckles impacting hard with my face. I stumbled back, swinging the masonry at him again and going for his head. He ducked it, lunging at me and the floor shuddered beneath us, making me lose my footing as he collided with my chest and took me to the ground, my weapon bouncing away across the floor as I lost my grip on it.

My back impacted with the floorboards and his fists crunched against my ribs in furious blows that stole the breath from my lungs.

But I wasn't going down easily. This man had caused Rogue unspeakable pain, had tried to put her in the ground on *our* land. I was one of her boys, her protectors, and I had to prove that I could fight for her and win. I threw my forehead up, smashing it down on his already bloody nose and he screamed to high heaven, falling off of me as he clutched his face.

I got up, running for his gun but a tremendous boom blasted above before I got there and the ceiling came down ahead of me, burying the gun and making my ears ring so loud I was deafened.

I stumbled away as debris continued to fall and strong arms wrapped around my legs, knocking me to the ground. Shawn crawled up my body, waving his phone in my face and showing me the screen so that I could see he still had a few more bombs left to detonate as he started fucking monologuing at me and I was kinda glad I still couldn't hear anything. Though as his fist cracked against my face, my hearing cleared and his voice drove into my head.

"-because I'm a god here on earth and nothing can take me from this world until I'm down with it. So where's my girl, pretty eyes? Where'd you stash my prize? Where'd you stash that sweet, sweet pu-"

I got my hand up and throat punched him, before following up the blow with a fierce punch to the head. I rolled us over, tasting blood in my mouth as I knelt either side of him and turned into nothing but a wild beast as I punched and punched and swore to kill this motherfucker here and now.

"She's not yours!" I roared. "And she never was!"

He growled as he fought back, his fist slamming into my kidney then he pulled a knife from his belt and I lunged off of him to avoid the swipe of it.

I grabbed a piece of piping from the ground, wheeling around and swinging it at him. He ducked back with a curse, side stepping again and again as we moved in a circle and I tried to land a hit on him.

He whistled low, raising the knife in one hand while tucking his phone into his pocket. "I don't lose, boy. That's a fact you're gonna need to learn real quick."

"You'll lose today," I promised as the ceiling trembled above us and my heart didn't even quake with fear. Worst case scenario, I'd keep him here long enough to die with me when the building came falling down.

"Hey boss! There's a way out up here!" someone called and I turned my head, praying it was a Harlequin, but finding a fucking Dead Dog there instead with two more at his back.

Shawn grinned victoriously and I lunged at him with the pole in a last desperate bid to end him, but those three assholes rushed me, wrestling the weapon from my grip before I got close.

"Keep hold of him, boys," Shawn commanded and his men forced my arms behind my back, immobilising me.

Shawn smiled through the blood pissing from his nose and coating his teeth. "Told ya."

"Shall we kill him, boss?" one of the men asked, placing a cold gun to my temple.

My heartbeat quickened and fury pounded through my aching limbs at me failing my girl once again. *Useless fucking waste of space.*

A roaring, groaning noise sounded from somewhere above us in the Dollhouse and I knew we were out of time. This place was coming down, right fucking now.

"No," Shawn decided. "Take him. Let's get the fuck out of here."

They turned, dragging me along and I fought as hard as I could to get free, but the assholes wouldn't let go. They forced me into a run as lumps of the roof came crashing down and I forced my legs to move around several twists and turns, knowing our time was almost up. But then they led us out of a back door and I turned my head in panic as they dragged me towards a white SUV parked up in the dark lot.

The Dollhouse gave one final beastly groan and the remainder of the roof collapsed, followed by the top floor and the one after that.

I was dragged away, my throat burning as I shouted my family's names and panic tore me apart from the inside. Rogue was in there, my brothers too. And I couldn't live in a world without them in it. They had to survive this, they had to, and I just prayed to any fucking god who was listening that they'd protect them.

I was shoved in the trunk of a car and everything went dark as Shawn slammed it shut and before I could even begin to try and fight my way free, I was being driven away to an unknown fate with terror in my heart over what I might have just lost from this world forever.

CHAPTER FORTY THREE

I was taken to somewhere cold and dark, left with a linen bag over my head for what I guessed was at least an hour, maybe more. My body was bruised and battered and I was in desperate need of water as I sat with my hands bound behind me and my head hanging low.

I thought of Rogue, Fox, JJ, hell even fucking Maverick and I prayed that the safe where I'd put Rogue had been strong enough to withstand the building coming down, but who really knew? The not knowing was even worse than being tethered to this wooden chair at the mercy of Shawn Mackenzie, because I didn't much give a shit about what happened to me. I'd already faced the worst fear of my life by being outcasted from the Harlequins, banished forever to live a life alone. Nothing came close to beating that, but if they were dead, I would gladly die here at Shawn's hands, no matter how long he took carving me up.

Footsteps eventually pounded this way and I focused on keeping my heart rate steady as the bag was tugged from my head.

"Hey, sunshine," Shawn purred, standing in front of me looking freshly showered in a white wifebeater and jeans, his nose all patched up from the break with white strips taped to his skin. There were plenty of bruises on him which I'd put there, though it wasn't much of a consolation prize.

I looked around, finding myself in what I guessed was a basement, a leaky pipe in one corner apparently the source of the dripping that had been pounding into my skull ever since I got here.

Shawn twisted a thin knife between his fingers, drawing my attention to it as he pulled up his own wooden chair and sat in front of me, putting his booted feet up on my knees.

"Have you heard any news about the Dollhouse?" I demanded. "Did the Harlequins get out? Rogue?"

"Nope, I'm afraid they're all dead," he said with a smile and my heart crushed to dust as panic seized me and made my head go into a tailspin. He boomed a laugh. "I'm just kiddin'. I don't know shit, they're still diggin' survivors outa the rubble. You're my backup plan though, pretty eyes."

"How?" I spat.

"Well, ya see, if Fox crawls out from the bones of that building, then he's gonna be missing one of his right hand boys who knows everything about him." He leaned in closer, cupping his hand around his mouth. "Or should I say boyfriend, eh?"

I shook my head at him with a sneer. "You took the wrong asshole, Shawn. Fox kicked me out of the Harlequins for betraying him. He wouldn't pay a penny to get me back."

Shawn smiled wickedly and the look sent a trickle of dread into my gut. "I don't want pennies, boy," he said and his mouth fell flat. "You're gonna give me every single detail you have in that pretty head of yours about the Harlequins' routines. And if Fox is worm food, then I'm sure you have plenty information on Luther that'll satisfy me, hm?"

"I'm not going to tell you anything," I snarled.

Shawn took his feet from my lap, gripping the sides of his seat and dragging it forward so his knees were pressed to mine. He leaned close so he was looking me dead in the eye, no hint of mirth on his face. "Oh you will, Chase Cohen. Because I'm gonna peel you apart piece by piece if you don't. You're gonna scream so loud, the kangaroos on the other side of the world will hear ya. But no one will come, no one but me with my shiny knives. So would you like to change your answer, boy?"

My jaw clenched and fear slithered under my skin, but I wouldn't break no matter what this asshole did to me. I'd lived in a house with a monster worse than him, who could twist my very heart beneath my flesh. But this monster could only break me on the outside and he was asking the one thing of me which I would never, ever give up.

I'd already lost all there was to lose, and now I would stand as a wall between my family and this piece of shit for all eternity. If this was what it took for me to have some worth in this world, then I'd suck it up.

"My answer is final," I told him with no hint of a waiver in my voice and I leaned closer to speak right into his face, showing him he didn't intimidate me and that my demons were far darker than his. They'd already seen what hell looked like and they could face it again and again. "I'm not going to tell you anything," I repeated.

He stared at me for a long moment, leaning back an inch with a sigh. "That's a real shame," he muttered then raised his knife to point it directly at my right eye. "So which one of your pretty, pretty eyes can you live without, Chase Cohen? Is it the lefty or the righty?" He swung the knife between them, back and forth like a metronome and acid built in my throat, my fingers locking into fists behind my back. *I'm not afraid.*

"Can't choose?" Shawn pushed, that twisted smirk of his lighting his lips. "Sure is a tricky choice. They're both my favourite shade of blue. But you've pissed me off quick, boy, and I can't let you get away with that."

He continued to swing that knife side to side and I held onto every scrap of good in my life as I retreated to the sunshine of my past, listening to the birds sing and my friends laugh.

"Sure you don't wanna choose?" Shawn pressed, but I zoned him out, retreating further and further into a place where he could never touch me. A place full of hope and freedom, where five kids had days and days in the sun stretching out endlessly ahead of them.

"Okay then, you leave me no choice," Shawn chuckled. "Eenie, meenie, miney..."

AUTHOR'S NOTE

Soooooo, a little birdie told us (actually several little birdies) that our recent cliffhangers 'weren't too bad'. Now I don't like to point fingers, but you know who you were. So in thanks we decided to end this book like this. And I'm sure that you're all cool with it. Just like the characters are cool with it. And the universe is cool with it. And most importantly of all, fucking Shawn is cool with it.

...

Still here? Sure you don't hate us too much? Oh, I do love a nice glutton for punishment such as yourself!

So far as the writing of this book goes, all I can really say is that it was a whirlwind. Rogue and her boys swept us away and the words just flowed like lava over a village of happy little lambs who never saw the eruption coming. Two weeks. Two motherfucking weeks, one trip to a farm (because the shitting world is only opening up from freaking covid at last in the UK - woohoo) and a whole lot of drama on the page and that's what it took to get us here.

But don't worry, we won't leave you hanging long – we will be back to Sunset Cove VERY SOOOOOON. But if you need to come scream at anyone then you should do so in our reader group where all the best people we know come to talk books and yell at us when necessary, so if you're not there already then come join the us :)

Love you dude, from Susanne & Caroline x

ALSO BY
CAROLINE PECKHAM
&
SUSANNE VALENTI

Brutal Boys of Everlake Prep
(Complete Reverse Harem Bully Romance Contemporary Series)
Kings of Quarantine
Kings of Lockdown
Kings of Anarchy
Queen of Quarantine
**

Dead Men Walking
(Reverse Harem Dark Romance Contemporary Series)
The Death Club
Society of Psychos
**

The Harlequin Crew
(Reverse Harem Mafia Romance Contemporary Series)
Sinners Playground
Dead Man's Isle
Carnival Hill
Paradise Lagoon

Harlequinn Crew Novellas
Devil's Pass
**

Dark Empire
(Dark Mafia Contemporary Standalones)

Beautiful Carnage

Beautiful Savage

**

The Ruthless Boys of the Zodiac

(Reverse Harem Paranormal Romance Series - Set in the world of Solaria)

Dark Fae

Savage Fae

Vicious Fae

Broken Fae

Warrior Fae

Zodiac Academy

(M/F Bully Romance Series- Set in the world of Solaria, five years after Dark Fae)

The Awakening

Ruthless Fae

The Reckoning

Shadow Princess

Cursed Fates

Fated Thrones

Heartless Sky

The Awakening - As told by the Boys

Zodiac Academy Novellas

Origins of an Academy Bully

The Big A.S.S. Party

Darkmore Penitentiary

(Reverse Harem Paranormal Romance Series - Set in the world of Solaria, ten years after Dark Fae)

Caged Wolf

Alpha Wolf

Feral Wolf

**

The Age of Vampires
(Complete M/F Paranormal Romance/Dystopian Series)
Eternal Reign
Eternal Shade
Eternal Curse
Eternal Vow
Eternal Night
Eternal Love
**

Cage of Lies
(M/F Dystopian Series)
Rebel Rising
**

Tainted Earth
(M/F Dystopian Series)
Afflicted
Altered
Adapted
Advanced
**

The Vampire Games
(Complete M/F Paranormal Romance Trilogy)
V Games
V Games: Fresh From The Grave
V Games: Dead Before Dawn
*

The Vampire Games: Season Two
(Complete M/F Paranormal Romance Trilogy)
Wolf Games
Wolf Games: Island of Shade
Wolf Games: Severed Fates
*

The Vampire Games: Season Three
Hunter Trials
*

The Vampire Games Novellas
A Game of Vampires
**

The Rise of Issac
(Complete YA Fantasy Series)
Creeping Shadow
Bleeding Snow
Turning Tide
Weeping Sky
Failing Light

Made in United States
North Haven, CT
09 September 2022

23898494R00311